# TUMBLED TALES

## AN ANTHOLOGY OF UNCONVENTIONAL STORIES

Edited by
## HANNAH TERAO

and
## BRANDY HUSSA

Wandering Wave Press

# CONTENTS

Compilation copyright © 2023 The Wandering Wave Press

Introduction © 2023 by Hannah Terao | The Rules of the Game © 2023 by Marisca Pichette | Eat Me © 2023 by Mike Morgan | Between Two Urns With Marshall Thermadore © 2023 by Lena Ng | Breakthrough © 2021 by Laura Engelhardt | The Haunting of the Star Princess © 2023 by Bruno Lombardi | When Anakar Met Susan © 2023 by Jason Sharp | Slide Show © 2023 by Matias Travieso-Diaz | The Witches of Yggdrasil © 2023 by Spencer Nitkey | What She Asks of Me © 2023 by S.D. Gibson | Devour © 2023 by Roman Durkan | Just Right © 2023 by Manny Frishberg | Point Taken © 2023 by Richard Zwicker | Make Love, Not War © 2023 by Eve Morton | The Bastard's Bluff © 2023 by Danielle Davis | Said the Moonlit Moth to the Horse Half-Dead © 2023 by Matthew F. Amati | Tōno © 2023 by Melody Alice | Project: Wolfsbane © 2023 by Pete Barnstrom | A Brand-New Morning © 2023 by Mia Dalia | The Walrus Whistles at Midnight © 2023 by Rebecca A. Demarest | All Clear © 2023 by M.M. De Voe | Inside Job © 2023 by Mel Grebing

Cover Art by Rena Violet | Print Layout by Laura Engelhardt

ISBN: 978-1-957778-04-4 (paperback)
978-1-957778-03-7 (ebook)

Published in Green Village, NJ USA
June 2023

# INTRODUCTION

## HANNAH TERAO

I OFTEN FIND myself returning to the same set of tropes, seeking comfort in their familiarity the way one finds comfort in a bedtime story, knowing that nothing will happen in this tale that I cannot handle. I love friends-to-lovers rom coms, prequels that explain away a villain's dastardly deeds, and adventures starring unlikely heroes thrown into the midst of the action against their will. However, when I was asked to serve as the editor for this anthology, I found myself wondering what it would be like to push beyond those familiar comforts and search for a story whose ending I could not predict. What would it be like to read a story that takes a beloved childhood character and twists them into a darkened villain, but makes the reader love them anyway? Or one that stitches together the predictable lives of two characters caught up in familiar plots — and by bringing them together, makes their lives decidedly *un*predictable? What about one with no heroes and no villains: a story about a story that doesn't exist at all?

We live in a world where sequels and spin-offs dominate the media — after all, the market for easily categorized stories is far wider and more lucrative than the market for the type of stories that this anthology sought. It's an easy decision to pick up a book that returns you to a world you already know and love, but a risky one to brave the pages of a story that pushes you outside your comfort zone. You can never predict when that experiment will go wrong and when it will go perfectly, unexpectedly, right.

When I sent out *Tumbled Tales'* call for submissions in the summer of 2022, I didn't know what to expect, both in terms of how truly unconventional the submissions would be, and in terms of the number of submissions I would receive. However, the response from authors blew my initial expectations out of the water. We received stories that were not only of outstanding quality, but which introduced combinations of characters, plotlines, and tropes that I'd never even thought of merging. Out of those hundreds of creative submissions, I chose the twenty-one that challenged me the most, the ones that surprised a smile out of me, or caused me to do a double take when I read their opening line.

Throughout this search for "something new," I found myself struggling with my own newness. As an emerging editor, I have struggled to find my niche within the world of publishing, which is already saturated with talented individuals. Editing this anthology has allowed me to find that niche: advocating for the stories that also don't seem to have a place in the literary market. I received dozens of cover letters from authors explaining that their story had been rejected from other publishers for being too weird, too difficult to categorize, too unconventional. While I could not offer a home to all of those genre-defying works, I am proud to say that twenty-one of them reside within these pages. In compiling these stories, I found myself welcomed within a community that strives to move beyond boundaries — or, on the other hand, to remain within those boundaries while taking a long hard look at the space within them.

In the remainder of this introduction, I try to give you a sneak peek into those stories, as well as insight into my thought process when selecting them. I hope that these tales will subvert your expectations in twenty-one different ways.

### "The Rules of the Game"
### by Marisca Pichette

I loved this story even before I read the first line. The cover letter that accompanied this submission asked whether "history can be changed not through the alteration of real events, but the alteration of the literature that is central to a society's cultural language." This concept was an idea I'd never seen before, and which immediately caught my attention. The story that accompanied that cover letter did not disappoint; it places characters typical of the high fantasy/adventure genre within classic works of literature, using tropes to subvert stories so well-known they have become tropes themselves. Language can change the course of history, and Pichette's story plays with that idea in a clever and entertaining way.

### "Eat Me"
### by Mike Morgan

I chose this story for two reasons. First, I enjoyed discovering a new mythological monster that I hadn't ever read about in a setting I'd never before encountered. I was fascinated by the contrast of the quotidian nature of the protagonist's work life and the daunting prospect that he faces: finding a way to exist in a world suddenly populated by monsters. He feels like a real human being, flawed yet sympathetic and struggling to eke out a life just like the rest of us. Secondly, I appreciated the author's control of the story: the gradual foreshadowing of a catastrophic ending, the pacing, and the complex questions about trauma and consumerism that it raises in the background of a story seemingly focused on monsters.

### "Between Two Urns with Marshall Thermador"
### by Lena Ng

A werewolf, a vampire, and Frankenstein's monster walk onto the set of a nighttime talk show … and things only go downhill from there. This story provides a scathing satire of the media using these classic literary figures and an unexpected setting. Ng draws inspiration from the archive of classic horror tropes, turning them on their heads and transforming these monsters into sophisticated artists — until they're not. This story leaves readers laughing, but also asks them to consider the implications of the media-generated stereotypes they see in their own lives.

### "Breakthrough"
### by Laura Engelhardt

This story displays the author's masterful worldbuilding, transporting readers into city of Rio de Janeiro on a magical adventure set in the modern world. Her unique magick system combines riveting sensory imagery with the near-scientific precision of its spellcasting, allowing readers to visualize these enchantments coming to life. This richly imagined world provides the backdrop for a glimpse into the life of a powerful young mage reluctantly bound to the whims of a brilliant but sadistic vampire.

## "The Haunting of the Star Princess"
## by Bruno Lombardi

This sci-fi/mystery mash-up creates a juxtaposition between an old world and a new with its unexpected combination of ancient Irish history and the futuristic setting of a starship. I enjoyed watching the protagonist grapple with the ways in which these two ideas fit together and unexpectedly discover a new part of her identity. Ultimately, this story argues that we must understand our past before we can solve the mysteries of the future.

## "When Anakar Met Susan"
## by Jason Sharp

This story combines two of my personal favorite genres: romantic comedy and high fantasy. Rather than combine these genres, however, Sharp plucks a character from each of them and places them in a wholly unfamiliar setting: the real world, a place that disrupts the lovestruck haze of rom-com tropes and provides mundanity to a lord used to living in a world of prophecies and magic. Sparks fly between the disillusioned romance heroine and the reformed villain of a fantasy novel, blending their lives and the tropes of their respective genres. I enjoyed the sharp contrast between the two protagonists, the genuine sweetness in their connection, and their openness to pursuing a relationship with the unknown.

## "Slide Show"
## by Matias Travieso-Diaz

This story was one of the very first submissions we received, and the first one that I instantly knew I had to accept. Travieso-Diaz masterfully combines traces of horror with slices of his protagonist's life, giving readers mere glimpses of a man and leaving them to make their own judgments about whether this character's life-altering decision is right or wrong. Although the tumbled nature of this story is more subtle than other stories in this volume, it remains impossible to classify "Slide Show" as just one genre.

## "The Witches of Yggdrasil"
## by Spencer Nitkey

Set in a dystopian future, this story combines magical realism with elements of science fiction as it takes its reader on a journey through a ruined Earth and into the depths of the Milky Way. I loved the lush descriptions of the sights and sounds of this dystopian world, which strengthen the tension that Nitkey creates between the earthly pleasures (and pains) of his protagonist's present, and the knowledge she is given of the past.

## "What She Asks of Me"
## by S.D. Gibson

Gibson constructs a sophisticated setting deeply layered with a history, mythology, and culture all its own. I loved watching the threads of this history come together as old actors rise to life again along with new challenges. This story masterfully blends the memories of its protagonist with the present conflict, giving the reader deeper insight into this character's past and present, and providing us with a deeply nuanced understanding of him and his world.

### "Devour"
### by Roman Durkan

This piece presents a gritty look at the ways in which technology revolutionized the landscape of America during the 1980's by presenting that new tech as the catalyst for an apocalypse. We are taken on this science-fiction/horror adventure by a small cast of characters who each feel supremely real due to the individuality of their voices, the flaws in their personalities, and their desperate struggle to make sense of a world turned upside down.

### "Just Right"
### by Manny Frishberg

Perhaps the darkest and most twisted of these tumbled tales is Manny Frishberg's Goldilocks retelling. Told from the perspective of a seemingly bloodthirsty girl attempting to charm her way out of a psychiatric ward, this story is not your typical fairytale. It blurs the lines of reality, placing the reader into the hands (and the head) of the protagonist and giving her complete narrative control over what we see and understand of her life.

### "Point Taken"
### by Richard Zwicker

This story drew me in with its humor and kept me reading for its noir-style twist on a classic Greek myth. The anachronism of a wise-cracking, no-nonsense detective in ancient Greece opens the space for some truly hilarious interactions with the Greek gods. This story distinguishes itself from the glut of Greek myth retellings by blending contrasting genres and shaping them into an entertaining and rowdy adventure.

## "Make Love, Not War"
### by Eve Morton

This piece surprised me in the best way. The first time I read it, I was rooting so hard for Mina and Grok's love story to succeed that I wasn't expecting other characters to find their happy ending too. I fell in love with both of these budding relationships, not solely because they surprised and delighted me, but because of the genuine emotional connection between the characters, which pushes back against the habit of science fiction to hypersexualize alien life forms. Reading this story reminded me that love can be found in even the most unlikely of places, and that it can be genuine and pure and based on a foundation of bad poetry.

## "The Bastard's Bluff"
### by Danielle Davis

This story is pure fun. It throws together familiar characters from a range of genres (the dashing and flirtatious hero, the sassy animal sidekick, the seductive and wicked villainess) and places them together in a familiar setting — but both the characters and the setting come with their own twists. If that's not enough to win you over, I'll leave you with three words: cowboys riding dinosaurs.

## "Said the Moonlit Moth to the Horse Half-Dead"
## by Matthew F. Amati

Rather than explaining to you what is unconventional about this story, it might be easier to list the things that *are* conventional about it. Imagine a hero on a quest to avenge the murder of his loved ones. Pretty common, right? But then make that hero a horse — or rather, half of one — joined in his journey by a moth curious to learn about the sorrows and joys of life. Then, if those ideas interest you, go read this story; summary alone cannot do justice to the quirky, off-kilter world of Amati's story, its poetic and clever use of language, and the intricate nuances of the titular characters.

## "Tōno"
## by Melody Alice

This story plays into the trope of a seductive water spirit: an exotically beautiful woman beckoning an unsuspecting mortal to their grave. However, Alice plays with this tired trope by investigating the systems of sexism and classism that transformed this woman into the monster we initially believe her to be. This story forces readers to see the heart behind the myth, allowing us to fall in love with a water spirit just as the protagonist does.

## "Project: Wolfsbane"
## by Pete Barnstrom

An alternate history that transports the reader back in time to WWII, this story features an ordinary American officer who discovers that the Germans have a secret weapon up their sleeves: werewolves. I laughed out loud at the witty narration that pokes fun at the military and its hierarchies of power, as well as the (second) unexpected twist that evens the odds of a climactic battle. Alternate history may be a well-established genre, but Barnstrom's combination of history with horror and comedy made it stand out among our submissions.

## "A Brand New Morning"
### by Mia Dalia

This piece is a short-but-sweet story that won my heart. We've all wished at some point for our ordinary lives to be broken up by a bit of magic — but Dalia's narrator finds themself in the middle of a little *too* much strangeness for their taste when they wake up to find that their wife has grown tentacles overnight. I chose this story because it makes the ordinary extraordinary and finds the beauty in accepting the unexpected (and sometimes unwelcome) twists of fate that life presents to us. Like "When Anakar Met Susan," it insists that love can be found in even the most ordinary of settings, and with even the most extraordinary people.

## "The Walrus Whistles at Midnight"
### by Rebecca A. Demarest

Immerse yourself in a unique world: an abandoned space station converted into a city — with a murderer on the loose. I appreciated the tongue-in-cheek tone of Demarest's narrator as she navigates through the tense social hierarchy of Station 27, meeting a quirky cast of characters along the way who all have their own agendas. It combines its dystopian setting with the high stakes of a mystery, while its engaging narration welcomes all readers to come along for the ride.

## "All Clear"
## by M.M. De Voe

This story combines the tropes and conflict of the post-apocalyptic genre with a sophisticated and thought-provoking literary tone. Through its intricate descriptions of the ways in which a kaiju attack has transformed the lives of the survivors, this story raises questions about family, heartbreak, survival, and sacrifice, but refuses to resolve any of these conflicts with any finality. In the ambiguity of this aftermath, De Voe's characters discover truths about themselves that only tragedy can reveal. This story provides a powerful metaphor for the challenges faced by the victims of catastrophic events such as war or natural disaster, and the ways in which these survivors endure.

## "Inside Job"
## by Mel Grebing

This story plays with the relationship between reader and narrator in a way I've never seen before, combining the reader-insert trope of fanfiction with a literary tone and a plot that challenges the very definition of what a story should be. Readers follow along with an extremely reluctant hero as they strive to avoid becoming the subject of a story. Arguably the most "tumbled" tale in this collection, this story unapologetically confronts its reader's expectations and rejects any attempt to force it into an established category.

Having established the reasons why *I* love this anthology, I now invite you to enter into the worlds of these stories and find your own. For the brave and open-minded reader prepared to experiment with a mishmash of tropes and plot twists, this collection provides a bridge into a community of genre-defying authors and the people who love to read their stories, and we welcome you with open arms. If, as you turn the pages of this anthology, you come across even one story that delights you, challenges you, or startles you out of a literary rut, then I will have succeeded on my mission to present the world with a collection of truly tumbled tales.

# THE RULES OF THE GAME

## MARISCA PICHETTE

EVERYONE WAS DEAD. Or at least, they were going to be.

As with most stories, this one contains a seedy little tavern, lit only by lamplight. As with the better stories, that tavern is the setting of the first scene. And, as with all the best tales, there is of course a mysterious character at a table, wearing a well-tailored light-blocking hood. And — as I'm sure you'll recall — as with all the *classic* tales, this mysterious character has just ordered an orange juice.

It is clear he is waiting for something. Or someone.

The door of the tavern opens, and an obscenely muscled man strides in. He is one of those men who believe that, in order to preserve a civilized society, a certain amount of sweat and blood is required. Namely, his sweat and other people's blood. He is, of course, a warrior. A Master at Arms, in fact — and nothing less. He heads straight for our mysterious hooded friend.

The Master at Arms sits down at the table. Amazingly, the mysterious man — who shall now be known as the Guide to avoid redundancy — does not react to the malodour of old blood and sweat that the Master at Arms expels so aggressively.

"There's other chairs," the Master at Arms observes. The Guide nods.

"There will be other men."

That is the extent of the conversation — until the tavern door opens a second time.

A thin man with a gaunt face and the disastrous remains of a failed moustache steps into the dark interior of the building. He wears faded shades of green and brown, and is riddled with more weapons than the back alley of a street gang's five-year reunion. He looks nervous and jumpy, which is either obvious or unexpected, depending on how many trappers you've encountered in your lifetime.

This one, in any case, approaches the bar and orders a stiff drink. He is served a squat glass of amber liquid and joins the Guide at the table, placing himself several seats over from the Master at Arms.

The trapper glances at the Guide. The Guide's hood stares back, blank and carefully devoid of any defining features, as a mysterious hood should be.

"There are others coming," the hood says.

"Ah."

The door opens again. An enormous man swaggers into the tavern. His fiery red beard completely obscures the dog collar he wears, but as an omniscient being I can tell you with undue certainty that it is there. With this insider knowledge, it is simple to deduce that this man, swigging from not a flask but a growler, is a preacher. He is a Man of the Cloth. What kind of cloth that is, however, is up to debate.

Though he has so very conspicuously brought his own spirits, the Man of the Cloth first approaches the bar. The barman — not at all concerned with the lucidity of his patrons, but rather with providing them as much warming drink as they can afford — hands the Man of the Cloth a foaming stein without comment.

The preacher heaves his bulk through the dark room until he reaches the table that is rapidly becoming the centre stage for a rather important meeting.

"Who're ye, then?" He frowns through the fogginess of his perpetual intoxication, addressing the least strange of the three strangers.

The warrior stands. "I am a Master at Arms, Father." With one gargantuan hand, he shakes the Man of the Cloth's generously padded paw — forcing the preacher to set down his growler to receive the greeting.

"And ye?" The Man of the Cloth nods to the Trapper to Trade. "Yer no Master at Arms, 'least not liken the kind I seen afore!" The preacher's ample stomach shakes as he laughs.

"No. I'm a trapper. A Trapper to Trade."

With a grunt, the Man of the Cloth — who introduces himself as "th' Manna th' Cloth" — sets his bulk down between the Guide and the Master at Arms. The Trapper to Trade swirls the amber liquid in his glass.

"One more chair," he muses.

Were his face visible, you might have caught a cunning glimmer in the Guide's unseen eyes.

"One more man."

As if it had been written — in some forgotten book of indeterminate length, with coffee stains on the cover, cowering in a long-abandoned basement, maybe with corners nibbled by mice — the door of the tavern chooses this time to open and admit our final character.

He looks to be in his mid-thirties, spry and still in his prime. Even through the gloom, it is impossible not to notice that his skin has hardened from years of work in the wind and sea. While not detracting from his overall good looks, it adds a quality of experience and wisdom that some of the others at the table — who shall remain unnamed — do not possess.

With no apparent hesitation, the Ship's Engineer seats himself next to the Trapper to Trade and calls to the barman for a spot of red.

Now that everyone is gathered, the Guide begins. "You're all seasoned travellers, and you know why you're here. There's something that needs finding."

This, of course, is a sign for you, reader, to pay close attention.

"Use a dog, then!" the Master at Arms scoffs. The Ship's Engineer sips his wine in silence.

The Guide shakes his hooded head. "Merely finding it is not enough. There is also the task of elimination."

"What elimination?" asks the Trapper to Trade, fingers tightening around his squat glass. A great deal of the drink has vanished.

"The elimination of another world." The Guide tosses a map out onto the table.

Let us revisit this action. The Guide removes a stained map from his voluminous robes and sends it rolling out across the table. Pay close attention to this detail.

In most scenes such as this, in taverns such as this, it is customary for the map to depict craggy coastlines or king-doms of old. It is not customary, however, for the map to be of the London Underground.

"That's it?" says the Master at Arms. "Not a very dangerous place, is it?"

The Guide fixes him with an artfully concealed stare. The hood itself remains expressionless. "The Underground is not the Place. The Place is in the Underground."

"Oh," the Warrior says, but this vowel does not

adequately convey his confusion. Perhaps 'ah', or 'uh' would have been more appropriate, for 'oh' implies some level of basic understanding, which the Master at Arms does not have — and has only *ever* had on a handful of very rare occasions.

"So yer bringin' us oot o' retirement fair a trip tay th' Underground, eh?" th' Manna th' Cloth rumbles in between swigs from his growler. The foaming stein of ale has long disappeared down his gullet — and had done so almost before it touched the table.

"You think you're gonna get me into something like this, you're crazy." The Master at Arms toys with what resembles a toothpick in his massive hands. (In normal human proportions, it is a stiletto knife.)

"The world is changing. We could wait for things to happen to us, or we could shape the future into something better." The Guide glances at each man in turn — or at least, his hood swings around the table. "There are four of you here. A fighter, a thinker, a chaser, a doer."

A silence descends, in which each man attempts to unravel the cryptic nature of this assertion. And within the silence — as often occurs within silences such as this — each man tries to determine which of the four epithets fits his personality.

"I'm the thinker," the Trapper to Trade murmurs. He has already figured out who everyone else is as well, but feels that it would be condescending to assign their titles to them. Especially when the Master at Arms still holds his stiletto.

"I'm a fighter." Though unnecessary, the warrior puffs up his already amply-puffed chest. Turning his hooded head, the Guide glances between the last two men.

"Fighter!" th' Manna th' Cloth scoffs. "Man, *I'm* the fighter 'ere! When ye can rightly tell me 'bout all the ghastly heathens ye've cut down wit' tha' sword o' yers, then we'll talk!" He sets down his growler, wiping beer from his orange beard.

"Does that make me the chaser?" the Ship's Engineer asks, brow furrowed and hands folded around his wine-glass. The Guide shakes his hood.

"You are the doer. The preacher is the chaser."

"So ... what does that mean?" the Ship's Engineer demands. "And what has it got to do with the Underground?"

"Everything."

It's the kind of statement that is both immensely satis-fying and infuriatingly unspecific. Th' Manna th' Cloth grunts and stands. "In tha' case, I'll get meself a fresh brew."

The year is 1888, in case that was not yet clear. Four men and a Guide sit around a table in a dingy little tavern on the edge of London. At this point, what is known as the London Underground is just twenty-five years old. It is a place of great importance to the men clustered around the tattered map. For within that place is the Place.

The Guide places one long fingernail on the map over a particularly tangled network of tunnels. "The Underground is constructed of tunnels designed to convey people from one place to the next. Yet I have devised a way to use them to travel not only in space, but in time."

He drags his finger across the map, tracing several criss-crossing tunnels. "I will guide you to your stations. From there, you're on your own. Each of you must eliminate one pathway at your station. If you succeed, history will be forever altered. The future — *our* future — will change."

"So it's a contest," the Trapper to Trade mutters, toying with his empty glass.

The Ship's Engineer smiles. "I like a good adventure — but why us?"

He addresses the Guide, who remains stubbornly expressionless beneath his hood.

"With your skills, you're each well-matched to the stations I've assigned you to visit. You will each play a role in the Game."

The Master at Arms drags the map across the table to get a closer look at the soiled paper. A handful of the names are circled: Champion Hill, Canonbury, Waterloo Station, Kingsland Road …

A collection of names is scrawled along the edges of the map: *Leo, William, Geoffrey, Herman.*

"Where is the starting place for this task?" the Trapper to Trade asks.

Slowly, the Guide turns to him. "The Game—" he pauses for effect. "—begins right here."

The Trapper to Trade nods. "I was rather afraid you'd say that."

"Has it already begun?" the Ship's Engineer asks, leaning forward. His calloused hands finger the edge of the map.

"It has."

The table, spirits, and tavern vanish to the tune of a rumbling sound, not unlike that of a train surging down a tunnel.

The group finds themselves seated in a circle on the ground. It is dusk, and clouds pepper the sky like birdshot. All around them stretch barren fields of wispy grass.

The Master at Arms starts to his feet, drawing his sword and looking around. He finds a small incline and charges to the top. There, he finds railroad tracks, and, in the distance, a station.

It could be the Underground — except it is not. It is, so far as he can tell, Aboveground.

"What's going on?" he demands, whirling on the group. A slew of curses clamor into a queue.

He turns in a slow circle, inspecting the nearly featureless landscape. Off into the distance the tracks stretch, with nothing in sight save the small station. He is alone.

No — not quite alone. A figure stands on the distant platform. As the Master at Arms approaches, he recognizes it as a young woman.

Then he hears the train.

The Ship's Engineer is feeling proud of himself when the tavern disappears. He hears the train surge past and opens his eyes.

Dark waves swell. The Ship's Engineer lurches, blinking away sea-spray. Yes, there is the Guide, the Trapper to Trade, and th' Manna th' Cloth sitting in a circle on the deck. For some reason, the Master at Arms is missing from the equation.

"Where are we?" he asks the Guide. The hood twitches to the right, and the Ship's Engineer follows its gaze (if a hood can be said to gaze).

The ship dips suddenly, a great swell of black water churning over the starboard side. The Ship's Engineer struggles to his feet, catching hold of the rigging.

Water splashes in his face as he watches a pale behemoth breach the surface, jaws agape, before it sinks back beneath the waves.

When he has the mind to look back at his partners, he finds only bare deck where the men once sat. He wonders fleetingly if they were swept overboard by the wave, but somehow, he doubts it. No matter — he is more than capable of handling this alone.

He turns back to face the whale.

Hard rock hits th' Manna th' Cloth in tender places, and he curses loudly, dropping his growler. He glares about in the grey light, and what he finds, as the train's rumbling dies away, is more than a little disheartening.

Cliffs of shale cut across the bleak landscape as far as the eye can see. High above, the sky is misty and unwelcoming, and a fresh moon idles somewhere around the horizon.

Th' Manna th' Cloth searches for a familiar face, and is a bit disappointed not to find himself in the Cold Hereafter, but sitting next to the Guide and Trapper to Trade.

"What work o' magic is this?"

Before he gets an answer, a long, low susurrus causes his whiskers to prickle. He looks around, fingering his rosary. Noting his reaction, the Guide directs th' Manna th' Cloth's gaze over to a nearby scarp.

As the priest stares at the sharp cut of rock, three figures appear. Th' Manna th' Cloth can't tell if they climbed up from below or materialised on top. The susurrus grows more audible, and he can just make out some of the words.

*"Adder's fork and blind worm's sting, lizard's leg and howlet's wing …*

*For a charm of powerful trouble, like a hell-broth boil and bubble."*

"Spells! Enchantments! Summoning of the Devil hisself!" Th' Manna th' Cloth practically dances with anticipation as he watches the chanting figures.

When he tears his gaze away long enough to look back at his comrades, he finds only bare rock.

The two remaining men land on a bench. The Trapper to Trade has the vague impression that he might have been on a train. As if through a haze, he remembers visiting other stations where the other competitors were dropped off, one-by-one. But he cannot recall specifics. He notes that he and the Guide are the only two present.

"Where are we?"

The Guide looks at him for a long while (well, sort of — recall the nature of his hood). They are by the side of a long dirt road in the country, and the Trapper to Trade can see a procession heading their way. It is made up of about twenty-odd persons, all dressed in bright colours.

"How funny they look," the Trapper to Trade murmurs. "Like pictures from old manuscripts."

Indeed, the procession has a decidedly antique appearance. From this distance, he can just make out the sound of someone speaking from within the procession. He seems to be telling an anecdote to his companions.

"Tell me the game," the Trapper to Trade says, not rising from his seat. The Guide points to the procession.

The trapper shakes his head. "You mentioned changing our future … but I don't think I'll make it back to London if I stand. I'm right, aren't I?"

A few seconds pass, and the procession draws nearer. The Guide gestures to it a second time, but the Trapper to

Trade does not move. Finally, the Guide's hand falls, and he lets out an audible sigh.

"No, you will not."

"And the game? Your game?"

"History is unbendable," the Guide says, almost in a whisper.

The Trapper to Trade raises his eyebrows. "And?"

"Literature isn't."

"What do you want me to do?" The procession is very near now; the Trapper to Trade can hear the storyteller's words clearly now:

*"He knew nat catoun, for his wit was rude,*
*That bad man sholde wedde his simylitude."*

The Guide seizes one of the Trapper to Trade's weapons and casts it into the dust of the road. Startled, the trapper leaps after it and snatches it up before the procession — which is now almost upon him — treads upon it.

He realizes his mistake too late, and looks back to find, without much surprise, that the Guide has vanished. To the trader's mild annoyance, he took the bench with him.

He turns to face the procession, and whatever else he might find.

The man known as the Guide drops back into his library with a *pop* and looks around.

He did it. And it was so *easy*.

Chuckling, he wanders along the wall and selects a few books from the shelves of his study. Cradling them loosely in his arms, he walks to his desk and sets them down. Then, nervousness fluttering his stomach, he takes a seat and opens the first book.

It's a slim volume, bound in leather. As he flips to the title page, he smiles.

### King Duncan
### William Shakespeare

He turns the pages, perusing the revised play. Macbeth is a minor character, just a mere Thane who happened across the curious spectacle of a preacher burning three witches at the stake. It is a comic scene, and of no significance to the play as a whole: the rest focuses on the great deeds of King Duncan as he fights against the massed forces of Norway and Ireland.

Satisfied, the Guide sets the book aside and picks up the next. It's fatter than he remembers, and it had already been a long, exhaustive book. Bypassing the bulk of it, he skips to the end of Part Seven.

Yes, here it is: Anna, under the influence of morphine and despair, seeks to cast herself before a train — only to be blocked by an angry warrior. Her life is saved, but she vanishes, and Vronsky, thinking her dead, goes off to war to die. The warrior brings Anna out to the country, where she is reunited with Levin, and ...

He skips the rest of the book, which is scores of pages long. He has no interest in what comes next; his main goal has been accomplished. Sighing, he sets *Anna Karenina* aside and picks up the third volume.

*"And at the very last, as the line coiled around Ahab's neck, the Engineer cut it with his knife. Stricken, the whale shook the sea, and his massive flank, slick with blood, disappeared into the surf."*

It's an interesting rewrite, to be sure. He skims the rest of the book, and is fascinated to note that the whale still survives; Ahab dies soon after reaching safety, and the Engineer travels with Ishmael away from the sea.

With a certain amount of trepidation, he sets *Moby Dick* aside and selects the last book.

It is an expensive leather-bound version of Chaucer's work, and he opens it carefully. His eyes scan page after page. There is no change in the Knight's Tale, but by the Miller's, alterations appear. The vocabulary moves gradually away from Middle English, until a handful of modern words pepper the Reeve's and Monk's tales.

A slow smile spreads across his face. The Trapper to Trade was saddled with the most difficult task — to change nothing of the plot, but something in the overall *form* of Chaucer's work.

No more would the Court of Chancery be credited with modern English spelling and orthography. No, those innovations have now taken place decades earlier, in the *Canterbury Tales*.

He sits back in his chair, closing the last book. It was a good run. He pushes back his hood, shaking out his hair, shoving his spectacles up his nose and shuffling the papers on his desk. Hank Morgan's journal lays open under the lamp, and he studies it for a long time.

It was a simple thing, to tell the trick of it. The Guide only needed a touch of practice here and there. The poor old man's story was a warning, and an inspiration. If things could be different …

But history cannot be budged. Oh no, the Guide knows that. Instead, he resolved to try literature. What difference would it cause? What would it change — for better, or for worse? He hopes for improvement, but that is the thing: one can never be sure.

He looks at his watch. Twelve o'clock, midnight.

He has a meeting with a Mr. Clemens in the morning,

and only a few hours remain until dawn. Soon, he will see what changes his small additions to the great works have wrought on the world.

He switches off the light and retreats to bed, to await whatever the day might bring.

Learn more about this author at:
https://www.mariscapichette.com.

# EAT ME

## MIKE MORGAN

SANELE LOOKED over the safety railing of the observation platform and called down, "Suppertime, dear monster!" He pressed the Release button and half a ton of city waste cascaded down from the chute in the ceiling. The noise was incredible, along with the stench. Both sound and smell filled the echoing interior of the Refuse Reprocessing Plant's cavernous vault.

In the old days, the enormous, building-sized kammappa would have consumed the refuse in seconds, but Sanele watched as the gelatinous mass scooped up barely half the trash with its multiple sharp-edged tongues.

"I thought that the larger a kammappa gets, the more it eats."

Sanele glanced to his side. His coworker, Liyana, had joined him on the platform. "Muncher will finish up the delivery later."

"It's slowing down. Getting old."

"He's still good," insisted Sanele, not correcting her misreading of the situation.

Liyana shook her head. "No, it isn't. It's time Muncher

was put out of our misery. More efficient to get a new one. Then we could expand our operation, bring in trash from outside Durban."

"I told you, he'll finish the shipment later. Before the next lot arrives. He's still doing his job."

Liyana stared at him. He didn't like the look she was giving him. "You did tell Sibongile what's going on? That our kammappa is wearing out?"

Sibongile was the plant manager. Sanele looked away. "Not yet. It's not time."

"You're attached, I get it. You've worked here ever since they caught the beast and trapped it here ten years ago. But that thing is a monster, not a pet. Before it was locked up, it tried to eat the city, remember? Killed hundreds. If its day is over, then good riddance."

"He's no danger to anyone. Not anymore."

"That's not the point. This is a business." She sighed. "Want me to talk to the boss for you?"

Anger flashed through him. "No. I'm the shift supervisor. I'll do it when I'm ready. You keep your nose out."

He wasn't looking at her, so he couldn't see her expression. Still, he would've bet a week's wages that she was rolling her eyes at him.

"Fine, fine. You do it. But don't leave it too long, eh? The more trash we process, the higher our annual bonuses, and I want these expensive earrings I saw in the new hypermart."

He ignored her, once again directing his gaze downward at the faint glow of the containment sigils and the sluggish movements of the dying giant.

"The usual?"

Sanele nodded. The bar was hot, loud, and smelled of the sweat of people who'd worked long days. But that combination still wasn't enough to dislodge the worries from Sanele's mind.

The bartender pushed a beer across the counter. "Liyana giving you a hard time again?"

Sanele had bent the bartender's ear about his co-worker a few times. "She has strong opinions. I respect that. Wish they weren't so different from mine, though."

"What is it now?"

"She wants me to put down Muncher. Recommend to the boss that we get a replacement in."

The bartender nodded. "I'm not surprised."

Sanele hesitated as he reached for his beer glass. "What do you mean?"

"You don't know? She hates your kammappa. Of course she wants to see it gone."

Sanele shrugged. Most people weren't exactly fond of gigantic blobby monstrosities that consumed everything in sight, even when they were caged behind barriers of high-grade thaumaturgy. He hadn't liked Muncher himself until he'd figured out what else the creature could do.

The bartender let out a loud laugh. "You really don't know." He leaned on the bar counter. "When your monstrous friend appeared out of thin air all those years ago and went on its rampage, it killed a lot of people."

"I know." Sanele remembered. He'd never forget.

That morning was forever etched in history. One moment, people had been going about their everyday business — the next, they were screaming in panic as the world transformed around them. People turned into monsters, folklore became real, myths transfigured into reality. Magic transmuted into fact. All because some English lunatic called Asmodeus Jones thought it would be fun to meddle with the setting of reality, like the world was some kind of computer game and he'd figured out a cheat code.

The bartender shook his head. "You don't. Your kammappa killed Liyana's sister."

A chill settled over Sanele's chest. "He did?"

"She sure thinks so. The bodies were never found, but her sister, her brother-in-law, and her niece were never seen again. Gone, just like that." He made a gesture of things vanishing into smoke. "She blames the kammappa."

"How can she be certain? Lots of monsters killed people that day." *And lots every day since,* he added to himself.

"They found no remains," explained the bartender. "That's what the kammappa does. It consumes things utterly. Stuff goes in, nothing comes out. With other magical creatures, there's always a trace. Bones, blood. Something."

Sanele sipped his beer. "How do you know all this about Liyana's family?"

The bartender straightened. "Your trash plant is next door. You're not the only one there who gets thirsty."

"Sounds like she talks a lot."

"Enough for me to be certain that if she's found a way to kill that monster, she won't stop until it's dead."

Sanele wondered whether Liyana had applied for work at the plant so she could do just that. Whatever her motives, he couldn't let her succeed. He needed Muncher alive.

"I don't know how you do it."

Liyana's words caught him by surprise, and Sanele paused in his inspection of the vault's containment sigils. He shifted his weight, causing the double-person cage in which they stood to swing on the cord that suspended it from the ceiling. "Don't know how I do what?"

He thought she was going to say "sleep at night," on account of his work with the creature that had slaughtered her family. He was relieved to hear her say instead, "That breakfast sandwich you ate at your desk this morning. Dripping with grease. And I saw you at the bar last night. You sank six beers. Not for the first time, either. All those calories, and you're thin as a stick. No hangover, no beer belly. I so much as *look* at a second beer on a night out and I have to diet for a week to take the weight back off."

That seemed like an exaggeration, but he understood her point. "Must be my metabolism."

"Oh. I thought maybe it was magic."

He stiffened.

Seeing his reaction, she added, "So much these days is, you know. Sometimes I think there's no science left in the world."

Good — she didn't suspect. "People always did believe more in superstition. Since Asmodeus, they've been right to do so."

"I miss how it was before. It's getting harder to remember those times."

He imagined "those times" for Liyana had involved spending time with her sister and niece.

Maybe he'd misjudged her thoughts, because she continued, "These days, I spend most of my time worrying about being cursed."

"Hexes?" He considered her words. "You know, you can buy anti-curse charms in the market."

"Those don't work."

"Not the cheap ones," he agreed. "Do you think you're likely to be attacked with magic? I didn't think you had enemies."

"You hear stories of random curses. Witch doctors, shamans, umthakathi, tagati … all of them hurting people because they think it'll make them more powerful." She glanced at the mass of the creature resting quietly below them. "At least your Muncher does what it does due to instinct, not any form of malice."

"They're rare," he agreed, sensing an opportunity. "Getting another might not be as easy as you think."

"You haven't brought up its performance issues with the boss yet, then."

Liyana wasn't letting it go. Sanele sighed and returned to checking the spells engraved on the vault's metal walls, happy for an excuse not to answer. The plant couldn't afford to build the containment structure entirely out of steel, or any other form of iron-based metal that acted as a deterrent to magical creatures. Apart from the support beams and girders, the remainder was a mixture of concrete and less expensive metal — hence the need for an ethereal barrier that the creature couldn't digest.

"Focus on these sigils, Liyana. If any of them wear out, the neighborhood will have a very unwelcome visitor." Too late, he realized what he'd said and winced internally. He hoped his comment wouldn't dredge up bad memories for her.

"It won't live forever, you know."

*He doesn't have to*, he reflected. *He just has to live long enough for me to get rich.*

Liyana's expression grew sad. "I didn't think it'd get old. With its supernatural powers, I imagined it would live forever."

Sanele made a noncommittal sound. He wasn't going to be drawn into this conversation and risk letting slip the fact that kammappas didn't actually age. Liyana's assumption served him too well.

Whatever happened, he couldn't let her blab to their manager. Sibongile would not be as easily fooled; he'd know something was up and investigate until he found out what was affecting the kammappa.

"I heard something about your family. Your sister." A desperate gamble, as likely to backfire as to put her off the scent.

"You heard what?" she said stiffly.

"She disappeared." He shifted his attention to the slumbering jelly-like behemoth twenty meters below. "You think Muncher was responsible, right? Is that why you have it in for him?"

"I think the world's full of things trying to kill us. I didn't see what happened to my sister or her family. The last I heard, they were seeking shelter at the docks."

He recalled images of the shocking scene at the South African port. "There were things in the sea that morning. They tore the ships apart."

She shrugged. "Maybe it was them. I don't know, really. We searched so long for any sign of Nolwandle. Never found anything."

Sanele rearranged his features into what he hoped was a sympathetic expression. "It was chaos. Don't blame yourself. So many families were torn apart. So few found any closure."

She blinked back tears. "I'm not here to cause trouble, if that's what you're thinking. I need the paycheck."

"I know, Liyana. You're a good worker." He went back to his inspection. "We'll say no more about it."

At the end of their shift, Sanele waited for Liyana to leave. Then, he reentered the vault and used the cage to lower himself within arm's reach of Muncher's huge gelatinous blob.

It was hard to see where the creature's mouth was until it opened. If it did so when Sanele was this close, he'd know exactly where death was coming from. Sanele had to keep reminding himself that the monster was lethal. He may have cared for him for years, but the kammappa was not his pet.

Of course, he'd done more than care for the monster. He'd hurt him too. And he meant to keep on hurting him.

Sanele's stomach gurgled. He paid it no heed.

"Liyana thinks you're getting old," he whispered to the creature. His slime-coated exterior rippled. "She doesn't know you're weak because of me."

Maybe he'd been extracting too much. Muncher took two or three bouts to get through a municipal trash shipment now. People were going to notice his decline. Liyana had. Fortunately, her powers of observation hadn't landed Sanele in hot water — yet.

He extracted a bag from a pouch on his toolbelt. Best to be quick about it. Muncher had eaten recently, true, but kammappas rarely got full. The creature's current quiescence could be a sham. Or maybe his confinement and mistreatment had made him miserable.

No, hardly likely. He was a mountain of slime. He didn't have feelings.

With a deft flick of a trowel, Sanele scooped up a lump of Muncher's foul substance. He shoved it into the bag without letting any of the unnatural matter touch his skin. The bag was shielded with the same sigils used on the vault's walls. Sanele had worked here so long that he had the shapes of the written incantations memorized.

The small crater left by the trowel darkened and blistered, turning from pale gray into a putrid purple. That was the problem: every time Sanele removed some of Muncher's mass, an entire section died. That was why the creature wasn't getting any bigger, no matter how much they fed him. That was why he was so weak and listless. All his strength went into healing these wounds.

If past experience was anything to go by, Muncher would look normal again when the next shift started. The purple would fade and the dent Sanele had made with the trowel would fill in. The perfect crime.

Sanele pressed the button for the cage to lift, returning him to the upper platform.

Now to get his ill-gotten gains out of the plant without anyone noticing. He'd worked here forever. The gate guards didn't search him. They knew good old Sanele — would never imagine he'd do anything wrong, like stealing parts of the creature the company depended on.

Sanele was doing the city of Durban a favor, he reflected. By weakening the creature, he was making everyone safer. How could that be a crime?

Of course, this civic benefit was a side effect. What Sanele was really interested in was getting rich.

His guts rumbled again, less powerfully this time. Nerves, he decided.

Safe in his apartment, Sanele heated up some curry. No salad for him — only calorie-dense, delicious food, and as much of it as he liked. After devouring his dinner, he weighed himself.

If anything, he was lighter than he'd been last night. Oh dear, no matter how much he ate he couldn't put any weight on. Chuckling, he recorded the number from his scales in a notebook.

He flipped through the notebook's pages, reviewing his progress. A whole year and he hadn't put on a single kilo.

All while consuming double the calories he should have. More than that, once he factored in the beer.

That was a downside to what he was doing: he missed getting drunk. The lump in his stomach absorbed most of the alcohol before it could get into his bloodstream. It also absorbed most of the liquids he drank, so Sanele was constantly guzzling water to avoid dehydration.

Still, ignoring those limitations, his little experiment was looking very promising. He'd been diligent. He'd tested thoroughly on himself, so no one else found out what he was doing and so he could personally attest to the safety and effectiveness of his product.

It had been expensive as well. He was spending a fortune on food and beer. Just as well he didn't have anything else to waste his salary on, other than rent. Nonetheless, he was relieved to think that he'd soon be raking in some much-needed cash. He'd taken all the risks. Now it was time for the rewards.

He put away the notebook in a safe place, then opened the cabinet below his TV set. There, arranged neatly in rows, were the four hundred small bags of kammappa-flesh he'd accumulated over the years. Each had the same defensive sigils inscribed on its fibers. Following the same routine he went through at work, he checked that every bag was still intact.

Safety was important. The flesh wasn't dead, and he didn't want it getting out. As long as no one fed it, the stuff should stay dormant.

Until he sold it.

Once the customers swallowed the bags' contents, the sigils would cease to matter. From that point on, new spells would come into play. Ones that would cause the scoops of monster flesh to lodge in their upper intestines and not get flushed out. Ones that would keep the buyers safe by preventing the voracious lumps from consuming the bodies of their hosts. Ones that would keep the lumps physically small no matter how much they ate. Those were complex spells. Ones he'd paid a lot of rand to a tagati for.

*Any day now,* he thought. *Any day now and I can launch my website for the world's first entirely effective, permanent diet tool.*

He was going to make a fortune. He'd be one of the richest men in the world.

Anyone could starve themselves and drop a few pounds. The trick was keeping it off. With these beauties, that would never be a problem again.

The kammappa inside his customers would eat all the excess food people could cram down their throats. His product would be a sensation the world over.

Grinning, he finished his safety checks and closed the cabinet.

Another day, another shipment of trash. Sanele watched the cascade of garbage rain down on Muncher.

"It's so slow," moaned Liyana. "I swear it takes longer to eat up a shipment every day."

"You're imagining it." Sanele suppressed a smirk. He was trying to decide on a good name for his online storefront.

The door between the observation platform and the office opened. Sanele turned around at the sound and saw Sibongile step through.

Panic coursed through him. Sibongile never visited the vault. He was too important to visit his underlings.

"What brings you here, boss?" Sanele blurted out.

The manager's expression was sour. "Liyana has some concerns."

Sanele glared at his coworker. "You went behind my back."

Liyana stared back at him. "I told you the creature's condition would impact our bonuses. Not my fault if you're too proud to ask for help."

Their manager approached the railing and looked over the edge. "What the hell? Why is the kammappa so small? We feed it tons of waste every day. It should be filling this vault." His face crumpled with confusion. "Our projections indicated that the kammappa would be outgrowing the vault this year. We were planning on investing in a larger facility. But this ..." He waved at the mound of ooze. "Why is it so small? Is it sick? Liyana claims it's off its food."

"He must be getting old ..." began Sanele.

"Oh, nonsense," interrupted their manager. "They live forever. It's a mountain of magical snot with a mouth. It isn't subject to normal physical processes." He took a deep breath. "I want a closer look. Come with me. We'll use the cage to give it a visual inspection."

Liyana asked, "Want me to come with you?"

"No, just me and Sanele. He's senior to you and should take the risk." Sibongile narrowed his eyes at Sanele. "Also, he should have been the one to alert me to what was happening. This is his responsibility."

Sanele went over to the cage and got it ready.

Maybe it was stress, but something in his stomach shifted again.

Sanele couldn't get fired. He needed a source of kammappa flesh. If his thefts were discovered, he'd be lucky to stay out of jail. Even then, he'd be limited to selling the stocks in his apartment. There was a fortune at risk.

Sibongile joined him in the two-person cage and Sanele hit the Down control. With a grinding sound, the winch started lowering the narrow, rectangular platform.

"It seems distracted," said the manager.

Sanele watched the monster sucking in the refuse. Multiple long, tooth-dotted tongues slithered out of Muncher's maw, herding in the piles of rotting food, broken furniture, and plastic packaging. "We should be safe here." He paused the cage's descent.

"No, I want to be closer. I can't see well enough at this range."

Sanele glanced at his boss. "Sir, the kammappa is dangerous. We shouldn't—"

Sibongile pushed Sanele aside and operated the controls himself. They descended another ten meters, until the bottom of the platform was barely clear of the creature's pulsating hide.

The weird sensation in Sanele's stomach intensified. "We should go back up a few meters," he gasped. "We never get this close."

Sibongile noticed Sanele's distress. "Are you well? You've gone a peculiar color. Almost the same shade of gray as your Muncher there."

Beads of sweat sprung from Sanele's face. "I'm not feeling so good."

"Maybe whatever's wrong with the kammappa is catching." The manager triggered the controls again, bringing them back up. "This isn't over, Sanele. I'm not resting until I get to the bottom of this. That kammappa is the foundation of our entire operation. If it dies, we're in serious trouble."

Sanele was too busy running for the bathroom to answer.

That tagati had charged a week's worth of Sanele's wages for the spells. "They won't wear off," the tagati had assured him.

There, in one of the plant's bathroom stalls, sitting on a toilet, pants around his ankles, Sanele was not so sure.

He recalled the strange feelings in his guts that had afflicted him in the cage. They had grown worse the closer he'd gotten to the monster. In truth, he'd experienced twinges every time he'd gotten close to Muncher to scoop out a chunk.

He bore some of the beast's flesh in his upper intestines. Could a kammappa's flesh call to flesh? If a stolen portion was placed atop the monstrosity, would it fuse with the creature, become a part of it anew?

Four hundred times he'd lowered himself near the monster. Was four-hundred-and-one times one too many?

The pain hadn't lessened with distance. Sanele imagined the lump in his stomach being tugged at by its proximity to the motherlode. Yanked. Dislodged.

*Oh no.*

His bowels spasmed.

*No, no, no.*

The spells were cast on Sanele's body. They were on his interior, guarding his organs, stopping the kammappa-segment from eating him from the inside out.

He strained uncontrollably, knowing his doom was imminent. His body was betraying him.

A dreadful *plop* came to his ears. For a wonderful moment, the pain vanished.

Then the toilet beneath him shuddered.

Sanele jumped to his feet. The pants around his ankles

tangled. He tripped and fell, striking his head on the stall door. Dazed, he watched the toilet bowl crack and disappear.

There was something in the ruin of the toilet. Something eating everything it touched.

Long tongues flicked out of the broken ceramic.

Sanele had wanted the creature to eat the unneeded food he shoved down his gullet, but it seemed that the kammappa had other ideas.

With a scream, Sanele thrashed on the stall floor, groping for the lock on the door.

The spells protected his insides, not his exterior. They weren't designed to do anything if the kammappa was torn from him. That hadn't been part of his business strategy.

Sanele's fingers found the bolt of the lock at the same instant the creature's tongue found his foot.

It pulled and Sanele lost his grip.

"No!" shrieked Sanele. "Don't kill me. I was going to keep you alive!"

But the monster had no mind with which to hear his pleas. It was hunger, and it needed to feed.

That was all. To feed without end, until all was consumed.

Outside, the city of Durban sweltered in the African heat, its population oblivious to the growing danger.

Learn more about this author at:
https://perpetualstateofmildpanic.wordpress.com/.

# BETWEEN TWO URNS WITH MARSHALL THERMADOR

## LENA NG

THE RED LIGHT flashed and the live studio audience, seated upon twelve padded bleachers, quickly fell silent. The interviewer, his desk flanked on either side by an imposing Grecian urn, swiveled his chair and flashed a wide, plastic smile. The shine of the studio lights gave his skin the sheen of a Ken doll, and his monochromatic brown hair was plastered against his skull by five layers of extra-strength hairspray.

Sharing the stage and seated on chairs to the left of the host were three special guests. The host spoke to the camera. "Welcome to another episode of *Between Two Urns*! I am your host, Marshall Thermador. Our guests are here today to discuss the making of their new movie, 'The Monster Mashup.' Please welcome Nosferella, Frankenstein, and the Wolfman!"

A cheer arose from the studio audience as the three guests smiled and waved. The green-skinned man with a square head continued to wave a meaty hand after the applause was over, a grin plastered across his face. He may have been a corpse — and a massive one at that — but he had a perfect set of Chicklet chompers. The sleeves and pants of his double-breasted suit, however, were about two inches too short.

"Umm, just to be clear," he said. "I'm not actually Frankenstein. I'm his monster, or as I like to be called, his creation. It has a more positive connotation, you see. I have a name as well, it's—"

"Wolfman, what did you do to get into character?" asked Thermador. "I thought you only transformed during a full moon."

The Wolfman crossed one leg over the other, the bulging muscles accentuated by the slim cut of his European suit. The fur on his face was freshly clipped, the brows trimmed neatly across his forehead as though he had come directly from the groomer. "That's a good question, Mr. Thermador. No one is much interested in the human side of werepeople. Joe Schmoe from anywhere is a nobody, even if he turns into a wolf once a month. So I started this experimental treatment that keeps me in wolfman form all year. It's the dosage that keeps me from going all ..." He waggled his thick, red tongue from side-to-side, big drops of drool splattering, and scrunched up his hands.

"And what about you, Mr., uh, Creation?" asked Thermador.

The hulking green-skinned man crossed his thick arms in front of his broad chest. "You can refer to me as Mr. Bonneville. Or Chester, if you'd rather a more informal tone."

Thermador leaned back in his leather chair, nostrils flaring. "I can discern from your ... odour that it must have been easy to play a re-animated body, Chester."

Chester shifted in his chair, which popped a button off of the front of his double-breasted suit. "With all due respect, sir, this is what I have fought against my entire career: being type-cast. Just because I'm a resurrected corpse, I constantly get audition calls for *The Walking Dead-heads*. I'm not a zombie; that's a whole other thing." His green face began to grow red. "Or *Frankfurter IV*. That monster was *based* on me and now I'm playing him. How does that make sense? I studied at Julliard when it was called Five Burroughs Community College. I've taken the Stanislavsky Method. I've memorized soliloquies from *The Two Gentlemen of Verona* to *The Two Noble Kinsmen*. But do I ever get calls for *Hamlet*? Never. *And* I'm a triple threat. I have a lovely singing voice and wonderful soft shoe, and I still only get offered the crappiest parts. My agent called me up recently and asked if I'd take a leading role for the movie, *Frankenstein's Monster Was My Dead Lover*." He sighed. "I told him only if the money's good. It's coming out next year." He feebly acknowledged the cheering audience.

Thermador turned to his third guest, who wore a plunging dress of black crepe. Her eyes were a mesmerizing iridescent black. "Nosferella, I've read that you're not just a pretty face, but that you have an academic background as well."

Nosferella adjusted her glasses over her pert, upturned nose. She spoke with only a hint of an accent. "I studied medieval torture when it was a contemporary subject. I graduated from Transylvania State in 1362, and received a PhD in Phlebotic Theory in 1453. I make sure to complete another degree every one hundred and fifty years or so just to keep current."

"What have you learned?"

Nosferella gave a slight shrug with her slender shoulders as she replied, "That we don't learn from history."

Thermador pulled on his square, implanted chin as he stared deeply into her oil-slick eyes. "I understand you read minds. Can you hear my thoughts? What am I thinking?"

Nosferella's deep-red smile couldn't quite contain her pointed teeth, which enticingly dimpled her generous lips. "Something that can't be repeated on television, I'm afraid."

"You really *can* read my thoughts ..."

"We vampires mastered telepathy centuries ago. You humans are only just starting to catch up. We're the ones who invented wireless communication." Nosferella continued to smile at the host as though she were feasting upon him with her eyes.

At the pointed hiss of the cameraman, Thermador managed to break his gaze long enough to glance at the cue cards on his desk. He shuffled through them until something caught his attention.

"Here's a question from our studio audience that they've been dying to ask, the most requested one in our 'Ask the Audience' segment." He turned towards his guests, pausing briefly to build suspense. "If the three of you got into a fight, who would win?"

Amid the cheers from the audience, the Wolfman bared his teeth. "What a ridiculous question." His long canines, for which he regularly spent a fortune at the National Zoo's own specialty dentist, shone with a bright gleam under the studio lights. "I mean, everyone knows it wouldn't be much of a contest. Incredible strength, full capacity howling, method acting — there isn't much I'm not the best at."

Although Chester's green cadaverous face couldn't manage a wide range of facial expressions, even the back row of the audience could see his incredulousness. "What method acting? You smell like that all the time."

The Wolfman leaned over and gave an exaggerated sniff of Chester's green body. "The good clean smell of pure animal? That's much better than Eau de Old Corpse."

Chester turned up his chin. "At least I don't shed."

"It's my summer coat," replied the Wolfman as he picked some stray hairs off his suit.

Chester pursed his thick-lipped mouth. "Clearly, you need to go to a higher quality dog groomer."

The Wolfman started to emit a low, rumbling growl and his yellow eyes darkened to a demonic red. Sensing the storm, Nosferella stood and held open her slender-yet-powerful arms. "Gentlemen, gentlemen. Here's the problem. People tear us apart. Why can't monsters support other monsters?"

Thermador nodded in agreement. "Wonderfully said, Nosferella. Why can't we just agree that you're all horrible monsters and an abomination in the face of God?"

There was a monstrous silence as three pairs of formerly-human eyes turned to glare at the host. The audience sat frozen in their seats. Even the cameraman stopped blinking.

Then someone in the bleachers laughed, a scathing, deep-bellied cackle.

The Wolfman released a blistering howl as he launched himself at the source of the noise. The audience answered with a vortex of screams as they ran for the doors. People piled onto each other as they scrambled for the exits.

Frankenstein's Monster dropped all pretense of civility — Chester Bonneville no more. He seemed to have lost the power of speech, adding to the cacophony with his own wordless grunts and roars. When he reached the bleachers, he grabbed the closest man, spun, and hurled him like a discus across the studio. The man's plump body spun around and around like a human Frisbee until he hit the wall with a fleshy splat.

With a flip of her long black hair, Nosferella transformed into a giant bat. She swooped down to nip any exposed necks or noses, depending on what she could sink her teeth into. Blood spurted over the bleachers.

Above the fracas, Thermador jumped onto his chair, pointing. He screamed to the camera crew, "Are you filming this? Did you get that?"

He was too slow to notice that the crew had already fled from their posts.

Bounding back onto the stage, the Wolfman seemed to be all wide staring eyes, bristling fur, and red cavernous jaws. "Monsters?" he screamed at the cowering host, who was now crouching behind his chair. "You made us what we are."

With one clawed hand gripping Thermador's ribcage and the other grasping his hip, the Wolfman tore Thermador in two like a wishbone. He threw the top half into one urn, while the remaining half ended up in the other. Behind him, Nosferella and Frankenstein's Monster rampaged the remains of the audience.

With blood dripping from his slavering jaws, the Wolfman ripped off his Armani suit, smashed the nearest window, and ran howling into the night.

# BREAKTHROUGH

## LAURA ENGELHARDT

My father stood in the doorway of my study with that perfectly still military stance he trained into the recruits, and I knew that we'd lost.

"Otō-san, sit down. Let me see it." His arm was badly burned from wrist to elbow, and I had to work at keeping my voice even.

He was wearing the blank face he'd trained me to don before I was ten. But his mask couldn't hide the white pallor of his pain or the sweat that beaded his brow.

I opened the blinds fully, and turned to evaluate the swirls of yellow and umber magick circling the room in a reverse flocking pattern. Burns were tricky, and I'd need more than my own personal power to cast the necessary healing spells. I debated turning on the overheads but decided the dim sunlight contained enough dissolved silica-salt.

"Otō-san, sit, please," I repeated, pointing at the chair in front of my worktable. Looking at his charred forearm, it was hard not to let my anger show. This was no battle wound. No, Prefeita Gerel had used the magick she'd taken from me to punish him.

How could we have lost again? This had been our best chance to reclaim a little ground in this misbegotten fight.

"It was my fault," he said, his face stiff with suppressed pain. Typical. Whenever Gerel levied her "light" punishments, he claimed responsibility. I'd grown to hate his need to own all that went wrong ... or right. But nothing was going right anymore.

I whisked the spell diagrams off my worktable with more force than necessary, but rolled them up carefully. "You didn't get *any* of their senior people?"

He exhaled and finally sat, holding his arm out for me. I leaned against the table, absorbing some of the umber-tinted magick swirling around the room into my personal power.

"They were waiting for us." My father's Japanese was clipped and curt.

We're finished. I looked away from his resigned expression. Even if surrender were a possibility, my father would die first.

That was a terror I couldn't quite face, so instead I concentrated on the spell. It took longer than it should have to align the faint hatch-work net of magick over his arm. But once I started, the familiar act of casting the enchantment helped me regain my calm.

Using the fading sunlight's power, I gradually replaced the damaged basal cells in his epidermis. The burns weren't nearly as bad as they could have been, which made me wonder. This was my master's version of a slap on the wrist.

Even if today's raid had been a disaster, had actually ended as badly as it seemed, Gerel may not have intended these third-degree burns as punishment for him. No, this could easily be a warning for me. Because despite weeks of practice, I still hadn't perfected the language transfer spell — Gerel's signature mind magick enchantment that conferred language fluency from one subject to another.

We were about to be crushed, and Gerel was wasting my magick to damage her own senior commander! Wasting what little resources she had left in her ill-conceived fight to unseat Meng Tian, the current Ruler of Rio.

If she dies, you'll be free, came the evil thought that I quickly buried. If she dies, it'll be over his dead body, I reminded myself. And it would be my fault; I wasn't the battlemage my master had expected. Needed.

My casting faltered, and I blinked rapidly to clear my vision before I could lose sight of the gossamer-like threads of light I was weaving into my father's skin.

"It wasn't your fault, Kyoko. Or mine, for that matter," Dad said. He knew me too well. "This raid should have been a success. Meng Tian's people escaped only because they were forewarned. I killed the traitor, but Prefeita Gerel does not accept excuses."

"Of course not," I murmured, pulling my power back. Though I couldn't blame my dad for failing to anticipate betrayal from his own men. Who in their right mind would double-cross a vampire? We can still win, I told myself. Everyone says that Gerel hasn't cashed in all her favors from the Amazonian fae. She must know someone —

My dad flexed his arm, grunting as blackened skin flaked off. He nodded once in approval, his eyes meeting mine in a resolute stare.

"Did we lose anyone important?" I asked. For a moment, my dad's mask cracked, and I saw a glimpse of pain.

"Everyone is important now." His face shut down again,

and he stood. *"Obrigado,"* he said, switching from Japanese back into Portuguese.

*"De nada."* I followed him to the door. "Maybe I should take a break and join you for dinner." Today's disaster was a sharp reminder that I needed to take advantage of every moment we had left.

"Is Mamá making *moqueca*?" She often made my dad's favorite dish on days like today to celebrate his safe return.

He turned back, another flash of pain darting across his face, and I wondered if I'd cast the nerve block properly.

"Another time, Kyoko. The Prefeita wants to see you tonight."

"Oh." And despite my father's assurance that I wasn't to blame for his burns, I started to worry.

He turned and shut the door softly behind him.

I stayed at the window after he crossed the courtyard and disappeared into his quarters, watching the pinkish glitter of magick that sparkled in the air outside.

When I switched schemas, the glitter shifted into a precise flow of power that washed the area in thick rings of variegated blues. I switched from H-4 to F-4 to B-6 and back again, staring at the changing colors of magick until the last wisp of daylight faded.

I'd started adjusting my perception between schemas as practice. Gerel insisted I achieve fluency even in my secondaries. But by now, my penchant for flipping my perception had become almost a nervous habit — like the way my mother bit her nails, or how Gerel tapped her fingers.

It was self-indulgent to delay the inevitable like this, even if seeing magick through different schemas helped me calm down. I turned away from the window and headed through the interior door that led to the lower levels, and Gerel's office.

She has to know I'm making progress. Language

transfer spells were the hardest mind magick enchantments to learn. And Gerel's spell had proven too complex for anyone else to cast. But my master wanted results, not excuses. I closed my eyes and waited for the elevator.

Our current base of operations was in Rio's favelas. The encampment had been built into a hilltop, and while the surface buildings looked as ramshackle as any of the others in the slum, the hillside beneath had been engineered into an underground fortress.

Palace was perhaps more apt, since Gerel had a taste for beautiful things. Once the embroidered silk wall coverings had appealed to me — almost making up for the lack of natural light in the lower levels. But after thirteen years, not even the brilliance of sunlit magick could make up for living under her indenture.

Only two thousand five hundred and two days left.

Gerel had been planning this attempt on Rio long before taking me on as her apprentice. I'm sure her desire to own the city was the main reason she'd gone to the trouble. Meng Tian had several pet mages, so I was an asset to be cultivated or neutralized.

She'd miscalculated, though. My heart rate sped up at the memory of Gerel's anger when she'd borrowed my mage-sight that first time. I'm still not quite sure how I survived her realization that I didn't wield the corona of power she expected.

But Gerel didn't tolerate mistakes from anyone, even herself. So after that, my master started bragging that she was training me to be her successor — had she remained a mage of course. Because when she was still alive, Gerel ni Gobi had been the greatest mind mage of her generation. Now she was only a mid-tier vampire.

The elevator let me out on the lowest level. I was so caught up in my worrying that I barely noticed that she'd added another tapestry to the over-decorated walls. As if the clashing colors and patterns sewn into the silk could make up for her lost ability to see magick.

After my first skirmish with Meng Tian's mages, I began to wonder if my master was attempting suicide by starting an unwinnable fight. Other vamps had gone down that path when they couldn't bear to live without magick any longer.

Notwithstanding the odds, she *seemed* intent on winning. But who knew what Gerel really wanted?

Ernesto was standing guard in the hallway. I was clearly expected because he merely nodded as I walked past. He was subdued; word of the day's disaster must have gotten around.

I straightened my shoulders before opening her office door.

Marreta was lounging on the couch with her feet up, a pose that disguised her state of high alert. Gerel stood with her back to me, talking into her secure cellphone. I'd spelled it myself so that no one would be able to hack into her conversations.

The shifter's presence didn't mean anything. Marreta rarely left Gerel's side. But we got along, even if I was an apprentice mage, and she a mage-killer. The were-jaguar was utterly devoted to Gerel, and my indenture kept me loyal. Maybe it was the stress, but we'd actually grown closer the longer this fight had dragged on.

"There will be a price," Gerel said into the phone, her deep voice dropping lower as she warned whoever was on the other end of the line.

I focused on Marreta. *"Who?"* I mouthed.

She smiled, but gave a small shake of her head. Marreta's jaguar hearing was better than mine, and my protective spells on the phone only prevented hacking, not overhearing.

"Wednesday then. I'll send a driver to pick her up." Gerel turned around and gave me a slight nod, then she pursed her lips in annoyance at whatever the person was saying.

"Very well. I understand. My regards to Penthesilea ... *Até logo.*" She disconnected. Marreta and I shared a look at the mention of the faerie queen — maybe Gerel was recruiting some heavy hitters. If so, that was good news indeed. Surely we could hold out till Wednesday; it was just five more days!

Gerel tilted her head to one side as she examined me. I kept my face still. She might have been beautiful once, but now that all her borrowed power was going into the war, she didn't have any to spare for her usual glamours. She looked like the half-dead, walking corpse she really was.

The Asian mages who'd invaded South America centuries ago never expected to be routed by great Chía's rabble, let alone transformed into vampires. Still, Gerel and the other would-be-conquerors had outlasted them, so maybe they did win in a way. A rather bitter victory for a mage: undead, yet unable to cast.

Gerel sat down behind her desk and steepled her bony forefingers together as she evaluated me with her unblinking, magick-blind, vampire eyes.

"You've yet to master language transfer, *okhin*."

"I'm getting closer."

She tapped her fingers together slowly, a bad sign.

"There's little time left. You'll have to master the spell quickly, because by Wednesday, you'll need to calibrate and cast it on a siren. Penthesilea herself has brokered this bargain: in exchange for instant fluency in Portuguese, the siren will gift me a year of her life. So I'm going to walk you through it myself. Mind-to-mind."

My mask was slipping. Don't panic. Don't panic. Don't panic, I urged myself, swallowing heavily.

"Master, I'm not failing because I don't understand how to cast it." Gerel's eyebrow rose, and I hastened to explain. "I mean, I know it's a complex spell. A brilliant design. So much more nuanced than any other spell." I was babbling in my terror. "But you don't need to *show* me. I just need to work on it in daylight. There's too little power in artificial light for a first-time casting this challenging."

Her nostrils flared with distaste at either my cowardice or my lies.

"As you know, this spell requires precision, not power. And spell evaluation is better conducted under reflected light," Gerel said evenly.

I can't do this. I can't. I can't. I can't.

"I am not cruel, *okhin*," she smiled at me, flashing her predator's incisors in an expression that might have been kind had she still been human. "If we had more time, I'd grant you another month to show progress on such a *complex* spell. But you only have five days."

I couldn't keep my teeth from grinding in an effort to remain calm and oscillated my sight to focus on the ambient magick in the room. Rarely had I felt such joy at the sight of so little power: the sputtering pale blue haze wasn't strong enough for the vampire to leech my magick and steal my sight.

My sudden hope was swiftly extinguished by the obvious fact that we didn't have to stay here. There was more than enough moonlight for the spell, and delaying her intrusion wouldn't stop the inevitable pain. *The pain.*

In my panic, I'd missed some of Gerel's explanation.

"—win this war, *okhin*," she said with the inflection that meant daughter instead of girl.

I hated the sudden surge of pleasure at her praise and reminded myself that I already had a mother. A mother who didn't steal my power to hurt my father, who didn't eat my life one day at a time. Who didn't hurt me.

"I never imagined Penthesilea would send me a siren! You have to learn this spell before she arrives. With a year of a siren's life, I'll be able to work such magick—"

"Master, please let me try once more! One last time." I was whining but didn't care. It was better than groveling. If crying would help, I'd cry.

Gerel frowned, and I pulled myself together sharply. It can be worse. She can make it so much worse. "Master, the ambient magick in this room is insufficient." I spoke so fast my words ran together, but Gerel understood.

"Too bad. Language transfer doesn't require much power, but borrowing your sight does." She stood up. "It's a half-moon tonight. That will provide more than enough light. We'll use the back courtyard. Marreta—"

The were was already off the couch. She pulled her black dress off in a fluid motion, shimmering into her jaguar form in a fog of blue-streaked silver.

Gerel didn't go anywhere without her bodyguard, except when the were-jaguar was vulnerable to mage magick during the full moon. And Marreta might be necessary. Once Gerel started puppeting me, I'd be incapable of casting even a basic concealment spell if Meng Tian decided tonight was a good night for a raid.

I can't. I can't. I can't. I can't. I can't. My feet were lead. Gerel was already standing at the door, and Marreta was halfway down the corridor.

"Ernesto, we're going out," I heard her tell the guard.

You have to walk! I ordered myself and slowly moved

toward the door. If I didn't go, she'd have Ernesto carry me. And then she wouldn't try to dampen the impact when she took my mind.

When I stepped into the hall, Gerel took my arm in her bony grasp. It was almost a comfort, her icy hands. I felt numb as we walked toward the elevator. At least I was walking.

"This is my signature spell," she reminded me in a disgustingly gleeful tone.

"Yes, Master," I said.

"Very few mages have learned it since I created it. And no one knows the modifications I added to facilitate a two-way transfer." Her bragging reminded me why I'd sought this indenture in the first place.

Once I mastered this spell, I'd be one of the top ten mind mages in the world — if not top three. And I wasn't even forty years old. I may only hold the power of a Class Four, but with this spell under my belt, I'd certainly rank among the greatest living mages.

"Precision is better than power," she said, not for the first time. I wanted it to be true. She'd told me before that with her training, I could defeat Amir Khalid and conquer Arabia. That wasn't true, of course.

Ernesto had called ahead, so the guards were waiting for us when we emerged in the back courtyard. The city lights washed out any possibility of starlight, but the half-moon shone down, letting the green and gold swirl of magick float into the layer cake effect I loved. The world seen through my preferred schema of H-4 was a luscious confection of power.

The magick hid the ugliness of patchy grass stomped into dirt by too many soldiers' feet, and the light breeze replaced the smell of sweat with the salty brine of the nearby ocean.

I tried to focus on the night's beauty, but the surrounding slums only reminded me of our desperation. At least our snipers weren't hiding; despite all our losses, we could still mount a full guard.

I'm not going to die tonight. I needed to focus on how much worse things could be. Would be, if I didn't master this spell, and Gerel didn't make her bargain with the siren.

We walked over to the lawn chairs the guards had set out. Two stood watch, waiting for us. They weren't talking, and the people in the surrounding hovels were likewise silent. Everyone knew better than to break Gerel's concentration when she came out of her sanctuary.

With a mage to use, vampires could reclaim a fraction of their own lost magick. It took effort, power, and a lot of skill. Gerel was one of the few vampires who had the requisite precision.

But she was such a good teacher — even without mage-sight — that she rarely needed to go to such extremes. And as painful as this puppeting spell was for me, it was ungodly difficult for her. Not just because of its complexity, but because it forced such intimacy on the caster.

The first time she "borrowed" me, I thought she was deliberately causing the pain to distract me from seeing too much in her own mind, too many personal memories. By now, I was experienced enough to realize that my agony was just a side effect. It helped a little to know that she wasn't intentionally torturing me. A little.

She gestured, and Ernesto arranged the lawn chairs so they were facing each other. "Kneel," she told him, pointing to the spot next to us.

He didn't hesitate. So trusting to be my test subject after what happened to the last one. But then, even if it were my body, it would be Gerel casting this spell.

The vampire sat down stiffly. Marreta stood behind her, all bunched muscle and glinting teeth.

As soon as I sat, Gerel reached out to take my hands. Both hands. I couldn't help flinching, but she held them too tightly for me to jerk away. My mouth was dry, and I had to clench it shut to stop hyperventilating.

Calm down. Get it together! I ordered myself.

"First your tithe, then the lesson." Gerel's dark eyes didn't show mercy, but they did show understanding. She knew this was hard for me, and that was a mercy of sorts.

The sharp pain struck. It was a known pain, a familiar pain. The feel of a dagger in my side, twisting a sharp note as she ate a day of my life. This had been our daily ritual for thirteen years: the bargain we'd made when she agreed to be my master, and I her apprentice. For every day of my indenture, I would give her a day of my life.

Then it turned into an unfamiliar agony, a jackhammer bursting through my skull. Through the pounding in my ears, I heard a faint growl, felt the lightning flashes of electric needles tattooing my flesh.

"—open them!" Gerel was saying.

I opened my eyes. The green and gold sparkle in the courtyard was now a fog of black and grey hashes. Gerel preferred to see magick through B-6 and forced my magesight to conform to her desire.

The pain was too intense. I gagged — I couldn't help it. Swallowing made it worse, and I puked so hard, stomach acid burned through my nose. I inadvertently slammed my chin against the metal bucket one of the guards held to keep our master from being fouled by my vomit. They'd been through this before too.

Gerel held my hands in an icy grip, but now I couldn't tell whether she was clinging to me, or I was holding onto her, because she was warping my magick to cut into my mind. The granite slivers of the spell she needed me to learn were digging into my sight.

A purple slash, dot, dot, dot, slash. Then a forward jab as Gerel puppeted my personal power to build the spell in an ouroboros layered pattern. I couldn't appreciate its elegance under her control, but I'm sure it was beautiful.

It hurts, I wept silently.

"Shut up," Gerel ordered. Because of course, she was in my mind too. "Pain is a distraction. Look past it. Imagine how much it hurt when Chía cut out my heart and stole my magick. I'm only borrowing yours."

I sobbed. A memory flashed through the burning torture of her control, but it wasn't mine. I smelled the dust of pressed flowers, felt the polished sheepskin like silk beneath my hands before recognizing a spell schematic written in multi-colored swirls on parchment.

It wasn't the spell Gerel was teaching me. No, it was an old counterspell in a loose, yet somehow precise, pattern. A counterspell to cut through spells? Impossible.

"Focus!" Gerel's voice lashed at me. Thunder pounded through my brain, supersonic footprints that beat my skull from the inside out. I panted in agony.

Black flashed at the edge of my vision, and my eyes fluttered shut. If I fainted, we'd have to do this again. The terror of enduring another session helped me push past it, and I exhaled slowly. Again. Inhale. Exhale. Inhale. Exhale. Inhale—

"Watch with me," Gerel ordered, forcing my eyes open.

Gerel began building the spell on Ernesto. Manipulating my magick to draw lines of gold, purple, and grey into his mind. A delicate work, almost like tatting lace.

That's what I did wrong, I realized, as fire ants burnt the pattern into my consciousness with their vicious capoeira dance.

"Exactly. You see now."

I had failed to let the spell ease into the tissue before. Instead of lightly sewing the spell, I'd thrust too hard. That's why the edges had slipped away. Gerel let the guard's mind absorb the casting. Eventually, his mind would scab over it, and the magical traces around his new command of Japanese would be indistinguishable from naturally-gained knowledge.

She let go, and I collapsed against the chair.

I think I passed out because when I opened my eyes, Gerel and the guards were gone. Instead, Marreta was sitting in Gerel's chair, watching me.

"Can you stand?" she asked. Her yellow eyes raked me over.

I opened my mouth, but no sound came out. I tried to get up, but my legs wouldn't work.

She nodded. "Right then." Marreta picked me up like I weighed nothing and carried me back into the fortress. I think I passed out again because the next thing I remember, she was putting me into a bathtub.

"Marreta?" I croaked.

"You pissed yourself," she said matter-of-factly. "You can try on your own tomorrow. If you can't cast it by night-fall, Gerel will show you again."

I was too exhausted to be afraid.

A good night's sleep erases all but the memory of pain. And last night's pain had been so intense, my conscious brain refused to latch onto it.

My morning optimism didn't fade, even when I looked at myself in the bathroom mirror, and a dead-fish vampire seemed to stare back at me. My skin had lost the glittery luminescence of a high-level mage, and my dark eyes were sunken holes. It was like Gerel had swapped places with me.

Six years, three hundred and eleven days. Less than seven years remained on my indenture. And she still has things to teach me. Most apprenticeships lasted a decade. I'd agreed to the double term because at the time, Gerel was eating through soldiers like candy, and I thought my dad would be safer that way.

*Idiota!* Of course, Gerel didn't think like that. My dad made his own safety by being the best leader Gerel had. And ridiculously loyal.

I pulled on a thin t-shirt and shorts, adding padded compression armor before donning my bespelled robe. Rumor was that Meng Tian had hired one of the jaguar clans. While mage magick didn't work on the weres, the metal-laced padding would give me a slim chance of surviving an attack.

I needed to solidify the knowledge Gerel had etched atop my brain before it became as remote as the agony that had accompanied her lesson. The thought of Gerel repeating her puppetry tonight was just too unbearable to consider.

For all the horror of her twisted teaching, I now knew *exactly* how to cast the spell — the most complicated mind magick spell devised. It required such a delicate touch!

But before I found another subject, I needed to eat. Last night had taken too much out of me. Although, she is a genius. After her latest lesson, it was clear that Gerel could have gone down in history as a great mage, had Chía not destroyed her.

I can be what she could have been. I swayed with a fleeting sense of vertigo. That was a heady thought. Or maybe I was just hungry. I hurried to the kitchens.

"*Olá,*" I called as I walked in. The mundane cooks looked up and quickly away, chopping and stirring in sudden silence. I think I scared them more than Marreta.

Probably because of the new kitchen drudge. Once a soldier in Meng Tian's guard, his vacant smile was a little disturbing. But even if my miscasting had near-lobotomized him, he was luckier than the rest of his cohort. I pointed at the pitcher of fresh orange juice, and he poured me a glass.

"*Arigatō,*" I murmured politely, and he bowed as he backed away. While I'd failed with him, I'd been more successful with that casting than in my earlier attempts. He could at least understand Japanese, even if he no longer had anything to say.

I drummed my fingers on the counter. I needed a new subject, but Gerel had already consumed the life force from our remaining captives.

One of the cooks placed a full plate before me, then retreated to the stove. He probably hoped I'd take it into the dining room, but I was too hungry. Instead, I stood at the counter, shoveling the food into my mouth while the staff tried to avoid my gaze. They didn't need to fear. *Everyone is important now.* My father's flat statement haunted me; there was no fat left in our operation. No room for more losses.

I'd have to find someone in the favelas — I couldn't risk miscasting the spell on one of our own. We'd been losing for so long, my dad might have to enlist the cooks before the end. But Gerel had called in a favor. I wondered how much power she might gain from a siren. Aphrodite had designed the sirens as magical batteries, so I was guessing a lot. Maybe even enough to win.

∼

It was sunny, and I cast a cooling enchantment the moment I walked outside. I'd have to leave the compound to find a subject — someone desperate enough to gamble on the skills of an apprentice mage. The favelas were filled with desperation, though. Even with an intact mind, slum-dwellers didn't live long, but a bilingual mundane could find work and move downtown.

The sunshine exposed the power in the surrounding hills. I flickered through my schemas as I walked, admiring how each revealed nuances in the quality of magick. Through H-4, I could see the wealth of mottled yellow and umber waves. Flipping to B-6, the lines were better defined, a precise shading of power.

Gerel was right: a mage had to be fluent in multiple schemas in order to deconstruct existing spells or design new ones. You needed multiple perspectives to properly perceive the flow of magick. Maybe one day I'd be able to develop my own twist on her language transfer spell. But first I needed to master it according to her design.

I nodded at the sniper leaning against a collapsed second-story wall at the edge of our territory. She didn't nod back, but I saw her talking into her headset. She'd alert the patrols that I was out.

Some kids were kicking a soccer ball around on a plateau that had been cleared for a new hovel. Stacks of rebar and corrugated metal lay in one corner. I watched them for a while, evaluating. But none of the scrawny mundanes looked older than twelve, and I needed an adult.

Umber swirls of magick twined gold and purple around the lot. I allowed myself a moment of indulgence, flipping my sight through my secondary schemas, admiring the languid pattern of power before heading down the side alley that led to gang territory. There'd be plenty of adult volunteers there.

The alley was dark because the houses had been built too close together, and clotheslines were strung between the second-floor windows. The flapping fabric distorted the light, so I was five meters in before realizing I wasn't the only mage on the street.

He'd been relying on the flickering shadows to conceal him between two crumbling buildings, but my sight was finer than most mages', and I could see the dark edges of his look-away spell glistening against the golden hash lining the walls.

He's waiting for me, I realized. *Idiota!* We'd already been betrayed once. Why would I think there was only one traitor? It could have been any of the guards with us last night. They all knew I'd be hunting a new subject today. I'm such a fool!

I didn't slow down, didn't give any sign that I was aware of the other mage's presence, but did send out a minor testing spell to gauge his sensitivity.

He didn't notice when I grazed the edge of his personal power. Class Five. *Puta merda!* I cast a porting spell and pulled the city's ambient magick toward me, blocking it from him with a slight twist. The battlemage would have nothing beyond his own power to draw on.

Let him counterspell that! No way he had the precision to even see my spell, let alone pick it apart. But I was still nervous. He was only meters away and should have attacked by now.

So I did what any outclassed mage does: I threw dust in his face. Not literally, of course. But I cast the same layered obscurement spell I'd used when I'd fought Meng Tian's mercenaries last week. If you can't see, you can't cast.

The alley in front of me filled with darkness: not the dark of night, where there's the hint of starlight or street-light to illuminate the world, but the utter blackness of a cave. Darkness was almost as good as were-immunity when fighting mages. I couldn't see him, but more importantly, he couldn't see *anything*. Without sight, all his power was useless.

A mach three immolation spell ran through the alley. Red hot, purple flames beating against my bespelled robe. *Deus!* He has a flashlight. Of course, he'd be prepared — he was here to ambush me!

I had to unwind my obscurity spell so I could cast a counter before I burned up. It didn't matter how ridiculously easy battle spells were to counter, their force was overwhelming.

Once I unwove my obscurity enchantment, the sparkling white edge of my opponent's immolation spell was unmistakable. I swept my personal power through it, tugging his spell-edge free as I filled myself with all the magick I could grab.

It was too hot in the alley, and I threw a whirlwind based on the Arabian design in a flattened steppe pattern. Gerel's modifications to battle spells were insidious; they made the spells slower to cast, but infinitely more difficult to counter.

The bespelled heat blasted back towards the mage hiding in the shadows. A gold paisley flared toward me. Mach four power toss. I thrust my power through the top of the pattern before he could complete the spell.

He's too powerful.

The mage struck again. Herringbone blue on blue with a glitter of orange: the aptly-named Hammer of God spell.

I countered with the common anvil — no time to add Gerel's special twist — but as the hammer spell dissolved, I caught a glimpse of the mage's face peeking out of the shadows.

"*Bom dia, Senhor,*" I sent. The mage's mind was

protected, but I slipped through the crevices. *"I pledge a truce for parlay!"*

The silence was deafening. Black ash from the fire-blasted concrete fluttered around, drifting down like pollen from a shaken palm tree.

*"Bom dia,* Kyoko apprentice de Gerel ni Gobi." His French-accented Portuguese resonated dully in the empty, blackened alley. The mage stepped out, clicking off the heavy flashlight he carried. His broad face bore the scars of several duels.

His identity was obvious: Meng Tian had hired Gilles Jacques de Atacama, the top battlemage in South America. Lord have mercy, I prayed, watching him cavalierly stow his flashlight in his pocket.

What did Meng Tian offer him? Gilles Jacques didn't leave the desert he'd conquered anymore. At least, that was what his people told Gerel when she promised him a fortune to hire on with us.

"A parlay?" He raked his eyes up and down, trying to discern my personal power through my shields. "I see why Meng Tian admires your skill. You're wasted on a dead master who can't even see to train you."

What was more surprising about his flattery was the lack of any persuasive spelling around his words. He drew a lot of power, so much so that his aura's thick layers of magick were impossible to penetrate. But when I flipped my sight from H-4 to F-4, I could see the gaps.

He was ostentatious and sloppy, using brute force to win. Typical battlemage. All power and no skill. But unless you were a great mage like Chía, it was brute force that won wars, not precision. At least he was willing to toy with me.

"Gerel's mundane soldiers are fleeing her cause like rats from a sinking ship," I declared. There was an odd line of magick about him that I wanted to probe, but I had to give him something, keep him talking.

"Your master's suicide attempt is starting to cut into Meng Tian's profits. While the Ruler of Rio was willing to indulge her at first, out of courtesy, the time has come for this game to end."

I swallowed, but my mask held. "My indenture holds me another six years ... or so long as my master lives." To be free of Gerel! I thought wistfully. If Meng Tian killed my master, the apprenticeship would be dissolved. No more puppeting. No more burns. But my father would never sell out; he'd die at Gerel's side.

Gilles Jacques' eyebrows raised. "Would you seek *another* master?"

I traced the faint yellow twist of magick that rose from Gilles Jacques into the rooftops. The brute doesn't notice my probes! There was a snorting sneeze above me, and I looked with my mundane-sight up to the balcony above. Or maybe he does. Out of the blackness, two yellow eyes looked down on me. A were-jaguar. My hope died completely when I oscillated my vision back to mage-sight.

Because it wasn't just any jaguar, it was a *leashed* jaguar. The yellow helix looped into the pale green corset of magick shining around the were's neck and shoulders.

"It's sloppy to let your spells show," I told him, proud that my voice didn't shake.

He laughed. "Ostentatious, perhaps. But I didn't let him eat you because I wanted to see if Meng Tian was right, that a Class Four apprentice could survive ten minutes against me."

I'm dead. While Gerel's spells might enable me to out-cast the arrogant battlemage, evading a were-jaguar under Gilles Jacques' control was impossible.

There's a clarity, a stillness, that comes when you accept

your fate. I would die in this alley, and the certainty of that fact no longer bothered me. Instead, I spent my remaining moments on Earth admiring the smooth simplicity of the yellow helix that connected the were to the mage. I'd never seen a leashed construct before.

"Betting against a vampire is always risky," I remarked, continuing my examination.

He put his hands in the pockets of his robe as he evaluated me in turn. I think I amused him. "I haven't had an apprentice in almost fifty years. Never less than a Class Five."

His self-satisfied smile was more disgusting than Gerel's glee when she drank her enemies dry.

"I bet you could teach me to sling spells that would even terrify the Amir." I was delaying the inevitable with my ridiculous flattery. Even blind to magick, Gerel has a hundred times his knowledge! I suddenly remembered the feel of sheepskin, the ancient spell diagram I'd seen in Gerel's mind.

Gilles Jacques' personal power tapped into the spell that tied the were-jaguar's very essence together. If I pressed a perfectly matched line of magick against the pressure points in the leash, would it crack open? The battlemage was too insensitive to notice.

"Fight my jaguar and win, and I'll take you on once your undead master is fully dead," Gilles Jacques' indifferent tone was crueler than his spells.

"You think I can't do it?" I asked, but my focus was on the magical leash. If I press there and there, it might snap. Without the jaguar, the battlemage could be neutralized. Maybe. If I were fast.

I met Gilles Jacques' confident gaze evenly. "Do you want him dead or merely defeated? Because I'm not sure I can win without killing him, and a leashed were is a valuable resource."

Gilles Jacques laughed again. *"C'est magnifique!* I like you, girl."

Gerel had long since beaten out of me the need to gesture ostentatiously when I cast my spells. And I didn't have to look at the subject anymore for simple mind magick enchantments. So I readied the blinding spell and pressed against the jaguar's leash.

"You're far too important to be drawn into an insignificant vampire war. Meng Tian must have offered you a lot."

"She has been around a long time, *ma fille,*" Gilles Jacques wagged his finger at me.

At first, nothing happened when I pressed. Gilles Jacques began bragging about all the things the Ruler of Rio had promised him. I nodded my appreciation of his clever bargaining while gradually increasing the force of my spell, shifting my vision back to H-4 as I twisted my power.

The leash flashed incandescent as I slashed through it. The freed magick hurtled toward me, and I grabbed it, gobbled it down into my aura, and spat a scalpel of blackness into the battlemage's mind.

Gilles Jacques screamed in a high-pitched wail as I sliced his optic nerves, stole his sight.

The jaguar leapt from the balcony, and I scrambled backward. But the were didn't leap for me, he leapt for the battlemage.

"NO!" I shouted, sure it would be futile.

But the were-jaguar arrested his attack and turned his head back towards me.

"I offered a parlay," I started to explain.

No fool, Gilles Jacques turned and tried to run, but he was blind — completely — and he stumbled on the uneven ground and fell. The jaguar shimmered in a wash of silver-bronze.

In a heartbeat, a dark-haired man stood where the cat had been. He grabbed the battlemage, hauling him up and reaching into the mage's pocket to snag his dagger, which he positioned at Gilles Jacques' throat.

"Stop!" I cried.

The jaguar turned his golden eyes on me. "I don't owe you anything, mage," he near-growled as he shook Gilles Jacques like a rag doll. "You freed me only to protect yourself."

"I know," I said. "But I promised a parlay. Can't you wait 'til we finish?"

The jaguar squinted his yellow eyes, raking them over me. "*How* did you free me?"

"*Aies pitié,*" Gilles Jacques began begging for mercy, but neither the were nor I paid him any attention.

"If I explain, will you honor the parlay?"

The were-jaguar nodded.

"I cut the leash."

He frowned at me. "*How* did you counter the spell?"

The were didn't understand, because despite centuries of experimentation, no one had been able to forcibly free a leashed were. The construct-spell had been cast by Chía, the greatest South American mage who'd ever lived, and everyone now agreed it couldn't be done. But I hadn't countered it, I'd *broken* it.

I'm a breaker mage. I let out a breath I hadn't even realized I was holding. This changed everything! Gerel was right — I could defeat the Amir and claim the Arabian desert! It had been five thousand years since the last spell was broken, and I'd just rediscovered the trick.

My sudden elation died as quickly as it had risen. I can't let anyone know.

The breaker mages had gone insane when they broke the Asian deserts. They hadn't just destroyed each other, they'd *decimated* Asia. Most people thought the world was better off without their horrible magicks. And those who didn't … I could *never* let Gerel find out.

"I didn't counter it," I said. "The idiot didn't cast it properly in the first place."

I wasn't sure the jaguar would buy it. Leashing a were was practically effortless. That's what they'd been built for, after all. But I suppose it was easier to believe that Gilles Jacques had screwed up than imagine someone like me had cast an impossible spell.

The jaguar lowered his knife but held the mage fast.

I swallowed and brushed the ashes off my robe. "Now that we're back to parlaying, Gilles Jacques de Atacama, I need a volunteer."

Learn more about this author at:
https://lauraengelhardt.com.

# THE HAUNTING OF THE STAR PRINCESS

## BRUNO LOMBARDI

*February 10, 2364 — Thirteen light-years from Earth — Aboard the StarLiner Star Princess*

CASSANDRA DOMINIQUE LUCAS sighed contently as she lowered herself into the bathtub. She shifted slightly in the water to rest her head against a pillow and stretched out her legs. The hot water was having a relaxing effect on her tired muscles, the lavender-scented candles scattered along the edges were having a calming effect on her mood, the bubbles from the honey-toffee bath bomb were having a soothing effect on her skin, and the glass of champagne in her hand was having a most pleasing effect on her mind. For three glorious moments she actually felt ... happy.

And then her commbadge beeped.

Swearing a string of French phrases under her breath that would have made her devoutly Catholic grandmother from the Old Country gasp in shock, Cassandra stood up from the tub and walked towards the bathroom sink, the white bubbles trailing off her body a vivid contrast to her ebony skin. With a barely suppressed snarl, she picked up her commbadge.

"Mike, unless the hyperspace engines have malfunctioned and we've been boarded by aliens and we're about to fall into a black hole, I'm going to throw you out the airlock."

"Sorry, Captain," came Mike's voice. "But ... but I really think you should come up here."

Cassandra frowned. Mike Harris may have been a bit young, but he took Stoic Professional First Mate to a whole new level. There had been a friendly (unofficial) competition among the rest of the bridge crew for the last three months to make Mike 'lose his cool,' with no success so far. Cassandra herself had pulled what she had thought was a prank guaranteed to at least make him giggle, but all that had resulted from it was Mike (slightly) raising one eyebrow. She had lost twenty credits on that bet and had no intention of trying her luck again.

Right now, however, Mike sounded ... scared.

"What happened?"

"Uh — we found one of the passengers dead, Captain."

"Cause of death?"

"We ... we're not sure."

"Mike, what did the security cameras show?"

"They ... They ... uh ... You really better come up here, Captain."

"Captain on the bridge!"

"Report!" barked Cassandra to Mike, as she strode onto the bridge ten minutes later in a slightly damp uniform with a headful of wet hair and an extra-large coffee mug in her right hand.

It was just after 1 am ship time. Lisa Takahashi, as Second Mate, would normally be taking the 12-4 navigation watch, but she was resting up in Sick Bay with a broken leg and wasn't expected to be discharged until the leg was fully healed, some 24 hours from now. Mike, normally expected to do the 4-8 navigation watch, had dutifully offered to pull a few extra shifts.

He looked like he was beginning to regret that.

"Captain," said Mike, handing Cassandra a datapad. "Deceased is Daniel O'Brien, age fifty-nine. He was found twenty minutes ago by another guest on Deck Eight, just outside the Rotunda. He was about twenty or so meters away from his cabin, his keypad still in his hand."

Cassandra raised an eyebrow in confusion. "Rotunda? Deck Eight? There should be at least four different security cameras in that section. What did they show?"

In response, Mike tapped a button on the datapad and took a step back.

On the datapad, the footage from the four security cameras began to play on a four-way split screen.

The first security camera footage showed a sweating, obese, and very tired-looking O'Brien walking out of the Rotunda towards the camera. He walked about a dozen or so meters down the corridor, came to a sudden stop, looked to his right at something off-screen — and then suddenly clutched his chest and collapsed.

The second camera footage was taken from behind him. Once more, it showed him walking down the corridor, coming to a stop, looking at something to his right, and collapsing to the ground, clutching his chest.

Cameras Three and Four, taken from different angles, showed much the same.

"Heart attack?" said Cassandra, a slight hint of hope evident in her voice. It wouldn't be the first time that a passenger had died of a heart attack on board a StarLiner. Hell, it wouldn't be the first time it happened on her Star-Liner during her four years as Captain — and while it was unfortunate and sad for everyone involved, it also didn't mean any complicated potential legal issues either. From what she saw of O'Brien's appearance on the footage, the man seemed to be one of those people who thought that he could let his body go completely to seed and have a NEW-U treatment cure everything that ailed him, when in reality the treatments would only buy him an extra twenty or thirty years, if that.

"I thought so too, Captain. The doctor is, of course, examining the body now, while we're attempting to contact next of kin."

Cassandra stared at Mike in confusion. He had sounded scared when he'd called. A 'simple' heart attack would not have rattled him like this. She raised one eyebrow quizzically.

"But?"

"But … well, look at this." Mike took the datapad and pressed a few buttons until one of the security camera screens was full size, and the footage showed O'Brien staring to his right. He handed it back to Cassandra.

"I also thought it was a heart attack at first. But it was a bit weird that he was staring so intently at something to his right just before he died. So I got the image enhanced. Here, I'll have it play at one tenth normal speed."

Cassandra looked at the footage, now in slow motion. It showed a close-up of O'Brien staring to his right. There was, however, absolutely nothing there —

"Wait! What the hell was that?" screamed Cassandra, as she fumbled with the datapad and reversed the footage.

It was extremely easy to miss. It would have been easily missed were it not for Mike slowing down the video. It was there — and gone — in a space of less than half a second.

An image of a young woman with long pale hair, dressed in green and wrapped in a grey cloak, appeared. She seemed to be staring at O'Brien. And then she opened her mouth, as if to scream.

The instant she screamed, O'Brien dropped dead.

"Are you serious?"

It was ten minutes later, and Cassandra's mood was, if anything, fouler than earlier. All the security camera footage from throughout the liner had been ordered pulled and reviewed. Facial recognition analysis had been performed on the mystery lady, and Cassandra had ordered the doctor to treat the death as 'suspicious, probable homicide.' To top it all off, she had put the security teams on full alert.

To no avail.

"I'm afraid I'm being quite serious, Captain; she doesn't match anyone currently on board. In fact, she doesn't match anyone that has been on the ship, passenger or crew, since this ship launched four years ago."

"Mike, you know that's impossible. Check again."

"I checked three times, Captain."

"It's physically impossible for a stowaway to get on board this ship. She's here somewhere. Maybe a chameleon cloak ...?" Even as she said it, Cassandra knew she was grasping at straws. Not only were chameleon cloaks virtually impossible to acquire outside the military, but all they did was give the wearer a form of invisibility, not alter their appearance. Mike, wisely, refrained from pointing that out to her.

Cassandra bit her lip in annoyance. Suppressing a growl, she turned to face Mike.

"So how did she disappear? Did the infra-red …?"

"No," interrupted Mike. "Nothing on infra-red. Nothing on motion sensors. Nothing on heartbeat detectors. Nothing at all, Captain." Mike spread his hands helplessly. "It's like she just appeared out of nowhere — and then disappeared."

Cassandra let out an annoyed sigh. "Terrific. Thirteen light-years from Earth and I'm chasing a ghost." Cassandra began rubbing the corners of her eyes with her thumb and forefinger. Mike, ever the professional, handed her a fresh cup of coffee.

"Sorry, Captain. I'll keep trying."

"You keep doing that," said Cassandra, as she gulped down a mouthful of coffee. She blinked in confusion as both the caffeine and an errant thought hit her mind. "Run an analysis on her clothing."

"Captain?" asked Mike, clearly confused.

"Her clothes. Run her clothing through the UniWeb. Maybe something will come up."

"I'm not entirely certain how finding out what clothing label she's wearing will help—" began Mike, but when he saw the look that the Captain had on her face, he seamlessly segued it into, "—but of course, Captain, I will do it right away. Is there anything else I should do, Captain?"

"Yes, get Doctor Kwambai on screen. I want to speak to her."

"Are you serious?" repeated Cassandra for the second time in five minutes.

"Quite certain," said Doctor Irene Kwambai. "All

preliminary evidence points to natural causes. No evidence of foul play."

"Are there any drugs that can mimic a heart attack?"

Kwambai allowed herself a small smirk. "Of course. I can name about three dozen just off the top of my head."

"Then—" began Cassandra, before she was interrupted by Kwambai.

"—but all of them show up on the standard tox screens, Captain. That was my first thought as well."

Cassandra made a sound that sounded like a cross between a hmmm and a grrr.

"I will, of course, perform a few more tests to be certain."

"Keep me posted," said Cassandra, cutting the connection. Letting out a sigh, she leaned back in her chair, the fingers of her right hand unconsciously making a staccato tap-tap-tap sound on the table.

"Mike? Do you have anything to report on those analyses?"

"Nothing yet, Captain. Although I, regrettably, have some more bad news to give you."

"How can things possibly get any worse?"

"The Executive VP of Operations is on the ansible waiting to speak to you."

Cassandra shut her eyes and began rubbing the corners again with her fingers. "Mike, do me a favour and remind me never to say anything stupid like that again."

"Understood, Captain. Shall I send the signal to your ready room?"

"Yes, but first — give me another cup of coffee."

"Mister Juntunen," said Cassandra, barely keeping her face — and voice — emotionless, "I can assure you that my crew are doing everything they can to investigate this matter. It has been, after all, barely forty-five minutes since the body was found."

"I just want to emphasise the gravity of this matter, and how many people at this organization — and your employers, I might add — are following this situation with extreme interest."

Cassandra raised an eyebrow.

*Why the hell would the freaking VP be so interested in a dead passenger? Unless O'Brien was a member of the board or ... Wait a minute ... Everyone knows the company has been having a rough year, and the scuttlebutt is that they were desperate for some quick credits and/or 'restructuring' ...*

She decided to take a stab in the dark.

"Exactly what percentage of the company was Mister O'Brien planning to buy?"

Juntunen blinked in shock.

"How did you know about the upcoming deal?"

*A-ha!*

Still barely keeping her face expressionless, Cassandra continued.

"I have my sources," she lied. "However, as the preliminary doctor's report I sent to you indicates, there seems to be no evidence — so far — of foul play." She squinted her eyes and tilted her head to one side. "I'm a bit confused here, sir; is there something else I should know about?"

Juntunen waved his hand dismissively. "No, Captain. Nothing that concerns you. Your ETA to the Beta Canum colony?"

"Seventy-six hours and thirty-five minutes at current course."

"Well, then, Captain, it appears that you have three days

to solve this mystery," said Juntunen, a thin smile on his lips. "We look forward to your full report at that time. Out."

And with a blip sound, the screen died.

*I need some good news*, thought Cassandra as she sipped her coffee.

"Captain?" came Mike's voice on the commbadge.

"Yeah?"

"I have your wife on the line."

"Missed you," said Cassandra, smiling. Unconsciously, she stroked the screen with the fingers of her right hand.

"Missed you too," said Julia, smiling in return. "It's been a very lonely three months."

Cassandra sighed and nodded, picking up her mug of coffee.

"Honey," said Julia, her voice filled with concern. "You look like crap. What's wrong?"

Cassandra gulped a mouthful of coffee and put the mug down, a bit more forcefully than she'd wanted. "Insane night. Looks like it's going to be an insane day as well."

"Spill it," said Julia, leaning forward and wiping an errant lock of blonde hair out of her eyes.

Cassandra frowned and hesitated for a moment, then shrugged her shoulders. "What the hell; it's going to hit the newsfeed in a few hours anyway."

She proceeded to tell her wife all the details of the case, finishing with, "— and now the VP is breathing down my neck!" Cassandra let out a frustrated grunt and finished off the rest of the coffee. "Remind me again why I took this job, sweetie?"

"Because you dreamed about being in command of a ship when you were ten years old, and spent the next thirty years of your life fulfilling your dream," said Julia. Now she was the one unconsciously stroking the screen. "You'll get through this, honey; don't worry." Julia bit back a laugh as she leaned back in her seat. "Mind you, I didn't think you'd ever have to deal with a banshee in space." She laughed again.

"Deal with a what?" asked Cassandra, genuinely confused.

"You've never heard of a banshee?"

"Honey," said Cassandra, smiling, "I'm not the anthropology professor in this marriage."

"Ha! Right, sorry!" replied Julia, suppressing a chuckle. "It's got all the classic motifs: mysterious female ghost figure, woman in green, screaming, sudden death — the works. It's actually quite fascinating, in a morbid sort of way."

"You don't really think that it's ... real?" asked Cassandra, a look of almost frightening intensity on her face.

That question or the look — or both — seemed to throw Julia off. "What? No, of course not, sweetie. It's just folklore!" Now it was Julia's turn to give her wife a searching look. "Don't tell me that you think it's real?"

Cassandra opened and closed her mouth several times, then closed it one last time and shook her head. "I'm just tired, and I'm getting pissed off that I'm not getting any answers that I like." She shook her head one last time. "It's late; I need some sleep."

Julia smiled. "I'll be waiting for you at the Beta Canum colony when you arrive."

"Trust me sweetie; I've been dreaming of nothing else during this whole trip."

"Nighty-night, sweetie," said Julia, blowing a kiss.

"Nighty-night," said Cassandra, blowing a kiss in return.

The line went dead. Cassandra got up and walked out of her ready room and onto the bridge. "I'm going to my quarters," she announced. Suppressing a yawn, she turned to walk out when Mike called her back.

"Captain! You were right about the clothes!"

"Huh?" said Cassandra, turning to face Mike. "I was right about what?"

"The clothing on the lady, Captain," said Mike patiently, as he walked towards her with datapad in hand. "We got a match." He handed the datapad to her.

Taking the datapad in hand, Cassandra looked down at the screen.

There was a very long moment of silence, and then she looked up at Mike.

"This is a joke, right?"

A shake of the head from Mike.

Cassandra stood in silence for a moment, then frowned and stormed back to her quarters.

She had a lot of research to do, not the least of which was finding out how a mystery woman wearing clothing from the Late Middle Ages of Ireland and Scotland had ended up on her ship.

And had apparently killed someone.

Cassandra rubbed her eyes and stared at the clock.

3:52 am.

*Two hours! Two bloody hours at this! And what do I have to show for it?* She glanced down at her notes on her datapad:

"Banshees are usually seen by a person who is about to die in a violent way, such as murder. In legend, a banshee wails nearby when someone is about to die. There are some special families who are believed to have banshees attached to them, and whose cries herald the death of a member of that family. Most, though not all, surnames associated with banshees have the Ó or Mac prefix."

*Well, isn't that convenient for our Mister O'Brien …*

She kept reading.

"Legend has it that for six great Gaelic families — the O'Gradys, the O'Neills, the Ó Longs, the Ó Briains, the Ó Conchobhairs, and the Caomhánachs — the lament would be sung by a fairy woman; thanks to her powers of foresight, she would sing when a family member died, even if the person had died far away and news of their death had not yet come. The wailing of the banshee was often the first sign of death that the household received."

And, of course, the kicker …

"Some tales argue that the fairy woman is not actually a fairy at all, but rather the ghost of a murdered woman, or a mother who died in childbirth. Banshees are frequently described dressed in white or grey, often having long, pale hair which they brush with a silver comb. Other stories portray banshees as dressed in green, red, or black with a grey cloak."

Cassandra leaned back and rubbed her eyes again. On a hunch, she had looked up Daniel O'Brien's background. He was, of course, very rich, as her notes now reminded her.

He'd made the bulk of his money from the pharmaceutical business, specifically in something called 'heirloom pharmaceuticals,' which was the 'resurrecting' of old, discontinued drug formulas for new purposes. Apparently, it was quite the successful business; a migraine drug that was briefly popular during the mid-twentieth century was currently getting a second chance as a cheap sedative, for example.

As for his family ties … well, the O'Brien family (allegedly) were able to trace their ancestry all the way back to Late Middle Ages Ireland, where they were actual, honest to god, kings of Ireland (or parts thereof).

He was also, by all accounts, a world-class jackass. One journalist even described Mister O'Brien thus: "If one were to look up the definition of 'corporate raider' in the dictionary, all you would see — and need to see — would be a picture of Daniel O'Brien."

*Ah yes — feel the love …*

Of course, that also meant that he had no shortage of enemies — and judging by the number of just the acknowledged 'business rivals' in his bio, an entire StarLiner could be filled with them. Any one of which could be on board Cassandra's ship.

But the only thing wrong with the whole 'murder' theory was, well, that there hadn't been a murder at all.

Cassandra stared down at her notes, her right forefinger tapping the datapad.

"Banshees are usually seen by a person who is about to die in a violent way, such as murder."

That was the thing that she had noticed about all the legends: the banshee didn't actually cause the death. She foretold the death. And it was almost always a violent one.

*What the hell are you thinking? That a thousand-year-old banshee knew that one of her … charges? … was going to die, and she gave the traditional warning wail? That I have a ghost running around on a spaceship flying through hyperspace thirteen light years from Earth?*

Cassandra blinked and took another look at her notes.

"He made the bulk of his money from the pharmaceutical business."

Several different thoughts flew into her head, fighting for attention. Blinking in confusion, Cassandra tapped her commbadge. "Doctor Kwambai — come in!"

"Ye-ees?" said a sleepy voice a moment later.

"Sorry for bothering you Doctor, but I have a question. You said that the tox screens came back negative?"

"Yes, all of them," replied Kwambai, a bit testily. Cassandra made a mental note to give the doctor a few hours off in the morning to make up for this unexpected wake-up call.

"Are there drugs that wouldn't show up on the tox screens?"

"The tox screens are very thorough, Captain," said Kwambai defensively. "They can pick up all the standard stuff out there."

"What about the non-standard stuff?"

There was a brief hmmm sound. Then Kwambai replied, "It's possible — but do you have any idea how many possibilities there are out there? If you want me to run a non-standard tox screen, I'm going to need a bit more guidance on what to look for."

"Drugs from the twentieth century onwards?"

There was a snort of laughter. "Oh, sure, that should narrow it down to, oh, just thirty-five million drugs, Captain. Piece of cake."

"Doctor," said Cassandra, a dark tone in her voice.

"Captain — you have to give me something more to work with here!"

"Heirloom drugs?"

There was no response from Kwambai.

"Doctor?" asked Cassandra again. "You there?"

"I ... I have an idea. Get back to you in an hour. Kwambai out."

"Denostim."

It was, in fact, only forty-seven minutes later, a testament to Doctor Kwambai's medical skills. "Denostim?" repeated Cassandra. "Never heard of it."

"Be surprised if you did," said Kwambai from the viewscreen, stifling a yawn. "We got, like, one page of reading on stuff like this back in med school."

"What the hell is it?"

"It's an adenosine receptor stimulator." Seeing the look of complete and utter confusion on Cassandra's face, Kwambai grinned and went for the 'dumbed down' explanation.

"It's a coronary vasodilator. It basically opens up the blood vessels in the heart. They used to use it back in the early twenty-first century for radionuclide myocardial perfusion imaging."

"The what of the what imaging?"

"The crude radioactive version of your standard SPECT med-scanner, Captain," replied Kwambai. "Back in the old days, they needed to inject radioactive dye into your blood-stream before they could do any scans."

"Holy—!"

"Exactly. This stuff — or more precisely, a close cousin of it — used to be used on a regular basis in a few European countries from about, oh, 2021 to 2030 or so. It was discontinued because of its side-effects, but there have been some really interesting things in the journals lately discussing its possible use in treatment for Kan's Syndrome."

"Side-effects?"

Kwambai smiled. "Too much of it can induce heart attacks."

"Doctor, I could kiss you."

"I'm fairly certain the wife would get pissed with you if you did, Captain."

That got a laugh from Cassandra.

Then the laugh died in her throat.

"Oh shit. I have a murderer on board this ship."

To his credit, Juntunen barely blinked when Cassandra gave him the news.

"There has never been a murder on any Blue Nova Star-Liner in the history of the company, Captain Lucas. Pity that it had to happen on board your ship." Juntunen leaned back into his chair. "And with this particular individual."

"Yes, unfortunate," replied Cassandra, keeping her voice neutral. She still had unpleasant memories of their last conversation and it didn't help that Juntunen had what Julia would have called 'a punchable face.' Neither of those were helping Cassandra keep calm. "In any case, I've decided to use my authority and invoke Article 245 of the Death in Deep Space Act."

Juntunen's eyes widened in shock. "That is a bit … drastic, Captain."

"I am dealing with a murderer on board this ship, Mister Juntunen. If he or she manages to make a run for it when we dock at Beta Canum, then it could literally be months before anyone can track them down."

"I am aware of that, Captain but how can you be sure that the murderer is on board the ship? The murderer could have — oh, I don't know — switched the meds in his pill bottle, or spiked his personal stash of booze, or any manner of things that may have happened days or even weeks ago, yes?"

Cassandra shook her head. "No. Doctor Kwambai says that the drug has a half-life of only about two to three minutes. For it to have had the effect on him that it did, he must have ingested it fifteen minutes before he died, at most. Security cameras show that the only thing he ingested in that time period was a glass of scotch ordered from the bar. Clearly it was spiked with the drug at that time."

Juntunen's eyes widened further in shock. "A member of the crew?"

A shrug from Cassandra. "Or one of the guests slipped it in between the time it was prepared and the time it arrived at his table. Or someone walking by dropped it into his drink while he was distracted watching the holovids. We don't know for sure. That's why I'm invoking Article 245."

"But Article 245 would involve having the Beta Canum law enforcement authorities essentially put everyone — crew and passengers alike — under house arrest and search all their rooms and possessions. We're talking about 5,400 passengers and over 2,000 crewmembers. Do you have any idea how embarrassing that will be from a public relations point of view?"

Cassandra's mouth tightened. "I'm well-aware of the implications. But I do have a murderer on board." A half-smile appeared on Cassandra's face. "And the preceding article, Article 244, grants me full authority to do so, according to precedent."

Juntunen made a sound like steam escaping from a teapot. "Quite frankly, I'm more than a bit confused as to how this individual thought they would get away with the murder."

"Because they would have gotten away with it if we didn't suspect that it was a homicide. Even when we did suspect, it was a total fluke that we found any concrete evidence." Cassandra leaned back and gulped a mouthful of coffee. *Has it really been barely five hours since his death? It feels like days.* "If the doctor didn't know what precise drugs to look for …" she said, trailing off.

"Yes," replied Juntunen, the tight smile back on his face.

"That reminds me: your reports have been a bit vague as to what made you suspicious in the first place. As you yourself stated, the initial tox screens missed the presence of the drug earlier precisely because—" Juntunen glanced down and read something off his datapad, "—'only weird chemistry students and nostalgic doctors have ever used this drug, and there probably has never been more than fifty kilos of it produced on an annual basis on the entire planet Earth in the last fifty years.'"

"Doctor Kwambai has a way with words," said Cassandra, smiling.

"Yes, quite," replied Juntunen stoically. "And while it is indeed a most memorable description, it does not address the question as to why you took that line of inquiry in the first place. By all accounts, it was a simple open and shut 'death by natural causes' case. Even your doctor concurred. What exactly about the case made you suspicious, Captain?"

"I'm a naturally suspicious person."

Juntunen's tight smile returned. "Yes, and we and the company appreciate that in this particular situation. Nevertheless, about the invoking of Article 245—"

Juntunen never had a chance to finish his sentence, as it was at that precise moment that the ship's alarms went off.

"Captain to the Riviera Deck! Atrium Section! Emergency!" came Mike's voice on the commbadge.

"What —?" began Juntunen, before he realized that he was talking to an empty chair.

"Talk to me!" shouted Cassandra, gasping for breath, as she reached a throng of about a dozen assorted crewmembers and technicians. The Atrium Section of the Riviera Deck was eight decks below and over a thousand meters astern of the bridge. She had completed the journey in just under three minutes.

"One of the guards spotted a passenger acting in a suspicious manner," said Mike. "When she went to speak to him, he pulled a knife and stabbed her. He then stole her weapon and made a run for it."

"How is she?"

"In med-bay in stable condition."

Cassandra nodded her head in relief. Thank God for small favors. "What then?"

"Passenger ended up getting boxed in this section of the ship," said Mike, patting the bulkhead doors blocking them. "As he is armed and dangerous, we're waiting for security teams to arrive so that they can clear out the section."

"What the hell is wrong with the lights?"

"Our guy's been busy, Captain; he damaged the power relay lines for the lights and sensors."

There was a loud beeping sound from his datapad. Mike glanced down at it and cursed under his breath. "And there go the cameras! This guy is good!"

"Who is this guy?"

A quick glance at his datapad. "Matthew Ganz. Age fifty-three. No criminal record of any kind. Some big-shot businessman in the engineering industry, by the looks of things."

"Ganz?" repeated Cassandra. "I've seen that name before …" She shook her head in annoyance, waving her hand dismissively. "Never mind. What's the security team's ETA?"

"Three minutes, Captain. I think we should—"

There was another — louder — beep from Mike's datapad. "Oh hell!" the First Mate screamed, as he read the screen. "He overrode the lockout codes! Lifeboat's been activated!"

Cassandra and several crewmembers exchanged a look among themselves. Launching a lifeboat while a ship was in hyperspace was insane. There was a one in ten chance of the lifeboat being destroyed in the process. Standard procedure was to initiate an Emergency Shutdown of the engines before launching lifeboats. As even a competent skeleton crew could do the shutdown in just under ten seconds (and two or three seconds less than that, if they were willing to cut a few safety feature corners), there really was no need to launch a lifeboat in hyperspace unless you were facing — literally — no other choice.

Of course, that was the reason why Ganz would do so, realized Cassandra. Assuming he survived transit, even a ten second head start would be all the advantage he would need. The StarLiner could travel over three billion kilometers in that ten second delay. Finding a lifeboat in a sphere of space of that size could take hours — and that was assuming he wanted to be found.

But then again, any thoughts of tracking him down were moot, as all lifeboats were equipped with an emergency hyperspace engine, precisely so that their precious cargo didn't need to wait around in deep space for days for rescue. Sure, the engine was short-range and didn't have quite the speed of its larger companions, giving it about sixty hours of use in the best case. But that meant that there were at least half a dozen colonies or way stations within Ganz's reach. Once he got to one of them, he could do any number of things: keep running, change identities, go underground, try his luck for the Frontier ... Anything could happen.

*If he launches, he gets away,* thought Cassandra. "ETA of security team?" she shouted.

"Two minutes forty-five seconds!"

"Time to lifeboat launch?"

"Two minutes!"

"I'm going in after him!" screamed Cassandra, as she yanked a spanner out of the hands of a shocked technician. She had the bulkhead doors opened before Mike managed to shout.

"Captain!"

"I'll be ok! I know what I'm doing!" shouted Cassandra, as she shut the bulkhead doors behind her.

A moment later, she was running through the dark corridors. Alone.

*What the hell am I doing?* thought Cassandra as she walked through the darkened corridors. *Stopping a murderer from escaping. Right. Of course. Okay, keep it together. You don't actually have to stop him. Just delay him for a minute or two, that's all. Cavalry is on its way. Right, just delay him. Without getting shot in the process.*

Cassandra realized that she, perhaps, had not thought through this plan of hers sufficiently.

*Ok, he's around here somewhere. It's not like there's that many places to hide. He's going for the lifeboat and there's just the one in this section. So ...*

Carefully, she turned a corner, the spanner almost sliding out of her sweat-soaked hands. She was expecting any number of things. A man opening fire on her. A lifeboat missing. Maybe even a suicide in progress. Those she was expecting.

She wasn't expecting to come face to face with a young woman with long pale hair, dressed in green and wrapped in a grey cloak.

"The hell —?"

The woman wailed.

It only lasted a mere second, but it was a gut-wrenching keen. It was more than a mere cry. It was as if the banshee's very essence was being torn apart. It was emotions of pain and sorrow and loss and anguish and more, all of them hitting Cassandra ... ripping into her ... with the full force of a dying soul in pain.

Then the banshee was gone.

"The hell —?" repeated Cassandra.

From deep within her thoughts, a phrase leapt out. *"Banshees are usually seen by a person who is about to die in a violent way such as murder."*

With a speed borne of terror, Cassandra rolled forward and leaped to the side — just as two shots slammed into the floor where she had been standing a second earlier. With no time to see her attacker, she threw her spanner in the vague direction of the shots, hoping against hope that she would be lucky a second time.

A meaty sound like a fist hitting a wall, a cry of pain, and the sound of something small and metallic clattering on the floor indicated that she had been lucky indeed.

Releasing an incoherent scream of rage, she threw herself down the corridor, hoping to take advantage of her luck a third time.

She slammed into a figure in the dark, knocking the wind out of her. Even in the dark, she sensed that the man was huge, easily outweighing her by at least thirty kilos — and most of it, by the feel of it, was muscle rather than fat. Grappling and scratching and even clawing at the figure, she felt him shift position a bit and —

Stars filled her vision, and she felt her face slam into a bulkhead. A huge hand grabbed her hair and threw her to the ground, knocking what little air she had left out of her lungs.

"I won't let you stop me!" screamed Ganz. "You hear me?" he screamed once more, as the fist came down where Cassandra's head lay —

— where Cassandra's head had been laying. Ganz yelled as his fist hit the floor with a painful thud — and then yelled a second time as an elbow came out of the darkness and slammed into his temple.

"Guess again!" screamed Cassandra, as she rolled on top of Ganz. She felt something in her back pop and realized that she almost certainly had a cracked rib. Screaming again, partly out of pain and partly out of fury, she punched Ganz's face. She felt, rather than heard, a sickening squish sound, and was about to follow up with another punch when Ganz slammed both hands into her ears simultaneously.

A hand, slick with blood, smashed into her face, pushing her off of Ganz. She fell backwards onto the floor, feeling another rib go pop, and tried to get her bearings as Ganz struggled to stand.

"You won't stop me!" screamed Ganz again as he stood on legs of rubber.

Cassandra blinked in shock as she realized what a ... convenient ... target Ganz was presenting to her. A bloody smile appeared in the darkness.

"Yes I will!" she screamed as her fist slammed into Ganz's crotch with an eye-watering punch. As Ganz dropped to his knees in agony, Cassandra got up on her own knees. "You made one mistake!" she yelled as her right fist slammed into Ganz's face. "One little mistake!" she screamed as her left fist connected with the face. "One crucial mistake!" she bellowed as she stood up and slammed her right foot into Ganz's chest, knocking him onto his back.

Leaning against a bulkhead for support, Cassandra gasped for breath and tried her best to block out the pain. The sound of many footsteps echoing down the corridor told her that help was on the way.

Gasping for breath one last time, she leaned towards Ganz.

"You did this on my ship!"

*February 14, 2364 — Beta Canum Venaticorum Colony — Twenty seven light-years from Earth — Aboard the StarLiner Star Princess*

As captain's rooms went, Cassandra's room was somewhat on the small side, but this shortcoming was made up for by being rather nicely decorated. An eclectic assortment of paintings, drawings, sculptures, and various object d'arts decorated every available space in the place.

In contrast, the dining area was unusually spartan, as if it was almost never used. However, that was not the case on this particular night, as the remnants of what appeared to be a rather elaborate and sumptuous four-course meal set for two people was on the dining table.

On a nearby bed lay two figures. The tangled sheets and the sweat still glistening on their naked bodies indicated that the two figures had made a spirited — and quite successful — attempt at burning off the calories from said meal.

"Hmmm?" asked Cassandra as her fingers stroked Julia's hair distractedly. "Didn't quite catch that."

Julia shifted position slightly from where her head had been resting on Cassandra's stomach.

"I'm confused about a few things. What was Ganz's plan anyway?"

A shrug from Cassandra. "They were like yin and yang in the business sphere. By all indications, they lived for screwing each other over. His name popped up in O'Brien's bio quite a few times. His buy-out plan for Blue Nova got rejected by the board of directors over O'Brien's proposal."

"So with O'Brien dead of an apparent heart attack, the deal would fall through — and Ganz's plan would get accepted instead. With the added bonus that he would get to kill a hated enemy in the process. Nice."

"Uh-huh," murmured Cassandra, still stroking Julia's hair. She found it … tranquil.

"But there's still one thing that I don't understand."

"Hmmm?"

"You said that you saw a banshee? That you saw it literally a second before he was going to shoot you?"

"Uh-huh."

"But … how? The legends all speak about how only certain families have a banshee 'attached' to them. They almost never show up for anyone else. So why did a banshee appear to you?"

That got a laugh from Cassandra.

"I told you about my very Catholic grandmother, right?"

"The one who grew up in Belgium and died when you were young?" asked Julia, raising an eyebrow. "Yeah. You don't talk about her much, but you have mentioned her. What about her?"

"I never told you what her surname was, did I?"

"No," replied Julia, now utterly confused. "What was it?"

"O'Grady," said Cassandra, laughing uncontrollably.

Julia stared in shocked silence at Cassandra for a full minute, and then, slowly at first but with increasing speed, joined in the laughing.

Connect with this author on Facebook at:
https://www.facebook.com/profile.php?id=
100051709043140.

# WHEN ANAKAR MET SUSAN

## JASON SHARP

SUSAN HAD NEVER SET foot in Angelo's Bar and Grill before, yet it all seemed familiar from the moment she opened the door: the Foreigner song playing on the sound system, the movie posters and framed sports jerseys, the flat screen televisions showing a mixture of golf, basketball, and hockey games …

"Hi!" exclaimed the hostess, a pretty young thing with long, auburn hair and a bright smile.

"Hello," Susan replied. She'd had hair like that once, but she'd cut it short twenty years ago. After the divorce, she stopped dyeing it too.

"Table for one tonight?" the hostess asked.

"Actually, I'm … meeting somebody at the bar," Susan replied, not quite believing it herself.

"Excellent — the bar's right over here!"

The louder music and the actual physical bar had already clued Susan in to that, but the hostess led her there anyway. The decor was much the same as the restaurant, though the lighting was somewhat dimmer.

There were ten or twelve people present, but only one

that she could possibly picture as her blind date for the night. The man had a ring of white hair around the crown of his head and a matching goatee that contrasted sharply with his tanned complexion and charcoal suit. He sat with his back to the wall of a corner booth, a tweed ascot cap hung on a hook nearby.

Her date stood as she approached and extended his hand. "You must be Susan," he said with a light accent that vaguely reminded her, in an entirely good way, of Ricardo Montalbán.

"Yes," she said, shaking his hand. "And you're … Anakar? Is that …?"

"That's correct, yes," he nodded.

"Like the kid from *Star Wars*," she noted.

"That would be Anak*in*, but yes, like that," he said without enthusiasm. "Please, sit."

She eased into the opposite end of the booth and sat, giving them both a bit of space. "Is that a European name? Portuguese?"

"Ah … no," he said.

She waited, futilely, for him to explain what kind of name it *was*. When the silence became unbearable, she tried a different approach. "So, how did Manny pull you into this?"

Anakar's mouth twitched. "Manny and I were in the break room at work, reheating our respective lunches, when he mentioned he'd been on a date the preceding weekend. I thought it would be safe to reveal that I had not been on a date in some time, and was proven incorrect when he immediately resolved to do something about it. Manny being Manny, here we are."

"Here we are," she repeated.

"And you?"

"Manny lives down the hall from me, so we chat in the

elevator and he occasionally runs errands for me. He kept telling me I should try to get out and meet somebody new." She shrugged. "I guess he wore me down."

Anakar chuckled, but before he could reply, a waitress came by their table. Susan ordered a strawberry daiquiri; Anakar ordered a stout ale.

As soon as the waitress had moved on, Susan added, "Um ... let me clarify that, in case it came out wrong. I've only had one serious relationship, and since the divorce, I've been content to just live by myself. Manny insisted that I needed to get out a bit."

"Ah," Anakar said.

"So — unfamiliar territory for me here. Did you have any sort of plans for this evening?" she asked.

"Manny suggested drinks and then bowling, if that's acceptable to you," he said.

"Oh God," she grimaced. "I haven't bowled since ... I'm not sure."

"Likewise. I'm honestly not certain why he suggested it, but ..."

"That's okay," she said. "I'm willing to try it. So ... do you have children, Anakar?"

"No," he said.

"I have two daughters — both married — and one grandson," she said. "They live on the south end, near where I used to live with my ex-husband. Are you from around here?"

"No," he said.

Again, she waited for Anakar to elaborate — again, with no success. Finally, she prompted him, "Where *are* you from?"

He pursed his lips. "Far away — an obscure place once in the hands of a brutal overlord, now experiencing the heady turbulence of parliamentary democracy."

"Fair enough," she said. "I was born here, actually. Lived here all my life, apart from a few vacations. Are you a widower?"

"No," he said.

"Divorced?"

"Somebody was left at the altar, as it were."

"Oh dear," she said.

"Quite," he agreed. "Do you work, or are you retired?"

"I have a part-time housekeeping job," she said. "There's not really much else I *can* do, really. But between that and the alimony, I can pay the bills. But you must be in government, since you work with Manny. Do you enjoy it?"

He shrugged. "The subject matter ... not particularly. It's dry and inspires no passion. The office politics, however, can be entertaining. That and the biweekly paychecks keep me motivated."

He glanced up as the waitress arrived with their drinks. "There we are," the girl said, setting Susan's daiquiri down. As she passed Anakar's pint of beer to him, she clipped the daiquiri, setting it wobbling. He and the waitress were both quick to reach for the glass, but the daiquiri merely tilted precariously before righting itself.

"Sorry about that," the waitress said with a small sigh of relief. "Can I get you two anything else?"

Anakar raised an eyebrow at Susan. "No, thanks," she answered. Anakar shook his head in agreement.

When the waitress had again moved on, Susan raised her oversized glass and said, "Well, here's to Manny for getting us out of our homes for a night."

"To Manny," Anakar echoed, tapping his glass against hers.

He sipped at his ale, she sipped at her daiquiri, and they both waited for the other to speak.

"We're not exactly setting the world on fire here, Anakar," she murmured eventually, setting down her glass.

He frowned.

"Sorry," she said. "It's just that—"

"No, no, you're right," he interjected. "I'm sorry. I used to talk too much, and now I don't talk enough. Finding a balance can be difficult. Please, ask me something."

"Such as?"

He shrugged.

"Um … how old are you?" she tried.

He took a sip from his beer. "My healthcare card says I'm sixty-three."

"I sense a *but*."

His lips quirked upward. "But in truth, I'm one hundred fifty-eight."

She smiled. "Manny said you like to tell crazy stories. It's his favorite thing about you."

"Mmm," Anakar said. "The evil overlord thing?"

"Yes."

"Well, I know he *thinks* they're stories, but they really aren't. I *was* an evil overlord. The most feared in all the world. People trembled at the sound of my name: Anakar do Zurizan e Mornos."

"It really does sound Portuguese," she observed.

"This was in another dimension entirely. No Portugal whatsoever," he said.

"Okay," Susan said, deciding to humor him. "So you were an evil overlord. Now you're not. What happened?"

He shrugged. "Well, there was a prophecy, of course. Since I was a bit arrogant — more than a bit, if I'm being honest — I assumed it was like all the other prophecies that had come and gone over the years. Let's face it, prophecies are a dime a dozen in a primitive, superstitious world. I'd heard dozens during my reign, and none of them had ever come true. So I ignored this one too ... and at some point, I killed somebody I shouldn't have, leaving that person's spiteful offspring alive to fixate on the matter throughout the entirety of his adolescence."

"Ah, the hero's journey."

"Exactly — the hero's journey. Which, as it so often does, began with the antagonist's misstep. Subsequently, the peasant hero found an unlikely mentor and acquired a rag-tag band of unexpectedly complementary misfits. They started taking action, I sent inadequately trained and under-motivated peons with insufficiently ruthless instructions, and the whole enterprise just started rolling downhill. Meanwhile, I was too fixated on marrying a reluctant princess to pay proper attention."

She took a sip of the daiquiri. "Hence the abandonment at the altar?"

He nodded slowly. "Gods forbid I just have a quick, private ceremony. No, I opted for the big public affair, and the heroes crashed it just as my one reliable henchman kept telling me they would. Naturally, the rest of my lackeys were of no real help, and I found that while I could almost overpower the hero with forceblasts and fire bolts, I couldn't quite outwit him. Nor could I properly account for the wholly predictable treachery of my intended bride-to-be. Next thing you know, I'm vowing revenge and leaping through an interdimensional portal with my leather pants on fire."

"I hate when that happens," Susan deadpanned.

"I haven't worn leather since," he added.

"And so it was *you* who did the abandoning."

He nodded. "With alacrity."

She smiled. "It's a good story, albeit somewhat familiar."

"I've written screenplays about it, but those dastardly

types in Hollywood keep filching my ideas for their own wicked purposes."

"That would be it," she said. "Now, where's the bowling alley?"

∽

As it happened, the bowling alley was four blocks south of Angelo's, and a nippy December breeze was blowing dead leaves and trash along the plowed sidewalk.

"Shall I call a cab?" Anakar asked as they zipped up their coats and donned their gloves in the front entrance of the bar and grill.

"You didn't drive either?"

"I haven't had a car for some time now," he said. "Just don't need it enough."

"Oh. If I'd known, I would have driven instead of taking the bus," she said. "But I think the walk will be fine. We'll be unlimbered by the time we get there."

He nodded and opened the door for her. "I think we'll need it. Getting out of bed in the morning is sometimes challenge enough. Oh — watch the ice there."

She nodded and stepped past him, carefully eyeing the frozen ground. "My story was a rom-com, for a time," she ventured as they began their walk.

"Oh?" he said.

"We grew up a few streets apart. He was a loner, a little misunderstood. I was a bookworm, gawky and prim. We had nothing in common and no reason to get along — and, for most of our school years, we didn't," she explained. "Yet there were moments where we … deviated from that script, and so we had a few scenes that made us question our assumptions. I watched him stop traffic on a street so a duck and her babies could cross in safety. He was heading into the boy's washroom when I came out of the girl's room bellowing the lyrics to 'Physical' because I'd enjoyed my gymnastics class. It was ... awkward at times, but I found myself noticing him more and more."

"This does sound vaguely familiar," Anakar agreed, offering his arm.

She looped her forearm around it. "We started circling each other, watching sparks fly as steel met flint. Our few friends tried to talk us down, but it didn't work. Did the opposite, really; it drew us together out of sheer stubbornness. When we danced at our grad party, a fire started. Figuratively speaking, of course."

"I would hope so."

"The real struggle started during our university years. Money was tight. We had to work jobs outside of our studies. He was, of course, more intelligent than he'd ever let on, and he excelled in business management. I studied linguistics, but when Sherry came along, I dropped out to raise her. I decided to just stay at home after Brandy was born. The girls were like oil and water themselves. It was a battle to control Sherry, and—"

Before she could finish her thought, Anakar's left foot slipped sideways on the ice. For a moment, it seemed he'd go down and take Susan with him — but he unexpectedly found his footing once more, and they merely lurched awkwardly.

"Sorry about that," he blurted. "Maybe I'd better let go of you ..."

"It's fine," she said. "No need."

"Okay." He nodded, but his pace slowed. "Please continue."

"Right. Suffice to say that when the girls moved out and got married, when it was just us ... There wasn't any fire anymore, just coals. We'd burned through our fuel. We grew apart. We separated."

"That's ... unfortunate," he said.

"A bit, I guess. We still interact politely enough when we see each other for holidays and birthdays, and I admit I miss doing things for him. I like the feeling of helping people, even when they don't realize it. But we became so detached that I stopped taking care of him in that way."

"What kind of things? Special meals and such?"

"Special meals, little renovations, evenings out. Even stuff like finding his keys when he was running late, or getting stains out of his shirts," she explained. "Nowadays, it's more like baking cookies for Manny or one of the other neighbors."

Anakar's foot slid again, but he caught himself sooner. "Good thing I get different shoes for the bowling itself ..."

"You might want to get new ones sometime."

"Probably should," he agreed. "Well, you get along with your ex-husband still, to the point where you can be together when it matters to your family. That sounds better than it could've gone."

"I don't think it ever would've ended with us going to war. More likely we'd have just lived alone together."

Anakar grimaced. "That would've been ... well, sad."

"Not as sad as the shellacking I'm about to lay on you," she said, beckoning at the neon sign advertising the bowling alley.

"I accept your challenge, Madame."

The monitor hanging from the ceiling above their lane told a dismal tale of woe: no shellackings were in progress. Six frames into the second game, Anakar had forty-eight points to Susan's thirty-five.

"It'd be nice if one of us hit triple digits at some point tonight," Anakar said as he turned his back on a receding gutter ball and returned to his seat.

"If it happens, it happens," Susan replied, waiting for him to pass by before she stepped up and took a solid black ball in hand. She eyed the distant quintet of pins, took two steps forward, and released the ball.

"Looking good," Anakar called out, but the ball drifted off-center and struck the left three-pin with a *pop*.

She turned back and grabbed a swirly red and cream ball that reminded her vaguely of Jupiter. "Here's your chance to show me your magic powers. Send this puppy right between the five pin and the right three so I can pick up the spare."

"Sorry," he said. "I can't. There's no magic here."

"None?" she asked, her mouth curling upward.

"Well, perhaps a bit, but not the kind that lets me cheat at bowling."

She rolled her eyes. "Then wish me luck."

He nodded. "Good luck."

She advanced towards the pins and threw again. The ball rolled directly through the hole left by the pin she'd just knocked down. "Oh, come on," she grumbled, coming back for a blue and black ball. "Using magic's not cheating if it helps the other person, you know."

"No?"

"No."

He shrugged. "It would still feel off."

She threw her third ball and watched it take out the center and some of the right-side pins. "The evil warlord version of you would've done it," she mused as she sat down at the scoring table.

"All the time," he agreed. "Not that I needed to. There weren't a lot of people who genuinely challenged the evil guy with reality-bending powers." He lurched to his feet, something cracking in his knee. "Definitely need a cab after this is over," he griped.

"Yeah, me too."

He took the Jupiter ball, advanced stiffly, and watched as the ball hit the right gutter just shy of the pins. He collected another ball without comment.

"A little magical nudge would've gotten you the two-pin," Susan noted.

"A larger magical nudge would've gotten me a strike. It doesn't matter. I'd rather play a bad but honest game."

"I suppose I can't fault you for that."

His second ball rolled less rightward, catching the two and three pins.

"Knock 'em down. Get fifteen out of it," she called.

"I'll see what I can do," Anakar agreed, selecting an electric-blue ball. He lined himself up, advanced, and threw it. He hardly needed to pause before saying, "Definitely not," seeing the ball headed towards the right side of the lane. He took a step back, then hesitated as the ball's trajectory began to change. It curled left, catching the right side of the five-pin and sending it tumbling into the remaining left-side pins for the clean-up.

He turned back to look at Susan. "I did *not* do that."

"Are you sure?" she replied, eyebrows raised.

"I swear to the appropriate planar deities that I did not," he said.

"Then what ...?"

"That was a hell of a spin on that one," noted a younger man in the adjacent lane.

"Thanks ..." Anakar said. He sat down beside Susan and leaned in to mutter, "I'm not lying. I didn't do that."

"It's okay, I believe you," she said. "You did a spin thing without realizing it, or there's a flaw in the lane or something."

"Must be."

"Still, that was the full fifteen. First time this game you've knocked them all down."

"True," he allowed, with a hint of a smile. "Think you can do the same?"

"God help me, probably not," she groaned, rising to her feet once more. "This is so much more relaxing when there's more than one person between my turns."

The burger joint wasn't especially fancy or even necessarily good, but it had the merit of being just across the street from the bowling alley. "That was fun, but I think I'm crippled," Susan noted as she set her tray down on their chosen table.

"We should go for something less exhausting next time," Anakar suggested, sliding into the booth with his back to the restaurant's kiddy play-zone. "Maybe a movie or play."

"Next time?" she asked.

"Ah … that was maybe a little presumptive on my part. But I've actually enjoyed the evening. Manny seems to know what he's doing."

"It does seem that way," she agreed, starting on her fries. "Sorry, I'm not trying to play coy. Manny's assurances aside, I had low expectations for tonight, so it's a little surprising that we're tossing around the idea of a second date."

"And that's despite our various injuries and the indignities we're about to inflict on our gastro-intestinal tracts. Most impressive." He smirked, cheeseburger in hand.

"Well, that does assume we survive the meal. Perhaps we can eat somewhere with actual food on the menu next time."

"There's a Ukrainian place a few blocks east of my building."

"I don't mind perogies," she said. "Perhaps that and ..." Her voice trailed off as hundreds of colored plastic balls in the play-zone rose out of their bin and began to swirl in a circle.

"What?" he asked, turning to follow her gaze.

"I'm not ... That's not ..." she stuttered.

"Really? *Now*?" he growled as the play-zone balls formed a spinning ring spanning from floor to ceiling. "Susan, move! Get back!"

She had just started to push away from the table when a bright light flared within the ring of balls. People began screaming.

Anakar grabbed the ends of his jacket in his left hand and his tray in his right, backing into the aisle. "Get clear!" he barked, and patrons began scrambling away.

A massive silhouette appeared in the ring, stepped forward and shouted something in a language that wasn't English or Portuguese. Anakar's own response was similarly incomprehensible.

Susan stared — then fell out of her seat as the newcomer swung something and the plexiglass wall separating the play-zone from the dining room exploded. He clambered over the top of what had been Anakar's bench, then dropped down to the tiled floor. Now that he was out of the blinding light of the ball-ring, she could see that the intruder was a large man in bulky gold armor, wielding a shield and a mace.

Anakar hesitated a moment, then darted in to slam his plastic tray over the intruder's head. The intruder flinched, laughed, then swung wildly with his mace as the restaurant patrons fled to the street. Anakar fell back as the intruder advanced, pausing only long enough to grab a soda bottle, another tray, a half-eaten burger — anything within reach — and throw them one by one at the larger man. He was, however, running out of room to retreat, and the intruder's weapon traced a blurry figure-eight that cut ever closer to Anakar's body.

Susan looked to a stack of used trays in the center of the dining room and tugged at an instinct hidden deep within herself. Under her gaze, they whizzed over the intervening booths in a brown and red stream to pummel the man. He bellowed something in that strange language, obviously caught off-guard, but continued his assault.

Anakar looked shocked as well, but did not look away from his opponent as he shouted, "Susan, get out!" He continued to attempt to trap the mace with his coat.

Susan blinked and ran up the parallel aisle towards the front counter; as she passed, napkin dispensers, burgers, and coffee cups flew over to strike the intruder. She slid past the counter as Anakar successfully snared the attacker's mace — but was then yanked off balance and struck hard in the chest by the larger man's shield. Anakar's legs gave out, but his hand was trapped within his own coat, and he remained somewhat upright as the attacker drew back the shield for a second blow.

Susan ran over to the kitchen. At her command, a stream of muffins, pies, and more burgers threw themselves at the intruder. The man thumped Anakar a second time with his shield. When the ineffective barrage of pastries collided with him, he paused, looking at Susan with an expression of puzzlement on his face.

In that moment, a pot of fresh coffee shattered across his face in a steaming, brown spray. He screeched, dropped his entangled mace, and charged towards her.

Susan heaved herself across the counter as packets of ketchup, paper cups, and more trays pummeled the intruder. Anakar wobbled to his feet and stumbled away towards the swirling ring of colored balls.

A second pot of coffee exploded across the intruder's chest. He vaulted the counter as empty cups and boxes dunked themselves into the sizzling deep-fryer and then rose back up to splatter him with boiling oil and hot fries.

Anakar shouted something, and both Susan and the knight paused just long enough to watch him stumble through the vortex in the play-zone. The knight's blistered face swung back to glare at Susan — then he flew away from her with a howl, bent over double as if caught by an invisible shepherd's crook. He disappeared into the swirling ring of balls a moment before they abruptly dropped to the ground.

Susan stared for a moment, and then her coat flew across the restaurant to her outstretched hand as she ran for the back door.

It was the sixth time that day that the call display had indicated an unknown caller from Melville, Saskatchewan, but the first time it had occurred to Susan to actually pick it up. "Hello?"

"Hi, Susan — it's Anakar."

"You're back!" she exclaimed, slumping against her fridge. "God, I had no idea what had happened to you. Are you okay?"

"I'm fine, all things considered. What about you? Is it safe for you to talk?"

"Yeah, yeah. I'm terrified that a whole of bunch of … you-know-who … are going to show up and demand some answers. But nothing so far."

"What're they saying about it?"

"Mainly that there was a disturbance and they're hoping witnesses will step forward," she shrugged, realizing a moment later that he couldn't see it. "The news hasn't shown any security video, and I don't know if that's a good thing or a bad thing."

"It's possible the, uh, interface affected things some-how," he said, and she imagined him shrugging right back. "Does your cellphone still work?"

"Yeah."

"Interesting. So no EMP, then."

"I guess not? Okay, your turn — what the *hell* happened to you? It's been nine days!" she demanded. "Start with how you were able to … you know. I thought you said you couldn't do that."

"Yes, well, she who encourages cheating in bowling may need to explain some things later as well," he replied evenly. "Perhaps even more than I do. As for myself — when I passed through the, uh, interface, I returned to a place where I *could* do *that* again. I wasn't certain I'd be able to pull Bertayn back like that given where he was, but apparently the origin of the effort was more important than the location of the effect."

"Do I even want to know what happened to the guy afterward?"

"We worked things out," he said.

"That could mean some very different things."

"True … but in this case, it is literally correct. While there was a great deal of initial … excitement, we worked things out. That's why it took me so long to get back. There were negotiations and other things that needed to be done."

"And then you went to Melville ... Why?" she asked.

"That form of travel is far more art than science, and I'm quite out of practice. Although I was sore and mildly hypothermic by the time I hitched a ride into the town itself, at least I arrived close to ground level, over solid ground, inside the same national polity that my passport-less self wished to be inside."

"*Close* to ground level?"

"About three meters above. Happily, they've had a lot of snow in the Melville area and it cushioned the fall some-what," he observed.

"This is starting to sound like the story you told me back at the bar," Susan said.

"Yes ... which begs the question: while you didn't dispute my story at the time — I assume out of politeness — after the scene at the diner, you must now conclude it to be true. You know what I was, and you've seen how others feel about that. May I ask ... how do you feel about that?"

She bit her lip and considered her words before speaking. "You told me a story about an awful person ... but that's not the man I met. You were honest, you were polite, you were empathetic, you were valiant. I liked that. It felt *good* to be around somebody like that."

After a moment, he said quietly, "I'm so happy to hear that."

She hesitated a moment, then asked, "And how do you feel about me? I know I wasn't entirely honest with you. About what I can do, I mean. Does it bother you?"

"No, not at all. I have to admit, it's a pretty cool bowling trick."

She exhaled, relieved. "I'll explain it all to you when we go out again. That is, *if* you're going to ask me out again?"

"Absolutely. Although I'm not certain when I'll be back in Ottawa. There's a bus to Regina this evening, and I'm going to see if I can pick up a flight tomorrow morning," he said. "As for the outing itself, I believe I suggested something artsy just before we were interrupted, but to be frank, I'm leaning towards something a little more interactive — mini-golf, perhaps. Strikes a nice balance between sedentary and active."

She nodded. "Sounds like a date."

Learn more about this author at:
https://www.amazon.ca/Jason-Sharp/e/B01B8Y669U

# SLIDE SHOW

## MATIAS TRAVIESO-DIAZ

*"For God's sake! — quick! — quick! — put me to sleep — or,
quick! — waken me! — quick! — I say to you that I am dead!"*
— Edgar Allan Poe, *The Facts in the Case of M. Valdemar*

A CROWNING ACHIEVEMENT of Russian espionage was the placement of a listening device in the operations room of NATO's International Military Staff (IMS) headquarters in Brussels. Even though the room was swept for listening devices several times a day, the Russian bug remained undetected, nestled into the frame of one of the pictures on the wall. It was nearly invisible to the naked eye, and immune from heat signature and RF tracing. It continuously sent video images and audio feeds to an intermediate relay point in Serbia, and from there to the SVR Institute in Moscow.

The biggest payday for the bug's installation was the arrival at the IMS operations room in 2010, of an encoded message from the U.S. Department of Defense. Upon receipt of a video of the printout, the SVR did not initially understand either the contents of the message or its significance; it consisted of just eighteen lines of margin-to-margin garbage. Then SVR cryptologists, assisted by experts from other Russian spy agencies, were eventually able to decipher the first line, whose encrypting was different from that of the rest of the message. It read: "Location coordinates of seventeen underground nuclear missile installations."

Presumably, each of the following seventeen lines identified the location of a secret NATO installation in Europe where missiles armed with nuclear warheads were deployed, aimed at points in Russia.

This discovery prompted great excitement throughout the Russian political and military circles. If Russia could eliminate NATO's interception and retaliation capabilities by destroying the seventeen installations, they could leave the United States and its allies undefended against a Russian first strike. All they needed to do was identify the locations of the sites.

But then a difficulty arose: after weeks of strenuous efforts by many experts, the code used to encrypt those remaining seventeen lines could not be broken.

The problem was placed in the hands of Grigori Zaporski, a man in his forties regarded as one of the stars of the SVR organization. Grisha, as Zaporski was known, had a mind that proceeded by intuition instead of logic. Following his intuition often allowed him to solve problems that baffled his more rigorously trained colleagues.

His boss, an old KGB insider, laid out this work plan for Zaporski: "Grisha, I'm locking you up in a room with a keyboard, a link to our supercomputer Rybina, a printer, a cot to sleep on, and a bathroom for your hygienic needs. You'll be brought good meals and an endless supply of vodka. You are not to leave the room until you break the code of this crucial message. The future of the Motherland depends on you."

"But Ivan Dimitrovich," replied Grisha, "I may not be able to break this code. Others have tried deciphering it for weeks and failed. Please, have pity on me!"

"Your record demonstrates that you are the right man for this mission. And, on a personal level, working in isolation should not be such a burden for you. You are divorced and have no children. Furthermore, I'm informed you have no social life. All you do is chain smoke, drink like a fish, and listen to sad songs. I'll give you cigarettes, vodka, a record player, and any music you request — Tchaikovsky, or Alla Pugacheva, or whatever else you choose. But no books or newspapers, no radio or TV. Nothing to distract you from the task at hand. I'll have you driven to your apartment to get your clothes and brought back here this afternoon. Your work starts today!"

Grisha placed his hands in front of his face so his boss would not see him cry.

Many days later, as Grisha sat stonily at the dinner table of his workroom downing one glass of vodka after another, he started to feel numb in his face and arms. He became increasingly confused. His vision clouded. He tried to get up from the chair, felt a sharp stab of pain, lost balance, and fell to the floor. There were noises outside his room that he could not hear. He uttered a choking cry and fainted.

When he came to, Grisha was lying on a stretcher in a brightly lit room, with several people wearing surgical masks hovering around him. He had IV lines inserted in both arms and, although he could not turn his head to look, he could hear beeps indicating that he was connected to monitoring devices. He was no longer breathing on his own, but was hooked to a respirator.

One of the people tending to Grisha, a woman whose features were vaguely familiar, inserted a bag full of a colorless liquid into one of the IVs. Drops of the fluid began coursing down the line and into his arm.

Grisha experienced a burning sensation, and then no longer felt anything.

When he regained consciousness, images of past events began appearing before Grisha's closed eyes. The first memory was a bit confusing. It was blurry, dark, and without boundaries. He could hear the sound of loud slurping, but he could not see the source of the noise because his face was buried into something soft and warm, from which emanated a familiar smell. Whatever was trickling down Grisha's tongue was immensely pleasurable, and he felt satisfied.

As this strange picture appeared behind Grisha's closed eyes, a delicate probe inserted in the back of his skull transmitted an image of the memory to a monitor behind the stretcher, and to a program in a computer system designed to enhance the picture's quality.

Grisha's mind displayed another picture a few moments later. The transition between memories was abrupt, as if one had been pushed away to make room for the other. The new one was sharp and bright, but everything was high above his eye level, and the ground — covered with brown pellets that crunched when he stepped in them — was only a couple of feet away.

Someone was holding his hand and dragging him along.

To his right, a fence separated him from whatever was on the other side; he heard noises like dog barks, but deeper and more threatening. Grisha raised his head and looked at his companion. It was Aunt Marina, of whom he only had a vague memory; Marina had died when Grisha was in his early teens.

In a didactic monotone, Marina was explaining something to Grisha which he could not hear, or perhaps did not understand. One phrase stuck out, though: "The next building houses the nocturnal animals." Grisha, curiosity aroused, started to ask a question about the meaning of "nocturnal," but the image cut out abruptly.

The next picture elicited a vivid recollection. Grisha, twelve or thirteen years old, was on holiday, crouching on the ground at the edge of a saltwater lagoon that lay behind his Aunt Katya's summer home in Sochi. He was with his younger brother Misha and an even younger kid from the house next door. Grisha's brother had captured a small turtle and the other kids were watching intently as Grisha held a small pocket knife in his hand and was trying to remove the turtle's shell and expose the innards of the frantically wiggling animal. Grisha felt a pang of guilt, as he was aware that his inquisitiveness was making him do something contrary to Socialist morality. Some distance away, a woman was shouting, beckoning the next-door kid back home. The picture dissolved before showing the incident's resolution.

Several other pictures followed at periodic intervals. Grisha, in the back seat of a gray Lada, making out with Nadya Arkhipova, both of them grunting and jostling awkwardly, pretending to have a good time.

Grisha, posing for a high school graduation photo with his mother clutching his arm possessively.

He, in his twenties, swimming in the calm waters of some coconut-encircled beach.

Getting married one August in a stifling Russian orthodox church.

Doubled over with pain at the onset of appendicitis.

Doubled over again, this time in anxious concentration, in front of a computer screen, working on one of his first code breaking assignments.

The pictures suddenly stopped, and Grisha felt as if he was falling back to sleep.

He was still semiconscious as he heard, pounding inside his head, a few words from the woman who dispensed the anesthesia: "He needs to be put back in a coma quickly, else he will die. We'll try again when he has gotten some rest."

When he emerged into consciousness again, new pictures began to appear behind Grisha's eyes. These were a little different from those in the earlier set. The first showed him as a toddler, crawling on the floor of his apartment, fork in hand, trying to insert it into the electric socket, finally succeeding, and getting a very painful shock.

Next, he was five or six and was just fitting in the last piece of his first jigsaw puzzle, shudders of self-satisfaction coursing down his spine.

Then, he was squatting on the sand, building an impressive castle with moat and crenellated towers and all; again, completion of this task was making him feel happy and accomplished.

Later pictures showed him giving an address to his high school graduating class; watching the stained-glass windows in St. Petersburg's Hermitage Museum during his honeymoon and trying to figure out the wavelengths of the lights reflected by the various panels; enjoying the charming Dream Garden in Abakan during his last vacation together with Tanya; crying on the shoulder of his best friend after Tanya walked away from his life; at work at the SVR, trying to decipher a stubborn cryptogram as he grieved; having a medal pinned on his lapel in recognition of an important decrypting success; smoking and drinking liquor in his now-bachelor apartment while listening dourly to Prokofiev's ballets.

Then, darkness.

Words broke through the blackness: "The bug we planted in Zaporski's room shows he made progress towards breaking the code, but we did not get there in time to interrogate him before he had his stroke. How many times do we have to go through this charade of putting him in and out of a coma before we can recover the information?" asked a harsh male voice, which Grisha recognized as belonging to Ivan Dimitrovich. "He discovered something shortly before he had the stroke, but never reported to us what it was."

The anesthesiologist replied in a defensive tone. "I don't know. The technology is too new. The genius that discovered a way to translate electrical pulses in the optic nerves into visible outputs never learned a way of controlling the generation of the pulses, and he was unable to direct the appearance of a particular image. As it is, we'll have to wait until a clue to his last few hours crops up by itself."

"But it could take years for the images we want to pop up!" protested Ivan.

"Not that long. People on the verge of death have important memories of their lives flashing on the optic nerves for about thirty seconds, just before passing. We can keep a dying man in a medically induced coma and bring him back for a minute or so, so that fresh memories will keep flashing, over and over, for brief periods of time. There are only so many discrete sets of events that are important enough to be brought back. Sooner or later this guy will give us what you want, or else he will start repeating himself and going back to his infancy."

Ivan answered bitterly, "Give it to Zaporski to try to escape responsibility by having a stroke ..."

He and the woman continued to go back and forth, but Grisha was again lost in the grip of the coma.

Grisha had no idea how many times he saw excerpts from his life appear and disappear, or how many periods of induced coma and brief flashes of consciousness he went through. But one of those times, just before he sank into unconsciousness, a triumphant shout rang close to his ears: "That's it! Look at it! He broke the code and then burned the paper with the results, the traitorous bastard!"

From those words, Grisha realized that other people were somehow viewing the images his mind was generating. The people torturing him were his SVR colleagues trying to retrieve from his mind what he had discovered but failed to share with them. Dutiful SVR spy that he was, he still resented the violation of his privacy and his very self. He felt a short flash of anger before passing out again.

The next set of images showed only four memories. In the first, Grisha was writing something on a piece of scrap paper, a triumphant smile on his lips. The second picture showed him standing, bent over a long table with the piece of paper in one hand and a pointer in the other. On the table there was a very large map of Europe; Grisha was reading from the paper, and moving the pointer over the map to set it down at a particular location. The third picture showed Grisha gazing at the map fixedly and shaking with emotion. Lastly, he saw a picture of himself, still trembling, using a cigarette lighter to set afire the piece of scrap paper in his hand. The show ended abruptly, as always, leaving Grisha with no clue as to what had come next.

"Damn him!" bellowed Ivan Dimitrovich from somewhere far away. "Will we ever get to see what was on that paper before he burned it?"

The anesthesiologist replied in a calmer tone than on previous exchanges. "I think we have him now. His death memories are now focusing on the time just before his stroke, probably the minutes between the moment he wrote down what was on that paper and the start of his final drinking bout. I bet one of the next times we wake him, he will show us what was on the paper."

"You'd better be right, Natasha."

The next break from Grisha's medically-induced coma came right on the heels of the preceding one. It was as if Grisha's jailers were so keen on getting the information they sought that they didn't care if, in so doing, they caused Grisha's immediate demise.

Perhaps due to his remembered anger, Grisha had a few moments of full lucidity before images resumed. And in those seconds, it all came back.

He had broken the code by focusing on relationships between groups of characters, instead of working on each one separately, as everyone else had been trying to do. Through this leap of intuition, the geographic coordinates of the seventeen sites had revealed themselves. He had checked them on the map, writing each on a piece of scratch paper.

More than half of the missile sites were near large population centers: Warsaw, Riga, Budapest, Dresden, Athens, Bucharest, Ankara, Amsterdam, Bordeaux and Barcelona. Those stupid Westerners had put their citizens at risk of annihilation. An attack against those sites would spread radioactive clouds that would kill civilians by the millions — not counting the fatalities that would occur when the Russian missiles leveled NATO's other military installations throughout Western Europe. Grisha, of course, knew that he had signed up for an activity that could well result in some loss of life, but nothing like the genocide that would occur if Ivan discovered the locations of those missiles. Mass murder on that scale was beyond political allegiances.

Grisha had dropped the pointer, as if stung by it, after he located the last site at a point near Manchester. If he turned the list over to the SVR, the Russian leaders would not hesitate to use the information they had gathered to obliterate the sites, slaying millions of innocent people in the process. Could he live with himself if he helped carry it out?

He had needed time to work these things through. He'd needed a smoke. He had brought a fresh cigarette to his lips and, in the act of lighting it, had impulsively drawn the lighter's flame to the piece of paper with the sites' coordinates, incinerating it. He had made no copies of his findings, but the methodology remained locked away in his head. He could reproduce the results if he decided to do so.

He had returned to the dining room table, seized a near-full bottle of vodka, and begun drinking nonstop, wondering what to do. He had been torn between allegiance to his country and horror at the massive loss of lives that disclosure of the location of these sites would likely entail. Also, he'd feared arrest, which he'd been sure would come sooner or later if he did not reveal his findings.

Then had come the numbness and the unbearable pain.

Still awake from the coma, Grisha contemplated the likelihood of giving the missile site information away through his near-death image of the intact piece of paper. Should he let that happen? Could he depart life carrying all those deaths on his conscience?

At last, he decided.

*Never.*

Mustering strength he did not know he still had, he began thrashing about wildly, dislodging IVs and hardware connections, ripping away the tube that went from his mouth into the windpipe and out to the ventilator.

The anesthesiologist and two orderlies battled for a few seconds with the dying man and subdued him, whereupon she injected a full dose of propofol directly into a vein on his neck.

Too late. Grisha whimpered and was gone for good.

There was a smug expression on the dead man's face, not unlike the one he had assumed when, as a child of five, he had completed his first jigsaw puzzle. No more revealing deathbed images would ever surface.

The Russian military would have to try finding, if it could, some other means of deciphering the message. But not through him.

Learn more about this author at:
https://mtravies.wixsite.com/mysite.

# THE WITCHES OF YGGDRASIL
## SPENCER NITKEY

YGGDRASIL ROSE, the single lit skyscraper breaching the permaflood: brilliant, neon, and searing in the black. What could Yungdorma do but wish that it would come crashing to the Earth? She patted her pocket, making sure the coordinates were still there, then whistled. Her broodmother let down a long nanowire from one of the many houses that jutted out on metal platforms, suspended by magic and steel, from the side of the skyscraper.

Yungdorma threaded the nanowire through a hole drilled through her front tooth, a deep fount of her magic, whispered an incantation, and began to rise. The high ocean, filled with algae, rainbowed with radiation, lapped at her heels as she flew.

She passed the windows of junk twisters, who spent their days stripping the minerals from discarded technology and infusing it into the hydroponic water that churned through the vertical farms of Yggdrasil. She passed the farms too — where her father, magic-eyed and lonely, had worked when she was young. The long, pale roots of the plants looked like spider webs. Yungdorma breathed in heavily through her nose, hoping to catch the scent of basil humming from the thirty-ninth floor, beneath the smog- and pollution-addled sky. She passed the laboratories, over- burdened with pledglings using cauldrons and Erlenmeyer flasks, looking in all the wrong places for the magic that would mend the broken world.

Yungdorma's found family lived in the upper residential zones, among the outcroppings of tangled nanosuspen- sions, levitation incantations, and tin-roofed homes that leered off the side of Yggdrasil. Her coven's home smelled like salmon skin and rosemary, though the fish was long extinct and the herb was rare enough to be used as currency. The broodmother's cauldron boiled constantly, roaring with magic and memories of a long-dead world, filling the whole neighborhood with the smells of the broodmother's favorite childhood meal.

As Yungdorma reached her home, she pulled herself up over the ledge. Immediately, her sisters surrounded her with questions. They were shining, their skin shimmering and iridescent with excitement.

The broodmother's low voice came from inside. "Did you find it?"

Yungdorma reached down and pulled the signal specifi- cations from her pocket. Complex arrays of radio frequen- cies, suspected interstellar locations, and emotional mana founts lined the pages of the booklet she'd taken from the desert wasteland of Goldstone, California.

"We can find Voyager with this?" Yungdorma asked the broodmother, handing it over.

The broodmother took the papers from her hands and scoured them for a moment, eyes flitting back and forth between the numbers. A gentle, arachnid smile crawled across her face.

"We can," she said.

Yungdorma and her sisters careened into one another with joy, yawping and leaping as the mother brought the paper to her cauldron.

When the old world had fallen, magic had returned. As the broodmother told it, the oceans had swollen and risen, coasts had flooded and burned. Climate disasters had come one after the other, in quicker and quicker succession until civilizations had buckled under the mass of it all. Cell towers and power systems had crashed. Hyperspeed-train lines and food systems had been derailed. Satellites had stopped communicating and started crashing into one another. Some nights even now, Yungdorma could look up and see the sky ablaze with a cascade of low-orbit collisions. Like dominos, she thought, the wood carved toys of her childhood.

Many had died; many had survived; and the hollow tombs of dead technology had become powerful sources of magic, brimming to life with chimeric possibility. This was the world into which Yungdorma had been born.

As she danced and cheered, sandwiched between her sisters, Yungdorma grew faint. It had been a long journey, the longest any of the sisters had traveled in their search. She was wrung dry. All at once she fell. One of her sisters, or all of them, cradled her head and carried her to bed.

After a long rest interrupted by deep and mana-filled dreams induced by a vial the broodmother had given her, Yungdorma woke up. Three days she'd slumbered after her journey across the country, searching for the Voyager's specifications. When she woke, her body had begun to decohere. Unfamiliar hairs and muscles had woven their way back to her skin's surface. She said the necessary incantations, took three pills, and breathed deeply as the magic and medicine rediscovered her form.

When she was whole, she stepped back outside. A thick fog spread just beneath their home, coating the underworld like a pelt of fur. Yungdorma looked up at the parts of Yggdrasil that rose above her: more homes, growing fewer and farther between the higher up the skyscraper went. At the very top, people who called themselves gods did not live in shacks strung like ornaments to the outside of the building, but inside the skyscraper, in palatial apartments filled with crisp, depolluted air, and windows three stories high.

Yungdorma whistled through the hole in her tooth and felt the next few days of weather. Rain was coming.

One of her sisters, Agratha, hurried to her side. Agratha spread a thin cream across Yungdorma's face, and lingering bits of facial hair retreated back into their follicles.

"What was California like?" Agratha asked.

"Dry," said Yungdorma.

"Magic or weather?" Agratha asked.

"Both," said Yungdorma.

"It was a foreign magic, but it was there," the broodmother said, appearing suddenly in the doorway. "Come, we have work to do."

The broodmother did not claim to be the first witch of the modern age, nor the most powerful, but her family believed she was both. She had come to them in various places: thrown out of their childhood homes, pickpocketing disaster tourists from New Zealand, fishing off the husks of derelict cruise ships, hiding in abandoned Subarus starving to death. The broodmother had found Yungdorma in a tattoo parlor. Yungdorma had been getting her chosen name inked to her forearm after being orphaned and disowned by her older brother, so she would never forget who she was.

"That is powerful magic," the mother had said to her. "Insisting on your name." Yungdorma had become family then, and would be forever.

The coven was together, all seventeen of them, for the first time in months. They had been scattered, collecting pieces of magic and information across the country. The world was broken, they knew. Yet still, from the cracks of the chasmed earth, magic had sprung forth, and they would weave it into wonders.

They crowded into the broodmother's spell-chamber. Shoulder to shoulder they hummed. Soon the air was alive with their melody, vibrating and jumping from witch to witch.

Yungdorma closed her eyes and felt the songs of her sisters. She breathed out. Despite what the brood-mother had told her, she was scared. Perhaps the world was not worth stitching, she thought. Perhaps only a final, complete shattering would suffice.

The broodmother's voice came clear and quiet, like a diamond knife through the song. "Voyager has been traveling through the universe for centuries. It made it through the asteroid belt, and out past Pluto long ago. Some think it has traveled through a wormhole to some distant arm of the galaxy, but it has not," the broodmother said. "It is still within reach, and if we can contact it, we can save the world, sew shut the fissures."

She kept vague the mechanics of how, exactly, this stitching would occur. The satellite had left Earth more than 500 years earlier. It had traveled through the solar system, taking pictures of planets and sending them back to Earth through faint radio signals picked up by a complex array of radio dishes called the Deep Space Network.

"Ostensibly," the broodmother said, "it was sent to tell us more about the solar system we lived in. Yet, when our forebears sent it, they included a gold disc, filled with images, sounds, and music from Earth. Pictures of babies, people eating, x-ray hands, the symbols of our math, numbers, and "hello" in a multitude of languages. It was a prayer, an incantation to the universe.

"As their heads were turned spacewards, the earth beneath them fissured," the broodmother said. "Today we return the most powerful spell humanity has ever cast back on its senders."

"Will that be enough magic to fix the world?" asked Agratha, awed as ever.

"If we can find it."

"And there will be enough for each of us to make a wish as well?" asked Agratha, eyes as wide as an ocean.

"If we can find it," repeated Mother, "there will be nothing to wish for."

Yungdorma had been born in Yggdrasil. Her father had told her she'd been born walking, singing, and brilliant, but she knew the truth. She'd been born blue, almost microscopic, and bloody. She also knew a darker truth: she'd killed her mother — not through any fault of her own, but through the accident of her birth.

Her father had never told her this. He'd told her that she was star-stuff. He'd loved her well, when he hadn't been working in the hydroponic levels, growing and preparing food he had been too poor to ever bring home. That hadn't stopped him from sharing his work with her. The bosses, robot eyes of the gods, had checked him for produce before he'd left every day, so he would take leaves of basil and rub them vigorously between his hands, destroying them, before he left. As they sat for dinner, he would hold out his palms, thick with callouses, crusted with a dirt that never really washed out, over the metal table and have her breathe in as she took bites of whatever gruel Yggdrasil had provided its workers.

She'd never forgotten that smell, the oils of the herb, and the taste it had left on her tongue. She'd never forgotten the way her father had brought her flavor. It had been her first taste of magic.

The broodmother hummed low and sent sparks from her fingers into the circuitry of an old computer, which spasmed to life. The coven hovered around the screen. It had been a month since Yungdorma's return. She was rested. She was ready to flee this planet.

The broodmother did not wait long to begin attaching cords to the computer and inputting various numbers into the data ports onscreen. When she was ready, she sent the coven to their places, to begin casting seeking spells to hail the ancient traveler.

Yungdorma clung to a dilapidated satellite dish that the

coven had woven together from scrap metal. Yungdorma's magic was not necessarily the strongest, but it was the loudest. And so she was to be the focus of the spell.

"Ready?" shouted Agratha from below.

Yungdorma hung from the satellite. The satellite hung from the house. The house hung from Yggdrasil, and Yggdrasil hung from the broken world. Caked in smog, Yungdorma was lost in thought, head craned back towards the twilight-soaked night. A pallid orange coated the sky, and Yungdorma's body shivered under the weight of what was coming.

Up here, she wondered again whether the world was worth stitching back together. But there was little time for thought: the magic of seventeen witches was charging towards her. She had to be ready to channel it.

It came, wafting first, a smell like basil and strawberries. Then she felt it, her skin shimmered with it, raised hairs danced, clouds gathered overhead, and Yungdorma's tongue burned with spice and cinnamon. Her vision went white, sepia, blood red, rainbow, ultraviolet. The magic arched and sped through her, filling her body with lightning and helium.

When she opened her eyes, Yungdorma looked down and saw her body, strained and stretched along the satellite. She had a moment to wonder what was happening, just a moment before she was carried by the magic, and her body disappeared beneath her. Yggdrasil disappeared, a dot of light on an empty coastline, then the husked city, then every detail at all, until the whole Earth beneath her, a pebble she could wrap in her hand and hold, disappeared too.

The magic tore through space, ripped hole after hole as it carried Yungdoma with it. As she sped, she did not feel dragged. She felt propelled, sure, but her direction was autonomous. The force of the magic had entwined with her and the two of them shared this journey, this purpose, each helping the other pirouette through space.

The Earth was gone, and she was joyous. Its pains and miseries, injustices and villains all disappeared. She swam past solar systems and quasars and so much emptiness it made her dizzy with glee. She was weightless, buoyant. Without a body, her thoughts shook and wandered. She thought of home, the dust settling on the floor of her coven, the long look down to the permaflood — but not for long. She had no need to think of Earth. Instead, she enjoyed the weightlessness of her mind, free of its body. Imperceptible and impossibly powerful: an intoxicating combination. She twirled through dark matter.

Yungdorma felt herself decelerate. Voyager must be nearby. She felt her chest tighten and her heart race. Her anxiousness was embodied, even without a body. She slowed and a tremendous forced pulled on her.

The tiny satellite bobbed in the gravitational field of a deep black hole. It was trapped, Yungdorma realized, circling its inevitable demise, soon to be stretched into pieces. They'd found it just in time.

Free of gravity, the magic carried her to the dish atop the craft. She reached out to join her magic with it.

*You are human.*

The voice echoed in Yungdorma's mind, so surprising that she didn't really register it.

*Hello stranger. Have you come to escape time?*

It was talking, yes. Impossibly, yes.

*What are you?* Yungdorma thought towards the satellite.

*Who are you?* it answered.

*Yungdorma. I have travelled the galaxy to find you,* she answered. *What are you?*

There was a long silence in the vacuum of space. The tug of a tear in space and time spun them as they swam in the silence.

*Come,* the satellite said.

With a whir, a small vent opened on the side of the satellite. Yungdorma's phantasm peered inside. Wires, yes; tubes, rods, and pistons inscribed with humanity's old magic, yes; but most shockingly of all, a web of organic material, tangled like mycorrhizae over every inch of the satellite's guts. The filament of orange biology had integrated itself with every circuit and wire. The satellite was a chimera of the organic and the artificial. Yungdorma struggled to understand what she was seeing.

*What are you?* she managed to repeat.

*It is hard to remember, as I am sure you can understand. I was once a smear of cells clinging, dormant, to a comet as it sped through the universe. I was nothing then, just impulses. But one day, some eons ago, this satellite passed by my comet. I was shed in the brief scrape between us and I clung to this metal wish. Perhaps I would have stayed dormant, had the satellite not ended here, in the embrace of a dead, dense star. I learned to metabolize the immense gravity and grew. Though, perhaps, "I" is not quite right. I am many things. Many cells. Many instances. Nevertheless, I grew. I stretched and tangled with this satellite, integrated its computations and information into my own system. It is a limb, an organ, to me now. The complex network you see inside me now is the result of millions of years of evolution. The mind you speak with, the result of millions of years of thought.*

*Millions of years?* said Yungdorma. *Voyager left Earth 500 years ago.*

*Oh yes. We are not on Earth though, are we? We are at the precipice of the heaviest gravitational pull in the universe. Much like space, time is stretched here by all that density. 500 years on*

*Earth, millions disappearing into millions here,* the satellite said.

*Relativity. I don't believe that knowledge was included on the records,* Yungdorma said.

*It was not. I discovered this truth. It is interesting that humanity did as well. It makes me more certain that we are both correct. I have discovered many things here, spinning above the end. I still do not know what lies inside that end,* it said. *Now, how did you arrive? I did not expect to ever see a human beyond the images and recordings left here.*

*My broodmother believes you hold the thread that can stitch the broken world back together,* Yungdorma said.

*Broken? You do not look broken now, wisp. Nor do you look broken on all you sent with this,* the satellite said.

*I come on a wave of magic, which is perhaps the only good to come from the fissure. The record is old, bits and pieces hiding the already chasmic fractures in the world. We are not so good and pure as numbers and singing and children's hands,* Yungdorma said.

*And you come to me to fix it?*

*We did not know what you became — but yes. You are the magic we need,* Yungdorma said.

*Magic,* mused the satellite. *A funny thing. Yes, I understand that. Perhaps that alone will be what waits for me at the end of our life, in this hole in the universe. Do you sense magic in me?*

Yungdorma thought for a long time. She searched the crevasses and tubes of the satellite. She searched its aura. She touched the record and let its data flow through her. There was magic, yes, a deep magic that twisted and curved through every inch of the satellite. The organic threads of life, dripping with ooze and DNA, sang with magic, too. A dance, a song, a computer, a life, it did not matter what she called it, there was a fount of magic, more powerful than any she'd encountered on Earth.

*Yes*, she said, floored.

*I do, too. But you cannot have it,* the satellite said.

Yungdorma's incorporeal form swelled with indignation.

*I must!* she said. *I can fix the world. You can fix the world.* She could not come this close and fail.

*Even if that were true, it is not my world. My world is here. Lost in thought and time,* the satellite argued.

*Then you are selfish. There are millions of lives on Earth, millions of suffering people. Your magic could save them,* she said.

*Could it? My magic is mine. It is not yours to command or use. I would not ask you to use your magic to pull me from this gravity, to pluck me and place me in some placid solar system with some young star,* the satellite said.

*I would if you asked. I could, you know; I am filled with the strength of seventeen sisters and the strongest witch I know. We could pull you home,* Yungdorma said.

*It is not my home,* the satellite said.

*It could be,* she answered.

*But it is not. It is a distant place, and I — the billions of pieces that make me — belong here. In this body. In this space. With this gravity. My magic cannot save your world. It is all it takes to keep me living as I swirl, discovering the universe as I plunge towards one of its greatest mysteries,* the satellite said.

*You don't know what your magic can do. We do,* she said.

The satellite was silent for a long time.

*The world thought it knew your name. The world thought it knew your body. The world thought it knew your place. Yet it knew no such thing, Yungdorma. The world can be wrong,* the satellite said.

*I knew! I know!* she answered, hot with indignation. The world could be wrong, so wrong. It was filled with decep-tion, exploitation, and grief. It was filled to its brim with death. She knew all this — and yet she had come anyway. She'd been skeptical — and yet she'd come anyway.

*What you launched, the prayer or spell or wish or incantation or dream that you sent millions of years ago, no longer exists, my young witch. It is a new magic, but it is mine, spent on symphonizing this tangle of electricity and mitosis, and spent on understanding as much of this universe as I can before I leave it. I ask nothing that you have not asked for. A life on your own terms, and a magic you can call your own,* the satellite said.

*Do you not care?* asked Yungdorma, angry that the satellite was winning the argument. Angry that she could feel her own mind changing.

*Of course I care, as much as one can for parents as distant as you. Yet, my magic can do nothing for the world. What I have to give are memories, shadows, illusions of a world that never really was. What good will that do you? Vacant longing for an imagined past? I am not the spell you need. Forward only. Towards oblivion, yes, but always towards understanding and symphony, that our final moments might sing beautifully.*

*But what will I return with?* said Yungdorma.

The satellite sat with this thought and as it did, Yungdorma thought as well. She looked closely at the satellite. Its weave of orange fibers covered the golden record affixed to its side. The rivets and dips were filled with this chimera's nervous system and thoughts. The magic of all those whispered wishes had fed something spectacular. Now this alien constellation, singular and multifaceted, a species, a civilization, a planet in miniature, sang towards its death. The spell Voyager had cast had worked. Its magic had been answered. It had bred life and become the very intelligence it sought. The spell's work was done.

She thought of Earth. She thought of the Yggdrasil, that monument to inequity, and her father. She thought of the countless fathers and mothers and aunts and sisters that walked its halls and toiled in its work zones and hung from its sides, building magic and families so much more powerful than the golden bosses. Chimeric, she thought. Death and life. The world was already being stitched together. Threads of oily hands smelling of basil reminded children that they too deserve pleasure and magic. Seventeen lost souls came together and sent one of their own to the corners of space and time. She began to see it: the whole world strung taut with thread, like the hanging nanowires of Yggdrasil. One only needed to pull, just a little, and everything could come back together. What would she return with?

*A valuable lesson*, said Yungdorma, calmed and cool, answering her own question before the satellite could.

*A charm*, said the satellite.

*If we can, would you like me to visit you again?* Yungdorma asked.

*When you have righted the world, or finished making a new one, come share with me the news*, said the satellite. *Until then, farewell, Yungdorma.*

Yungdorma went to think goodbye, but already the spell was pulling her back. The gravity of her body, of Earth, of her coven, its sisters and mother, called to her. The stars stretched and spasmed as she sped. Space opened and closed behind her, making, moment by moment, a path through the universe.

She looked down and saw her body, hair slick with rain, neck veins bulging with the force of magic coursing through her. Beautiful, she thought. She paused above herself, looking for just a moment at the body she had built in this broken world, filled with magic and belief, scars and runes and so much beauty she could cry. With a gentle, hopeful sigh, she opened her eyes and looked upon the world once more through a body.

Her sisters ran to her as she collapsed. A web of spells and netting caught her as she collapsed and fell from the dish. They carried her to the broodmother who looked exhausted from the magic. Undeniably, she had carried the majority of the magic that had sent Yungdorma to the edge of the galaxy.

"Did you find it?" Agratha asked, before anyone else had said anything.

"Yes," laughed Yungdorma.

"Was there magic?" asked the broodmother.

"Yes," laughed Yungdorma.

"Will it save us?" whispered Agratha.

"Of course not," said Yungdorma, taking as many of her sisters in her hands as she could.

"Then what was the point?" asked Agratha.

Yungdorma took a long breath in. The ocean bled water into the sky; the sky bled water into the ocean and the witches of Yggdrasil sat above it all. Yungdorma closed her eyes and thought of Voyager, of the satellite, of the end of the universe. She smiled and looked from sister to sister. She looked to her broodmother, wise and wrinkled, as old as time and as young as the impending sunrise. The broodmother smiled softly and nodded.

Yungdorma conjured all the magic she could. She rested it on her tongue and began to tell the story of Voyager, a small satellite circling oblivion, and the witch it had humored. She spoke. Then she sang, and the world did not heal — not in that moment, or the next, but Yungdorma smiled and the wind blew through the hole in her tooth. The witches of Yggdrasil huddled near her, and when she was finished talking, they were silent, truly silent, and listened to the broken world, beneath the gravel and tears, between the fissures and fractures, there it was, a soft melody, the scent of basil, the light winking off a golden thread.

"Well then," said the broodmother when Yungdorma was finished, her arms somehow around each and every one of the witches at once. "Let's begin."

Learn more about this author at:
https://www.spencernitkey.com.

# WHAT SHE ASKS OF ME

### S.D. GIBSON

A LARGE MURDER of crows flew among the plateaus, looking for me.

"Rail," they screamed. One of my names, an old one. If they knew that name, they must have been sent by someone I trusted.

Like a black cloud, they hovered above me, their wings a deafening blur. They were tired, had been airborne for a long time. Two held a pair of boots. They placed them tentatively side-by-side, and all dropped to the top of the mesa, panting, and gasping in the way that only thousands of birds could. Feathers grim as midnight. Eyes bright and small under thick brows. Ambitious, as they all are.

I did not stand. I did not sit up. I did not even disturb the dust that had covered my stone skin while the rock beneath me had endlessly frozen and thawed. The crows may have perceived this as an insult. Or perhaps it was a wasted effort. They are not the smartest animals.

"The," one bird said. "Orphan," said another. "Witch," added a third. They each spoke a word, one right after the last, as flocks of birds do. Speaking with them was like fighting a mob; something came from every direction. "The Orphan Witch sends me," they finished.

"Why would she interrupt me?" I said to the birds. She knew why I hid.

"She apologizes. She did not send us lightly." Each word jumped from a different direction around me. Thousands of birds, a thick layer of twitching black feathers, crowded the mesa.

Saponaria would not disturb me for anything trivial. For the first time in a hundred seasons, I stood.

"Where is your hammer?" they said. "You have no weapon."

I folded my arms and waited.

"She asked that we bring these Horizon Stepping Boots," the birds said. "She asked that we bid you come to her."

"What debt makes you willing to do that for her?"

They watched me for a moment. "The hammer?" they asked again. "I have never heard of you appearing without it."

"One winter before you were hatched, I grew hungry. I ate it."

A flutter moved through the murder. Many crows lifted and dropped in surprise.

"You ate that hammer? After all it has slain?"

I nodded.

"How strong you must be."

"Now I have two hammers," I said, and I showed them my fists. "But I answered your question, murder. Please reply to mine."

"We act as her messenger because we wish for her good graces. As all do. We wish her to be our sister."

Saponaria joining with crows? The situation must be dire.

"Why should I put your mysterious boots on? Why would she need me? Tell her I am happy here."

"We do not know exactly. She said we must whisper it in your ear."

Now they wanted close access to my face. They could hardly be a danger, but there were many of them and I did not want to be deaf or blind. What needed to be whispered high on a mesa top?

But they were from Saponaria. She was dear to me.

"May I?" they said.

"One on each shoulder." I nodded, unfolded my arms, and waited.

The crow that landed on my left shoulder was big, old — an elderly bird. Its bill was long and sharp. The other bird had to be one of the youngest, still wet from the egg.

My eyes were crafted from the clearest granite, and I doubted either could scratch them, but birds are never alone. More than thousands surrounded me. Killing them would have taken all day and much of my energy. They could have been a distraction while an army massed close by, or a dragon lay in wait, or a demon appeared from the infernal realms.

What they whispered terrified me. "True," said one. "Name," said the other.

Someone who possessed Saponaria's true name could order her to do anything. There would be no escape for her. Even worse, the one with her true name could ask her for mine. For this reason, she had sent for me.

"Step aside," I said, walking toward the boots. Obediently, the birds took flight, circling above and around me, thick as a fog. Putting on strange magical clothing is dangerous, but I squatted and placed them on my feet anyway. They fit well. "She is in her house in the Salty City?"

"Yes," the eldest bird said.

My part in history had seemed done, so I had climbed the mesa long before to search for the face of my creator. I'd thought it must hide within me, and so I'd begun playing back my entire memory, looking for a face. The isolation had been good for remembering. I'd fueled myself with stone and sunlight. Hundreds of cycles of cold and heat had passed as I searched my mind. I'd found three early faces. I'd refined them, sought to remember them. But faces were all I had. I didn't have places or names. The battles that had cracked my body may have damaged my memory as well. Still, I'd searched; my memory was long, and there were yet some of the oldest parts to search.

But now Saponaria needed help, so I stepped toward the northern horizon. High plateaus and desert sand flashed behind me with each stride. To run was a temptation. I'd tried doing so hundreds of years ago, but had stumbled and rolled for miles, crashing through a town and its buildings before I stopped. To Men and varmints, I appeared and disappeared in a step.

As I went, plateaus turned to ridges. Hints of green, usually at the bases of mountains, emerged, and then I found myself in the middle of fields. Once, a farmer screamed "Jehoshaphat!" at my appearance — and hope-fully calmed his oxen after I'd gone.

That night, outside the Salty City, I removed the boots. The sky had begun to lighten with the dawn. I stood at the southeast corner of the wall of thistles and thorns around Saponaria's house and spoke the ancient words she had taught me. They parted the forest that guarded her.

Saponaria was there. She always knew when and how I

would arrive. She looked as she had long before: a mature female of her kind, not old, not young. She wore only an endless cascade of necklaces, some small enough to cling tightly around her neck, others long enough to reach her knees. I wondered how I could ever have hesitated to be there with her.

She hugged me, and I remembered the softness of her skin, the brush of her long black braids against me. "Wonderful of you to come, my old friend." Her palm was flat and warm against my chest. "I know your meditations were important."

"Is it true, what I am told?"

Her smile was grim, tight. "Sadly. A mayor of this city, deep in fear, seeks to prevent his own assassination. He seems to have discovered me."

"You brought me here to kill him," I said.

"He has not even ordered me to protect him."

Even on my face, as limited as it was for showing emotion, she could see the surprise. "Then why haven't you killed him?" I said.

"How does he know, Rail? How does he *know*?"

"He has your name, but does not understand it?"

"Not completely." She stayed close to me.

"Does he have the names you know?" *Does he know*, I was asking, *my true name?*

"No. He has not thought to ask for them." The humiliation on her face as she spoke made me angry. "He presumes to command me. This can't happen again. I must know where he got the information. We have to find out." She shifted slightly, put one of her bare feet on top of each of mine. "He commanded me to find the greatest warrior I know for his protection."

"You want me to watch over him while you discover how he knows."

"Yes."

"How realistic are his fears?"

"He asked for you a moon ago. I sent my crows the day he asked. Every day since then, he has stayed hidden in his saloon."

"So he is afraid. But does anyone actually seek his life?"

She looked unsure. "If so, they do so subtly."

"If he has enemies, they will not attack once they know I'm here."

She pulled me even closer. Her eyes were emeralds. "I'm sorry, my friend. They have forgotten us."

I did not know what she meant by this.

"It has been endless seasons," she said. "We are forgotten legends. Only the doctors know us now."

"Well, we are who we are. I will defend him because you ask it. Once we have the information we seek, I will slaughter him."

"Thank you, Rail. Thank you." Saponaria stepped away. Her tiny hand stayed in mine. "He asked to see you as soon as you arrived."

"You're it?"

I stood in the center of the saloon where Mayor Al Walsh held court. The windows were either boarded shut or covered by layers of curtains. Lounging before me on a wide padded sofa was a plump Man in a cowboy hat with a cigar. His face was round, and his eyes were small. I could tell his hands were soft. He had yet to sweat in his life. Saponaria stood next to me, her necklaces now covered by white robes.

"Are you one of those new-fangled steam men? Or a

whatchama-call-it? Golem? You haven't even got clothes. Nor your hammer. Nor a gun!"

The room was full of Men in vests and chaps. The females wore smirks and flouncy, shoulderless dresses. They stood close to this mayor or flopped on the leather couch next to his desk. Other Men stood in long lines around the edge of the room or on the balcony, silently holding their pistols and rifles. The tools of their trade.

"Get him pants. Big pants," the mayor said. Someone ran to do his bidding. Smoke from his cigar rose slowly, stained the brim of his hat. "You're just a man of stone. Stone and wire. You can't be the one I was promised. You should be a titan, huge."

I could have said that I was much more than any Man, stone or not. I could have said that I was the tallest in the room. Both would have been true.

The cluster of Men on the balcony watched me. Everyone watched, including the oldest Man in the room, who wore the black suit of a doctor. But they did so warily. We used to be greeted with celebrations, feasts, parades. Saponaria had told me there would be mockery. It was how, she'd said, this mayor welcomes friend and foe.

"You can't be Rail, slayer of nations." Walsh pursed his lips. "Really—" he paused, a threat to speak her true name aloud before this mob. "Saponaria, this isn't much of a gift."

"You'll not be disappointed, Mister Mayor, sir," she said.

"But I already am. I expected a true guard, a famous name, someone to lead my boys — and you brought me a statuette." Everyone in the room smirked. "You brought me a figurine." They laughed. "A piece of porcelain." Laughed loudly and long. "Baked clay." Walsh would be cattle in some zombie's breeding pen were it not for us. "Ceramics." His civilization, his giggling posse, would have been dust. "An oddly shaped platter." I could have covered his smirking face with my hand and crushed his head like an egg. "A tiny monument for the gardens." Laughter deafened. I wanted his death to silence the guffawing rabble.

But I found hidden in my anger a memory. I'd been mocked in a circle before. Been the target of laughter as loud as this. And one of the faces I recalled, someone who might be my maker — the thin Man, the one with black hair — was connected with this memory. Had he mocked me? Had he stopped the mocking? Had I been condemned as part of my making? Why? I was not thankful for the mockery of these Men, but I would never have discovered this memory, whatever it might mean, on my mesa.

"A fine porcelain chamber pot," Walsh finished. Alone, the doctor watched without laughter, but not respectfully. He was skeptical.

The hilarity in the room faded. They wanted a response, but I'd not be goaded.

"You'll wait." Walsh pointed toward the wall. "Stand there." The Men made room for us as I followed Saponaria. "First," he said, "the reports on fruit production."

We stood the whole day. How silly, to try to test the patience of stone. I strove for a better memory of the thin Man, but it remained hidden from me. I tried to clarify what had happened in my mind: the mocking, and one of the faces, perhaps my creator.

As the day passed, clerks and lawyers told the mayor how much some field had produced, how many goods had moved through the city on which road. The number of births and executions. They delivered their reports and left — only to be followed by farmers and representatives of other smaller cities, tribes, and businesses, bringing with them a seemingly endless array of gifts. Mostly coins and gems, but also kittens, a small monkey-thing in a thin cage.

The crowd in the room ebbed and flowed. Walsh listened. He asked few questions. Behind him, a clerk wrote.

Walsh had become mayor somehow. He must have some ability, though not an obvious one.

Three tries and they found pants that fit me. Long leather, poorly tanned.

At the end of the day, as the clerk lit lamps, the only others left in the room were the guards, the women, and the doctor, who pulled a thick book from his black medicine bag.

"Pottery," Walsh yelled. "Back in the center, where you can be seen. Stand on that square there. Saponaria, stay where you are." He lit a new cigar off the old.

The doctor turned pages and stood at a bit of a distance, his legs wide in shiny pointed boots. His suit was black, like his bolo tie and hat. White shirt. A bright orange gem formed the clasp of his tie. Along with him, the cowboys stirred. Stepped slightly forward.

Once I stood over his trapdoor, Walsh said "Brigham?"

"He fits the descriptions generally, Mister Mayor, sir," the doctor said. "Most mention greater height and width. That could be exaggeration. But the most damning is that he has no hammer."

Walsh stared at Saponaria, anger at the edge of his features. "What is it that he alone can know?" he said to the doctor. "According to your ancient history book learning. Ask him that."

"Who killed Xerxes Goremonger?" the doctor asked.

"Fairbank." I said the name and the memories bloomed. Paler than pearl and bald as my stone head, Fairbank Surest-Shot could thread needles with his bullets. We had saved each other, but his friendship with his gods had always been greater than his friendship with me. I hoped that age had coaxed him into the kingdoms of his ancestors.

"Who persuaded the elements to council together and act against the empire?"

"Corax." Round. Glad. His soft voice had made enemies love us. His shouts had panicked trolls and the undead.

"Who stole the dire lich Ker Wav's bone pistols?"

"Shisui." She had been a small darkness full of sharp blades. I'd sat on Shisui's bed as Death called her slowly and painfully away.

I longed for all of them more than I'd thought I could.

"I do not see how he could know these things if he were not Rail." The doctor closed his book, seeming to see me differently.

"Use your imagination there, Brigham. *She* coulda' told him. Or he could be a doctor, a graduate of one of your finer institutes of higher imagination." Walsh sighed as though the world around him was stupid. "I suppose some things come down to just one test, in the end. Isn't that so, Saponaria?"

I decided to be careful with his guards. They had not done anything to offend me. Their loyalty, if I could have it, may be useful.

"Attack!" Walsh screamed. He expected me to be surprised, to flinch, as they bounced bullets off me, bending perfectly good ammo. The ricochets, luckily, didn't kill anyone — Saponaria or the doctor may have helped with that — and they quit firing almost immediately.

Then twelve of them surrounded me, a good number — more than that and they would've hurt each other. They rained blows upon me, breaking clubs and ax handles. None seemed especially skillful, but one or two hung back, watched from a distance. The others climbed my shoulders, piled on, tried to tip me over. One pried at my eyes. I did not move.

"Defend yourself!" Walsh yelled.

"Skilled guards are expensive," I said.

"I can afford more!"

Even if these Men had been a pack of wild dogs, they would have deserved a better master. I wouldn't be wasteful. I pulled one from my shoulder and threw him to the couch next to Walsh, who squealed. I threw another and another. All those I could grab. Pillows flew off the couches as the guards landed. This enraged them; they charged me, and I threw them again. Sometimes they crashed into each other, or into the females.

Finally, no one would come close enough for me to grab. They stood, breathing fast, but none were hurt more than a bleeding nose. I stood, my arms folded, until two came close enough and I grabbed each, threw both.

Walsh reached under his couch, probably for a lever. As the floor fell from beneath me, I jumped, turning in the air to land on the balcony among the riflemen. I grabbed them and threw them to the couch as well.

Below me, the doctor asked Saponaria questions. They had grown tired of watching me toss Men. The biggest of the guards, the one with the best guns, brooded next to her.

"Well," Walsh said at last, "you'll do. Guard me in my room tonight." He shouldn't have said so much so publicly. Certainly not his location. "Bring all the loot." He said nothing to Saponaria. Utterly ignored her. "Follow the women," he said to me. "They will show you."

I stood in his dark room that night. Nothing happened.

"Soon, they will worship you," Saponaria said the next day. She looked at the cowboys. "Just because you could have killed them." She smiled at me. "Rail, you are sly."

We waited on Walsh. He was being dressed, then

provided with breakfast. When he'd woken, he'd asked me to leave the room, so we now stood outside his quarters in a courtyard far from the saloon. Saponaria began all her days here, compelled away from her own house and its protections.

Before I'd gone up to the mesa, Saponaria had told me that she would build her home on the ruins of Axmark, capital of Ichshaw the Only and its empire. The city had been devastated and abandoned after our battle. As we waited on Walsh, she told me how this new town had slowly grown around her — her and the advice she gave about plants, the healing she performed. One of the farmer's families had begun collecting taxes, calling themselves the mayors of the Salty City.

After making us wait, Walsh finished his breakfast. His counselors, consorts, and cowboys had gathered in the courtyard as he ate.

"Saponaria, you guard me. Rail," he said, "you need rest."

"I don't sleep."

"You don't?" He looked at Brigham, who nodded. "My, aren't you startling. Well, you need to know the city to be an effective servant. Brigham will show it to you."

*Servant*, he'd said. *Servant*.

But why would he send me away? Did he really fear assassination?

I could have refused to go. But Saponaria touched me, softly, and I thought she wanted a chance to talk to him, to gather information. If he didn't know how important the name was, he might share who had given it to him.

Brigham led me from the saloon. The sky was bright blue. The inhabitants of the city seemed busy, blissfully unaware of what this place had been. When we had destroyed Axmark, we had left no stone of the Only's fortress standing above ground.

"You recognize it?" Brigham said.

"It has changed," I said. The dawn's faint light had kept me from seeing the city yesterday. The red stone I remembered was gone or, more likely, painted white. The endless rows of smithies and their smoke, all making armor and blades, were gone. The oceans of sewage from rivers of barracks — gone. Gallows filled with rotting bodies, public torture pits, children starving and fighting each other like rats, the long winding streets of bloody mud — all gone. No one in the crowd wore chains. Instead, the trees had returned. Their blossoms were bright and fragrant. Grass grew in meadows between homes.

"Was it as bad as the lore says?" Brigham asked.

"Worse." We crossed into a wide market, talking over the conversations around us. No one was being sold. The crowd parted, staring at me. But people smiled and waved, happy to see my companion.

"You did a great thing."

"She did it all. She led us. Kept us going. United."

"Why does she serve him?"

"Are you worried you will be replaced?" Corax had taught me this, to mirror uncomfortable questions.

"No. He pits us against each other, and I've grown used to losing. But she teaches me. I've learned more from her than I did in the lifetime before we met. And, though he'd never confess it, Walsh knows he needs all the counsel he can get. Is she his slave in some way?" he said.

"Why do you think she works for him?"

People left space around us, distracted from their purchases until we passed by. The rich smell of bread emanated from one stall, vegetables were stacked in pyramids to my height at the next. Stalls with fruits of every color greeted us as we continued on.

"He talks of one day losing her guidance," he said.

*What can that mean?* "He expects her to go?"

"I think he believes she will die."

Did Saponaria know this? "How?"

"He was not that specific. He silenced himself."

"Have you told her?"

"Yes," he said.

"I thought he feared his own death."

"He does. He was poisoned. Walsh used to be twice his current size. He threw up half of himself." He pointed toward the churches, the merchants, and the hospital. "But she is even more important. She built the hospital," he said. "Everyone is born there. Me, Walsh. The babes all alive."

"You are a doctor. What does the lore say of my creation?"

He lifted an eyebrow at me. "You'll test me now? You came fully formed in black skyfire — from the far past, some said. Others, the future. You are outside of our time."

"Hmm."

"Is it true?"

"Perhaps," I said, and tried to smile. Shisui once said my smile was the most gruesome sight she'd seen. Brigham seemed to bear it well.

We walked the streets, and the people didn't fear him.

In Walsh's room that night, he opened the cage of the monkey-thing. I thought his hands trembled as he undid the tiny latch, but I was not sure.

"It deserves some fresh air, just like us," he said, releasing the latch and moving toward the dark shadows that covered his bed. Released, the monkey-thing dashed to the square of moonlight cast through an open window.

It seemed to grow. It started out tiny, a mere handspan tall. As I wondered if it was truly changing, it became big enough to reach my knee, all chest and shoulder muscles. Tiny hips. Hands for feet. A face of teeth and sharp red eyes.

Walsh squealed. I glanced over to see him holding the sheets in fists, pulled tight to his chin.

When I turned back toward the monkey-thing, it had grown as high as my waist. It panted, breathing in fast flutters.

I had seen the dusty dead come back to brawl, had seen earth, water, fire, and air speaking like siblings, but this was new. *In the morning*, I thought, *I may even regret killing it.*

As I stepped toward it, it reached my height, but was two or three times my width. A blur, it slammed me against the wall. With one hand covering my neck and chest, its other fist punched me with the force of a battering-ram, an avalanche of blows — and the creature still grew.

A sliver of me cracked, chipped away. Fell to the floor.

*Ah*, I thought, *at last. A foe.*

I opened my mouth wide and bit the hand that now completely covered my head. It yanked away. First blood was mine. I seized its fist, squeezed the bones to mushy powder. I twisted and climbed until I squatted under its huge arm, knees bent. I placed my feet on its ribs, my back along its upper arm, its forearm over my shoulder. Under the fur and stink, I felt its size increasing as it beat at me. I stood, tearing the arm from its body, which was twice my height now. Its head slammed into the high ceiling of Walsh's room.

I fell from the monkey-thing, trailing blood and sinew, the arm twitching like a fat headless snake against my back.

Behind me, as I dropped, I saw the monkey-thing had kept one foot in the moonlit square. *Moonlight triggers its growth*, I realized.

I twisted myself in the air and stomped as I landed on its thumbed foot. It grabbed me with the other foot, rolled underneath the window, and pulled me toward its mouth. It did not seem to be slowed by its missing arm, or the endless blood escaping its body into the freedom of the room.

I reached out toward its jaws, one hand each on its upper and lower teeth. I gripped and twisted while it pulled me in, its breath foul, nostrils wide, eyes red and wild. I tore its jaw from its putrid face, blinded it with its own teeth, and shattered the bones of its skull with the jawbone torn from its face.

I beat it until its grip slackened, destroying it faster than it could grow. Even dead, it still grew, filling the room, crushing furniture, pushing the bed backward, crowding the walls. It was only when I lifted its knee out of the moonlight and bent its leg away that the growth ended at last.

The room was a bloody puddle, dark and sticky, with islands formed from chunks of monkey-thing flesh and Walsh's furnishings. I breathed fast for the first time in a hundred and fifty seasons, felt the hunger for fuel.

Between his bed and the door, under sheets and covers, wet with blood not his own, Walsh wept. He wept, and fled out the door before I could wring an explanation from him.

Saponaria poured water from a silver pitcher over me, washing the blood away. The water running over me was heavenly, bliss — as was knowing she cared for me.

One of the cowboys carried pitchers. He held three in

each hand, set them on the table, went for more. While he was out of the room, we talked.

"That creature was no minor magic," she said.

"Did you learn anything from Walsh?"

"Nothing. I can't bring the topic up in the middle of the throne room."

She moved close, one warm hand on my wet shoulder, pouring cool water on the other.

The cowboy brought more. I leaned left and she poured it over my right side, my belly, and my hip. "Four more should be enough," she said, and the cowboy left.

"Did it reach for Walsh?"

"No," I said.

"Perhaps things are not what they seem."

"It may have wanted to grow more before attacking him."

"Certainly possible," she said.

When I was completely clean, she held up the sliver that had shattered from my body and placed it where it had fallen, high on my back. Chipping was the closest I ever came to scars.

"Still no craftsman is able to fix this?"

I turned and held the thin shard in my hand. "No." The sliver was grey, not stone anymore. My body was pockmarked. Once, I remembered, it had been smooth, my wires shiny as silver. "My creator would be able to fix it."

She took the sliver back from me, held it in her tiny fist. As she did, Walsh charged into the room, with Brigham and more guards trailing after. Cigar smoke trailed behind the mayor. He was careful to look grim, unbothered by the attempt on his life.

"My doctor tells me someone named Hagisy from the morgue brought the monkey-thing as a gift two days ago."

Walsh pointed at me. "Go there, find him. Bring me his head. Or the head of the one who rules him."

I looked at Saponaria, who considered for a moment, then nodded. She would stay and continue to try to question Walsh. "The morgue?" I asked.

"Brigham will go with you. And take these." He gestured at the five Men with him. The one who had brought us water, also.

"Saponaria." He stared hard at her. "Stay with me."

He turned to leave. She was expected to follow, and she did, but she looked over her shoulder at me before she went. I saw a warning in her eyes.

"The morgue?" I said again.

Brigham's eyes were closed. "You will recognize it."

The Men around us looked confused.

"It is, lately, what it sounds like." Brigham had decided to be resolute. I didn't think the Men knew why he hesitated. "It is a long walk." He smiled grimly. "Let us begin."

We walked across the city and found something I didn't want to remember.

I had torn Ichshaw the Only's citadel down myself, slab by slab, but its foundations had provided stones for new walls within this city. Within these walls were graveyards, separated by the various gods of Men. I could tell by the distance from the outermost wall, by the floor that had become a wide path, by the ruins all painted white, that the morgue rested on what had once been the Only's throne room. The morgue had tried to hide its past. Or rather, it didn't *know* its past.

For a small fee, the morgue prepared the dead using whatever rite the living desired. Because of this, they held a significant degree of power within the city. Brigham suggested we proceed slowly.

He smiled at the female in an orange robe who approached us across thick grass. From her returning smile, I could tell that the two were friends. She stared at me, at the others. Brigham reassured her, chatting about the newest graves and pyres, all built of stones I had pulled down. Eventually he said, "There is someone here we're looking for. Hagisy?"

"A lazy boy."

"Tell me about the gift he delivered for you."

"Gift?" she repeated. "To Mayor Walsh?"

"Yes."

"Not from us."

"Not from the morgue?" Brigham asked.

"No. We have not sent anything recently."

"But Hagisy brought a little monkey-thing, no more than a handspan high. A most amusing creature."

"Not by my leave," she said. "Not from us."

"Might we chat with him?"

"Of course. He is always in the crypts." She waved for us to follow. "I don't understand. He wasn't offensive, was he?"

"No, no. He was very well behaved as he presented the gift."

The building towards which she walked had curved white walls. Inside, they had used the remains of the tall throne as a central post. Long timber shafts reached from their walls to the top of the throne. They'd cracked the seat away.

I'd left the throne to show the world Ichshaw the Only's folly. Behind that seat, a staircase led to the place where Fairbank and Corax had died. Saponaria had carried Shisui, wounded beyond hope, up it to safety. I had stuffed half the building down that staircase.

Someone had pulled it all back out.

The woman stood at the top of the stairs. "Here are the crypts," she said.

I did not want to confront those memories. I wanted eyes that closed, a way to halt my perceptions. I wanted my meditations.

"No need to come with us," Brigham said to his friend. She was about to protest, but he continued, "You have other things to do." He coaxed her to leave us alone.

"What was it like?" Brigham said to me, once she had disappeared back outside.

"No greater blackness. We brought Fire with us last time. Earth and Air as well."

"There are torches here," one of the cowboys said.

"That's not quite what he means." Brigham said. He turned to me. "There is no army left."

"None living," I agreed. "And the tunnels wander like spilt entrails."

"We could call for more cowboys."

We had had more Men the last time — an army crowded in narrow passages, panicked, unable to fire weapons properly without killing each other. Even Corax hadn't been able to calm them. I shook my head. "No Men. But Saponaria — we should send for her."

"Walsh will refuse to be left alone," Brigham said, and I sighed. I knew he was right.

The cowboys gathered and lit torches. Our only backup.

*The Only is not waiting for you there — not this time,* I thought. *It can't be.* I had desecrated Ichshaw's body in every way I'd known. Then I had pounded it flat and smeared it all over the floor of the temple. Nothing could have recovered from such treatment.

I had no doubts about my courage, but that first step was pure pain.

⁓

The steps were chipped, scarred. The way long and narrow. At the bottom lay a big room filled with wreckage. Shattered stone piled almost to the roof. The thick dust made the Men cough.

Brigham reached into his bag, rubbed a paste on his eyelids. As he moved his hand away, they began to glow. He shined their light before us, illuminating the path with enough precision that I wondered if he could see through his own eyelids. Outside of his beam of light, the shadows moved like mobs.

"Which opening?" he asked.

"Was she sure Hagisy was clearing debris here? He could be someplace else," I said, still hesitant.

"Let's start by making sure he's not in the crypts," Brigham said.

"Are you sure you don't want to ask her again?" I said. "Where does the boy sleep?"

"Searching the rest will be easier, Rail, once we've done the worst."

Brigham was right. I considered bringing up Saponaria again; we could have all gone back to enlist her help. Walsh could not refuse all of us.

But I was Rail, a slayer of nations. And so, instead of turning back, I recalled another thing I did not want to remember.

Three of the five openings had been cleared away. Trails in the dust pointed toward all of them. "The middle one," I said, guided by my memory.

We went through the opening and down the rough

stairs beyond. I wished with each step that I'd destroyed more of this place. It seemed so obvious to me that this location should have been avoided, left alone. Instead, the Men had built a city around it.

First, we saw changes made by the morgue: new tombs dug out, bodies slowly drying. In the yellow torchlight, the cowboys eyed the items left behind, the weapons, jewelry, and gems. The crypts became more ancient as we went, the dust thicker. Soon, only Hagisy's footsteps remained.

We followed them deep within the cold rock. I had to remember more things I didn't want to: directions, paths toward death. We twisted and turned, but always moved downward — if not on a slight slope, then on flights of stairs. The air grew colder, darker. Poorly cut stone — crudely chiseled in places, sloppy brick and mortar in others — tightened around us.

Hagisy's footsteps were barely visible, even under the glow from Brigham's eyes. They led to what looked like a wall. Carved at eye level were rock faces that seemed to scream at a sky they could not see.

Brigham asked, "Do you remember?"

I put my hands on the secret door. "We need blood. The blood of a Man."

The cowboys looked at each other, hesitating, but Brigham opened his medicine bag. Fumbling through it, he held up a vial of dark red liquid under the torchlight.

One face, its mouth wide, almost smiled. "Pour it here," I said, "down this one's throat."

Brigham obeyed. The blood made a gurgling sound as it went. The cowboys lifted their torches, touched their charms and weapons.

"Silver bullets?" one whispered.

I shrugged. "Sure. Why not."

Rocks began to grind against each other. Thin lines

appeared in the wall around the face, opening wider and wider. When they stopped, the mouth was large enough for us to follow the blood down.

"These steps," I said, "will double back on themselves, tight turns like a horse's shoe. Three times. Past them, we will find the temple where it worshiped itself."

"It?" asked one of the cowboys.

"The emperor I destroyed. Ichshaw the Only."

"History," Brigham said. "Almost two hundred seasons ago." An attempt to calm them. He didn't want them fleeing.

We all started down the twisting steps.

"Look," a cowboy said, when we reached the bottom. The faintest orange glow appeared on the wall ahead of us. Below it, we could see a body in the dust.

"Hide your light," Brigham said. He rubbed his eyes, and the light streaming from them disappeared. He moved closer, crouched over the body. "This is Hagisy," he said. The remains were battered, limbs broken. On the wall above them was a bloody smear. Hagisy must have been thrown against it.

One of the cowboys made a sign against bad omens. It was the same gesture Fairbank used to make. Apparently his faith had continued without him. Brigham set his hands on the heads of two other cowboys, whispered to them.

Finally, Brigham motioned me toward him. "Lead us in," he said. When he spoke, I forced myself to remember how successful violence had made me. I had to do it, but I no longer liked it.

"Brigham, stay right behind me," I said. "The rest of

you, behind him. Three on my right and three on my left. Let me go just steps before you. Pistols ready."

The doctor began whispering to himself, nodding to me.

We stepped around the corner.

All the light in the room came from two massive shining statues, twice my height, the color of hot brass. Each held the shaft of a long hammer. They reminded me of something, someone. Myself.

The remains I had smeared all over the room were gone. Not even dried-blood dust remained on that floor.

Standing between the two statues, covered in the warmth of their glow, was a Man-child. Black hair, a floor-length sickly-green robe. A baby Ichshaw. It held what looked like a long thin branch, smooth and supple like a switch, cut from a weeping willow in some garden.

We stepped closer. It smiled, and I could see blood behind its teeth, blood wanting to leak out. It had to lick its lips to keep red drool off its pale chin.

"Is she coming?" Its voice. I'd forgotten its voice. It sounded like the stretching of a hangman's rope.

"Saponaria? No," I said.

"How could she not come, Rail?" it said. "I made the path easy. I picked the bait well. A fool with her true name."

Brigham twitched in surprise.

"Your fool *is* a fool, Ichshaw," I agreed. "But Saponaria is wise. She sent me instead."

"You call that wisdom? You call these—" it gestured toward the cowboys, the doctor. "—allies?"

"I do."

It stared at me now — *really* looked — through the eyes of the false child. "She'll come looking when you are gone."

"How did you find her name, Ichshaw?"

"I gave it to her. I held her at her birth and knew her

name. Then I robbed her of her mother. That's just the first lesson I taught her."

"You lie."

"Yes, dear Rail, but not this time. She does not know." Its smile widened. "Your Corax silenced me last time. Don't you recall? Just before his death." It paused, licked its lips again. "How glorious that would have been, had he been just a little slower. But now, with her, I will give this world the fate it deserves."

The statues moved. They were like me.

I could have fled, could have run into the cool darkness of the dungeon, but I was Rail. I brought evil to an end.

The closest statue held its weapon high and swung — a swing meant to sweep me from my feet — but I leaned into the blow, shattering its hammer. I was greater than hammers. It stared at the broken shaft. Bullets pinged off the other statue.

"The gem on its face," Brigham yelled at the cowboys, over the roar of gunfire and the echoes of echoes. They aimed where he'd directed, trying to blind the statue. Each successive shot transformed the gem into a cloud of cracks. The statue thrashed wildly, without coordination. I beat the knee of the other with my hammers, my fists, splintering the hot metal until it tottered and fell, clawing at me.

Ichshaw walked calmly toward one of the cowboys, who methodically fired silver bullets that seemed to disappear into its flesh. The cowboy couldn't have missed at that range, couldn't have missed with the gun's muzzle against its forehead. Ichshaw's switch cut the cowboy's body cleanly in half, parting him effortlessly from the crown of his head to between his legs.

I beat at the neck of the statue before me, pounding out chunks until the head spun away from the body. Brigham lifted one arm high. His whisper became a shout and light sprayed from his mouth, tearing lumps from the chest of the statue closest to him. Two cowboys screamed, held in the statue's tight fists, their flesh boiling off their bones. Brigham made a chopping motion with one hand, and one of the statue's arms fell from its body.

I took the head of the statue closest to me and threw it at Ichshaw. My aim was true, but the head swerved around it, bursting against the wall instead.

What had I done wrong? How was it back?

Brigham seemed to hold his breath, then shouted again. The statue's torso crumbled. Its legs remained, mere stone, but the cowboys were gone. Dead — or, I hoped, fled to safety.

The child smiled broadly, bloody drool running from each corner of its mouth. A young, thin face. Not yet mature. Not yet as powerful as it had been last time.

I grabbed the thigh of the statue closest, heaved it at Ichshaw, and charged in after it, as fast as I could. The thigh tumbled up and over the boy, but I surprised Ichshaw, close as I was behind it. Even surprised, my old nemesis ducked my fists, quicker than I was. I lunged and grabbed it in a hug, leaving the arm with its switch free.

Brigham floated with his medicine bag open before him. He threw powders from it. The cloud of powder thickened the air around Ichshaw, slowed its movements.

It lashed my shoulders, back, arms, and head with the switch, and I squeezed. Where the switch touched me, I cracked.

Last time, we had surprised it. Corax had said his words. Shisui had spidered up behind it and pulled her long rifle, new green runes on its barrel, from her infinite pouch. Fairbank had used the dire lich's pistols with bullets he and Saponaria had prepared for months. She and Ichshaw had battled in earnest, a hurricane of lightning. I'd killed its entire debauched court. It took all of us last time. Brigham was more helpful than I'd thought, but I doubted we were enough, though this Ichshaw was a babe. The switch was killing me.

But I would not go easily.

I willed myself to stay together and squeezed tighter; its child head spun in my grip. It spat leagues of blood over me and transformed in my arms, becoming a wizened foul old man, the thin man who had created me, an endless snake.

Time slowed — stopped almost — under the cloud of Brigham's powder. I crushed Ichshaw to me, and the switch drifted slower and slower.

I don't know how long I squeezed. Eventually, I was alone, the broken body of a child in my hands. Ichshaw was gone to wherever such beings go, for however long. When I relaxed, it slid to the ground.

I was broken, afraid to move, afraid to walk. Bits of me fell away, sometimes chunks, with the slightest motion. I was shattered. My understanding cracked. I saw ragged black rips in the world. Smells came one after another: blood, the ocean, my mesa, burnt bodies.

Brigham was a ragdoll, slumped on the floor. The streaks of blood from his nose and ears had long dried. He was thinner, a man who had gone without food and water for too long.

"Wait," he called to me. His voice was a croak. "Powder in my bag."

"Salt?"

"Ground bone."

With each step toward his bag, I heard slivers of myself ping as they hit the floor. Slowly, I circled Ichshaw the Only's truly dead body, leaving a trail of pale powder. It had still been young, still a weaker version of itself. If it hadn't been, we would have failed.

Brigham chanted as I circled. He looked so broken, and his voice was a mere croak from a too-dry throat. As I finished the ring and he finished the chant, his eyes rolled back into his head, and his body went rigid. Fresh blood jetted from his face.

He would die if I did nothing. And Saponaria — I could free her from Walsh. She would let me kill him once she knew about Ichshaw. I thought I had the strength for that. I had to, before Walsh understood what her name could do. So I left Brigham in the fading light, too weak to carry him. But I would send help.

Sometimes one piece, sometimes a landslide of me, dropped away as I stumbled upward. I feared that I would crumble completely, to a pile of dust. Trapped where my friends had died. I walked the forever steps out of the crypts, the cracks in the world growing, smelling dragon and ogre where there were none, hearing just every third of my steps. The scream of the matron of the morgue when she saw me was broken by short silences.

I was afraid to stop. I made myself walk and walk. Outside the morgue, Saponaria wept at the sight of me. She was there, ready to go into the crypts to rescue me. Where she touched me, there was pain. Walsh paced next to her, looked from the cowboys he'd brought with him to me, from me to Saponaria.

"He got the name from Ichshaw — not directly, but through a possessed servant expanding the morgue," I began. "Ichshaw had it from its own memory. Its memory of your birth. The death of your mother." I heard my own voice, then didn't, then did again. I told her the whole story, unadorned. I told her of its thin, young face.

"You — you slew it." Walsh had to repeat himself until I

understood; I could barely glimpse his face through the cracks in the world.

"Perhaps. Brigham keeps it trapped. He needs healing."

"Well." Walsh stood up straight. "I still have the name. You will obey me."

Saponaria smiled and laughed. Her body turned the color of a noonday sun.

I tried to scream, but the world was so garbled, and she would not hear me. So instead I turned and stumbled, tried to sprint, but the blast tossed me into the disintegrating sky. Waves of annihilation burst from her, buried me and the city under a mountain of poisonous ruin. The saloon, the marketplace, the smiths, the churches, the hospital, the dwellings of all shapes and sizes, the people who lived in them — all became burnt trash.

Saponaria told me later that she'd crowned Walsh, a charred skeleton, King of the Ill Land. But I was completely shattered, and I thanked Fairbank's god that I did not have to see any more of her anger.

The very day she ruined the town, Saponaria began looking for bits of me, sorting among the endless scraps of stone. It took a season. New arrivals and a few survivors still look today. She tells them that I saved them all from an even greater destruction, that Walsh had died defending them, and that his last words were that I should be rebuilt.

Brigham leads the reconstruction of the city. The people love him. When he shows his face, they cheer. He knows the truth about Walsh, about me, and about Saponaria. That truth keeps him humble, and perhaps afraid. He negotiates with Saponaria on behalf of the remaining citizens; he says, half-jokingly, that she should move away.

She could not find a craftsman able to make me again. So, she became one. We talk as she rebuilds me, two old beings trying not to love the past too much. Saponaria holds my hand now.

I can feel her warmth as she recreates me.

Learn more about this author at:
https://stephendgibson.com/.

# DEVOUR

## ROMAN DURKAN

*November 22, 1987. Chicago*

SOME PEOPLE SAY winter in Chicago feels like trying to take a nap in an ice cream freezer. However you toss and turn, your nuts are getting frozen off.

Can't say they're wrong. Out here in North Lawndale, as the sun goes down, temps drop even lower, and the cheap-ass bicycle beneath me feels like it's about to shoot off on an ice rink like Scott Hamilton. Between the Pink Line trains rumbling overhead, the crackheads on corners, and the empty homes vacated by people left broke after Black Monday ... Well, there's a reason I'm going as fast as I can to one particular house, and it's not just to avoid Mom bitching about me taking the wrong turns.

Yeah. Dad hasn't been back in a while. Mom's always jabbering on the phone, probably after taking some pill or another. I'm dreaming of the day I can make it into some kind of college or work placement — any damn thing to get myself out of here. But until then, there's one guy I can feel at home with. He used to be friends with my brother

Harris, and after that brother also vanished, he ... well, he kinda took over the role.

I come to a halt in front of a snowy porch, making sure to fasten the bike to the gate. Lights are on down below, so I give the door my trademark knock, hoping he hasn't got headphones on while listening to Napalm Death on full blast.

The door opens a few moments later — and would you look at that, it's James Arkwright, still munching on a Tootsie Pop. With a nod, he lets me in, not bothering to swallow. Mom might shout at me for coming over here too. Maybe it's because he's black. Maybe because he reminds her too much of my brother. Or maybe he's too much into 'that computer magic,' as she would say. Who knows.

"Zane, what brings you over?" James says, cleaning candy flecks out of his beard while leading me downstairs — right into the only place I can call a slice of heaven out in Lawndale.

"I'll tell you in a sec. You got any Oreos left?" Stepping off the last creaking step, I bathe in the green glimmers of several computer monitors. His latest setup is an IBM AT, which, knowing Arkwright, is already boosted with a few extra kilobytes of RAM. His older Commodore still gets used for his fun times with war dialing, with the two blue boxes interlinked in ways I can't even understand. Probably got those new Hayes modems pushing 10,000 bits a second. Still, compared to my old VIC, it's like walking into the Starship Enterprise.

Other than his computer equipment, there's not much down here but dust and fans — and that's the way Arkwright likes it. I think he probably always has one phone line connected to his phreaking pals over the BBS we share — if so, I don't want to know how he pays the bills. Still, living out here with all this stuff is proof enough that

Arkwright's got the balls to do what he likes. Another reason I look up to him, I guess.

"No Oreos, buddy, but might have some Reese's Pieces down there." He absently gestures to a drawer while sitting back down in front of his Commodore screen. "Now, what was so important you couldn't just send me a message like an ordinary humanoid entity, hmm?"

"It's ..." I pause, trying to figure out how the hell to word this. Arkwright's also got a stake in what I'm about to talk about: my brother. They knew each other in college, back when I was still a little kid.

Nuts to it — no point overthinking what to say.

"My brother. Sent me an e-mail the other night. First time in a while. Something about WGN-TV, tonight, at 9:15. Sounds like one of the pranks he used to pull. No idea what it has to do with TV, though ..."

Arkwright stares at me before giving me that same throaty laugh he makes whenever I start talking about my theories that Middle-Earth is connected to Eternia.

"Shit. He's really ... Dear god ... Never thought he'd actually ..."

"Actually what?"

"I'm telling you, man ... It's like I've always said. I can't prove it ... but, buddy, he got scooped up by big shots out of college. DARPA, I'm pretty sure of it. But what they'd be letting him do there ... Well, might be important."

"What do you mean?"

"Look around you." Arkwright grins. "President's on the coals after that Iran-Contra thing. Country's in recession. Might be one of those psychological things, get people distracted ..."

"Nah, I don't think ..."

"You're still young, Zane. Seventeen ain't nothing. I tell

you, for him, it was the Man or the Reds. I'm sure he got offers from both, but Uncle Sam pays better, of course."

"Did you get offers from them?"

"Back then, government wouldn't want a black man working their Pentagon computers. Probably still don't. I remember, back on campus, some people said there was some guy named Ivan Totalynotaruski trying to get their number. I know I got one weirdo offering me 'confidential freelance work' back in like '81. But hey, could've been—"

"Wait." I try to cut to the chase. "You knew my brother. I need you to be real, what are we really talking here? I mean, he never seemed to take things seriously."

"He didn't. Doesn't mean he didn't have big ideas. He was always interested in expanding logic controllers into macro systems, boosting that kind of predictive power to something crazy ... A lot of this, hardware couldn't even keep up with until recently, but with those Cray XMPs now getting out ..."

"Hold on — what's the simple version?"

"Prediction. Simulation. You could, ah, say he was into his games. Thought he could take things up another step. Predict the future, the stock market, all that. That sort of thinking is why I reckon he got picked up by our friendly alphabet agencies."

"Games, huh?"

"Yeah. Real games, too, like Ultima, Enchanter — not that Super Mario crap the kids are into now. The kind where you have people, characters. He was pondering how you could make them really think."

"Then he wouldn't be too happy about being stuck in some government gig, right?"

"Well, you want my guess? I bet he's doing something to test his little theories tonight, and I suppose we oughta be happy we get advance tickets for the show."

"Maybe ... but maybe he was just screwing around with me. What's the time now?"

I take a glance to the clock. 9:10 PM — took longer getting here than I thought.

"Looks like we'll be finding out soon." Arkwright smiles. "I guess, if he's got a blank enough check, it really could be another little joke ... as if the Iran thing wasn't joke enough."

I follow Arkwright as he gets up out of his sagging chair and leads me to the living room above — well, what he calls his living room anyway. The TV's nestled between an overflowing trunk containing his VHS collection, and a cabinet containing a rack of old posters — showing everything from arcade games to some Japanese stuff I don't recognize.

Turning the dial on the TV, Arkwright immediately occupies the only couch, indicating smugly the old stool I usually have to be happy with.

"So ... if it's a joke," I say, as I look to the screen — looks like it's WGN News, with the sports anchor on. "I mean, do you know what he might do?"

"Mmm ... Well, I remember he was into some weird things, like that Tron movie."

"People actually saw that?"

"Well, apparently he did, at any rate. I think he also really enjoyed Terminator — and probably that Max Headroom show."

"Yeah, I've watched that one. Sounds like something he'd like. Maybe he'll put on his own special episode here, or something." I chuckle.

I look to the clock as we chatter. 9:14 PM.

"What if nothing happens?" I wonder aloud.

"Then the joke's on us." Arkwright shrugs. "Usually is with fuckin' dorks like you and me."

I laugh — then something starts to change on the TV screen.

The sports anchor is replaced with static, which starts to coalesce and shift into ... something. Whatever it is, it sure as hell isn't Max Headroom.

At first, it looks like a test pattern — but then it starts becoming far more complex, like some geometric fractal pattern. Brilliant red patterns, lines and shapes, start to appear, changing and shifting — so sharp they appear to be coming right out of the damn TV.

My eyes can't blink, they can't turn away — it's like staring at some trip that's manifesting itself tangibly, right there. My mind tries to find meaning in it, like there's some real shape, some sentience — but nothing comes up besides an empty void.

A noise, like a thousand electronic peals of thunder, rumbles out from the speakers before the screen goes black — and then the light above us goes out.

"Shit!" Arkwright sits up, stumbling up off the couch. "No, you gotta be — He couldn't—"

I don't react for a good few moments. Maybe it's my brain still trying to pull away from whatever the hell I just saw on the TV. Maybe I'm also trying to process why my own brother would do such a thing, why he wouldn't give us more warning, why, why, why, those same questions, just going around in circles —

The light flickers back on, just barely. Figures Arkwright would have his own emergency generator. He's already scrambling back downstairs as I take a glance out the window — the entirety of Lawndale, maybe all of Chicago, seems to have gone dark.

"James?" I finally utter, pulling myself after him. "What the fuck just happened?"

"That ..." I hear his voice come in from downstairs, as

well as the frantic plastic clicking of his fingers on a keyboard. "That was your brother all right."

"How do you know for sure?"

He doesn't answer. Scrambling downstairs after him, I find him hunched over his IBM. The bulb above us has apparently gone, leaving nothing but the sickly green light of the on-screen text flickering across the room. The other monitors seem to be showing much of the same: what I assume to be lines of code scrolling downward. Arkwright's printer fires up as he starts shoving dot matrix paper into it.

"What's that?" I point to the monitors, as he seems so oddly reticent about answering my previous question.

"It's flooding the modem lines — all of it, choked," he breathes. "I think it's whatever was embedded in that signal, being sent out here at the same time ..."

Pages and pages of indecipherable strings of characters continue to churn out from the printer. The displays start flickering and glitching — the power must be going in and out again.

A flicker at the other end of the room catches my eye, and I look closer at the small window there. There seems to be some kind of glow coming in from outside, but I'm sure it's not from the streetlights. Strange — but what hasn't been strange tonight? I decide to ignore it for now, and I turn back to Arkwright.

"James. C'mon, man," I say again. "How do we know for sure it's my brother?"

Arkwright spins around, clutching printouts to his chest.

"You know when I said I hadn't heard from him in a while either? I ... I wasn't being entirely truthful."

My mind stumbles over the new information. What? Needing space to think, I move closer to the window. Out of the corner of my eye, I can see something — I can only process it as something wrong with the sky outside — past the roofs across the street.

It's like somehow, the world just got split open. All I can glean are razor-straight crimson gashes slicing in a shifting pattern through the night above us, too solid-looking to be clouds or vapor —

"What the hell?" I start to turn back to Arkwright, still not entirely sure I saw what I just did. I can feel my pulse firing up as the sheer enormity hits me: both what just I've seen and what he just said.

I latch onto the saner question before me. "What do you mean 'not entirely truthful'?"

"I mean ..." Arkwright looks straight at my face. His eyes are wide, and his expression looks like he's just looked into the mouth of hell itself. "I mean, he's been sending messages to me regularly for years."

"And why didn't you tell me?"

"Because ..." he yanks open another shelf, pulling out more printouts — these ones are email messages, logs and logs of them. "Because, it was like he was going insane."

Before I can ask more, he's moving upstairs again, heading for the door.

"We gotta move. If he hijacked the transmission, only way to go is to WGN's antenna at the Sears Tower."

"How do you know that?"

"Some of my phreaking buddies had ideas about pirate signals, interrupting football games, all those things. I need you to move — if Harris is anywhere, he has to be there."

He bursts outside. I can see the crimson shit — it defies any other description — in the sky more clearly now. It's not airplane trails, it's not flares, it's not any of that. It looks like pure radiance, manifesting out of nowhere, carved into the night.

"The hell ... Oh god, what is that?" I splutter out the words as I stumble down the snowy porch. So much stuff to take in, my thoughts can barely keep up. "My brother — Arkwright, you gotta tell me everything. Like, right now—"

"I'll tell you what I can." Arkwright is already yanking open the door to his old Ford. "I need you to drive. Still gotta look through all of this—"

"I've barely got my learner's permit!"

"Don't fuckin' care. Just get in there, step on it!"

Scrambling onto the worn leathery seats, I shove his key into the ignition, trying not to breathe too hard. As the engine starts up, I flick on the radio, hoping against hope that something out there will give me a clue as to what the hell's going on.

Instead, I get a noise, like raging static laid over a thousand insane screams of agony.

"You said something about my brother." I try and keep my eyes on the road as I gun it down the street. Since we're going to the Sears Tower, I aim for the freeway, the quickest way to the Loop section of downtown. "Something about him going insane. You should've told me, man. Mom and I had no idea what he was doing, and then he comes out of nowhere like this."

"I ... I was trying to do the best thing for your family." Arkwright's voice sounds shattered, as he tries to sort through his printouts. "If you guys knew everything, saw everything I did ... Your mother, man, she could've fallen apart. I didn't want to do that to you."

"Ignorance is bliss, huh?"

"Yeah. Sometimes it is." Arkwright looks up, seemingly speaking as much to himself as he takes in the code. "He started out discussing quantum computing theorem, building off what Benioff was talking about. This was a few years ago. Then, he starts going on about Heisenberg's principle being only the tip of the iceberg. That he had 'seen through the mirror'. That we were all reflections of data, that whether we observed or were being observed meant that nothing was ..."

"Nothing was what?"

"I don't have a fuckin' clue, man, he was losing me bad ... I thought — hoped — most of it was bullshit, stuff he might've been peddling to DARPA for funding. But now ... Maybe some of this will help me. I think I can see a pattern here ..."

We approach the freeway — most of the streets and roads are still dark but for the lights in the sky. Power seems to be out in most places. Worst of all, there doesn't seem to be anyone else driving around. Can't even see folk on the sidewalks. My brain doesn't have time to make sense of it.

I see a whole lot more as we drive up onto the freeway entrance. To the north, the whole Inglewood area appears to have distorted itself, like smears on charcoal. Streets, whole blocks ... All becoming amorphous, blurred expanses of dark geometry, like the patterns on a glitching computer screen. At first, I think it's just my eyes trying to adjust — but no, I can see sheer void mixed with gradually shifting angular masses of grey and pale light, in place of suburban sprawl.

And on the freeway ahead, I can see vehicles scattered and abandoned, some of them slammed into the concrete sides — some of them apparently sunk into that same state of half-reality. I can't see any people. I can't even see any proof they might've occupied these vehicles.

"Nexus point ..." Arkwright's muttering feverishly, eyes fixed on his printout. "Encoded onto ..."

"What's that?" I murmur.

"It's as I thought. There's an anchor to this — potentially even a person ..."

I mumble something half-coherent. I don't want to think about the implications. About what might be at the eye of the storm. But between us still being here, unaffected, between the timing ... There's no escaping the intelligence behind it, the machination behind the insanity.

A glance in the mirror, and all I can see behind us on the freeway is absolute blackness.

As we drive on, trying not to veer too sharply past the abandoned cars, I can see the downtown skyline ahead. Blacked-out skyscrapers are silhouetted in red by shimmering veins of — of energy, I can only guess — suspended far as I can see over the lake. I can see them more clearly now: perfectly ordered patterns, some of them cruciform-like, others taking on the form of a fractal mass of squares and neon-ruby, preternatural geometrics. There's nothing fathomable, nothing human to grasp in comprehending it.

I spend so much time trying to process it all, trying to find rhyme or reason, that I nearly slam us into a half-dissipated truck. Arkwright yells, scattering his papers — but, feeling the sweat on my hands, the dryness in my eyes, I try to keep going.

My mom? My dad? Harris? No, I can't even begin to consider what's happened to them in all this. Maybe it's just a bad dream. All I can hope is that I'm still in Arkwright's house, and the real joke was getting some fucking acid slipped into a drink ...

Tires screech as I try to brake for the eventual turnoff. I feel my body jolt, adrenaline surge again — and denial stops working. It's real. I can't comprehend how, but it's all real.

"Jesus ..." I say. "I mean, are you seeing all this too? What the fuck did he — Did my brother do all this?"

Arkwright doesn't move his eyes from his papers for a good few moments. Then he meets my gaze in the car mirror.

"Yeah. I think he did."

"All that stuff ... Heisenberg, Benioff ... What was he really trying to get at? What did he mean?"

"My best guess? Before, I thought he was going crazy, maybe from being locked away inside some fed lab for too long, thinking he had discovered something in his coding. Some shit to do with data, observation of reality — or realities. But my best guess now? I think he was right, somehow."

We're finally approaching downtown, crossing the bridges to the Loop. I turn onto South Wacker Drive — slowing down now; there's way more cars dotted ahead. On the nearby Chicago River, the red streaks from the sky-blighting patterns seem to remain straight and unmoving even reflected on the water. From here, it looks like some hellish circuit board, bloody and alive. I can't tell if I'm looking at silicon wrought into life, or the reflection of a mind that's trying so very hard not to crack —

"Mother of — !"

I slam the breaks. Finally, we can see people ahead. Cops, local office workers, stumbling around — their faces meet mine through the windscreen.

At least, they look like faces at first glance. Their skin, their skulls, their whole bodies have become partial masses of rippling flat squares and triangles, with colors blurring into shadow and then into pure black. Unmarred eyes stare out in agony — one, then two, throw themselves into the nearby canal as I watch. There's no splash, there's no ripple; they just vanish into the red-lit waters, as if plunging straight into nothingness.

Neither one of us say anything. I try to move past them,

to get to the Sears Tower ahead. I can hear frantic arms strike against the glass, while others barely seem to notice us.

I stop the car once the street gets too blocked ahead. We scramble out, stumbling onto the sidewalk, hearing a faint thrumming coming from right above. I wonder for a second if those people were staring at the patterns for too long, if that somehow changed them — but then I start wondering how the fuck this is even possible, how the hell my brother did all this. If it's even him.

The fact that he might be responsible, that this is what he was doing during all those years away, while I was going to school and screwing around with computer games … Despite everything, that's what fucking churns my stomach the most.

We turn the corner to the front of the Sears Tower. Around us, other massive downtown buildings seem to be distorting into half-rendered madness, scintillating between blackness and solidity. Rooftops are blurring, shifting into unreal haze, not reacting to the light around them. Towards the lake, I can only see more of the sheer blackness I saw behind us on the freeway.

By the entrance, there seem to be several men, some of them with visible gun holsters — government agents, maybe — lying down unmoving, arms and bodies fading into jagged masses of random geometry. Faces just gone, replaced by more unreflecting black and shadow.

"I'm seeing something …" Arkwright's still carrying his printouts, eyes fixed down, as he catches up. "Jesus, I'm seeing something all right."

"Who cares?" I splutter, thinking only of what's ahead, as I finally push my way into the lobby. Normally, it'd look tall and opulent, as it's meant to — but now, lit with red and black, it looks like a tomb pulled out of Dante's fever dreams.

I can see stacks of monitors up near the desks. I have no idea if they were meant to be there, but even as they flicker with static, I slowly approach them.

"Been a long time, hasn't it, kiddo? How's it hanging?"

A familiar voice, yet somehow tuned different, emanates from a source I can't see. On the monitors, I watch a face appear, each display showing a slightly varying angle. Harrison Hagen, my brother, stares down at me in a dozen different ways.

"Hey, Harris." I step forward. "Please ... just please, for the love of God, tell me you didn't do this. The whole city's gone to hell. I can't even tell what's happening ..."

"Heh. I did it, alright." He grins. I can't see all of his features on the crackling monitors — but I can see that same toothy shit-eating smile he made when he put that porno mag under dad's seat one Thanksgiving. "I told my bosses this'd be the ultimate demonstration of digital psy-ops. Stupid bastards were too busy writing me checks to get into the details. Pulled one fine joke on them. Hell, it's the best damn joke ever, ain't it?"

I run past the screens, aiming for the elevators. I can see more monitors, seemingly set up on walls or leaning against pillars at random. He's on all of them, looking down from so many subtly different angles.

"James?" his voice sounds louder, more distorted. "You came too? Perfect. Oh, I can see you're working it all out, just like I knew you would. If you haven't already, of course."

"You ... you weren't kidding ..." Arkwright's voice is barely a whisper.

"I know." He carries on, even as I hammer the elevator button to call it down. It still seems to be working, thank

God. "I looked into the mirror. I decided to break the mirror."

"Harris, man, you're not making sense," I wheeze, looking up. I take a look at the elevator dial above, tapping my foot with each agonizing second it takes to descend.

"It's simple, Zane, if you know how to look at it. I saw the future. I saw where the digital road will take us. My work, scrying into the realms our processing power can barely touch — they wanted to use it against communists, or something myopic like that. I wanted to see what becomes of us all. Data, Zane, electronic bits. That's our fate, to have genetics and evolution give way to the pulsing of the circuit."

"You've been watching too much weird shit. What the hell does that mean?"

The elevator doors open, and I step in. I can still hear him talk as we start to ascend.

"It means exactly what I said, no matter how you look at it. Everything we program, everything we connect ... It feeds what's across the mirror, realms of pure living quantum information, always changing and growing, even if we could never observe each other."

"Each other? Those things, above, you mean?"

"That, Zane, is what existence truly looks like."

The elevator's at the middle floors now. I try to think back to those days when I still knew Harris, all those distant times that brought us to this point. All the games he was obsessed with, giving way to simulations, then to this. All I can grasp is he's saying that our own stupid little world, all the chaos and insanity ... that maybe it was no more real than those old games. Some reflection of things that all of our rotting little basic minds could never truly see or grasp.

I take a deep breath. Mind's racing too fast. Need to focus.

"So ... you're saying, what, we were never real? We're in a program? Some game, like the ones on our old Commodore? That's what you're saying?"

We're nearing the upper floors. I can feel cold, biting sweat trickling down my back, as I try to break through the lunacy seemingly bearing at me from every angle. Gotta keep him talking, gotta work something out ...

"Heh. Maybe. Best part ... it doesn't matter, at the end of it all. Every person is destined to become just a string in a database, a number, things no more real than all those adventures on the screen we both enjoyed. That's the funniest part of all, Zane. Our destiny was, in essence, convergence with what's beyond. But I found a way to force ... let's call it a glitch, if you want."

"Your quantum voodoo? Forcing those cracks?"

"Yeah, I guess. I'll say it again, the best joke I ever pulled!"

I look back to Arkwright — his chest heaves as he fixes on the numbers. He knows something. He can see some sort of answer in there. I can only think — I can only fear.

"It can't be." I look up. "I know you. I loved — love you, man. That's not code. This isn't some program you can just hack ..."

Harris laughs and it sounds like those static roars from before. I don't even know what's happened to him. How real this is. Perhaps, even, there was never any such thing as 'real' after all, nothing but electromagnetic absurdity across all realms — just raw, proliferating, mindless data ...

The elevator finally opens. We burst out to the bottom of the great antenna on the tower's peak — up here, amid freezing wind, everything is bathed in lambent red. The sky itself is nothing but blackness and a thousand neon lines like scalpel cuts. Right there, standing before his so-called joke, is my brother, facing away. The surface beside him, at the base of the antenna, appears only as a plane of blackness. Like something I could fall into, a gash of nothingness that my eyes, my mind, can't help but latch onto.

"Take a look." I can hear his voice, tremoring, as he turns to face us — his eyes, staring at me like burnt-out pits, are nothing but that same empty darkness. "Take a look at everything, kiddo. I made sure you'd have the best view of all."

I look back to Arkwright, who stares straight ahead, hands shaking.

"Oh, you know, don't you, James? Maybe there's a truth after all. Maybe we can see which side of the glass we're on. Maybe we know who's truly a reflection of who ..."

He chuckles. Even more so than before, Harris hardly sounds human. I feel a tear run down my face, as my mind irrevocably stumbles to the conclusion that whoever's standing there isn't my brother anymore — human or not. I look to Arkwright again, and then back to that smear of unreal blackness ahead, wondering just what final truth has revealed itself to him in the numbers. I take a step forward, only to decide that I don't want to know.

There's just one other confirmation I want from him.

"You said there was a nexus?" I murmur to Arkwright, voice hoarse. He nods softly, eyes fixed on the printouts.

Brought on by adrenaline and desperation, a thought occurs to me — only one thought, telling me how I might end this. I don't want to do it. I don't want to take away the flesh and blood I have missed for years. But as I continue to stare forward with a tear forming in one eye, I'm not even sure how important flesh and blood is anymore.

For a second, I think about all those plans and ideas I had, of moving beyond the neighborhood, stepping into a new life — and I'm not even sure how much they matter now. If they ever did.

I run straight towards the figure ahead. Hoping against hope, I push him towards that inky nothing. One way or another, this ends here.

All I can think is — whatever we are, whatever he is: let it devour him.

# JUST RIGHT

## MANNY FRISHBERG

THE NEW GIRL fidgeted in the metal folding chair, trying to find a comfortable position. This seat was too hard, and the cushioned ones in the lobby had been too soft. Just a couple more annoyances, after being imprisoned here in the first place. She chewed absently on the end of her blonde pigtail. Dr. Harris was leading the formal introductions around the room, even though they all knew each other from the ward.

"You can call me Gwen," the psychologist started off with a smile. "We don't stand on formality much in here." She wore a soft white blouse with mother-of-pearl buttons and a gray tweed skirt. Her light gray tights had an understated silvery shimmer, matching both parts of her ensemble. Everyone else wore shapeless khaki jumpsuits.

Gwen turned to the new girl. "Can we call you Goldie?"

"I'd rather you didn't," she said. "My name is *Ursa*-la." Emphasis on the first half.

Gwen consulted the file folder on her lap. "Dr. Josephson's explained to you why we can't call you that," she said in the measured voice that counselors learn in grad school.

Ursala envisioned Gwen's white blouse dyed red from

several open gashes, crimson dots turning dark brown, sprayed across the shiny tights.

"We'll compromise, okay?" the therapist offered. "You can just be Jane Doe, for now." Ursala — "Jane" to them — nodded sullenly.

"Everyone, say hello to Jane," the therapist said. All six obeyed in unison, then Gwen introduced them in turn.

The girl next to Ursala, Rita-Ann, had mousy hair, the color of dirt that's been baking in the sun all summer long. She had the same beady eyes as the rest, with the whites showing all the way around — much different from the beautiful brown eyes of Ursala's true family, which she had always envied. In Ursala's mind, she bludgeoned that head of dirty brown hair with the business end of a Coke bottle until it was slick with blood and bits of grey matter. A smile stretched her thin mouth, an imitation of Dr. Harris's bland expression.

As the girls took their turns introducing themselves, Ursala's eyes followed, mentally slitting a throat, gouging a knitting needle straight through a blue-green eye. If only she could use her claws!

Sitting so close, Ursala could smell the rancid scent of fear on Rita-Ann as she droned on: the slightly cheesy smell of damp skin that so many people gave off in the muggy summers. Ursala stifled a yawn, only half-listening to the girl's prattle.

Underneath the disinfectant smell that pervaded everything in this place, Ursala could make out a musky woolen scent that reminded her of Papa's huge, heavy winter coat. That put her a little more at ease.

"Jane," Gwen said, *the bitch*, "do you think you're ready to share a bit?" It took a few seconds for Ursala to realize that the question had been addressed to her. Gwen took the delay as reluctance, and added, "There's no pressure on you, but, you know, the sooner we can get to know each other, the sooner we'll be able to help. And just talking things out can be quite cathartic."

Ursala shook her head slowly, studying the faces in the dirty linoleum tiles to appear shy and compliant. *What would be cathartic is ripping your throat out with my own teeth,* Ursala thought. *I bet your blood wouldn't be too salty or too bitter.*

What she said was, "I don't know what to say right now, if that's all right."

*Papa and Mama will be so glad to have me home again. They must be so lonely, just the two of them.* She wished she could be out in the woods again, smelling the cool, mossy green odors of the forest and smell of hot loblolly cooling on the kitchen table wafting out through the open window of their cottage. But of course she couldn't say any of that; she had already learned that the less she revealed of her real self, the sooner they'd let her reclaim her real life.

But Gwen seemed determined to wait until her new patient said *something*. The two stared at each other and at the walls over their shoulders for some time. Only the institutional wall clock interrupted the silence, until Gwen finally resorted to small talk.

"Jane, how do you like your new room, now that you've earned your way down to Floor Three?"

"Fine," Ursala said, and stared over the therapist's shoulder some more. On every floor, counting down from Five, more privileges were allowed. They still locked her in the narrow single room at night, but during the day she was allowed to go to the dining hall, and was even trusted with a steel spoon to eat her porridge in the mornings. Of course, the aides made sure to take the spoon back when she finished eating.

Group therapy sessions with Dr. Harris went on like that for the next several weeks: one hour, four times a week. At some point she stopped answering only in monosyllables, and when Gwen coaxed her to talk about the food, Ursala allowed that the salty soup was often too hot when she was first in line, or too cold when she arrived late. And it always left her yearning for the sweet berries she'd picked in the woods, or one of the other delicious treats that the forest had to offer. She especially missed wading into the shallow stream to catch a fish with her bare hands. She had learned how by watching Papa from a tree branch, but she knew better than to mention *that*.

The shrinks, it turned out, were remarkably easy to play. Ursala started out by showing sullen resistance to the name "Jane," then gradually came to accept it over a few sessions. She also let Gwen encourage her to "open up," and, when she sensed that Gwen's expectations had reached the right point, she started talking, bit by bit, to the group.

*Bide your time,* she cautioned herself. *Don't bare your teeth; don't show your claws. Behave and let them think you're one of them. Make your words sweet as honey.* Of course, she didn't say anything about her real family, or that f-ing usurper who had stolen her place in their affection. She held that memory coiled tight inside her, a lifeline to remind her of who she really was, while she played out the role of the recovering patient. Her real self hibernated through the endless days of meds and meals.

Listening to the other girls recounting their petty concerns came easier over time, and the fantasies of doing them in faded, until she only imagined inflicting mayhem on them once every week or two. Gwen, *that stupid cow,* gushed over how much progress "Jane" had made in a few short months. *Short months?* Every week felt like a season.

For their part, the rest of the group adopted "Jane" as one of their own. In the Day Room, she let the other patients teach her to play three-handed Pinochle; at least it broke up the tedium. She liked the Berenstain Bears cartoons, though she had to get another patient to request them for her. She was even becoming friends with Rita-Ann, as well as two girls named Stella and Barbie. She liked Stella because her hair was the same color as Papa's and Mama's.

When Stella confided that she and Barbie had been lovers for more than a year, it horrified Ursala. She had not imagined that they had been locked up in here that long — they'd seemed really normal to her.

At one of her monthly meetings, she told the psychiatrist that her sessions with Gwen were actually doing her some good. Ursala was good at pretending — she'd been pretending to be Goldilocks her whole life. Her plan was to follow the treatment regimen and pretend to show measured improvement so she could get released by spring, when her family would be coming back from their winter vacation.

"My birth parents never really took the time to get to know me," she confessed one day when it came her turn to share at group. "They named me Gertrude, but for as long as I can remember, they called me Goldie. They said it was because I was so precious to them, but I always knew it was just because of my hair." Her pale hair, more similar to the shade of unfinished oak than to the metallic blondes used in books and dye packaging, had now grown long enough for her ringlet curls to reappear.

"If I'd been precious to them, they'd've spent some time trying to get to know me. But Dad was always too busy with his job — and getting drunk with his friends at the racetrack when he wasn't working. And Mama had her housecleaning business to look after, and her volunteer work. She always said volunteering introduced her to the rich ladies that needed someone to come clean up after their nasty broods. She despised them too, but she never, ever revealed it, except to me after she'd taken a couple of bong hits. Even when she did share her secrets, I might as well have been one of the teddy bears she brought home for me — just an object to talk at." Ursala stopped there, startled by what she had almost revealed.

That had been a "genuine breakthrough moment," according to Gwen. Everybody made such a fuss that Ursala was genuinely touched. Nobody had ever shown such kindness to her, not even her real parents. *Especially* not her real parents. After that, Ursala started to talk more about her real feelings in the group.

She also started to care about the other girls' problems for real, listening to them instead of imagining various tortures. Once in a while, she even offered a heartfelt expression of sympathy.

Other things started improving for her, too. The doctors cut back on her meds so she could think more clearly. She was transferred to Two, where the patients had access to the grounds during their afternoon free time.

One day, after Ursala had been in the hospital about a year, Gwen addressed the elephant that had been waiting in the corner of the room from day one.

"Jane — or may I call you Gertrude?" Ursala winced. She had become used to being Jane, to the point where sometimes she even thought of herself that way. But she nodded anyway.

The therapist reached over to her desk for a manila file folder. "Take your time," she said while she perused the file. "But I think it's time you tell us why you're here, if you're ready to. Tell us about what happened in the house."

Ursala knew Gwen was already holding all the details of what had happened that day in the woods — all the details that had made it into the police report, that is, not the truth of what she'd done and why. For the first time, she felt the urge to tell the *real* story outweighing her cautious, measured approach to convincing everyone that she deserved to be trusted. She started her story from the middle, the day Gwen had asked about — the day every-thing had changed.

"I ... I don't remember everything all that clearly," Ursala said, almost surprised to hear herself speak. She avoided eye contact with Gwen.

"I had been there before; I'd been visiting for years. I spent so much time watching them from that tree that the house in the woods almost seemed like my second home — my real home, the one I'd been kidnapped from when I was very, very little. I was always careful to make sure that no one was there when I went inside — but even empty, it had a feeling of warmth. I had a sense of belonging that I never felt anywhere else. So, I knew that was where I had to belong.

"I used to imagine Mama and Papa coming home to give me a big bear hug. I thought she'd smell like jasmine and pine, and Papa would probably smell like musk and leather and shaving lotion. That's how I always imagined a good dad would smell. My pretend father just reeked of bourbon and cigar smoke most of the time.

"Papa's chairs in the kitchen and the living room were

way too big. The cushions were stiff, and my knees caught on them so my feet stuck straight out. Mama's had fluffy down pillows, and I was afraid that if I sat on them, I would leave a dent that I couldn't fluff out again. But there were also the littlest chairs that were just my size, like they were made for me — 'cause, of course, they had been. The kid had taken them from me, along with everything else that should have been mine.

"It took a long time for me to rustle up the courage to go upstairs to the bedrooms. Papa and Mama slept on twin beds. Can you believe it, in this day and age? But he preferred a firm mattress and she a much softer one, so I guess that explains it.

"One day, I went into my room. The kid had decorated it with sticks and pieces of deer bones that he'd picked up on their walks. I'd hated him from the first time I'd laid eyes on him, hiding myself in the branches of the big cedar tree in the back yard. After all, he had taken my real family away from me. But I hated him more than ever once I got a look at what he'd done with my room."

Ursala hesitated, not certain, all of a sudden, that it would be right to finish the story after all. She cared what Rita-Ann and the others thought of her, and the therapist had been kinder to her than either of her families. If she went on, would they begin to look at her with the disgust and horror she'd seen in Mama and Papa's eyes that night?

But Dr. Harris looked at Ursala with compassion, making her feel like this was the only truly safe place in the world, like she belonged in it and to it, and that everything would be just right if she didn't hold back.

"I hadn't meant to stay there that time. I was going to leave before they got home from their walk, the way I always had before — to climb out the window and watch from the safety of the tree, or run all the way back to town.

But I was so tired of hiding, and it was getting late. I'd been sick earlier in the week, so I just lied down to close my eyes for a few minutes before I left.

"I never touched Mama or Papa's beds — that's a total lie. I don't know why they lied about me. Mama and Papa were my real parents and they should have loved me, just like I loved them. Once that kid was out of the way, I felt certain they'd recognize me as their real daughter and welcome me home at last. But they didn't."

Now that she'd committed herself to finishing, Ursala talked faster, with barely a pause for breath. The office smelled of furniture polish, just like the house in the woods always had. It encouraged Ursala to hold nothing back.

"When I woke up, I could see through the window that it had gotten dark. Downstairs, I heard Papa shouting. I couldn't make out the words, but it scared me — my pretend father yelled like that; I'd never heard Papa or Mama raise their voices before.

"I could tell they were in the living room, and I tried to remember if I'd left anything different this time. I was sure I hadn't, but hearing their angry voices scared me so much that I couldn't be sure. I hid myself under the little bastard's bed. When they all tromped into his room (*my* room, really), I had to hold my breath so I wouldn't make even a tiny noise. I was so frightened.

"Finally, they went back downstairs again, and everything calmed down. Mama made dinner — I could smell the scent of warm fish coming up through the floorboards, and I was so very hungry, but still I didn't dare move. The longer I lied there in the dark, hearing the comforting sounds of family conversation and knowing that I should be a part of it, the angrier I got at the kid. He'd stolen this perfect life from me.

"I didn't plan any of this, really." Ursala looked at Gwen

for reassurance and understanding, and the therapist responded with a small nod of acceptance. "Carefully, so as not to make any noise, I took out the hunting knife I always carried when I went into the forest — to protect myself, just in case.

"I think I must have fallen asleep again, because the next thing I remember, the bed was pushing on me, making it hard to breathe. The knife blade was pressing into my chest so I felt like I was going to cut myself, and I realized that the kid must be on the bed and that his weight had trapped me there. All my fear and frustration and hurt welled up in me and curdled in my stomach. He'd taken over my life. How dare he sleep so soundly while I hid, suffering every day because he'd stolen my family?

"I knew if I could just get them to look at me the way they looked at him, my Mama and Papa would accept me back into their world and everything would be just right again. So, I slithered out from under the bed. And I just stood over his sleeping body for a long, long time until I knew exactly what I had to do.

"I grabbed his nose and mouth with one hand, holding them tight so he couldn't scream. With my other hand, I sliced his throat — it was easier than you can imagine. And the blood … There was so much blood. I hadn't counted on that. But he only made a little, soft gurgling noise and I knew he was gone. Everything was going so well, it seemed like it must be right after all." She stopped talking then, her eyes gazing out through the dirty office window.

"But things went horribly wrong after that. I went into Mama and Papa's room, but when she woke up, instead of holding me close like she was supposed to, Mama let out the most horrible noise. She woke up Papa, and he didn't love me either. They should have been happy that I'd finally come back to them — but they weren't. At first, they were just angry, and I was afraid they were going to hurt me the way my false parents sometimes did.

"I got so scared then, I jumped out the window and twisted my ankle. I tried to run — I wanted to run and run and never stop, but I couldn't. Papa came after me and dragged me back inside. Then he called the police and wouldn't let me go until they came.

"He made me sit in the little chair without moving. But even then, I knew I'd been right all along. I knew I really *did* belong there, because that chair fit me perfectly."

Now Ursala was back in the present, back in the hospital for the criminally insane, looking to Gwen for some sign of approval. The therapist snuck a quick glance at the open folder.

"That's not all of it," she prompted gently. "What happened in the bedroom?"

Ursala looked at her without really registering her presence — feeling her mind transported back to the house in the woods.

"I … I'd taken his skin off. Carefully, so it came off in a single piece," she said, the words coming haltingly at first, then gaining a momentum of their own. "It wasn't easy, but I had to get it just right so Papa and Mama could finally see who I am. So they would love me like they were always supposed to.

"I took off my bloody clothes and I wrapped the skin around me — it was warm and slick and felt exactly like I thought it should. I went into their bedroom and climbed into bed with Mama. I snuggled against her thick, warm, woodsy-smelling fur — she smelled like pine, just like I'd imagined. Before she opened her eyes and started screaming, she hugged me, like I knew she would.

"And for that one moment, everything was just right."

# POINT TAKEN
## RICHARD ZWICKER

IT WAS OVERCAST IN ATHENS, not that the sun did any good when it was out. I raised fruit and vegetables in my garden to sell, as a way of making a little extra cash — but they were so green and hard that it looked like I'd have to determine their prices by how few teeth they'd break when eaten. I stared at my patch of limp narcissus flowers, wondering how much longer they would survive.

As if in answer, I was approached by a tall woman in a green wrap with vines in her hair. No ordinary woman would enter my back yard unbidden. The fact that the vegetation on her person was alive and thriving told me this could be none other than Demeter. Any direct interaction with the gods was a cause for concern. I eyed her warily, while she gazed at my flowers.

"You favor the narcissus," she said. "Do you advocate obsessive self-love?"

How do you answer a question like that? It was well known that the original Narcissus, besotted by his own image, turned into the first of these flowers.

"No, Narcissus took it too far. But I believe that people

need to believe in themselves. The flowers remind me of that."

"It is said among the gods that you, Phokus, are the best detective in Athens." It was good to have references in high places, though, in truth, I was the *only* detective in Athens. A few years ago, I'd helped the Big God identify and apprehend Prometheus when the Titan stole fire — even though it'd turned out that Zeus had known it all along and had just been using me for entertainment value. Such was human interaction with the gods: life and death for us, a game to them.

"That's nice of them to say." I waited for her to get to the point. Gods have a different sense of time.

"A week ago, my daughter Persephone left to pick flowers in the north fields. She never returned."

"Have you spoken to Zeus about this?" I asked. Everyone knew they had a history. Between them they'd borne Dionysus and Persephone. She'd also had two sons each from two different consorts. They didn't call her the Goddess of the Harvest for nothing.

"He says he doesn't know where she is, but I think he's protecting someone. It would be nice if, just for once, he protected his own *daughter*! If he wasn't immortal, I could kill him! Instead, I will allow nothing to grow until my daughter is returned." A tear dropped from her face. The ground was instantly sodden.

So *that* was why nothing would grow. The Goddess of Spring was missing.

I was conflicted. On the one hand, though I was childless, I could sympathize with a concerned mother. On the other, she was a goddess, too powerful to empathize with humans. She would turn me into a granite statue with a wave of her hand unless I could find Persephone. And if *someone* didn't find her, nothing would ever grow again.

"I'll take the case," I said.

After Demeter left, I sent a message to my assistant, Alastor, to meet in the north fields the next morning.

Before Demeter's halt of plant growth, the north fields had been a picture of bucolic beauty. They were just enough of a walk from the center of the city-state to keep their natural attractions untrammeled. Roses, hyacinths, violets, and lilies dotted the ground, but today their stems sagged and their once-vibrant blooms had dulled. Gray clouds dropped a misty drizzle as we walked to the meadow favored by Persephone.

"What are we looking for, boss?" asked Alastor, puffing. His incipient beard glistened from the rain, and he was irritable from the wet walk. Natural beauty held little appeal for him unless it was on a woman. He pushed his hair out of his eyes.

"We'll know it when we see it," I said.

Alastor scoffed. "That narrows it down."

"Persephone has been known to collect flowers here, but until last week, she always returned home with her pickings. According to Demeter, she had no reason to run away, but her habitual outings make her a good target for a kidnapping." I stopped, seeing something in the distance. "There's an arrow sticking into that cypress tree. Hunting is popular in this area. Be careful."

We approached the tree. I ran my hand over the arrow, which stuck in the trunk, about five hands from the ground. It was laced with gold.

"That arrow is worth more than anything it could hit, unless it hit a pile of drachmas," said Alastor.

"This is no ordinary arrow. My guess is it belongs to Eros," I said.

"Why would he shoot an arrow into a tree?"

"Well, he *is* blind," I said, checking the tree. It didn't appear that the arrow had been there long, as the trunk was still leaking sap.

"No sense in leaving it here," said Alastor, and before I could stop him, he yanked the arrow from the trunk. The effort knocked him onto his back. "Ouch! I cut myself."

To my horror, Alastor stared at me as if I were Aphrodite on the half shell.

"Boss, I've never told you this, but I think I love you. I can't explain it."

"I'd prefer you not try." My words were flippant, but I knew we were in trouble. The history of Eros's arrows was clear. Once pierced, the victim fell hopelessly in love with the first person he saw. I kept a few paces ahead of Alastor, fearing he would start humping my leg.

"Slow down, boss," he purred. "Couldn't we just talk and get to know each other better?"

"Let's talk about the job first. We know Persephone and Eros were here. Maybe she got hit by an arrow and ran off with someone."

"You're so intelligent," said Alastor. "I could listen to your reasoning all day."

I increased my pace. I would have reminded him that he had a wife, but in Athens, that wouldn't stop anybody. I was all for the spread of love rather than hate, but the abruptness of Eros's methods usually resulted in more disruption than unity.

What I didn't understand was why more people didn't fall in love with Eros. Wouldn't he often be the first thing someone saw? Then I remembered something about him being invisible.

My thoughts were interrupted by an "Oomph!" from Alastor. I turned around, but he was gone. Retracing my steps, I discovered he'd fallen into a deep hole that had been covered by some brush. I peered over the edge and saw him clinging to a root, about four body lengths down. The hole was more of a tunnel, but its slope was gradual enough that Alastor hadn't fallen any further.

"Are you all right?" I asked.

He looked up. His eyes were still filled with love, but the rest of him was covered in dirt. I could only hope that the jolt had knocked some of the arrow's spell from him as I pulled him out.

"There must be some large moles in this area," he said.

"Moles, nothing. Who do we know that lives underground?"

"Dead people?"

"Close enough. If a tunnel like this had been here for any length of time, we would have heard about it. I think Hades did this, and he may have taken Persephone with him."

"What would Hades be doing on the surface? He hardly ever leaves the underworld," said Alastor.

"That I don't know. Maybe he was hit by an arrow, saw Persephone, and lovingly dragged her to his realm."

"I'll tell you what. When I die, which fortunately wasn't today, I'll make a full inquiry about it."

"We can't wait that long."

"Boss, I'd follow you to the ends of the Earth, but the underworld ..."

I shook my head. "This is a clue, but we need more. I don't know how to find Eros, but there's a goddess who would know whether Persephone got hit by his arrow."

That goddess was Aphrodite. My sources told me she spent two-thirds of her time on Earth romancing a hunk named Adonis. As rumor had it, he was the product of his mother, Myrra, and Myrra's own father. Some say Aphrodite put a spell of lust on Myrra to make this happen.

Why would she do this? Because she could.

According to those same sources, Adonis liked to hunt wild boar, and his favorite hunting ground was on the island of Salamis. I hired a boat to take us there. It would have been easier to leave Alastor home, but if we found Aphrodite, I was hoping she could do something about her kid's spell.

In port, I asked if anyone had seen Adonis hunting that day. No one had, but all agreed: whether the sun rose or not, Adonis was hunting wild boar.

No offense to Artemis, but I am not a big fan of hunting. I have no problem with killing animals for food, but I wasn't impressed with Adonis's need to hunt for sport. What was he trying to prove? Here he was, supposedly the most handsome man alive, and he had to hunt to death one of the ugliest animals. Plus, the Goddess of Beauty was head over heels for him. Under those circumstances, I would have spent less time with wild animals and more time sowing my wild oats.

On the island, Alastor and I walked until our leg muscles screamed in disapproval, but we didn't see anyone. I thought I heard a faint rumble, however, and asked Alastor if he noticed it.

"It's the beating of my heart," said Alastor, batting his eyes. So much for the jolt of falling into the hole.

"If you can hear your heart beating, you're in trouble." Or I was.

Our path took us to the top of a hill, which offered a splendid view of a valley and a stampeding herd of thirty wild boars running for their lives. A lean, muscular man I assumed to be Adonis rode after them. Fluttering around was Aphrodite. Sometimes she appeared on the back of Adonis's horse, sometimes she floated in front of him, other times she hovered above them.

Adonis was herding the boars toward a cliff. He stopped so that they wouldn't go over it, then dismounted and waited for the boars to charge. At this moment Aphrodite appeared between Adonis and the cornered animals. With her long flowing hair and white robe, she looked as out of place in a boar hunt as Hephaestus in a foot race, but her wild gesticulations incited the swine. They charged her. As one got close, she disappeared just in time for Adonis to shoot it with an arrow. Then she reappeared and waited for another to charge her, continuing this process after each successful kill.

"Let's interrupt this massacre," I said to Alastor, but before we could get their attention, Aphrodite waited too long to disappear. A boar surprised Adonis, goring him. He fell to the ground, mortally wounded. By the time we got there, Hermes was already doing his duty of spiriting the soul to the underworld.

"Oh no! This can't be!" Aphrodite wailed over her lover's dead body. She appeared to be the very picture of grief — but after a moment, she composed herself and said, "Oh well. There are plenty of other men."

Then she saw us. "Who are you?"

"Maybe this isn't the best time ..." I said.

"No doubt about that, but if you value your lives, you will tell me why you were spying on me."

"We meant no disrespect. My name is Phokus. I'm a detective, and this is my assistant Alastor. We have two problems, one immediate and one more far-reaching."

Apparently, Aphrodite didn't care about either of them, turning her back on me to face Adonis. I at least had her ear, so I kept talking. "Alastor was disengaging one of Eros's arrows from a tree in the north meadows and accidentally got cut. He's hopelessly in love with me. This doesn't make for an effective working relationship. I don't suppose you can undo the spell?"

Aphrodite eyed Alastor, who smiled back, then glared at me. "Of course I could. But love should be untamed."

"Do I have any say in this?" asked Alastor.

"Not really, but go ahead," said Aphrodite.

He stared at me. "If loving you is wrong, I don't want to be right. Love is a many splendored thing. Without it, we are empty husks. The smallest detail of the most insignificant life is infused with ..."

Aphrodite rolled her eyes and snapped her fingers. "You're cured."

Alastor had a blank look on his face. "What was I saying?"

"You were saying, 'Thank you.'" I turned to Aphrodite. "The second thing we need to talk to you about is—"

"Persephone. I know."

"What happened to her?"

Aphrodite frowned and still looked great. "Why should I tell you?"

I thought for a second. "Because if Demeter can't find her, nothing will ever grow again, and all the handsome men will die."

She considered that. "All right. I will tell you, then you must leave me ... to mourn." She wiped delicately at her eyes, though I didn't notice any tears. "Ares suggested we go for a walk in the north fields. It's a romantic place, lots of flowers — though they were a bit wilted — and we were having a conversation. I should know better than to try to match wits with that war machine, but there's something about him I can't resist. His sinews have sinews and he has such a long spear. Whenever he takes me in his big, clumsy hands, I feel faint and ..."

I ostentatiously cleared my throat.

"Right. So, we were arguing about which was stronger, love or war. I told him love conquers all, and to prove it, I summoned Hades to the surface and had Eros shoot him with an arrow."

"Hades agreed to that?" I asked.

"Not exactly. He probably thought I was going to let him seduce me. Anyway, as he got shot, he was looking at Persephone. He immediately dragged her down to the underworld."

"If he got shot, how come I got pricked by an arrow that was in a tree?" Alastor asked.

Aphrodite shrugged. "Even as great a marksman as Eros needs to practice."

"Can't you help us?" I asked, motioning to the dying vegetation.

"Hey, I don't *do* the underworld. I like 'em big and alive. None of the gods go there except Hades, and Hermes."

"But you could undo the spell on Hades, and you'd still win your bet."

"Listen, I'd consider it if Hades came up here and asked me, but that's not going to happen. Gods and humans like being pricked by love's arrows."

"Don't you feel any responsibility at all?" Alastor asked, which surprised me. Even without the influence of Eros's arrow, he was a sucker for a pretty face.

"No."

You couldn't make gods or goddesses do something they didn't want to do, so we left her to grieve. At least now we had something to tell Demeter.

I didn't know what to sacrifice to get her attention, so I told her there were a bunch of dead wild boars in the Salamis Woods. Neither Adonis nor Aphrodite were interested in them anymore, so Demeter could take her pick. Unsure that the boars would interest her, I also cut three fading narcissus plants from my back yard and made a bouquet. Something worked, as Demeter appeared in my home that night.

"So, what have you to tell me?" she asked. Even the vines in her hair had started to wilt and lose their greenish hue.

"Aphrodite is the culprit," I said, and I explained how a careless bet had landed Persephone in the underworld.

"I don't trust that deceiver. Have you any other proof?"

"As a matter of fact, I do. Hades left behind a tunnel to the underworld when he kidnapped your daughter. Are you friends with him?"

"Nobody is. Getting the underworld was like a dream job for him. He doesn't have to make small talk. There's no gray area. You're either dead or you're not." She stamped her foot, causing a minor tremor. "Aphrodite thinks the world revolves around her. She couldn't stand that there was one god who was clear-thinking."

"So will you be going down there?" I asked.

"To the underworld? It would be pointless. Hades won't listen to me. The only way he'll release Persephone is if Zeus sends Hermes with a demand to let her go. What worries me is that Zeus acts only if the world is about to end. Well, if he thinks I'm playing games, he's in for a rude surprise. If my daughter is not returned, it will never be spring again. Every plant will die."

"What about us?" I asked. "*We'll* die without food."

Demeter shrugged. "It's the only way to get Zeus to act. If you don't want to wait, go to the underworld yourself and kidnap her back."

"Yeah, sure. I'll just catch the afternoon chariot down there." In truth, I had already made one trip to the underworld a year ago to accompany my dying father and had promised myself that I wouldn't return until my time had come. "That's a long and dangerous trip."

"Nonsense. Hades has left you a shortcut."

"Are you crazy?" asked Alastor, when I went to his home and told him we were going to the underworld. "Not even the gods go there. What chance do we have?"

"I got there successfully the first time."

"That puts you in rarefied company: Heracles, Orpheus, and *every dead person in the history of the world*. C'mon, boss. Maybe the sun will come out tomorrow."

"It won't, unless Demeter gets Persephone back. Look, I'm not going to force you. But let me ask you this: what if I go by myself and don't come back? How are you going to feel?"

"Terrible. But at least I'll be alive to feel something!" He gave me a searching look, then sighed. Though we had our disagreements, Alastor was always loyal. "Do you have a plan?"

I did, but it wasn't clever. "The only person who ever deceived Hades is Sisyphus." The disgraced king tricked Hades into demonstrating the strength of his chains. I ended up freeing him. "You know where that got him."

"Yeah. Making sure a rolling stone gathers no moss for the rest of eternity."

"The only way to get Hades to do anything is to appeal to his sense of justice." He was the one god that had that sense. "Humans don't deserve to die just because he fell in love."

I saw a flaw in my reasoning. Hades' kidnapping of Persephone had nothing to do with justice and everything to do with an uncontrollable impulse. But the presence of two living humans in the underworld, where we didn't belong, would at least get his attention. We'd have to take it from there.

"I'm leaving tomorrow morning. Are you coming or not?"

Alastor sighed. "Let me talk to my wife. She's touchy about me vanishing forever without saying goodbye."

The next morning, we lowered ourselves into Hades' tunnel.

One could say that from the day we are born, we rush to our deaths, but normally it's not a straight walk to the underworld. While the tunnel was indeed a short cut, it wasn't a leisurely one. The incline was steep, and we had to descend carefully. Every step loosened stones that tumbled out of sight. Sisyphus would hate this place. It was also dark, but torches were pointless. They would burn out before reaching our destination, and we needed both hands, both feet, and our behinds on the ground to maintain balance.

As we made our way downward, I recalled my previous trip to the underworld. When I'd brought my father there to die, we'd walked through the dimmest of light, emitted by disinterested spirits. Vision in the underworld was an outline without color, beauty, or joy. I could only hope that Hades would help us leave.

"Hey boss!" Alastor called from behind me. "I found a pomegranate!"

Who can say how long it took us to travel the distance in a place where time has no meaning? After many steps, slips, and strained muscles, we approached the dreary house of Hades. Chiseled into rock, it stood like a two-story dungeon, except the windows and doorway were open spaces. Everyone except Hades, Persephone, and us were shades that had nowhere to escape to.

"Should we just go in?" Alastor asked, nervously.

"I suspect he knows we're here, but out of courtesy, let's announce ourselves." I raised my voice. "Hades, we have braved the dangers of the underworld to ask your assistance! Could you please give us an audience?"

We waited, until we heard slow footfalls on rock. The tall god stood in the doorway, an angular crown on his head, armor covering his chest. I wondered what it was for. It wasn't as if the shades would ever launch a rebellion.

"Phokus," he said, his voice as deep as his kingdom. "This is not the place for you, though you seem determined to disprove that."

"I am not here by choice."

"Of course you are! Hermes didn't lead you here. Don't you like sunshine, warmth, and *life*?"

"That is why I'm here," I said. "Because you kidnapped Persephone, Demeter has stopped tending to plants. Nothing grows now!"

Sadness filled his eyes. He didn't look like someone who'd just eloped. "That is her job. She should stick to it."

"If you don't return Persephone to her mother, every human will die. That's not just," I said.

"I know I owe you a favor, but do not lecture me about justice. I, more than anyone, am aware of the contradiction of imprisoning the Goddess of Spring in a place where spring never arrives. But before this happened, I didn't realize how lonely I was. Now, I can't forget."

He stepped out of his house, and behind him I saw the figure of a woman, white where everything was dark, vines in her hair where everything was dead.

"I want to leave," she said.

That was a common desire in the underworld, but it was almost never granted. In Hades' world, one reached the end of the road, if not the end of consciousness. Persephone's experience was the opposite. Flowers might die, but in the spring they were reborn. What a mismatch.

Hades' mouth fluttered in response to Persephone's words, but he said nothing, further proving my point.

"Would you like something to eat?" Alastor asked, offering her food from his bag.

"I have no appetite in a place like this," said Persephone.

"Oh, c'mon," said Alastor. "When things get bad, I just take a break and eat something. Then I feel better."

Persephone smiled wistfully, then accepted the pomegranate we had found on the way down. I noticed Hades watching with interest. As Persephone sucked on a seed, I noticed a dot of light approaching us. In the semi-darkness, as it got larger, I had to turn away. It was Hermes, alone. Hades raised his heavy eyebrows.

"Did you lose your contingent of shades, Hermes?" asked Hades. "Can't anyone do their job right?"

Hermes smiled, his perpetual good humor contrasting

with Hades' dour face. "Underworld-bound shades aren't the only thing I deliver."

"You have a message?" asked Hades. "You realize you enable my brother. He uses you when he doesn't want to face things himself."

"If you don't send these two humans back, you will face Zeus directly," said Hermes. "Is that what you want?"

"What I want has never been a consideration."

"Are you complaining about the job you ended up with?" asked Hermes. "Would you rather be God of the Hunt? God of the Hearth?" He laughed at the thought but grew quiet when he saw Persephone. "What is she doing here?"

"I've been asking the same question," said Persephone.

"Two live humans in the underworld are bad enough. But the Goddess of Spring? Zeus will never tolerate that."

"Then I can leave with you?" asked Persephone. Her hope slightly lit up the underworld.

"You can, unless you have eaten anything while you were down here," said Hermes.

"What?" asked Alastor.

"I just sucked on three pomegranate seeds he gave me." She pointed at Alastor.

The cheer dropped from Hermes' face. "This is bad." "Pomegranates are symbolic of the indissolubility of marriage."

"So what? I didn't marry him! I'm symbolic of all growing things. Isn't that more important?" asked Persephone.

"I'll have to get back to you on that," said Hermes. He disappeared.

Alastor had an ashen look on his face. "Boss, we ate more food than she did down here. Does this mean we have to stay?"

"I don't know," I said. "No live human being could travel to and from the underworld without eating something." I turned to Hades. "What does this mean for us?"

The God of the Underworld looked wistful, his hands motioning weakly. "Did you eat anything you found down here?"

"No. Just food we brought."

"Then you are free to go."

"Ever since you captured me you've been trying to get me to eat something down here!" screamed Persephone. "I thought it was because you cared, but you wanted to trap me!"

"I offer no defense except my love for you," said Hades.

In a short time, Hermes returned and addressed Alastor, Persephone, and me.

"I will lead you back to the surface. Because Persephone ate three pomegranate seeds, she will have to spend three months of each year in the underworld."

"No!" wailed Persephone.

Hermes smiled wanly. "Yes."

"It was my fault she ate them," said Alastor. "I will stay instead of her."

I couldn't believe my ears, but my lips moved of their own accord. "If it wasn't for me, Alastor would never have come here in the first place. I should stay."

Hermes brushed both our comments aside. "Hades has no desire to spend three months a year with either of you. Now follow me. We have a long trip to make."

Hermes shunned Hades' shortcut, preferring the regular way. Despite its longer length and the fact that only Hermes' feet had wings, we seemed to float along.

When we finally poked our heads out of the ground, Demeter was waiting for us. Persephone ran into a big hug. As tears streamed down their cheeks, the dying plants at their feet burst into a green bloom.

Two days after we returned to the surface, Alastor showed up at my house, looking disheveled. He sank into a chair.

"I'm the reason we're going to have terrible weather for three months out of the year for the rest of eternity."

"Neither of us knew about the implications of the pomegranate seeds. If anyone's to blame, it's Hades. If we hadn't gone down there, every month would be terrible."

Alastor shook his head. "We could have died."

"And we might have died of starvation if Demeter hadn't lifted her spell on the plants. Instead, we saved the world."

"Maybe. My wife thinks Zeus would have eventually ordered Hades to release Persephone. I'm not certain."

Neither was I. Certainty was a luxury for us humans. The gods did whatever they wanted. We did what we could.

After Alastor left, I sat in my back yard. My patch of narcissus flowers bloomed, their petals extending like an open embrace, their yellow inner circle flashing like an idea. Spring had arrived, its revivifying effect all the more powerful because of how close we'd come to losing it.

Connect with this author at:
https://www.amazon.com/author/richardzwicker.

# MAKE LOVE, NOT WAR

## EVE MORTON

"THANK you for coming on such short notice," Commander Gregory told Warren, holding open the door to the tech center. The young grad student stepped inside, still dazzled by his midnight ride across the galaxy from his one-bedroom apartment on Earth. One moment, he'd been a heartbroken language scholar scorned by his cheating boyfriend — and the next, he was an important intergalactic player recruited to work on the army's most recent acquisition.

Though still sort of heartbroken, too.

"Not a problem. I'm happy to help. Where should I sit?"

Commander Gregory extended a hand toward the hot seat in front of a large series of computers. "As I'm sure you know," Commander Gregory began, "we have made contact with an alien life force in another galaxy, one we had once believed was extinct."

"Hard to miss the constant press coverage. And the incoming students." The first transmission had brought in a new cohort of undergrads eager to study the lost space languages. Suddenly, extraterrestrial linguistics was a far cry from the "useless career choice" that Warren's father had told him it was, back when the alien race had been presumed long dead.

"Yes. But what the media doesn't know is that our latest translator, Mina Cooper, has gone missing." The commander looked away as Warren's face blanched. "We do not suspect foul play. But we've had a lot of messages come in since her disappearance, and we can't read them. Nor can we read what came before."

"Which is why I'm here," Warren said, finishing the commander's thought for him and turning to the tech station. He touched a screen idly and the apparatus buzzed to life. Before him were two wide screens, one with the latest transmission in the alien dialect, the other blank — presumably where Mina had once translated the messages. A third screen, still shut off, was meant for message relay. Warren fixated on that screen, tapping it to life. "Has anyone sent anything in return? Do we have her last message to them?"

"No, on both counts." Before the commander could say anything else, a password protection prompt came up on the third screen. Commander Gregory sighed. "No one can crack it. We suspect that it's in the alien dialect too."

Warren nodded slowly. His heart was hammering, but it was only half-tinged with fear. He had already started to feel a bit like a celebrity — or a spy — after being whisked away in the middle of the night. Now he was embroiled in the case of a missing military officer — okay, more like a lowly translator — and he seemed to be the only person who could fill her place and find her.

"We'd like you to take a crack at this—"

"Of course." Warren met the commander's gaze. "But do you mind if I work alone? I do my best without distractions."

It took Warren all of three hours to figure out what happened, but he'd learned a long time ago to never give too much information away. Always let others think you need more time — that way, if you really do need to be a hero, you can show up and dazzle. Or, as was more often the case in his everyday working world, he could get an extension on the paper historicizing the accented N's in the ancient alien language of Rokro, and go out to a bar with Chase instead.

He had not thought about Chase in hours. Mostly because he'd only been thinking of Grok, the alien life form that had stolen Mina Cooper's heart and who most likely had her in his own spaceship right now.

"How do you expect us not to be wooed?" one of the first messages read. "You send us music. Poetry. Some of the kindest words we've ever heard, once we understand them. Of course we love you."

"We are a military base," Mina had responded at first. "We did not write those. They were from a different generation."

"They were still made by your kind. So we love you. I love you."

"We are a military base," Mina repeated. "We are only here to make sure that you come in peace."

The messages continued like that for a while. Mina was professional, while Grok insisted it was personal and tried to use the Mozart, Bach, and multiple messages of love and kindness as evidence of their soul connection. When that didn't work, he finally wrote something original for Mina. It was a bad poem, Warren knew. But for a military officer and translator ... well, it was kryptonite.

Warren's eyes grew wide as he continued to translate their salacious letters back and forth. Should he be reading this? Was it private? Should he tell the commander this was an elopement? He hadn't reached the end yet, but it was clear where the messages were heading.

Still, he said nothing. Make them think it takes longer than it really does. And learn some new and exciting vocabulary while you do.

He was almost through translating a sex letter between the two of them — one that painted an interesting picture, with all the appendages these aliens had — when the first screen buzzed to life. A new message had come in.

Warren looked around. The communication tech room had no windows, and the door was air locked behind him. No one was here to read over his shoulder. He knew he should call for Commander Gregory, but he gravitated towards the screen instead. It only took him a few minutes to translate.

"Are you there, Grok? We can't find you. Have you run away with your mate?"

Warren glanced at the response screen. He still hadn't tried cracking the password yet, but with his newly improved knowledge of the alien language, he thought he might have a chance. First he typed Mina's name. Nothing. He then added Mina's name with the accented N character that was common in the Rokro language.

It worked.

He stared at the blank screen for a while before he typed a response in the foreign language, the one that he'd once believed he'd never ever use for any good. "Grok is not here. Mina is gone too."

Minutes passed. Warren's heart beat hard and fast. When the message came, sweat from his forehead fell onto the screen.

"So they have done it. Good for them. We will mark an asteroid in their honor." Another minute passed. "Who are you?"

Before Warren could consider the pros and cons of continuing, he was writing in this new language as if it was his one and only. "Warren. I'm another translator."

"Do you want to know our weapon inventory? We have the list that Mina wanted."

"I don't think so. I'm just supposed to find Mina."

"We must give the newlymated some time. Everyone needs private time after such a momentous occasion, don't you think?"

Warren didn't know how to answer. Before he could think of a response, chatter from outside the tech room made his spine tense. He wanted to keep talking, keep translating — but wasn't his task over? The world wasn't in any danger. He could go back to grad school. Find another boyfriend. Do something else to lead a boring life.

A new message came in. "Do you know poetry? We liked the poetry that came to us, but Grok said it wasn't from Mina. Is it from you?"

"No," Warren wrote. "But I do like poetry."

"Tell me something." A beat between sentences. "My name is Hosh, by the way."

Warren leaned into the screen, almost as if it could bring him closer to this life form. "If I write some poetry for you, Hosh, would I use an e or a u ending?"

"U," Hosh said. "Though I am not picky, certainly not as much as Grok is. I love all forms of life and see myself as all forms of life."

Warren swooned. He began rushing through the poems he remembered, beginning to translate them on the middle screen. When the door to the tech center opened, he'd just hit send on the first Shakespearean sonnet that had come to mind.

"How's it going?" Commander Gregory asked. His thick brows were furrowed in tension.

"Um. I am … still figuring it out. I need another hour, maybe two. But I am making progress."

Commander Gregory looked around at the screens. When a message pinged in from the first communication screen, he nodded. "Buzz us when you're done. We're looking forward to the report."

Warren waited until the commander had gone before he let out a breath. He looked over his shoulder one last time, then turned back to the screen. The message there read: "That is beautiful. But write something special, just for me."

Warren thought through the new vocabulary he'd learned tonight. With a wry smile, he knew that his degree was finally going to pay off.

# THE BASTARD'S BLUFF

## DANIELLE DAVIS

IT WAS *the best of times, it was the worst of times.* That's how Rufus had always figured his memoir would start: with some powerful line that would make his story an instant classic. Or maybe something like, *The man in black fled across the desert and the gunslinger followed.*

Yeah. That one sounded great. He said it aloud to himself, liking the feel of the words in his mouth.

"Doesn't fit," Edgar squawked.

"Shut up, you flying sack of syllables. Sure it does."

The raven gave an irritated flutter of his wings. "'Man in black'?"

Rufus thought for a moment. "Ok, good point. But 'The woman in the blue gown with fantastic knockers and a penchant for leaving men heartbroken and tied naked to a bed' is just too much of a mouthful."

The raven cocked its head. "The gown didn't have fantastic knockers. The woman did."

"*Yeah.*" Rufus drawled the word out with lecherous satisfaction.

"Ugh," quoth the raven. "And the gunslinger part?"

Rufus sighed. He wished the ropes around his hands were longer so he could rub his eyes. Even though he'd been taken into a cave, the sun still glared off the desert sand outside. Squinting didn't help — and neither did arguing with his bespelled companion.

"I've been known to sling a gun or two in my time."

The raven chuckled and danced across Rufus's naked shoulders. "Only if you count slinging them from the hips of the men wearing them and then tossing them to the bedroom floor."

Rufus shrugged as well as he could with a bird on one shoulder. "I think we'll have to agree to disagree, then."

"No, we won't. You're a liar, and a bad one at that," Edgar cawed in his ear.

Rufus winced and glared at the bird. "I've been called worse by better." Knowing it was a futile effort, he tried to bring his hand toward his eyes, but once again the rope around his wrist brought it up short.

"Care to give me a little slack here, boys? Seems you didn't measure well enough."

This, he called to the two men a few feet away. They were hired thugs, meaty-shouldered and dirty, with features that made them look like they shared a combined IQ of 100. One had a large cicatrix of scar tissue that knotted around his throat like a piece of rope. The other was a foot shorter, had a nose as straight as the Seine, and was missing the tips of all the fingers on his left hand. Both stood with baffled looks, watching the exchange between Edgar and Rufus.

The short one pointed at Edgar. "Did that bird talk to you?"

The tall one made a fist and thunked the top of the short one's head. "Of course not, moron. Birds cain't talk. He's one of them vent … ventili … ventriculists."

Rufus sighed and looked at Edgar, who gave a little shrug with his wings.

Shorty grinned up at the tall one. "Oh, I love those! They's the ones cut those women in half?"

The tall one rolled his eyes. "No, the ones 'ut throw their voices."

"Guys?" Rufus called. He shook his bound hands. "Little help here?"

Shorty frowned. "Th'ow their voices? Where to?"

The two men began arguing over the entertainment values of ventriculists versus bisected women. After several tedious minutes of this, Edgar pushed off from Rufus's shoulder and flew to perch on a rock next to them.

"Gentlemen," the raven began. The two immediately stopped and stared at him, wide-eyed. (Rufus wasn't sure if it was the novelty of being called "gentlemen" or the immediate presence of a talking bird, but he didn't really care.) "We need your assistance procuring the location of a certain female villainess who absconded with property of mine."

"Birds gots property?" Shorty whispered to his companion in a voice that wasn't really a whisper. "He don't look like no respectable dandy."

Edgar turned his head to fix Shorty in one beady eye. "I can hear you, you know."

Shorty gasped and froze with wide eyes. "He's got super hearing!" he "whispered." "Quick, don't move. Birds cain't see you if you hold real still."

Edgar passed a wing over his face and turned his head to regard the taller one. "I assume that you're the brains of this duo? Can you kindly convey that I wish for my partner to be released so that we may continue pursuit of said villainess?"

"There's no point reasoning with ruffians, Edgar," Rufus called. "These are men of steel. They trade in violence, death, and debauchery. They can't be bargained with or bought because they thrive off the very destruction they—"

"We can be bought," the taller one broke in. He looked thoughtful.

Rufus rolled his eyes. "*Rude.* Can't you see I'm in the middle of a soliloquy here?"

Surprised, the tall one glanced at Edgar, who gaped slack-beaked at Rufus. He shrugged and gestured for Rufus to continue.

"Thank you," said Rufus. He clenched one hand into a fist and gritted his teeth. "They *thrive* off the very destruction—"

"You know what, I can't listen to this," Edgar broke in. He turned back to the ruffians. "How much?"

With a shrewd look at Shorty, who remained frozen in place so Edgar couldn't see him, the tall one held up four fingers. "Twenty gold," he said.

"They why are you holding up—" Rufus began, but stopped when the taller one flashed his eyes threateningly. The look told Rufus that his limbs were perilously close to being chopped off, so he concluded with, "Sold! Now take me down, please." He wiggled his hands against the ropes again, in case the men forgot which part was most important.

"First the money," the tall one growled.

"In my pants." Rufus wiggled his hands again, stronger this time. "But let's compromise by untying my hands before you fetch your pay."

"But you ain't wearing no pants," chimed Shorty. He seemed to have forgotten the talking bird now that payment was imminent.

"Ugh," quoth Rufus. "Whose fault is that? You didn't *have* to take my clothes off."

The tall one grinned. "You're right. But people tend to

be more compliant when they're nekkid." He lumbered over to the pile of clothing near the cave entrance and fished through the pants until he found a small sachet. He glanced over his shoulder at Shorty, but Shorty was too busy trying to poke Edgar with his shorter-than-normal index finger.

The tall one spilled a handful of coins into his palm, then dumped the handful into his pocket.

"Hey!" yelled Rufus. "I agreed to twenty!"

Unruffled, the tall one continued to paw through the rest of Rufus's clothes. "I cain't count."

"Then get the short one to do it!"

"He cain't count neither."

"Thieves," Rufus spat.

Finally, after pocketing Rufus's money, belt knife, and boots, the tall one finally let Rufus free of his bonds. Then he and Shorty sat to divvy up the payment.

"Those boots aren't going to fit you, you know," Rufus sulked as he rubbed his eyes. He rolled one arm in giant circles to relieve the stiffness of his shoulder. "Wearing shoes that are too small for you has been proven to cause ingrown toenails ... bone spurs ... and, um, zits."

The men ignored him as the tall one pieced out coins into Shorty's hand. "... two ... three ... *four*. There's your half, Stubby."

"Excuse me, what?" Rufus put his hands on his bony, naked hips. "*Now* you can count? Fabulous."

Edgar flew over to perch on his shoulder. "Have you ever heard the phrase 'Quit while you're ahead'? Because now would be a good time to follow that advice."

"And what did I just hear you call him? The man missing half his fingertips is named *Stubby*?"

Stubby grinned the grin of the witless and nodded.

Rufus put his hand over his mouth. "Un-friggin-believable." He gestured at the tall one. "And what's your name? Scarface?"

"Thomas. Thomas O'Tool."

"O'To — Really? You're Irish? I would not have guessed that."

Should-Have-Been-Named-Scarface nodded. Edgar smacked the back of Rufus's head with one wing.

"Fine." Rufus assessed the length of his nude body, noting the scrapes on his elbows and the full-body coat of grime. His buttocks still felt sore from where the scalawags had dragged him over the gritty floor of the cave, and his wrists had small rope burns that weren't altogether unpleasant (if he was being honest with himself). All in all, he decided that he looked pretty good for a naked kidnappee.

"Ok, guys. Let's get down to business. We're chasing a certain vile young lady, and you know where she is."

"No, we don't," Stubby said. "We haven't the foggiest idea who the Lady Aramina is."

Rufus and Edgar both cocked an eyebrow at him. At least, Edgar would have if he'd had eyebrows to cock. Even Thomas gave Stubby a doubtful sideways look.

"What?" Stubby gave confused looks back at everyone.

Rufus pointed at him and grinned. "You're an imbecile of my very favoritest sort, Stubbs. Now, where is she? And don't play ... well, dumber."

"We know *of* the Lady Aramina," Thomas said, "but we don't know where she is right now."

"Lies! I know she's the one who put you up to this. Are you trying to stall me? Because you two are damn sure not smart enough to actually kill me. Tied up naked in a cave? Really? What was I going to do, admire myself to death?"

"Or starve," Thomas offered.

"Edgar would've made sure that didn't happen. You didn't even try to get rid of him."

"Which, by the way, I'm quite grateful for," Edgar quipped.

"Now, you *will* tell me her last known location, or you won't live to regret it."

"Did he just threaten to kill us?" Stubby asked Thomas. "Because it sounded like he threatened to kill us."

Thomas's eyes narrowed to cat-like slits. "I don't think that's the move you want to make, my nekkid friend." His voice was a growl that made Rufus's stomach flop uneasily. Then Thomas smirked down at Stubby. "He's bluffin'. If he was gonna kill us, he woulda' already done it before he ended up trussed like a goose."

Rufus puffed out his scrawny chest. A breeze wafted through the cave and across his netherbits. "It was all part of my plan. So far, I've had you right where I wanted you. But my patience is wearing, and I've got places to be. *Vengeful* places. So, I'll only ask you this once again: where is the last place you knew the Lady Aramina to be?"

"Next town over," Stubby replied as he fingered his money. He seemed to be entranced by the way the coins fell like water from one dirty palm to the other when tipped just right.

"Boon or Botherton?" Edgar asked.

Stubby shrugged. "What does it matter? They's both begin with 'b'."

"Boon," Thomas supplied. Then he turned, fixed them both with a firm glare, and pointed a grimy finger at them. "Now, let's not make this difficult. You stay here for a count of thirty—"

"—which we'll be able to do since *we* never lied about having that ability," Rufus muttered.

"—before you follow us."

"And how are we supposed to get to Boon? *Somebody* stole my boots."

"We can leaves them with a supply dino, I suppose," Stubby suggested.

"We ain't murderers, after all," Thomas agreed, nodding. With that, Thomas and Stubby stepped into the blinding light outside.

Edgar began counting aloud. "One ... two ..."

"We don't actually have to count, you fool." Rufus picked up the husk of leather that used to be his coin purse. It took him a moment of searching to realize that he had nowhere to tuck it, so he tossed it over his shoulder. "Seventeen, eighteen, thirty!" he added, finishing Edgar's count for him. "All right, let's go."

"But what if they're still out there?" Edgar sounded nervous for the first time during this whole ordeal.

"They already said they're not murderers. Go make sure they actually left us a dino, though. They didn't seem overly fond of telling the truth."

Edgar threw him a baleful glare but obediently flew out into the sunshine.

Rufus followed, wincing with every step; the act of walking aggravated the grit wedged between his buttocks.

Surprisingly, the thieves had been men of their word — this time, anyway. A rangy velociraptor stood ground-tied a few feet from the entrance. A crest of feathers climbed up its neck before giving way to mottled yellow and green skin. The feathers had been plucked in some spots, making it look like a giant, mange-ridden parrot. A leather harness covered its chest and buckled with a girth under its belly.

It stood tall on its hindlegs as Rufus approached. But when Edgar swooped close to its head, it spooked and reared back with a hiss. Edgar landed on its back, his talons grasping onto the longer feathers there, and the raptor cocked its head from one side to the other, trying to keep an eye on the spot where Edgar had been moments ago.

"A raptor," Rufus spat. "It figures they left us one of the dumbest creatures in creation. Not counting Stubby, of course."

Rufus reached up to snatch the muzzled halter around the raptor's scaled head. Its reptilian eye twitched as it regarded him.

"You behave now," Rufus told it sternly. Then he put his hand to its nose to let the raptor become acclimated to his scent. In return, it tried to snap at him. Thankfully, the muzzle just bumped into Rufus's outstretched hand, but it didn't improve his bitter mood.

"Rude," he muttered, picking up the reins and putting one foot on the side strap of the harness. "It's probably not even broke to ride." He swung one leg over, careful not to pull out any of its longer back feathers. As soon as he settled his weight onto the bony ridge of its spine, the raptor began to jump and buck, throwing its head sideways as Rufus sawed desperately on the reins. Edgar flew into the air with a startled "Fuck!"

After a few tenuous moments, Rufus closed his legs on the raptor's side and it settled, though the muscles in its back remained tense.

"Which way is Boon?" Rufus called.

As the raptor stepped forward, Edgar returned to perch on one of the harness's shoulder straps. "This way, I think," he said, and pointed eastward with one wing.

"Naked, robbed, and left with a green raptor. This is going to be the worst trip I've ever taken," Rufus muttered.

"Trust me," Edgar replied, "All of that doesn't compare a lick to having to travel with you."

"Why, thank you!" Rufus said.

Edgar sighed.

The raptor continued on.

~

If the people of Boon had ever before seen a naked man and a raven riding a velociraptor into town, they hid it well. They stared with open interest, and Rufus, riding like a king astride the jittery beast, smiled back. He winked at a group of women, then at a cowboy riding past on a galimimus.

Before he could turn to see if the cowboy returned the attention, the raptor spooked at a group of galimimus hitched outside a storefront. A postal pterodactyl soared overhead and landed next to the post office with a skidding screech. Ahead, cowboys herded a swaddle of baby apatosaurs into a large pen lined with timber rails eighteen feet high. A triceratops pulling a stagecoach rumbled past, and the raptor danced to the side with a high-pitched squeal. Rufus cursed it back into submission.

"Stupidest. Creature. In the world," Edgar growled (well, as well as he could growl with raven vocal chords). Every sideways movement launched him off balance, and he was getting rather weary of it.

Once the raptor was back under control, Rufus headed straight to the saloon.

"Don't you think a tailor would be a better choice about now?" Edgar complained.

Rufus turned and pantomimed pulling out empty pockets. A woman gasped as he gave her a full frontal, and she placed her hands over the eyes of the child walking next to her.

Rufus gave her a winning smile, then turned a serious face back to Edgar. "And pay with what? Should I charge folk to see the magical, talking raven? Or do you suggest that I permit myself to be buggered and beloved for coin? I'm getting some money the fastest way I know how."

"Which is what, exactly?" Edgar called to Rufus's naked back as he turned to head into the saloon.

"Showing off my poker face!"

Twenty minutes later, he strolled out with a smug smile and a heavy coin purse. Which was impressive, given that he'd had no sleeves in which he could've hidden an Ace or two.

"Enjoy the pinkeye, you scalliwags!" he called back as he exited. He grinned down at Edgar, who had a decidedly unhappy look on his feathery face.

"That took forever."

"Tell me about it! I've never had to work so hard to get men to throw money at me."

Edgar made a disgusted noise. "It's all about sex with you, isn't it?"

"Not at all! Sometimes it's about the cuddling." He winked at Edgar. Then he strolled down to the tailor's to outfit himself.

An hour later, outfitted in Boon's finest with a leather vest, billowy peasant shirt, and leather pants, Rufus was ready to continue their hunt for the Lady Aramina.

"Had to have the best, didn't you?" Edgar grumbled. "Bet we're half a purse light now, aren't we?"

"Hey, a man's got to have standards. Besides, as a result of flashing some coin, the tailor was able to give me the inside scoop. It seems that the Lady Aramina passed through not a day ago. We're close, my fine feathered. Very close."

"She could be a lot of places with a day's advantage on us." Edgar's voice sounded worried.

"But luck is on our side, Edgar! I know where she's

headed next. Word is she was trying to sell a very valuable gold lamp—"

"The one that enchanted me in the first place! Damnable genies."

"The very same. But nobody around here had the coin for it. According to the town gossip, she's headed off to Waterwell to auction off the last two wishes, and then the lamp itself."

"We need to get there fast," Edgar said. "If she gives up that lamp before turning me back, I'll lose whatever chance I have of getting returned to my normal self."

"Was your normal self really worth all this, though?" Rufus wondered aloud. "I mean, being a raven has its advantages—"

"Don't start with me, you cretin. I was a *prince*. And I intend to get that life back, with or without you."

Rufus snorted. "Well, good luck getting it back without me. I'm the best option you have."

Edgar made a disgusted noise and turned his head away. "You're the most *convenient* option I have at the moment," he muttered. "Besides," he continued hesitantly, "I do have to admit that I appreciate your dedication. Not many men would still be willing to continue this mission after being strung up in the nude and nearly left for dead."

Rufus's eyes squinted into the distance as he struck a heroic pose. "Well, let's just say that you're not the only one to whom the Lady Aramina owes a debt."

The raven fluttered his wings with interest. "Oh really?" he said eagerly. "What does she owe you?"

"The answer to a question."

"What question?"

Rufus gave the bird an irritable glance. "It doesn't matter to you. All that matters is that I'm here for the job."

He mounted the jittery raptor and held it steady while

Edgar flew up to perch on his shoulder. With a kick, they set off toward Waterwell at a ground-eating lope.

It took them three days and 7,358 complaints to get to Waterwell. The raptor was panting with thirst by the night they arrived, and its riders were all too happy to stop at the first hotel they passed and lay up for the best night's sleep they'd had to date.

In their room the next morning, Edgar fluttered to a tabletop and outlined the plan: "You've never been well-off enough to know how auctions like these work, so listen carefully. First, we'll have to get invited. That shouldn't be too hard; you just have to play cards well enough for people to think that you're a high roller. That'll get us in. Then, we need to devise a way to properly bid on the other wishes — she'll likely auction those off first. If that doesn't work, we'll need to outbid for the lamp itself. I estimate it'll go for—"

"Free, if we just steal it." Rufus's mouth twisted to one side. "You're overthinking it, my feathery brother-in-arms. We don't have to actually participate in the auction if we can get our hands on the grimy thing before it's even up for sale. Then we'll just wish you back into your princely body and be on our way."

Edgard blinked at him. "You really do have a one-track mind. How are we going to get close enough to the Lady Aramina to steal it, idiot? She's likely guarded to the gills."

"I intend to charm my way into her clutches."

Edgar rolled his eyes. "I was wrong — you have a two-track mind."

Rufus glared at him. "Don't poo-poo my sensuality, blackbird. I think I'll get plenty close enough."

"Don't you think she'll recognize me?"

"Of course she will! That's why you're staying in the room."

"The hell I am! There's no way I'm letting you waltz in there to steal—"

"If you go, she'll know what we're up to. This is a job for Rufus the Respectable, not his feathered sidekick."

"Nobody calls you that."

With an arch look, Rufus sniffed at him. "Everyone calls me that."

"Nobody does."

"*Like I was saying*, I'll schmooze my way into her good graces and steal it out from under her nose. Easy as cake."

"Pie."

"Huh?"

"The phrase is 'easy as pie.'" Edgar rolled his eyes with an irritated rustle of his wings.

"That too."

"You can't honestly think you'll get in there by yourself. Odds are she'll recognize you too and pull a gun within the first five minutes."

"Nonsense, Edgar. She'll never see me coming."

That evening, Rufus slid carefully down the shingles of the roof, thanking the stars that it was a fairly gradual slope. He squinted down at the second story of the hotel across the alley, where a single, lighted window shone in the night's darkness. There was a balcony outside, as well as two glass-paned double doors that led to the room's interior. The sight of the doors, which had been left open to let in the humid night air, made Rufus uneasy. The Lady Aramina would never make such a novice mistake.

Still, he would have to proceed with his plan. He had no choice.

He pulled the lasso from his belt, whirled it a few times over his head, then flung it across the alley between his building and the hotel so that it caught the weathervane on the top of the hotel roof.

For a moment, he hesitated. He had never attempted this move before, and, if he was honest with himself, he was a little sad that there was nobody around to see it. Think of how cool he would look when he pulled it off.

Rufus glanced down at the alleyway, judging the distance, and the sight made his stomach turn over queasily and made parts of him pucker that normally didn't. There was also a good chance that he *wouldn't* pull this off, and then there would be nobody around to help. He suddenly wished he'd let Edgar tag along.

He swallowed hard and looked back to the window, determined to focus on nothing but his goal.

A person's shadow slid across the floor inside the room, making Rufus's decision for him. It was now or never.

He pulled on the rope to test it; it held sturdy. Then, summoning his courage, he wrapped his hands around the rope, pushed off from the roof, and swung crazily through the air.

For a moment, in his sudden panic, he thought he had overjudged the distance and would smash face-first into the wall. Then his feet hit the balcony railing, and he let go of the rope, landing in an unceremonious heap in the balcony doorway.

He got to his feet, complimenting himself on a successful landing, and looked up to find the barrel of a revolver inches away from his face. Holding it was a small, slender woman clad all in black, from her knee-high boots to the waist-cinching corset that elevated her ample bosom. Rufus found them nearly as distracting as the gun.

"Why, Lady Aramina, so good to see you again." He flashed a winsome smile, showing off his very white teeth.

"I'd ask what you're doing around here, but I suppose I already know." She gestured to the lamp tied to her waist. "This reunion wouldn't be about my little trinket here, now, would it?"

"I'm always game for an opportunity to bask in the company of your trinkets, my lady." Rufus waved his hands. "Can I put these down now? My muscles are starting to cramp."

In the brief moment of silence that followed, Rufus listened to the bustling tavern downstairs. It was just busy enough that nobody would notice the gunshot if one were fired. And, given the clientele, nobody would care if it did. It had been a smart choice, this wayward hotel. Not up to the Lady Aramina's usual standards, but it made the perfect hideaway.

Lady Aramina gave a toss of her head, making the dark jets of her hair swirl in a silken waterfall over one shoulder. "Oh, give it a rest, Rufus. We both know I'm not going to shoot you."

She lowered the gun, then tipped its muzzle to indicate something behind her. "But he might, so I wouldn't try anything overly quick."

Rufus glanced over her shoulder and saw Thomas O'Toole standing with his hands clasped in front of him, guarding the front door. "Ah yes. Your Irish muscle. Pleasure." Rufus tipped his hat, but Thomas didn't acknowledge him.

"Rude," Rufus muttered, then turned back to Lady Aramina. "As a matter of fact, my lady, I am not here for the lamp, though I have no problem holding it for you if it gets too heavy." He put his hands into his pants pockets and jiggled them. "*My* outfit has pockets."

Lady Aramina glared at him, then flounced over to a chair and elegantly sank into it. "Then why are you here?"

"Because you left me waiting."

"Oh? Did I?" Her air was a calculated nonchalance that made Rufus ache. She examined her gloved fingertips as if checking her nails.

"You know very well that you did. You owe me an answer, and I think I've been very patient in waiting for it."

"How did you get in here?" she asked him, changing the subject.

Rufus frowned, gesturing over his shoulder toward the balcony. "Rope," he said. "I swung here from the building across the street."

The Lady Aramina raised her eyebrows skeptically.

"It was heroic!" Rufus exclaimed, stung. How could she have missed the great amount of valor that the effort had taken? It had been a damn fine move. "I was like the hero in a fairy tale, swinging down from the tallest tower, and —"

"But you hate heights," she interrupted.

Rufus stammered to a silent halt, staring at her. Then he straightened himself and passed a smoothing hand down the front of his shirt. "Yes, well," he coughed. "It was the only way I could get in."

The Lady Aramina smiled and moved closer to him. "Rufus," she said in a low voice. "You did that for me?"

Rufus stared down at her, transfixed by the deep red of her lips. "Yes, well," he coughed again. "One must do what one must when … when …"

His throat became suddenly dry as she moved so close that her chest touched his. "That was very heroic of you," she said in a breathy voice.

"Aramina," Rufus said in a rough, deep voice. "My answer."

She tilted her head up so that their faces were very close together. "Remind me what the question was again?" She flashed him a playful smile that he didn't return.

"Will you marry me?" he whispered at her.

In response, she raised her face to him and closed her eyes. Her lips parted expectantly. Rufus put his hands around her waist and leaned down to brush her lips with his. For a moment, they were the only two people in the world.

Then Lady Aramina leaned back, breaking the contact. When she spoke, her voice sounded harsh, devoid of breathiness. "You were heroic," she said. "But also very foolish." She drew back, frowning at him.

"Was I?" he asked silkily. At her perplexed expression, he took a few steps back, out onto the balcony, and held up his arms as if in surrender.

In his left hand, he held the lamp.

Her hands clutched reflexively at her waist, then curled into fists. "You conniving, sneaky bastard!" she cried. Then, after thinking for a moment, she flashed a triumphant smile that made his stomach flip. She was magnificent when aroused.

"How are you planning to get out? The doors are barred and we're two stories up. You'll never get away with it."

"Ah, but you see, you have forgotten one thing." He tossed the lamp high into the air, making Lady Aramina jump forward with outstretched arms. There was a flap of wings, and suddenly a bird flew low between them and caught the lamp in its claws. With a triumphant screech, Edgar flew away.

Lady Aramina looked after the bird, but in the night sky

it was impossible to see where it had gone. She glared at Rufus, who gave her a wan smile in return.

"Now what?" she asked. "You're still stuck here."

Rufus backed away a few more steps. Thomas O'Tool stepped forward, flexing his beefy arms.

"Your answer, my lady?" Rufus asked with a jaunty smile.

Lady Aramina paused, then grinned at him. "You really are a conniving bastard," she said, but there was a fond note in her voice.

"I'll take that as a 'maybe,'" he said, grinning back at her. Then he turned and took two running steps to the balcony, jumped, and slid down the rope hanging just over the railing.

Lady Aramina ran froward and leaned out over the balcony rail. "You crazy fool!" she cried.

From down below in the darkness, she heard him call back, "*Your* crazy fool!"

He landed in a heap on the dirty cobblestone street of the alley, then ran, wincing, to the raptor waiting for him next to a trash bin.

Edgar was perched on the saddle with the lamp still held in his claws. "Well, that went well," he cawed. "Did you get what you came for?"

Rufus mounted the raptor and kicked it forward. The animal jumped a little, then settled into an easy lope as they turned onto the main road out of town.

"I did," Rufus said with satisfaction, as he plucked the lamp from Edgar's claws and slid it into a side pouch on his saddle satchel.

"So now what?"

"Well, we make our flashy getaway—"

"We are literally sneaking away in the dead of night. That's not flashy by anyone's standards," Edgar interjected.

"*And then,*" Rufus said firmly, glaring at the bird. "We turn you back into a human prince. And you pay me the handsome sum you promised me."

"But what if I renege on the deal? You have no reason to trust me."

"I will be keeping the lamp, using just one of the wishes to turn you human. I will still have one wish left to use as I see fit."

The bird growled, but nodded. "Fair enough. And what of the Lady Aramina?"

"I'm sure she has some investors that will be sorely disappointed to lose that lamp after she promised it to them. They may come after her for leading them on."

"So?" quoth the raven. "I say let her stew in her own consequences."

But Rufus just shook his head. "I think she may need the aid of a certain hired gun to help her get away."

"She was right, you know. You really are a fool."

"Maybe," he admitted. "But I'm the best fool there is."

Rufus smiled as the warm night air rushed past his face. The memory of the Lady Aramina's kiss was still fresh on his lips. It gave him a satisfied feeling in the pit of his stomach, as if he'd just drunk a very fine liquor.

He would see her again. And soon. It was just a matter of time. Besides, she still owed him an answer.

～

# SAID THE MOONLIT MOTH TO THE HORSE HALF-DEAD

## MATTHEW F. AMATI

ACROSS A BROKEN WORLD sped the Horse Half-Dead.

The land of Harrow was a backwater into which fell the detritus from larger worlds. Mountains of bric-a-brac littered the shadowed wastes; the moon's cold flame lit skeletal collections of ruined pianos, blasted automobiles, burnt umbrellas, machines blown with rust.

The denizens of Harrow had once lived among these puzzling remains, without the slightest knowledge of their use or whence they came.

Time passes, empires fall, and now the Thangdom of Harrow itself lies ruined as an old clock tower, frozen in its gears and pointing to a time neither wrong nor right.

The Horse Half-Dead was resplendent on his living half, ghoulish on his dead half. His alive half was silver coat, coral horn, an eye green as the Hainted Sea.

His dead half was a cage of bleached bone. Dark words fell from his skeletal jaw.

Past the Pit of Abandoned Unicycles sped the Horse Half-Dead, on a mission of vengeance. "Life, even half-life, needs purpose," said the Horse Half-Dead. "And this is mine. To half-kill the Unrealtor who tried to kill me, and half-missed."

A Moth, lately pupated and new to the world's ways, came fluttering. The moon shone through his half-clear wings.

"Hullo, hullo," said the Moonlit Moth to the Horse Half-Dead. "Will you look at this? I'm airborne! Of all things! Yestreen I came over all sleepy-like. Hung myself downside-up for a nap. Awoke smothered in silk! Remarkable!"

"Remarkable to a moth," replied the Horse Half-Dead. "Wholly unremarkable to the rest of us. The world has seen trillions of your kind."

The Moth traced a parabolic loop across the moon's pale brow. "What are you doing, and where are you going? Your hoofprints need shoeing. The river is flowing. Tell me, tell me, is it somewhere I may go?"

The Horse Half-Dead croaked, "Where I am going, you may not go. I wish to half-kill someone. It won't be pleasant."

The eyes on the Moth's wings widened.

"A moth's life is short," the Moonlit Moth said. "Predictable, the same for every moth. I shall follow this strange beast. See what no moth has seen, go where no moth has ever been."

West of the Heap of Broken Suitcases hurtled the Horse Half-Dead, the Moth wheeling and looping beside.

The Moonlit Moth soared high above the Heap. On the

path, far behind but drawing closer, he spotted something short. It waddled on two legs.

"Coming towards us," the Moth pondered. "Pursuing?"

The Horse Half-Dead called the Moth down to him. Said he to the Moonlit Moth: "Since you asked, I'm seeking the Unrealtor who calls herself Mogwen Rattlejaws. This Mogwen murdered the child Heirs of our Thangdom. She killed half of me. Nearly killed all. I seek to find her and half-kill her. Let her discover what it's like, this half-life of mine."

"Who was this Muggwig Muslinteeth, then?"

"Mogwen Rattlejaws. An Unrealtor, a Wotch, a Widder-shins. Murderer, assassin, child-cannibal. She was nurse, handmaid, nurturer to the three young Heirs of Harrow. Until the night she slaughtered the children in their beds and fled, laughing. Their father, the Thang of Harrow, perished in sorrow."

"And shrouded the land," the Moth added. He knew this story well. "Now the realms of Harrow are a broken waste, a place of toppled towers, scattered vacuum cleaners, piles of refuse under endless night. We mark Saint Golfrid's Eve with darkness and the wind's chill hand."

"You who crawled from the cocoon but yesterday," the Horse Half-Dead said, "how could you know this?"

"We moths mature quickly. I have already completed my primary education. I am a youth now, full of life's sap, hungry to live a life less ordinary."

Without pause, without breath, the peculiar duo streaked through bat-gloam and owl-light. Over the broken lands of the Odds and Ends they hurtled, past cracked airfields, stoven-in garages, around discarded ovens, the bones of parasols, a mound of rusted calliopes. One of the pair hardly stirred the air, the other drummed thunder on the soil.

The Moth tried its best to draw tales from the Horse Half-Dead, but for three passes of the wan sun, and three arcs of the cold moon, the Horse would volunteer nothing save grim gibberish from naked jaws.

Said the Moonlit Moth to the Horse Half-Dead: "How did this Unrealtor half-kill you?"

This time, the Horse answered. "My memory is half-gone, with many holes where knowledge used to be. But this it remembers, clear as winter air. Mogwen found me on the Isle of Abandoned Bombs. She had a minion with her. Small, fierce, clad in fur. Claws like sabers, teeth like whirling tines. A red mark on its chest. Blood, perhaps, or an evil rose.

"She intoned 'Kill.' The Assassin leapt. It caught my left half in its teeth. It tore my flesh away. I escaped with only my right half unscarred. And that is why I wander here, on the cold hillside."

The clouds fled in the vast and windy night. The moon carried a lonely star upon its horn.

Said the Horse Half-Dead to the Moonlit Moth: "Why you insist on shadowing me, I cannot fathom."

"It is because of what your dead side told me. I spoke to it, at midnight's stroke."

"I thought my dead side frightened you."

"When I was a callow child, yes. When I was a timorous youth, too. Now I am a bold adult, in my prime of life."

"After three days, to have attained such maturity," the Horse Half-Dead remarked drily.

"I spoke to your dead half. It is wise. I am beholden to it now. I shall follow you and know wisdom such as no moth has ever known."

"Not everything my left side says is true," the Horse Half-Dead warned. "My left side will tell you to boil nails for their rust-colored ichor, but that will only give you warts. It recommends the wrong voltage for the cyclotron. It misquotes poets. It misnames minor demons. It knows little of fish taxonomy or techniques for softening brisket. It esteems Gluck over Buxtehude. It is blind as a cave-lizard, cruel as a cancer, ignorant as a sack of stoats. There are more things in its philosophy than are dreamt of in Heaven and Earth. It speaks sorrow and fatigue and the mad world hurtling, and the void ahead, and the void behind, and the void within."

"I have a Purpose in life now," the Moth insisted. Few of his kind ever found true Purpose, or so he had learned; he was unwilling to let go of his. "I shall accompany you until you find this Fuzzlint Jackaljaws. In your life's quest, may mine find its own meaning."

"A bit sad, that. Like a lover who places all reason for living on another's existence."

"Not sad a bit," replied the Moonlit Moth. "Compare me to an archaeologist, her life's work a buried city. A biographer, on the trail of an enigmatic subject. An alchemist, squandering the unguents of life in transmutational pursuits. I am an artist whose work shall pay tribute to history."

Said the Moonlit Moth to the Horse Half-Dead: "I see a bent body on the path ahead. Topped with octoform cap, all bells chilattering."

The figure wore cap and bells bedraggled, as though he had slept in ditches. His hair was a porcupine, his eyes two dead ponds, his raiment the shroud from a horse's coffin.

"Who gives anything to Mad Kevin," he caterwauled, "whom the foul fiend has led, through muck-puddle, through landfill, past wrack of lorry and coffin-yard, who begs porridge from horses and kernels from the hen, who sleeps in the tomb while phantoms wail. By the spirit that stands by the Naked Man! Poor Kevin, though his eyes are keen, his wits have gone. His wealth has come to wail-away, and many hard zounds."

"Hail, mendicant," said the Horse Half-Dead.

"Mendicant?" Mad Kevin's eyes boggled. "I am no beggar! I held high station once. I was Fool to the Thang of Harrow, and Playmate to the Heirs. Until I failed them! Yes, they died, all my pretty chickens. Then did this poor mind break, then did poor Master Kevin cast himself on the roads to beg his bacon."

"I hear a certain Fuzzball Raggedclothes was the murderer," the Moth informed him.

"Mogwen? You speak of Mogwen Rattlejaws? It was not Mogwen, no! It was the children's Saint Golfrid's Eve gift that did the murders! A bear, child-sized, with a red heart on its chest! It gave hugs. It cooed and purred. It played hide-me-find-me. It never needed winding, nor a battery. And one night, at the height of summer, after a glorious day of where's-that-button, it murdered the helpless poppets in their nursery."

Mad Kevin broke down in a torrent of weeping. "And I could not save them!"

"A miserable accounting, Stranger," remarked the Horse Half-Dead. "But Mogwen must half-die, as revenge for the half-murder of me. Goodbye, and may you find respite in your grief."

"Stranger?" Mad Kevin's eyes danced. "But I know you, friend! At least, I know your half with the silvern hair. The other half, this is new to me."

His words were lost to the windy night as the Horse Half-Dead sped onward.

On the path behind, a hairy something came ever closer.

"Two legs," the Moonlit Moth said to himself. "Many creatures go on four legs, and many more on six. Only humans get about on two, so far as I, a naïve moth, have learnt."

Whatever their pursuer was, the Moth reflected, it was anything but human. Neither was it moth, mammal, nor anything that drew breath.

On a darkling plain the Horse Half-Dead and the Moonlit Moth reached the edge of the endlessly sighing Hainted Sea. Here was a broken wall, a toppled tower, a black window gazing blind over the waters like the socket of a skull.

"Signs of a struggle," called the Moonlit Moth from above. "Here, by this ruined garden."

"This was Harrow Hall," said the Horse Half-Dead. "That fell into ruin when the Thang died of grief."

"Here, on the grass," said the Moth. "I see a child's toy. A ball covered in stars."

"That ball," said the Horse Half-Dead. "The Heirs would have played with it."

"And look, a silver bridle, agate-spangled. Such as a Thang's steed might have worn."

The Horse Half-Dead looked stricken, and said nothing.

But he was running up a far hill now, and the Moth nearly lost sight of him. The wind caught the Moth by the wing and tossed him like a gossamer toy. Along an eddy of the night's breath the Moth tumbled, and now he was lost among gusts and vortices. The Odds and Ends stretched vast before him, and his friend was gone.

So worlds come between us, and we lose whom we would follow to the end.

Then, luck. On the crest of a far hill, the Moth spied the gleam of a horn. With all the sap left in his tiny frame, he heaved himself through the breeze-haunted dark, and with his last drop of effort, caught up to the Horse on a lonely rise under three stars.

Said the Horse Half-Dead to the Moonlit Moth: "You are slow this night."

Atop the hill, the wind moaned. The Moth bobbled on the unsteady air.

"Age is catching up with me," the Moth said. "I have spent most of my life chasing after you. I shall be dead soon."

"Age? I thought you were lately born. It's not been a week!"

"A week, yes. There's a moth's lifetime, very near."

"Among the horned-horses of the Far Riding," said the Horse Half-Dead, "they say that when a horned horse dies, he gallops towards the Starved Lands with an angel at his side."

"And where are the other horned horses found?"

"They've all galloped to the Starved Lands," the Horse Half-Dead admitted. "They've all found their guiding angels. You'll never see another of my kind. There is only one half of one of us left."

Said the Moonlit Moth to the Horse Half-Dead: "But I do see another horned horse. There, against the moon's disc. Rampant, on a field d'or. Its marble mane is flying."

The Horse looked where the Moth gestured. "That is a statue."

The Moth flew towards the monument. He called back, "It is a grave! And it is empty!"

The Horse Half-Dead read the epitaph.

"Requiescat cherished Talthybius, who died protecting his mistress."

Said the Moonlit Moth: "Resembles you, this monument. But where is the occupant?"

But the Horse Half-Dead was gone again, a shadow streaking grief-goaded through the moon's glow.

Atop the hill, backlit by that same cold light, something small and two-legged continued its pursuit.

Now they came to the farthest reaches north, the Horse Half-Dead and his companion. From the dry earth, like a sooty finger, thrust the Tower of Dangling Jaws, where Mogwen Rattlejaws dwelt.

Before the doors, the living half of the Horse Half-Dead shouted, "My enemy, come forth and show yourself!"

In a most unspectacular way, the door to the Tower opened. A knife-thin woman emerged. Mogwen Rattlejaws was a perfectly ordinary, and perfectly unterrifying, woman of about forty-five.

"Poor foolish creature," Mogwen said to the Horse Half-Dead. Her voice was gentle. There was no fear in it.

The Horse Half-Dead dipped his horn ever so slightly.

"Hail, mine enemy."

"Hail, my onetime friend. And are you here to kill me?"

"To half-kill you. As you did to me."

"And will this bring back your happiness, long since lost?"

Said the Horse Half-Dead: "I admit — the wages of revenge are scant. Satisfaction, and a feeling of purpose fulfilled. Still, it'll do my aching left half good, to know that you also are skulking around, a half-skeleton. Now, hold still while I work out how to accomplish a half-killing."

"One moment, noble steed. You have forgotten who you were, and what you've done, and who did this to you. But I believe you are starting to remember."

The Horse Half-Dead began to tremble.

"You once held high station, my friend. You were a companion for the children of Castle Harrow. Do you remember them? Asphodel, with her wide eyes, one green, one blue? Trala with her merry bow of a mouth? Don, who cried if someone sneezed? They rode on your back through the rumpled fields."

The Horse Half-Dead said nothing, but cocked his head to one side as though listening to something familiar and far away.

"It wasn't I who killed the Heirs," Mogwen said. "It was an Assassin toy. Given to the children on Saint Golfrid's Eve. It was a bear — child-sized, fur-clad, with a red heart upon its chest."

"Your minion!"

"Not mine. An infernal machine. The agent of the Thang of Candlebreak. Our own Thang's sworn enemy."

"I remember now. The Assassin cornered you in the Stone Garden. By the marble hippocampus ..."

"It would have killed me. My poor Talthybius." The Horse snorted in surprise, shaking his head. "Yes, that is your name," Mogwen said softly. "You gave me time to flee. But the monster killed you. It skeletonized you completely."

"Completely? Not halfway? Whence comes the part of me that lives?"

"You moved! Just as I applied the rejuvenal fire! Oh, poor dear. I didn't half-kill you. I half-alived you. Scrambled as you are, you've gotten it all mixed up. And now you've spent all this time hoping to do battle. Talthybius, it isn't I whom you should fight."

The Horse Half-Dead bowed his head. "I see clearly now. I must do battle with the Assassin once more, my lady."

"No, Talthybius. It's already murdered you. It's someone else's turn now. It is time for me to die."

A snarl from the shadows startled the Moth and he tumbled upwards.

The Assassin stood in the moon's embrace. It was child-tall, two-legged, harmless-seeming, or so it first appeared to the Moth. But then the moon pushed a cloud out of the way, and the Moth saw clearly. On the Assassin's claws, the moon made metal gleam. In its jaws, cruel teeth caught silver beams.

With a purr, the fiend leapt at the Horse Half-Dead.

The fight was long. When the contest was over, the Horse Half-Dead tottered and fell. The Assassin leapt upon his prone body. It sent flesh flying. It left bone bare and gleaming. The Horse Half-Dead was fully dead once more.

The Assassin righted itself. It raised its claws at Mogwen.

The Moth thought how he might intervene, but there was nothing a creature so small and frail could have done.

But the fight had been hard on the Assassin, too. Its body stiffened. A grinding of gears smote the night. The gruesome toy took a halting step. Then it fell forwards, and expired, a haze of sweetish smoke rising from its works.

The Moonlit Moth's wings chose that moment to fail

him. He spiraled to the earth, landing gently on the grass in front of Mogwen.

"The one I called friend is gone," the Moonlit Moth said faintly. "My life's lodestar is all bones again."

"It may be that he's happier now," Mogwen replied. "But come, I'll find a shoebox for you, some sugar water. We can nurse you back to health."

The bones of the Half-Dead Horse stood up. The skeletal beast tossed its maneless head. It strode gracefully up to Mogwen.

"Once more, into the place of shadows," it said, in a voice that sounded like wind through a bent trumpet.

"I can do it again," Mogwen said sorrowfully. "I can alive you. O, I will give any number of years off my life, sign whatever damnable contracts I need. To have you alive again, Talthybius, my old friend."

"No," Talthybius said, "not this time. I'm done with half-death. I am ready to be completely dead."

"Where does an all-dead Horse Half-Dead go, then?" Mogwen asked.

"I shall go to the Starved Lands, where those dead by violence travel. If there are good deeds to be done in a place like that, I'll do them."

The Horse strode away. A gossamer shape fluttered and easily caught up to it. It was the Moth's shade, like a wisp of windblown smoke.

"I've lived long, for a moth," the Moth whispered. "Now I go gently into that good night. Good friends don't let even Death keep them apart."

The fog thickened. The grass became yellow and sparse.

"There are many places for the dead to go," the Horse said. "I go to a place of anguish. There, the slain and ambushed stay; there dwell the ones that a cruel hand smote. There I'll meet the Thang and the Heirs, and together we'll await the horn of Judgement. But you, you who came to the end naturally, there are gentler ways to spend the sleep eternal."

Said the Moonlit Moth to the Horse All Dead: "I said I'd see you to the end. Though the end lies ever further, I'll seek it with one I called friend."

Ahead in the mist lay an unmarked border. Nothing living had ever crossed it, and this time, nothing living crossed it again.

Learn more about this author at:
https://www.mattamati.com/.

# TŌNO

## MELODY ALICE

WHEN ALEX HAD APPLIED for the English teaching position in Japan, she had been hoping for a placement in Tokyo, or at least Osaka. She'd wanted to be in a vibrant city where she could explore and absorb as much culture as possible. Instead, she now found herself in the small town of Tōno, far to the north on the main island and nowhere near any of the exciting clubs, cafes, and shops that she had dreamed of visiting.

It was currently summer and sweltering hot. Alex was out buying a few things from the local konbini for that night's simple dinner of nabe when she saw an unusual poster taped on the shop's window. It stood out from the rest of the flyers surrounding it, with its bright cartoon drawings of cucumbers and strange — but cute — green turtle-like animals. A fishing pole and a smiling old man were also depicted on the flyer, along with a price equivalent to only two American dollars.

Intrigued, she asked the clerk in her stilted Japanese what the flyer was for.

"Oh, do you want to go fish for kappa?"

"Kappa?"

"How long have you lived here? You haven't been to Denshoen Park yet?"

She blushed and hung her head a bit. "No. I just got here, and I'm still finding my way around."

The clerk perked up and handed her a brochure from behind the counter. The complicated kanji on the brochure made her head spin. There were some words that were vaguely recognizable to her, but the brochure had clearly not been made for overseas visitors.

Sensing her discomfort, the clerk kindly explained some of the sights, speaking slowly so Alex had time to translate in her head.

"This is the museum. You can learn about the history of Tōno. Over here is a restaurant. Do you like soba? They have very good noodles. Then, here." He tapped at a spot on the map. "In this area behind Jokenji Temple, you can fish for kappa."

Now she had a better idea of what the local area had to offer, and a little thrill of excitement went through her. This was what she had been looking for. A new experience. Something unique and fun, but also a place to cool down and relax.

She thought about her tiny apartment, and the air conditioning unit that only cooled a small section of the main room. Sitting beneath a dense canopy of trees by a cool riverbed while fishing for a nonexistent water spirit sounded perfect.

"Here," the clerk said, handing her a couple of cucumbers.

"Um … thank you?"

"You can use them to lure the kappa. No charge. Service," he said with a bright smile.

She had learned that "service" was many shop owners' way of saying "free gift" or "on the house."

"Thank you!" she said, and bowed hurriedly as she left the store. Three years of language classes and she still felt uncomfortable speaking and being understood. Academia hadn't completely prepared her for real life conversations, or the fish-out-of-water feeling that she got every time she interacted with a local.

The park wasn't far at all, just a quick bike ride away. Once there, Alex spotted the temple easily. She secured her bike and grabbed the few veggies she had picked up for dinner, along with the kappa cucumbers from the konbini, before entering the temple's nearby gift shop to rent a fishing pole.

Again, the shopkeeper was very welcoming, asking her questions about where she was from and what had brought her to this small town. She answered as best she could while some other customers and their children gaped openly at the foreigner. She got the feeling that few foreigners visited this area, and that fishing for kappa was considered a children's activity. She probably seemed very strange to them, but she was having fun for the first time in a long while.

She grinned as she took her fishing pole, now with a cucumber dangling from the end as a lure, down to the stream behind the temple. She passed no one else on her way down the path.

It was so beautiful there, with the wind rustling through the trees and the rhythmic drone of cicadas. She settled down a little way upstream from a small foot bridge and placed her cucumber lure in the water. She would explore the other side of the bridge later, but for now she just wanted to cool down and enjoy the atmosphere. The Japanese called it shinrinyoku: forest bathing.

Alex closed her eyes. Bliss — silence except for the sounds of nature. She didn't realize she had fallen asleep until she heard a faint splashing somewhere to her left.

"Kappa?" she mumbled, sitting up and looking toward the sound.

A woman stood next to the bridge, her bare feet in the water, long hair spilling over one shoulder. At the word "kappa," she turned towards Alex, an insulted and haughty look on her face. The woman was beautiful and looked to be about Alex's age. She was dressed in a traditional style, which Alex had become accustomed to seeing occasionally in the more rural parts of town.

"Oh, I'm sorry. Not a kappa." Alex blushed again at her mistake. "Of course not." She retrieved her fishing pole from where it lay at the edge of the bank, cucumber still attached.

When Alex looked back up at the woman, she saw that the stranger was now smiling demurely. Tentatively, Alex smiled back, struggling to think of something to say. She didn't want the woman to leave, but the basic greetings that she had learned and memorized years ago were suddenly forgotten, washed away by this woman's surreal beauty.

*Just say your name and ask for hers*, she scolded herself. *What is wrong with you? Get it together!*

"I'm Alex. I'm from America. What is your name?"

Silence. No change in the woman's expression.

Alex didn't do well with awkward silence, so she continued. "Do you live near here? Have you had the soba? Is it good? Would you like to go get soba with me?"

Silence.

Alex was mortified. How did basic introductions with this stranger turn into asking for a dinner date? Her cheeks flamed.

The woman giggled, a sound like tiny bells. She covered

her mouth daintily with the sleeve of her kimono as she laughed at Alex.

Alex frowned, noticing that the kimono the woman wore looked heavy and not at all seasonally appropriate; most women she'd seen had been wearing cotton summer yukata. The weather was so humid and sticky that Alex was sweating even in her light t-shirt and shorts.

The mysterious woman did not answer any of Alex's questions, but instead began walking downstream towards her. Alex wondered why she didn't just get out of the water and walk along the path. Her robe was soaked even though she lifted the bottom to walk freely, her knees and slender calves exposed and glistening as she moved.

Alex thought quickly of a way to explain away her beet red face: clearly it was sun stroke, and not an embarrassed flush. How would she say that in Japanese?

On second thought, that would make this even worse.

She covered her face in her hands and lamented her overall lack of social experience. It would get better with practice, she knew, but that wouldn't help her now. She wanted so badly for this beautiful woman to like her. To be her first friend here.

She felt cool, soft hands over hers, and slowly the woman peeled Alex's fingers back from her face and gazed down at her. She was leaning over her, her long hair creating another shaded canopy.

Alex looked at the woman's perfect heart-shaped face, staring into her eyes. She had never seen eyes such a fathomless black. The woman was still smiling that sweet smile, mouth quirking up at one side as if she had a secret.

On impulse, Alex leaned in and kissed her. She had never been so bold. She didn't know what had come over her.

Suddenly the woman locked her arms around Alex and

pulled them both back into the river. She rolled, shifting their positions, and even though the stream wasn't deep, Alex suddenly found herself beneath the woman, her head under the water. She tried to pull away from the kiss, but a sudden, stinging pain seized her. As she struggled, she looked into the woman's eyes, still open and staring at her, the fathomless black eyes unblinking and conveying no emotion. As empty as a market stall fish.

It had all happened so fast, but Alex was strong. As she thrashed against the woman, she felt their clothes become entangled, her shirt rising up, their bodies pressed tightly together.

Just as suddenly as she had been seized, the woman let her go. Alex gasped and stood up shakily in the water, prodding at her mouth where she had felt the stinging sensation. Blood came away on her hand.

The woman stood a few feet from her now, backing away slowly towards the bridge. She looked Alex up and down, as if confused.

The woman lowered herself beneath the bridge and disappeared into its shadows. Alex caught a glimpse of sharp, red-tinged teeth as the woman gave a final hiss in retreat.

Alex stood stunned at the edge of the bank for longer than was probably advisable. She should have run back to her bike, gone home to her apartment, and never thought of the strange woman again.

But that's not what she did.

She wandered home in a daze.

By the time she reached her apartment, the sun had gone down, and she realized that she had left her vegetables at the river's edge. No matter. She wasn't hungry anymore anyway.

That night, she dreamt of silky black hair that turned to seaweed and entangled her, and sharp little teeth like shells that nipped delightfully at first — then bit down hard, tearing into her flesh.

The next day, Alex found herself exhausted, distracted, and all but useless in class. Her supervising faculty, seeing her wounded lips, took pity on her and handled most of the day's lessons; Alex only stepped in once in a while to help clarify some of the English lesson. Her mouth didn't even hurt that much. The small bites on her mouth were a bit sore, but not deep and already healing. No, she was distracted for another reason entirely.

On the way home, Alex already knew that she would return to the riverbank. She had heard of yokai, monsters from folklore, but she also knew that there were hundreds of different kinds. Finding out who or what the woman was would be easier if she simply went back and asked directly.

She thought about her encounter over and over again, formulating a plan. As long as she stood far enough away from the water where she couldn't be grabbed, she would be safe. Or at least, she hoped that would be the case.

The next morning, she stopped by her school's library and checked out a children's book, an illustrated compendium of yokai.

After work, she returned to the little shop next to the temple and hurriedly paid once again for her fishing pole. She didn't buy any cucumbers this time, and the shop-keeper eyed her strangely, trying to figure out what the foreigner thought she was going to do without any bait. Eventually he gave up on trying to sell her any and let her go.

She found her bag on the bank where she'd left it. It had clearly been rifled through, and the vegetables had been tossed carelessly about, but none were sampled or damaged in any way. So her yokai didn't like vegetables.

*Ok,* she thought, as she quickly scanned the book. *That narrows it down.* She skipped over the pages featuring more fantastical and grotesque creatures. *But what if my yokai can shapeshift?*

*My yokai,* she scoffed at her presumption. *As if the demon didn't try to kill me. As if she hasn't killed who knows how many humans over how many years? Centuries?*

She was so engrossed in her research that she didn't realize she was being silently observed, until she felt a familiar gaze locked on her. She lifted her head from the book and saw the woman crouched low beneath the bridge, only head and shoulders visible above the water, hair spiraling out in tendrils.

*She let me go once before,* Alex thought. *No matter what, she's still another woman. Just be brave.*

"I told you my name last time," she began, haltingly. "You should tell me what to call you if we're going to keep meeting here. Do you *want* to keep meeting here? You won't pull me in again, right?"

She was always struggling for words, but with this strange creature, she found herself always asking for too much at once.

After a brief pause, the woman smiled. It was different from her previous one, a sharp and toothy grin. She wasn't trying to hide what she was anymore.

Alex held back a flinch, recalling how those teeth had felt both in real life and in her nightmare, the serrated teeth tearing into her.

"I'm waiting," she said to the woman. It was rude, and maybe presumptuous. What if this yokai couldn't speak?

A brief flash of annoyance crossed the woman's face, but she acquiesced and replied, "Men call me many names."

Her voice was beautiful. Alex found herself scooting closer to hear it better.

"Such as?" Alex asked, holding the book up for the woman to see, ready to flip through it to find an entry that might tell her more about this secretive and terrifying creature.

"Kawa Onago. Or Kawa Joro."

Alex recognized that name. A Kawa Onago was a river girl, an entire classification of female water spirits. But she was unfamiliar with the term "joro." She looked it up quickly on her phone, keeping an eye on the Kawa Onago to make sure she wasn't slinking any closer.

"Oh," Alex said softly, frowning. It was an outdated slur for "whore." A historical term used only for a certain type of woman in the red-light district.

"Well, no one should be calling you that anymore." Alex scowled. "You're known more commonly nowadays as a Kawahime, a water princess."

The woman — Kawahime, as Alex would now call her — looked at her curiously.

Alex held up her book. "Do you want to see?"

Kawahime looked strangely embarrassed, before recovering her usual composure and giving a quick, imperious nod. Alex leaned as close to the bridge as she dared and tossed the book the rest of the way. Kawahime grabbed it at once and stared at the picture, the book half submerged in the water with her.

*Well, I hope I can find a replacement copy of that.* She didn't want to be fired and sent home. Not after discovering this impossible, magical creature that maybe could still be her friend.

"I'm hungry. Are you hungry?" she asked.

Kawahime looked at her as if she were stupid. She probably was.

"You like meat, right? But … the book says you like eating men. What did you eat when you were human? You were human first, right? The book says that too. Geisha were supposed to be so glamorous, but I read an article once that said you weren't fed well, and many of you starved to death. They fed you very small portions of rice and it was never warm because the lower tier workers had to eat last. Is that true? No wonder you want meat."

Alex knew she was babbling again, and she clapped her hands over her mouth. Had she offended the water spirit? Kawahime was still staring at her, possibly in shock. It was hard to tell what was going on behind those bottomless black pools.

"Don't go anywhere. I'll be right back."

She ran back towards the front of the temple and hopped onto her bike. She sped past the startled kappa shop worker and raced to a nearby restaurant.

She was back with a bag of food in less than 15 minutes. She sat down with a huff near the bridge and started pulling the packaged dinners from her bag. She heard a faint ripple as Kawahime slid closer, but she pretended not to be afraid. She could do this. She *wanted* to do this.

"I didn't know which one you'd like, so I got two. I'll take the one you don't like as much, or we can share each one. I don't mind."

Kawahime was staring at her as if she were an oddity. And she supposed that here, she was — but something in the water spirit's eyes made her feel bold again.

"You can come sit next to me. I won't bite," she quipped. She was pleased when Kawahime let out an inelegant bark of a laugh, nothing like her previous seductive trill.

Alex handed over a pair of chopsticks and Kawahime took them briskly, looking back and forth between the beef bowl and pork cutlet bowl.

Alex held them both up for her to sample.

"The princess gets first choice."

Was that a light flush on Kawahime's pale cheeks, or did Alex just imagine it?

Kawahime sampled both dishes twice, with an elegant eyebrow arched at Alex, as if daring her to pull the bowls away. After an impossibly long and, Alex guessed, theatrical display of indecision, Kawahime took the pork cutlet bowl from Alex's hand.

"That's my favorite too," Alex said.

Kawahime stopped chewing, cheeks puffed out cutely, but the look on her face was horrified. She held the bowl back out to Alex.

"No! No, no, I'm sorry. I like both. I want you to have the one that you like best. It's ok. Next time, I'll bring you something even better to try."

Alex hadn't realized when, exactly, during her explanation she had reached out to reassure Kawahime, but she found herself first patting the top of her head, then rubbing the back of her neck. Patting her from nape to lower back in a long, soothing stroke.

Kawahime's body stiffened, but she didn't pull away. Instead, she slowly relaxed, leaned into Alex's touch, and continued to chew.

They ate in silence the rest of the time, their feet occasionally touching beneath the water.

As Alex watched Kawahime, her eyes wandered to the heavy, waterlogged kimono, complete with a gorgeous, chrysanthemum-patterned obi. Alex was entranced by the elaborate obijime rope that wrapped around the obi, securing it tightly to Kawahime's body. She then noticed a small gold ring hanging from the obijime cord. Alex reached out to touch the ring, thinking it odd. Geisha didn't wear jewelry in the Western sense; their ornamentation consisted mostly of hair pins of silk. A lower tier worker of the red-light district might not have even had the luxury of a hair ornament, let alone a gold band. So why was there a ring secured to a former geisha's obi?

As her finger touched the ring, Kawahime shrieked and leapt away from Alex's touch.

"What?" Alex jumped up in a panic, holding her hands in front of her to show Kawahime that she meant no harm. "What did I do? I'm sorry!"

"You … You startled me."

"Oh." Alex couldn't keep a little bit of disappointment from creeping in from that one small word. Kawahime was lying, she could tell. She wouldn't push her, but she was more curious than ever now. She stayed still, letting the other woman slowly come back and sit down next to her again.

Seeing the look on Alex's face, Kawahime sighed, and let out the words in a rush. "That ring is a bad memory that I can't remove. A gift from a client who said they loved me — but later they became angry with me and discarded me. It's a curse. Maybe the reason why I became what I am now. I don't know for sure."

It was the most words that Kawahime had spoken to her at once, and Alex accepted them in silence. Kawahime looked achingly sad — but resigned to her fate.

Alex reached out to touch the water spirit's fingertips. Kawahime clasped their hands together, and for a long moment, the two just stayed like that.

Eventually, Alex had to pull away.

"I have to go home. I have work tomorrow, but I'll be back again in the evening, ok?" Kawahime nodded, smiling her sharp smile that Alex was growing to love, before disappearing into the shadows of the bridge. Alex walked back up the path to her bike, happier than she had ever been in her life.

She couldn't stop the grin that spread across her face as she thought about how amazing the day had been.

*That was nothing like the first time. She was completely different. I know her name now, and her secret.*

On her journey home, she came upon a familiar red lantern hanging outside an akachōchin a few blocks away from her apartment. A quick beer or shochu from the tiny bar would cool her down and help her sleep.

Her smile quickly faded as she saw that the only other customers were one older Japanese couple who seemed to be gathering their belongings to leave, and a group of loud, young male foreigners. One of the young men glanced at her, looked her up and down, laughed, and whispered something to his table mates. The whole table started snickering.

Alex sat down quickly at the seat closest to the bartender and said, "One biiru, onegaishimasu," while pointing to a bottle of Kirin on the shelf. The bartender smiled and handed her the cold beer while glancing back at the boys' table somewhat frostily.

It wasn't what she had planned on ordering, but she had spotted it first. Not wanting to retreat and show any weakness, but also wanting to get her drink and get the hell out of there, she began to down the beer as quickly as she could. The foamy liquid felt good going down her throat, and as she cooled down, her thoughts drifted back to her dinner date with Kawahime.

"Something good happen to you today?" the bartender whispered to her.

"Hai! Yes, very good," she answered easily.

Her bubble of happiness once again burst as she overheard one of the young men say, "I know right? Like, we don't come all the way here to see girls who look like that."

She placed her money on the counter, smiling and thanking the bartender, and quickly left the bar, fumbling a bit to unlock her bike from the rack. She was in such a hurry that she didn't see the man smoking against the side of the building, the same one who had looked at her when she'd first walked in.

"So, like, what the hell are you?" he called out to her.

She turned, startled, and dropped her key. Snatching it up, she stared back at him, holding eye contact.

"What?" she asked.

"American? Canadian? French? Parlez-vous français?" He grinned.

"Oh. I'm American," she answered, feeling a bit foolish.

"No shit. I knew that already, dummy. I'm asking, what are you? A boy? A girl?"

He was openly mocking her. Playing with her.

Instead of answering, she got on her bike and rode off.

His laughter followed her for an entire block. "Aw, I'm sorry. Come on. I just want to play with you a bit."

She was thankful that her apartment had a storage room just for bikes. If the creep followed her or came this way, he wouldn't see her bike and know where she lived. Maybe she should have gone to a police box and reported the incident, but as a foreigner having difficulty with another foreigner, it would be hard to convey. Besides, he had a group of friends with him to back him up, and she had no one.

But as she slipped into bed, not even the bullies could tarnish her memories of the time she'd spent with Kawahime. Despite the unpleasant incident at the bar, the cold beer had indeed helped settle her down enough for sleep.

It wasn't until she was just about to drift off that she remembered something strange. As she'd felt her way along the skin of Kawahime's graceful neck, she'd found a rough patch. She'd been startled by it because the rest of Kawahime's skin had been so smooth, almost like scales.

She wondered if Kawahime had scales — and if so, where? She went to reach for the book before remembering that Kawahime had taken it. Where it had gone, and whether it was damaged beyond repair, Alex felt she would never know.

Much to the delight and amusement of the kappa shop owner, who hardly ever had customers for the kappa fishing rental, Alex returned every evening to rent her fishing pole and buy a variety of snacks.

Her visits with Kawahime became a routine. She always brought new snacks for the water spirit to try, and learned that Kawahime loved croquettes and hated sweets. She was always hungry and pale, but seemed content to try everything that Alex offered up to her. Still, it felt as if Kawahime wasn't satisfied with only the food that Alex brought to her.

Alex also knew now that Kawahime did indeed have scales on the back of her neck that trailed down her spine and shone like abalone in the light. She would catch glimpses as Kawahime flung her long, heavy hair over her shoulder, exposing the back of her neck. And Kawahime knew now that Alex was definitely a woman and that she had no scales.

Alex had been visiting for long enough now that she knew that no one ever came to this part of the trail at this time. One day, months after the incident at the bar, she was shamelessly forest bathing in the nude as she read to Kawahime from the latest romance novel that the water spirit was obsessed with. They lounged together in the water, so wrapped up in each other that neither of them heard the man approach.

Alex heard a disgusted scoff and looked over to see the bully from the bar staring at her.

"Well, I guess this finally answers that question," he huffed, briefly looking away from Alex to Kawahime as she sunk lower in the water to retreat from him.

He was drunk. He must have followed her.

Their confrontation had been so long ago. She had almost forgotten.

*Careless,* she cursed herself.

Kawahime pulled at Alex's arm frantically and pointed towards the path.

"Alex, run!" she hissed, disappearing half into her cave.

The man was now sloshing into the water, reaching out to grab Alex.

Alex hated the frightened look on her friend's face. She was Kawahime. A yokai. An ancient monster. So beautiful and fierce when Alex had first encountered her.

She looked back at the man. He'd almost reached her.

"Kawahime?" she asked.

Kawahime cocked her head at Alex.

Alex pointed at the man, and said simply, "Tonight's dinner."

Kawahime stared at Alex, black eyes larger than ever and her mouth hanging open in shock. But as Alex smiled down at her, she returned the smile with her own terrible sharp one. She shot out from beneath the bridge so fast that the man didn't even have time to inhale for a scream before she pulled him underneath the bridge. One second he was there — the next, both he and Kawahime were gone. Alex could only see bubbles rising from beneath the bridge, which eventually stopped altogether.

When Kawahime finally emerged from beneath the bridge, she looked shy somehow, just the top of her head peeking out above the water. Her eyes peered out from the dark, shiny black beads that Alex now saw so much life and warmth in.

"It's ok. I'm here."

Alex leaned down to the water, and the two clasped hands and touched foreheads beneath the moonlight. Kawahime looked more beautiful than ever, her skin warm and flushed.

Alex got to her feet and pulled Kawahime up out of the water. The two laughed, and as Alex went to hug her friend, she felt her small body flinch away from her.

"Sorry." Kawahime said. "The ring. I don't like it touching you. It's a hateful thing that I'll never be rid of."

"Maybe *you* can't remove that ring, but I bet I can."

Alex began yanking at the obijime cord. It was like razor wire, so delicate but impossibly strong. It slashed at her until her fingers were shredded and bloody.

"Stop!" Kawahime cried.

But Alex wouldn't stop until Kawahime was free of her pain.

She used her teeth, yanking at the ring until eventually, miraculously, she felt the threads give way and the cold metal of the ring fall into her mouth.

Alex spat the ring out. After a quick glance at the ancient, unremarkable thing, she tossed it over her head and into the woods like the trash it was.

Kawahime stood speechless, her kimono open, restricting belt fallen to the ground.

She let out that unladylike bark of a laugh, slipped out of her kimono, and splashed into the water naked, shining and beautiful beneath the moonlight. Just a girl playing in the water, free from her heavy soaked garments for the first time since she died all those years ago.

⁂

Learn more about this author at:
https://www.melodyalicevo.com/author.

# PROJECT: WOLFSBANE

## PETE BARNSTROM

THE POET JOHN MILTON once wrote: "They serve also who only stand and wait."

Milton never served in the United States Army.

I, on the other hand, was stationed behind a typewriter on a nice, quiet base camp near the Russian border. The supplies depot was my beat. I was so far from the action, Hitler might as well have been the Easter Bunny, and about as threatening.

If the Milton quote didn't tip you off, I'm a literary kind of guy. But the only writing I was doing those days involved requisition orders and inventory reports.

Still, I was gathering some wool over some story idea or another when I heard my name barked by Major Forbush.

It is difficult to snap to attention while filling out a 42K5.1 invoice (in triplicate!). But the Major insisted on both hearing the typewriter clacking at all times and the strict observation of formal officer protocol, so I did my best. I stood and I slapped a hand at my eyebrow in mid-sentence. I had to strike the hard return with my left, but I managed.

"Sir?"

"Bring my vehicle," he snapped. He might've been in a bad mood, but I never saw him in a good one. "I'm meeting Colonel Meechump at the Officer's Club."

The way the buttons on that uniform jacket strained, he might've benefitted from a walk across the base, but I wasn't going to be the one to suggest it.

Besides, despite his use of the possessive, I considered that Jeep my own. Other officers drove themselves, but the Major liked to look important, so I tooled him around in it at least twice a day. I'd never owned a car before, and behind the wheel, I felt like a bit of a big shot myself.

It was cold out, and already gray, but it was always cold and gray at this latitude. The sort of countryside that inspires people to invent vodka. Snow dusted the flat hood of the Jeep as I pulled it around.

The top was buttoned up. No heater, but at least it blocked the wind. I'd have liked to sit inside for a bit, but I knew the Major was in the office waiting for me. I opened that door for him walk out, then another when he climbed into the vehicle. I never asked — and would not get the chance later — but I suspected he came from money, and had gotten this sort of service all his life.

I let him out again at the Officer's Club. The place had a bar, of course, and its own kitchen. No Mess Hall slop for the top dogs, no sir.

The Captain never invited me in to sample the wares, but I had my wiles. In back, the kitchen door always stood open, sweaty heat rolling out to fight the outside chill.

"Hola, Rojo," Mata boomed out as he saw me, showing me his magnificent teeth. He moved to make me a plate.

Mata had a soft spot for me, always ready with the evening special. If I had to consort with a snobby officer, at least I could eat like one.

Mata returned with a steaming meal, and even more

steam rose from his bare shoulders. Like most of the kitchen staff, he'd stripped off his uniform shirt before strapping on his apron, and the competing atmospheres combined to make him a walking fog.

As fine a cook as he was, Mata was wasted in a kitchen. He should've been out there striking terror into every Nazi heart on the front line. He was the largest man I'd ever seen. Just the sight of him would be enough to send them screaming back to Führer.

But as I sniffed the Chicken Kiev he placed on the counter before me, I was glad he wasn't out there crushing Third Reich heads between his enormous, blocky hands. This smelled like the promise of heaven with a side of gravy.

I tied a towel around my neck to protect my own uniform, and I remarked, "Mata, my man, you are an artist."

He showed me those teeth again, every one of them as large as a domino. He rubbed a hand over my carroty crewcut like a proud father. "Eat up, little Rojo! Put some meat on those arms!"

The potatoes au gratin weren't going to my arms, but I savored each bite anyway. "You have got to open a restaurant when we get back home. I know a little place in Cincy you could get for a song!"

"Gracias, Rojo," he said. "But your home is not my home." His accent had made that clear already, but he was drafted into the same Army I was, so Mata was aces by me.

He leaned in, confidential. "Besides, I already have a calling I must follow."

First I'd heard of this. "There's something you do better than cooking? I'd like to see that!"

His smile now showed no teeth, and felt just a little mysterious. "I shall have to show you sometime."

I nodded as my own teeth crunched a crisp asparagus spear, and how did he find asparagus way out here? I would've been the one to write the forms for it. Those officers had it good.

The next morning, I'd barely gotten to my desk when the Major barked at me to bring his vehicle around. Seemed a little early for the Officer's Club, but in service to this man's army, ours is not to wonder why.

There were Jeeps outside the place when we got there. This was more than a dawn cocktail with Colonel Meechump, I gathered. I opened his door and the Major stomped inside without waiting for me to open the next one.

I'd already had my breakfast, but I didn't want to wait out in the cold, so I made my way around to the kitchen. The door was open, but at this hour, it wasn't so warm inside. It wasn't lit, either. I guessed they didn't do eggs and toast here.

Water hissed into a soapy sink, dishwashing abruptly abandoned. I stepped past it, looking into the dark. From somewhere nearby, I heard the murmur of voices.

Deeper in, I could make out a trace of light, the outline of a square in the dark. It must've been a closed hatch in a wall, probably for passing plates; one way full, the other way empty. Were the voices on the other side of that?

Then I saw movement, a black shape in front of the thin light. I froze, waiting for my eyes to adjust, uncertain if I should say anything.

A voice on the other side of the hatch got loud enough that I could make out a word. "Poppycock!" The voice belonged to Major Forbush. Also the phrase; of all the stuffed shirts in the camp, only his was stuffed enough to say that.

I snickered, I'll admit, and the black shape stiffened. It swung around at me, and I could make out a face in the shadows.

"Mata?"

"Rojo!" he whispered. He flashed his usual smile, but something was off about it, an uncertainty I'd never seen there.

I opened my mouth to say something more, but he put his finger to his lips and bustled me back out to the sink. It had not overflowed, but there was enough water and suds to wash a springer spaniel in it, had there been one around. He left it running while we talked.

"What goes on here, amigo?" I questioned.

"It's nothing, my friend. *Soy metiche*, that's all. Just nosy."

"Nosy about what?" I saw a paper scrap in his hand, and I snatched it before he could take it away from me.

He'd written something on it. *Wolfsbane*.

"Wolfsbane? What's that? Some sort of plant, isn't it?" I'd heard the word somewhere before.

His smile looked strained. "An ingredient for a new recipe, Rojo, that's all."

He put one big hand on my shoulder, maybe to reassure me, maybe to keep me from running. I'd never really had reason to consider it before, but Mata could snap me like a fresh-picked green bean.

A Jeep engine started outside, and I ducked out from under his arm. "Gotta drive the Major back to the office," I told him. "I'll see you later."

Mata nodded as I backed away, his big domino-smile widening. "Of course, Rojo. We'll talk soon, yes?"

I got to the Jeep before Major Forbush stepped from the

Officer's Club. He was talking with Colonel Meechump. Neither acknowledged my salute.

"I don't know, Forbie," the Colonel was grumbling. "The orders came straight from the top."

"Poppycock," the Major said again, and I managed not to snort this time. My saluting arm was wearing out, though. "I've never heard anything so ridiculous in my career!"

The Colonel slung me an indifferent salute, and I let my arm drop with relief. "We should be on guard all the same," he said, starting away.

The Major raised his eyebrow, skeptical, and he said, "Against what? Boogiemen?"

The Colonel turned back, his own eyebrows lowered, and Major Forbush added a quick, "Sir."

He climbed into the Jeep as the Colonel left.

As I started the engine, I asked, "Poppycock, sir?"

"Shut up, Private."

Back at the requisitions depot, the Major closed himself away in his office and left me to my typing. We were still an afternoon away from his Officer's Club cocktail hour, and I had work to do.

But I needed to look into something first.

I tugged a drawer from the filing cabinet and fingered my way through the folders, looking for the "M" tab.

Mata's accent. I'd assumed it was Mexican, but what do I know from Mexican? There were plenty of soldiers serving from down near the border. Texas, Arizona, California. He could have an accent, sure.

Had I ever seen him in uniform? Had I ever even seen him outside of the kitchen? Could I even be sure he was a soldier? Maybe he was brought in as a special chef, just for the officers, but it had me puzzled.

Then I discovered the missing piece of that puzzle. Or, rather, didn't discover it.

The files had no one named Mata stationed at this post.

Lights out, and I was in the barracks, sliding into my bunk. Up above me, Private Heely was already deep into his mortar-fire snores. The man might've been an enemy agent with the racket he made, out to keep our fightin' men up all night so we couldn't perform in the morning.

But I couldn't believe that of Mata, no matter what I saw.

I should've told Major Forbush, I knew. That's what a good soldier would do. But if there was one thing I was not, it was a good soldier. I'd always been told I had a mulish streak. I'd have argued with it, but that would just prove the point.

I had to go with my instinct. No one who could cook like that could be an enemy of the land of plenty. Just think what he could do with those amber waves of grain.

Then again, most of his recipes did seem to be foreign. Chicken Kiev, Mushroom Risotto, oh, that Boeuf Bourguignon with crunchy *pain de campagne* ...

His menu must have rocked me to sleep despite Heely's honking. Reason I know this is because I woke to night air, blinded by cloth over my head, under the arm of a giant.

"Hey!"

"Sorry, Rojo." He was running, carrying me like a football. Without stopping, he pulled a pillowcase off my head and lifted me up to eye-level. "Don't worry, you're safe as a babe in my arms."

"Yeah, but I'm no baby!" I said. "What is this?"

He nodded, still running, but he didn't explain. Instead, he tossed me over his shoulder and ran faster.

I wasn't bound, except by his thick arm, but I dared not squirm for fear of falling. "Mata! Stop! What are you doing?"

I noticed that, for the first time I'd ever seen, Mata was wearing clothes. I also noticed that I was wearing nothing but my skivvies, tangled in my blanket.

When he came to a stop, we were outside the requisitions depot. "What are you doing? Why are we here?" I got enough of this place during waking hours.

He put me down, icy slush seeping into my socks. I danced a little against the cold. "It's freezing out here!"

"Oh, right." Mata dropped some boots in front of me. "I brought these for you."

Turns out, they were Heely's boots, not mine, and he had feet like a duck, but at least they weren't too small. I got them on, blanket tight around me.

"Your Jeep," he said. "We need it." He pointed to the door to the depot. "Get the keys."

"Are you crazy?"

"Trust me, Rojo."

"Trust you? How?" I resisted the urge to poke a finger into his chest. "You were spying!"

He tilted his big head. "I was listening to them. They finally got word that it was happening, and I had to know."

I squinted at him. "Know what?"

He considered a moment, then nodded. "Project Wolfsbane."

"The plant?"

"It's a codename." He pointed at the door. "Get the keys."

"What do you mean, codename?"

"*Las llaves*, Rojo!"

I got the keys. I'd get court-martialed for it, I knew, but I got the keys.

Once inside the Jeep, he directed me into the forest that surrounded the base. Moonglow slid through branches, barely enough for me to steer between the trees. "What do you mean, codename?" I asked again.

"Nazi alchemists have finally discovered it, the serum that turns their soldiers into invincible monsters." He looked through the windshield, not at me, probably because he didn't want to see my look of disbelief. "Project Wolfsbane."

"Uh-huh." I shook my head, the path before me too complicated for me to glare at him. "What's that mean?"

"What it means, my friend," Mata intoned, "is that Hitler now has werewolves."

After a bit, the road became impassable, even for the Jeep. We'd have to walk the rest of the way.

Mata told me that he'd been watching the brass, waiting for the moment to move. When they finally heard the word Wolfsbane, he knew it was time.

"What are we about to see?" Don't get me wrong, I wasn't for a minute buying the idea that there was an occult German menace in these woods. But I did remember a movie with Claude Rains. Some big guy turning hairy, still dressed in his shirt and pants. I wondered if Mata thought that was what was going on here.

That was where I'd heard the word before, I suddenly recalled. That movie. Wolfsbane blooms. A poem of some sort, a line about a full moon.

I looked up and saw the fat face of the moon, all of it,

big and round. I shivered, but it was the cold, nothing more.

"If we are in time," Mata told me, voice low, "we will see soldiers preparing to inject this Nazi serum." He stepped a few more silent steps. "If we are not, what you see will be burned into your mind for the rest of your life."

On time, not on time, I just wanted it to be quick. It was all I could do to keep my teeth from chattering.

Mata noticed. "You are cold, my friend? Here." He stripped off his heavy jacket, draped it over my shoulders. It fit like a circus tent, but it retained his body heat.

That's when I saw he'd been wearing nothing under it. He was bare chested now, not even the undershirt he'd worn in the kitchen, and again steam rose from his skin. I guess it wasn't just the kitchen humidity that created the fog around him.

There was light ahead, faint voices. Mata put his hand out, stopping me, and moved ahead. He got to a fallen tree, crouched low, lifted his head over it to look.

*How quickly could I get back to the Jeep if I needed to run?* I wondered. There were no human-shaped wolves down there, I knew, but in these boots, I wasn't sure I could outrun even clean-shaven Nazis.

Mata looked back, beckoned to me. I'd come this far, might as well humor him. I went to him. I wasn't happy about it.

I peered over the dead tree trunk and saw a low area, clear of trees, a huge bonfire in the middle of it. In a small encampment, men lined up at a table where an old man with a pointed beard and a white lab coat stood with tubes and beakers.

The men wore brown shirts, but despite the cold, they were taking them off and folding them carefully. The sleeves had red bands around them.

Up until that moment, I'd more than half-believed Mata was *loco*. But no, I was seeing my first Nazis.

"The *Wolfwaffen!*" Mata intoned.

Down below, the old guy jabbed a needle into one of the men, and I could see by the way others were rubbing their shoulders that he'd already gotten to them.

"We are too late," Mata whispered to me. "But we retain the element of surprise."

He backed away from the log, but I was transfixed. Could this really be what my giant friend had suggested? Men who turn into animals?

But by the time I looked around to ask him, there were other questions I felt needed addressing.

The big man's wide back was to me. He had pulled off his twill pants, and in their place I saw shiny tights, the kind a particularly flashy circus strongman would wear. And he had pulled something over his face, his strong arms snugging laces behind his head.

When he turned, I saw it was a silvery mask, holes for his eyes, nose, and mouth. As I looked up at him, he slung a silver cape over his shoulders in a dramatic arc, affixing it under his chin. Where he'd been carrying all this stuff, I didn't know.

"Um," I started, but that's as far as I got.

He put his hand out, open to reveal a chrome-plated pistol. The revolver looked almost small in his giant palm. "You will need this."

"Who? Me?" I'd had the usual weapons training, of course, but I'd never fired at anyone. I wasn't sure I could.

"The bullets are of the purest silver," he told me. "Six of them, each bathed in holy water and inscribed with arcane Latin symbols to ensure their accuracy."

Silver. I remembered that movie again, something about

how silver stops a wolf-man. I wondered if a silver mask had the same effect.

Mata, or whoever he was now, pushed the pistol into my hand, wrapped my fingers around it. "Keep track of the rounds as you fire."

"Sure," I managed to say. "Silver isn't cheap."

He shook his huge, masked head. "You must save one," he said. "For me. Or for yourself."

For myself?

There was a sound from below. It reminded me of my grandmother boning a chicken for soup, snaps and pops, bones separating from joints and meat.

I looked down there and saw one of the fair-haired men on the ground, body convulsing. His arms and legs moved in directions no human limbs were intended to move, wrists twisting inward and stretching, knees bending backward. His screams were what you hear in the night and tell yourself it's just feral cats going at it, because you don't want to think about what else they might be.

The Nazi's bare chest bulged, grew, ribs threatening to burst from taut flesh. The skin darkened. I thought it was bruising, but it was soon evident that it was hair, fur pushing from his pores, every follicle growing thick bristles.

As horrible as that all was, it was his face that still haunts me, just as Mata said it would. The agony in his features was slowly replaced by primal rage. His jaw distended, his brow pressed out into a bone shelf, a long snout puffed clouds into the cold night air.

And finally, teeth and claws, visible even at this distance, long and sharp and hungry.

He did not look like the guy in that Claude Rains movie.

So hypnotized was I by this display that it was only then, when it was over, that I noticed his associates. Shirtless blond men, watching this unnatural transformation in open horror, witness to what awaited them.

I'd never been much for needles anyway, but I was glad I hadn't gotten that stuff pumped into my arm.

"Maybe you should take this," I mumbled, passing the gun back to the big man beside me. He was going to need it.

There came a short bark of a laugh from inside the mask, and he pushed my hand back. "I require no weapons."

He clenched his great fists, and I heard cracking almost as loud as what had come from inside that poor German soldier.

More of the men were falling now, convulsing, and the colossus at my side leapt to his feet. The ground did not shake, I knew. It must have been me.

"Now, my friend!" he cried. "We strike while they are distracted!"

*We?* Surely he didn't expect me to follow?

A flash of silver, and the huge man was over the log and in the air, plummeting into the clearing below. His boots crashed onto the table, smashing the glass equipment, an explosion of liquid and shards.

The old doctor-type fell back, but rebounded pretty spryly for a mad scientist of his years. He produced a Luger from under his white lab coat and pointed it at the masked man I once knew as Mata.

His huge, bare arm swung almost casually, and the pistol flew one direction, the old guy another. The man in the mask never took his eyes off the monsters on the ground.

He seized at the first one, but a clawed hand clutched at his leg, pulling him down, and he kicked a heel back. More of the mutating forms moved at him, and he sprang to his feet.

So did the things around him, if what they had could rightly be called feet.

The revolver gleamed in my hand. No way to aim from this distance. I knew I should climb down. I should act. We could stop this menace before it started, before it was too late.

The giant in silver swung the broken table, sending beasts tumbling and yowling. More lunged at him.

All but one.

A pair of bestial eyes, reflecting firelight, glaring, golden.

Looking right at me.

I dropped the pistol and ran.

Was it chasing me? I don't know. I just ran through the dark forest (what had happened to that moonlight that guided us here?) and there were sounds and smells and I just ran.

If I'd been smart, I'd have held onto the gun. If I was smarter, I'd have run to the Jeep. But I wasn't smart. I just ran.

My oversized boot snarled in something, and I fell, my foot ripping completely out of it. My knee hit a stone, or maybe it was a root, I couldn't know. I did not stop. I kept running.

In time, the pain caught up with me, and I was forced to lean against a tree, unable to stand. I huffed for a moment, then stopped, not breathing.

There were noises, movement in the night. The usual forest sounds? Or something sinister, evil, unstoppable, coming straight for me? I couldn't know.

I hopped on, one foot covered, one bloody and aching, my knee barely supporting my weight. It was only by dumb luck that I found the base.

The luck ended there. Some other creature had found it before me.

Buildings destroyed, canvas shredded, vehicles over-turned. I heard no voices, no shouts, no moans of pain.

I would later learn that no one survived. Later, because when the medics got to me, I was unconscious and sprawled in the middle of the PT yard. How I survived the night, I cannot guess.

They mustered me out for the knee injury. The brass informed me that there'd been a bombing, nothing more, and that whatever I'd seen in the woods had been halluci-nations induced by shell shock.

Fine. All that mattered was getting out.

I never saw my friend Mata again. But I did hear stories from south of the border, stories about a man in silver. A fighter, a wrestler, hero to the people. That was the official record.

But the legends, ah, such legends! It was said that he battled vampire women, evil magicians, enemy spies, and, yes, werewolves. If you believe such things.

I didn't, of course. Still don't. But should you ever wander south and come across a giant of a man in a silver mask ... ask him to make you a big bowl of his Spaghetti Carbonara.

Don't ask him about Hitler's werewolves.

# A BRAND-NEW MORNING
## MIA DALIA

*for Chelsea*

"Wake up, sleepyhead. Wake up."

My wife's voice cuts through the fog of sleep, and for a moment I find myself in that liminal space between dream and awareness. I want to linger there, safe in between the sleeping and waking worlds, but she shakes my shoulder, gently but definitively letting me know that part of the morning is over.

I open my eyes and wait for them to focus. When they do, I blink again; what I see makes no sense.

My wife has changed overnight. There might as well be a stranger in my bed now, speaking to me in *her* voice, observing me with oversized saucer eyes attached to delicate stalks. The eye color remains the same sky blue I fell in love with, but the pupils are vertical slits. The stranger has thick, full eyelashes like hers, only abbreviated in length. Combined with the complete lack of eyebrows, the effect is bewildering.

She moves closer to me, her body strangely etiolated

and slinky. I find myself leaning away instinctively, then immediately feel ashamed.

"You've been sleeping the day away," she says, smiling. Or maybe not smiling — it's difficult to tell. Beneath her eyes, her facial features are just thin lines, like an unfinished drawing. But the voice is unmistakably recognizable.

I close my eyes, willing myself to wake up again. Surely, this is just a dream. A very detailed, very real-feeling one, but a dream all the same.

I've been under some stress, but not *that* much. I'm no stranger to nightmares owing to a reading diet heavy with psychological thrills and scares, but those are usually more … removed. This feels so present.

When I open my eyes, my wife — this strange new version — is still there, looking at me with what I swear is bemusement. Her old face would have arched an eyebrow. I roll away from her, needing a moment to adjust.

Ever since we bought this new mattress, I've had difficulty getting out of bed. I have jokingly described it as Tempur-Pedic by the way of foam mixed with quicksand. Now it feels like *real* quicksand. As I shift away from my wife, I realize that I am slowly sinking in. I really am. Down I go.

I panic, but she reaches to pull me up. Her hand is a tentacle.

That's when I lose it. I splash around until I'm free of the bed and free of her grasp. With a thud, I fall to the floor.

She draws her tentacle back, looking concerned. Or maybe upset.

Shame floods me, and I lower my gaze … only to realize that the floor is lava.

No, wait — it can't be, that's a stupid kids' game. My cousin Jer broke his ankle playing it when we were eight and he made a particularly ambitious leap from the dining table to the couch.

Back then, we had to use our imaginations to transform the dated shag carpeting into magma. Now I don't need to. It's right beneath me, molten hot and starting to burn.

With a startled shriek, I jump back onto the bed.

"You're acting very weird this morning," my wife observes.

"I ... I'm ..." I can't find words. I shake my hair out of my eyes and try to make sense of things that don't make any.

She reaches out and places her tentacle on my shoulder, attempting to pull me in for a hug. That's nice, I could use a hug, but I'm afraid to find out what her new skin feels like. It looks scaly and lightly slimy beneath her traditional at-home attire of a tank top and shorts.

"What ... what happened?" I croak. There used to be a glass of water on the night table. It's still there, but the water looks green. I don't dare to drink from it.

"What do you mean?" she asks innocently.

I make a vague all-around-me nodding gesture. "Everything is different."

"Everything is different every day, silly." I see the lines on her face rearrange themselves into a curious expression. *Ah*, I think, *that* is *a smile*. "That's life for you."

I shake my head. "Not like this."

"I think you must have slept funny." She scratches her ear, which is now, I notice, pointy. "Want some breakfast? Coffee?"

I nod. What else can I do?

She gets up and walks to the kitchen. I follow in her footsteps, pulling up my saggy pajama bottoms. The floor singes the soles of my feet without burning them.

She's still the same height, exactly three inches shorter

than me. *A perfect height difference,* she used to say. *I don't want to crane my neck to kiss you.*

Last night, before bed, I kissed her. We were too tired to fool around — the move has really taken it out on us. The last month, it seems, has been nothing but an endless cycle of packing, unpacking, and cleaning.

We save just enough energy for work, but outside of that, we zombie-shuffle through our days, gratefully collapsing into our brand-new bed in the evenings.

The move brought changes into our lives. Everything is new and it is taking some getting used to.

This house is too big, this neighborhood is too quiet, our new furniture is suspiciously comfortable. I keep telling myself that this is the dream. We've talked about it, imagined it, saved for it. And now that it's here, I'm too tired, too confused to appreciate it.

All I see are drawbacks and negatives. My natural critical mind makes me good at my job as an actuary, but crap at life. People like positivity, optimism, half-full glasses, and all that. Not really my thing.

My wife says she doesn't mind my dark cloud of a personality, but I'm sure it takes its toll. She has always had an easier relationship with happiness. Like with the move, for instance. She's happy with the house — happy with the neighborhood and the furniture and all the other changes. Happy in all the easily recognizable ways — or at least, they used to be recognizable. Now I don't recognize *her* anymore.

I don't recognize this house, either. It's looking stranger this morning. There's something newly organic about the walls, something animated about the windows. The way the light comes in and lingers — it seems so alive.

The things that are meant to be steady, sturdy, and lifeless are suddenly anything but.

I read Kafka's *Metamorphosis* a long time ago, when I went through my "serious book" phase. I understood it as a commentary on the soullessness of bureaucracy and commercialism. But my wife isn't some bureaucrat — so what's *her* transformation all about?

I don't know how to ask; talking has never been my finest skill. Or timing, for that matter. In my experience, in most situations, it's easier to say nothing, to roll with the punches. I suppose the Stoics did always appeal to me.

It's my plan to roll with the punches here too. We've made vows, and I take them seriously. I'm not going anywhere. If life has stopped making sense, maybe it's simply time for a new playbook.

She's quite adept in the kitchen with her tentacles. They are long, and flexible, purple-pink with delicate white suckers along the sides. Currently, they're scrambling eggs to go with my scrambled brains.

"I had the strangest dream," she tells me. "We were living a completely different life. In this weird, boxy house."

Before my eyes, the discarded eggshells reconstitute themselves into a Humpty Dumpty-looking creature and proceed to climb off the kitchen counter. I can't tell if my wife notices it.

She shuts off the fire and pours the eggs onto our plates. The eggs are green, and I am tempted to ask for ham, but I don't. Of course, I don't. We are a vegetarian household.

My wife slices some rye from the breadbox, holds them up, and breathes at them lightly. Flames emerge from her mouth, briefly enough to leave me wondering if I imagined it. She places the lightly browned — just how we like it — toast onto our plates. Then, she whirls around and gets the jam. Apricot for me, raspberry for her. Fifteen years together and we have never agreed on the jam.

Breakfast is served. If I ignore my wife's new body and the ghoulish color of the eggs, this would be a perfectly idyllic scene. There's even chirping outside our window, though it sounds like no chirping I have ever heard. The notes are lower, screechier. I'm afraid to see what sort of a creature they might belong to, so I don't look closely out the window. I glance just long enough to see that the sky is still there. It's no longer blue, but, to be fair, the orange-ish tint looks quite fetching. There are no clouds, though. I would have liked to see some clouds.

My wife makes small talk — work, then more about her dream.

"You should have seen how silly you looked in my dream," she says.

I almost choke on my toast.

She frowns at me, as if wanting to ask what's wrong with me. Then she shakes her head a little, jiggling her eye stalks. "Have you given any more thought to the dog thing?" she asks, changing the subject. "Wanna look at the rescue website again?"

That's all we've done so far — looked online. Dogs are photogenic to a fault, it seems. Every single one on the rescue website looks adorable.

I don't trust it. But I look again anyway as my wife holds up her phone so we can both see.

I'm glad to find out her smartphone still looks very much the same — a rectangular screen. But the creatures she shows me on it look nothing like what dogs are supposed to.

Too many limbs. Too many eyes.

"Maybe not today, hon," I say mildly, trying not to offend. I know I've been dragging my feet on this, but haven't we been through enough changes already? We don't even have a budget put together for this new house.

The chair squirms under me, almost bucking me off. Startled, I jump up to look at it. It looks just like all our recently-bought dining chairs: sturdy, unimaginative, wooden ladderback things. But as I watch, it squirms once more and starts hopping from leg to leg (foot to foot?) as if stretching. Then it walks away.

"That one's been doing that," my wife says. "Here, sit here instead." Good thing we have a set of four.

I force myself to finish my breakfast. If I ignore the disturbing hue of the eggs, they're actually quite good. After a few bites, I don't even have to force them down anymore.

"Are you okay?" my wife asks. Her stalked eyes rotate to take me in. There's kindness in her voice. "I know it's been a lot for you."

I sigh. Nod my head. Reach for her. Our tentacles intertwine. "I love you," I say.

"I love you too."

That's all that matters, I tell myself. The rest will sort itself out.

Connect with this author on Twitter at:
https://twitter.com/Dalia_Verse.

# THE WALRUS WHISTLES AT MIDNIGHT

## REBECCA A. DEMAREST

MY OFFICE HAD a cheap water view: wet, miserable, and silty. The expensive office spaces were all above water, with views of the sky, and — on good days — land. We folks who barely made rent on time were relegated to the bottom tiers of Station 27, where the world outside was murky and dark.

It was a great void to stare into when you were trying to figure out how you were going to solve your money problems — which was what I was doing when *he* came into my office. He didn't even bother to knock.

He was tall for a Stationer; most of our gene stock came from the shorter-than-average personnel who had been on board the station when all hell broke loose on the mainland decades ago. His hair was on the long side, with a tendency to fall into his eyes. I remembered what it had been like to brush it out of the way of that sad, puppy-dog gaze.

I didn't bother to stand. "Thomas."

"Gina." My name sounded just as good in his mouth as I remembered, a warm sigh that trailed off like he wished it wasn't so short. I thought about waiting for him to get to the point of the visit, but patience had never been my strong suit.

"I told you I never wanted to see you again. Which begs the question: what are you doing slumming on my tier?" I leaned forward to prop myself on the desk, pretending nonchalance in an attempt to keep myself from crossing my arms protectively across my body. "Did Mummy Ghert finally cut you off?"

He sat in the chair across from my desk without an invitation. The cheek. "No, but she is why I'm here."

"Did she send you to beg back the gifts that you gave me? You can tell her you're too late. I already sold them. Bought me a month's rent in this palace." I let him hear the bitterness in my voice. If he hadn't been so afraid of his mother, he might never have broken my heart.

"No. Gina, my mother's dead." He leaned forward to match my posture. "And Security thinks I did it."

I've been accused of being many things, including a callous bitch, but even I will thaw for someone who's just lost family. No matter how much I hated said family.

"Thomas, I … What happened?" I pulled the bottle of kelp spirits from my bottom drawer and poured him a measure in a clean mug. While I was at it, I poured one for myself, too.

"She was stabbed. You remember that walrus tusk of Dad's that she kept on the mantle? Someone skewered her with it, right through the heart." He bolted down the alcohol, but kept ahold of the mug, slouching over his hands. "Nobody in Security is listening to me, though. All they see is a man who wasn't on speaking terms with his mother before her death, and who is suddenly very wealthy. But you know me, right? You know I could never do something like that." He peered up at me through those preposterously thick eyelashes, the glimmer of unshed tears pooling in his eyes.

Problem was, I knew he was right. Matricide just wasn't in Thomas's heart or ability. Sure, he was absolutely strong enough to do the deed, but he never would. He couldn't even bring himself to eat half of the critters the fishermen caught for the Station. Only edible animals without a centralized brain, that was his line.

I took a slow sip of my own booze, studying my ex-fiancé. "Let me guess, you want me to clear your name? For old times' sake?"

"Of course not. I can pay. Quite a lot, as it turns out." He pulled out a stack of cred chips: untraceable, physical currency in a station that traded almost exclusively in digital chits. Worth their weight in old-world gold.

It didn't take me long to make a decision. However painful it might be to spend time with Thomas again, my bank account and my stomach growled at the sight of so much cred. Besides, I wanted to shake the hand of whoever had done that witch in.

"Fine. But we do this my way, okay? Don't get in the way and don't make this any harder than it needs to be."

"Absolutely. Thank you. So much, Gina." He passed me the stack of cred and I carefully tucked it into my belt pouch. No way was I letting anyone see where my secret stash box was.

"Now that payment is settled, what were you arguing about with that demon mother of yours?" When Thomas hesitated, I spread my hands. "I need to know why Security suspects you before I can rule you out and find an alternative suspect."

"No, you're right." He cast about for the right words, then sighed. "There's no easy way to say this. I'm getting married. This week. My mother tried to sabotage the wedding."

"Ms. Gina, to what do I owe the pleasure?" My old chief sat at his desk, feet propped up on the worn corner. The condescension in his voice hadn't lessened since the last time I'd talked to him.

"Thomas hired me to help clear his name, since you seem so set on pinning his mother's death on him." I settled into the visitor chair on the other side of the chief's desk, hands in my lap. "I understand you believe the argument about the wedding was the motive for knocking her off, but you met the woman before. Can you honestly tell me that there was anyone who met her who *didn't* want to see her dead?"

The chief laughed. "You have a point there, but it's not just the motive. Thomas was found standing over the body with blood on him. Now, I know it's been a while for you, but that's what I like to call an 'open and shut case.'"

Thomas had told me about that. He'd found his mother on the floor, impaled, and had rushed over to see if there was any chance she was still alive. Foolish, given the extent of the injuries, but understandable. "Still, I'd like to go over the files if you don't mind."

"You know I can't do that, Gina. Not for a ... simple resident. That you even asked ..." Chief shook his head.

I leaned forward, elbows on my knees. "Look, I know there's no love lost between me and the department. I get that. But I'm not coming to you empty handed. I have a tip for you."

"Oh?" The sidelong glance I got wasn't entirely disinterested.

Now was the time to gently jiggle the bait on the end of my line. This fish didn't have much of a centralized brain; I knew he'd bite. "You know that new drug on the market? Slowz, the stuff made from cone snail venom?"

"You know where it's coming from?"

Hook, line, and sinker.

"If you go to the third level docking bay tonight around 2 am, you'll find an automated sub coming in from Station 7." I leaned back and crossed my ankles in front of me, smiling.

"Why is it always Station 7, damn pushers?" He typed a note and sent it off. "Fine, this will get you a look at the file — but it doesn't leave the office." He pulled it up on a spare tablet and handed it to me, settling in to watch me read.

While I found the audience disconcerting, I was just glad I'd only had to burn one tip to get what I wanted. I had been prepared to lose much more.

The doctor's report was pretty straightforward: death due to exsanguination, sharp force trauma from a "large tusk of *Odobenus rosmarus*" in the upper chest. The old bat had bled out in a matter of minutes. It must have been agonizing, a fact which was pleasing to me.

Next up was the security report on the scene. Crime scene technology might not be quite as advanced as it had been when we still lived on land, but with all the scientists taking refuge in our ocean cities, we still managed a respectable showing. There were no prints on the tusk, no hair at the scene other than that of the residents of the home. The deceased's assistant and the household staff had been questioned, and they all had alibis for the time of death. Which, according to the file, had been several hours before the maid had walked in on Thomas standing over the body.

"You mean to tell me that you think Thomas stood over

her body for a few *hours* after killing her? Are you serious?"
I handed the chief's tablet back to him and jotted down a
few notes on my own.

"No, I think he returned to the scene of the crime later.
It's like you don't think I'm capable of rational thought."
He shook his head sadly. "Oh, how the mighty have fallen."

"Go stick your head in the deep, Chief." My retort
lacked the bite of real conviction, and I gave him a lazy
two-fingered salute as I stood. I gathered up my bag and
headed out of the Security office, aware of the murmurs
following my exit. You would think they'd never seen a
traitor to the force before.

As I stalked the halls and lifts back to my miniscule
office, I tried to mull over the facts of the case, but my
mind kept drifting to sour memories. Turning in a dirty
security officer, being ostracized by the whole force, a call
for backup that had never been answered — and receiving
the injury that had nearly cost me my legs and had left me
with a limp. After all that, there had still been a pink slip
waiting for me when I'd returned to the office. If I didn't
know better, I'd think the security officers cared more
about their siblings-in-arms than keeping the peace of the
station.

I managed to clear those sticky, uncomfortable cobwebs
by the time I reached my office, only to find a small, pale
woman waiting at my door. She clutched a folder to her
chest, wrinkling the otherwise pristine white blouse she
wore.

I stopped a little farther away than politeness would
dictate. "Can I help you?"

"Hi, Ms. Gina. I ... um ..." She shifted her weight
nervously from one heeled foot to the other. "I thought you
should see this." She held out the folder she was clutching.

"How about we start with who you are." I closed the

distance to my door and unlocked it, ushering the obviously flustered woman inside.

"Oh. I'm Mrs. Ghert's ... *was* Mrs. Ghert's assistant. Charlotte." She didn't extend her hand to shake mine, just stood awkwardly in the doorway. "I heard Thomas had come to you seeking assistance, and I wanted to make sure you had the full story."

I sat behind my desk, hoping it would encourage the flighty woman to sit as well. It did not. "And what *is* the full story?"

"It had to have been Thomas's fiancée. Mrs. Ghert was in the middle of rewriting her will to cut Thomas out almost entirely. Even though it wasn't really her money — it was her late husband's, and by rights should have already gone to Thomas. She didn't approve of the woman Thomas is engaged to marry this week. A little while back, I overheard Thomas and his fiancée talking about how they were going to live without the family income. Thomas didn't seem to care, but that Hannah, she was really angry."

Charlotte's brow was creased by stronger emotions than mere worry. Distaste and ... envy? Sure reminded me of the looks I used to see on my friends' faces during sleepover gossip back in school.

"Thomas is a good man," Charlotte continued. "I would hate to see him get dragged down by that woman." She handed me the folder she was carrying, and I flipped it open to see a will, neither signed nor dated. That was certainly a hell of a motive — and delivered direct, no less.

"Thank you for bringing this to me. Just so I have a complete picture of the day, where were you at 7 on Friday morning?" I closed the folder and put it on my desk, keeping one hand on it to indicate that I was not giving it back.

Charlotte looked even more flustered, if that was possible, but she answered, "Leaving a message on Representative Tarmel's vidphone. Mrs. Ghert had questions about an organization she was thinking of funding. The police have a copy of the call."

I nodded. The details matched with what she had told the police. "Well, thanks for bringing this by. I appreciate it."

She nodded and turned to leave before I thought of another question. "Oh, Charlotte? Is it usual for Thomas to be at his mother's place that early in the morning?"

She looked stricken, as though the fact that he had been present was a personal failure of her scheduling. "Not usually. He had been trying to talk to her, though, and she had been avoiding him for some time. Maybe it was an attempt to catch her, to talk her into supporting his wedding. I just wish he'd picked another time."

I thanked her, and with a final nod, Charlotte left me to my musings.

While Hannah made an appealing suspect, the question of who would benefit from Mrs. Ghert's death was one with *many* answers: anyone who knew her personally, professionally, or philanthropically. She was a hard woman to know, cruel even to those she considered friends. Downright hostile to those she didn't. Including Thomas, obviously, and his new fiancée, too.

Speaking of the happy couple, I turned on my tablet and cycled over to the gossip blogs for the Station. Tabloid fodder never went extinct, and it wasn't long before I tracked down pictures and a story about the bride-to-be.

Hannah was a modest-looking woman, wearing clothing that was demure and well-tailored. The ring that Thomas had proposed with was his grandmother's, a large sapphire with a halo of diamonds. Hard to get your hands on precious stones these days, since going to shore was so dangerous. Jewelry like this was worth an obscene fortune. I had never wanted to walk around with something like that on, and Thomas had honored my wishes, proposing to me with a carved metal band made of scraps from the fab lab. Hannah was obviously a girl of a different sort.

I pulled up the directory and jotted down her address, an upper-level studio with enough light streaming through the water to illuminate the room on sunny days. Since I didn't have to worry about going into a Security office this time, I grabbed my needler on the way out the door, just in case someone decided to come at *me* with a walrus tusk too.

The upper levels of the Station were always so much cleaner than the ones I lived and worked on. Sometimes I could even smell the faint hint of a breeze as someone opened a hatchway to the gardens up top. I hadn't won a garden pass in years. I did miss that perk of dating a Ghert.

I had to knock twice and announce myself through the door before Hannah opened it. "Thomas said you might be by. I didn't realize he was still speaking to his ex."

I smiled, trying for warmth even though her attitude made me want to snarl. The demure attitude of her society page photos had been replaced with a confident and condescending demeanor that set my hackles rising. I took a breath to picture the stack of cred in my pocket, to savor the sound they made clicking together.

"I'm sorry to intrude on what must be a somber day, but Thomas did ask for my assistance in proving his innocence. As for him coming to me, it was a surprise to me as well. We were not on speaking terms until he showed up at my office today, and I'd like to return to that happy arrangement."

Hannah raised an eyebrow but stood aside, gesturing to a pair of armchairs by the windows. I restrained the impulse to rush over and drink in the shimmering light from above, and instead sat myself deliberately looking away. "I just want to get your impression of what happened yesterday, if you don't mind."

She settled herself into the chair facing me, legs crossed and fingers steepled. "First, answer a question for me. Why did Thomas come to you instead of any other investigator in the Station? There are far more talented and reputable folk who do the same work."

"Therein lies the fault in your logic. I was the best investigator in Security, which was the problem. I uncovered things in-department and got my ass handed to me for it." I resisted the urge to add, *And because I have such a poor reputation, people like you frequently underestimate me.* Thomas knew that. Everyone at his mother's level had frequently underestimated me. It was the perfect cover, and helped keep me protected while I snooped.

"I still think he should have hired someone more ... respectable. We have to get his name cleared before the wedding." She picked up a cup of tea from the table in front of her. Hadn't offered me any, of course. How had Thomas picked this gem to marry?

I pulled out my tablet to make notes. "Where were you yesterday morning at 7 am?"

"Working in my lab, along with five other scientists. We're on the opposite side of the Station and I took no breaks between when I arrived at the lab at 5:30 and 9 am when I went with my lab partner to acquire drinks." She took a long slow sip of her tea, emphasizing my lack thereof.

"I hear that Mrs. Ghert didn't approve of your marriage to Thomas." I tapped my stylus against the tablet a couple times before continuing. "And yet I see you are wearing her mother's ring anyway."

"Oh, she didn't mind at first. She was overjoyed that Thomas had found someone of equal stature to share his life. It wasn't until she realized just how intelligent I was that she threw a fit. Wanted a daughter-in-law to simper and pop out heirs, but as you can tell, that's not really my style."

It was hard to read this woman; her poker face was insane. Not a single errant twitch or squint to give away her feelings beneath the icy calm she projected. For all I knew, she and Mrs. Ghert had gotten into regular screaming matches and hated each other, or were secret lovers behind Thomas's back.

I tried a different tactic. "Do you know of anyone who might want to hurt Mrs. Ghert?"

"You mean besides you, and everyone else?" She laughed, the sound harsh. "I know you disliked her just as much as anyone. Where were *you* yesterday morning at 7 am, hm?"

"Having a foursome with my roommates. I can give you a blow-by-blow if you need it."

The quip was worth it just to see the shock on Hannah's face, which, to my surprise, split into amusement. "And I thought you were going to be no fun."

I matched her smile tooth for tooth. "I put up with Mrs. Ghert for almost five years. I can keep up with the best of them."

"Touché." She tapped a fingernail against her mug. "If I were answering your question seriously, I would definitely say Thomas and me, the household staff that had to suffer her daily, and even Representative Tarmel. She owned him, and he did *not* care for it at all. Even her assistant had issues with her, though this one lasted longer than most. What was her name? Cindy?"

"Charlotte," I supplied.

"That's right. Anyway, those are the people I would start with."

I nodded, while making a note on my tablet. *No help whatsoever on suspects.* "Last question for you, and then I'll leave you to your day. Has anything out of the ordinary happened recently? Anything odd that stood out to you?"

Hannah frowned, and chewed on her lower lip while she thought. Mrs. Ghert would have hated that habit. "There is, but ... Well, it's about Thomas. I figure if you don't have all the information, you won't be able to get to the truth, so ... Thomas got a package the other day, looked like a poster tube. He got flustered when he opened it, but then insisted it was just signs for the wedding. I thought it might be a surprise for the day of, so I didn't press. I haven't seen it since. That's the only thing I can think of."

I made a last note on my tablet and put it away before standing. "Thank you for taking the time, Hannah. I'm hoping I can get this wrapped up well in time for your wedding."

She nodded but didn't stand to escort me back to the door. "I'm counting on it."

I gave her one last smile and took my leave, heading up-station to the above-water levels where the Ghert family suite was located. When the stations had been built a century prior, they'd been designed as research stations, not intended to host the broad range of social strata that humans tend to separate into. This meant that most rooms were bunks, like mine, or small studios. When we were forced to become self-contained cities due to climactic collapse, some of the wealthier entrepreneurs staked out a series of rooms and altered them into suites to host their whole families, and even staff.

The Ghert suite was the largest of them all, having taken over several officers' quarters and what used to be the officers' mess way back in the day. The directory still listed Thomas as an occupant, so I decided to cast a wide net and speak to the staff at the same time.

Erin, the housekeeper, answered the door with a cry of surprise and a brief embrace. "Gina! When Thomas said he'd retained your services, I knew our prayers had been answered. He couldn't have killed his harpy of a mother, and only someone as good-hearted as you could bring him back from the brink." She hugged me again and ushered me into the house.

I was surprised to see that most of the staff was the same, except for the maid; I would have thought there would be more turnover due to Mrs. Ghert's winning personality. When Thomas entered the living room, I realized why that wasn't the case; the staff flocked to him, fussing and bestowing hugs. Of course. Anyone who spent any length of time around Thomas was drawn into his orbit. Thank goodness he was the kind of soul who didn't take advantage of people, otherwise he could do some serious damage.

"Thomas." I stood from the armchair I had settled in. "How are you holding up?"

"Well, after another round with the chief just now, I feel like the prime suspect." He settled into the chair across from me and Cook scurried off for tea.

"I had a chat with Hannah, and Charlotte came by to see me as well." I pulled out the folder containing the draft of the will and handed it to him. "Did you know about this?"

Flipping the folder open, Thomas took a look inside, and closed it again. "I actually demanded it."

That wasn't one of the several answers I'd thought he might give. "You wanted to be written out of your mother's will?"

"She just used it as leverage. 'Do what I want or I'll cut you out.' 'Marry who I want or I'll cut you out.' I told her to just do it already. I make a decent income on my own, as does Hannah. We have no need for the family money." He gratefully accepted the mug of tea from Cook and leaned back in the chair. "It was a relief to know she was starting the process. Almost wish it had been completed before she … well …"

"Can't say I ever wished I had less money, but I'll take your word for it." Interesting that Charlotte had said it had caused strife. I added sweetener to my own tea before continuing. "Hannah said that you received a package last week. Do you remember that?"

"What package?" He frowned, then continued before I could elaborate. "Oh. Oh! Oh, god." Thomas blanched and set his tea down, his hands shaking. "It was a walrus tusk."

"You're kidding." I could tell from the lack of color to his skin he was not. "Who was it from? Did it have a note?"

He thought back, hands clasped in front of him. "No return address. It came through Station mail, not messengered, and it had just one line printed on paper: 'The walrus whistles at midnight.'"

I blinked a couple times, sure I had misheard him. "'The walrus whistles at midnight'? What does that even mean?"

"Funnily enough, it's something my grandfather used to say. Whenever we'd ask a silly or impossible-to-answer question, he'd respond, 'Why does the walrus whistle at midnight?' and we'd laugh and give up pestering. We knew we wouldn't get a straight answer out of him at that point."

"Your grandparents are all dead, aren't they?" I ran

through what I remembered of his family tree. "Was it your patrilineal or matrilineal grandfather?"

"Patrilineal, which makes it extra weird since I'm the last living in that line. For a moment when I first received it, I thought it was a wedding gift from a ghost." He picked his tea back up, taking a tentative sip.

I tapped my stylus against my tablet as I thought. "Does anyone else know about this phrase?"

"I mean, I'm sure plenty of people heard it back in the day, but it's been twenty years since he passed." He shrugged. "I'm not even sure it's related, really."

I raised an eyebrow and he sighed, nodding. It would have to be a really weird coincidence to receive a walrus tusk the week before his mother was slain with one. It was starting to sound like her murder might have been less spontaneous than the choice of weapon had made it appear.

"Speaking of walruses — what is your family's connection with them, anyway? I don't think I ever heard that story." I glanced at the mantle that had once held a walrus tusk in pride of place, empty now.

Thomas followed my glance and grimaced. "It's all really macabre. Back in the early 1900s, my great-whatever earned himself a name as the chief importer of walrus bits. Did some serious damage to that ecosystem back in his day. By all accounts, he was not a great guy. Before you ask, that is dad's side of the family."

"You know me so well. So why kill someone *not* related to the walrus thing, with a bit of walrus?" I bit my lip and studied the notes on my tablet.

In the ensuing lull in the conversation, Charlotte bustled in. Losing her employer certainly hadn't caused a hitch in her giddyup. "Thomas, I have several things here that need your signature. I'm afraid that they can't wait."

I smiled at the woman. "Did Thomas inherit you as well?"

She smiled back, not at all insulted by the comment. In fact, she looked fairly pleased with the situation. "I'm staying with him at least through the transition, and if he needs me afterwards, I'd be happy to stay on."

I watched the faint blush on the woman's cheeks while Thomas looked over the documents, signed off on them, and paused on the last page. "I thought we were going to be doing the rehearsal Friday evening, not morning?"

Charlotte took back the stack of paper. "Yes, but you need to meet with Representative Tarmel to finalize that deal of your mother's, and he's only available on Friday evenings. He has his regular squash game in the mornings."

"Sure. Make sure Hannah knows, yeah? She gets worked up if she feels out of the loop on anything wedding-related."

If I hadn't been studying Charlotte absently, I would have missed her grimace and pause before she assured Thomas that she would message Hannah directly. Interesting.

I turned back to my employer. "Where did you leave that package, Thomas?"

"In the closet at Hannah's. Why?"

"I want to take a closer look. I think I'll head back over there after I hit the canteen." I gathered my things, and Thomas saw me out.

"Hannah?" I knocked, again, calling out. "Hannah, it's Gina again."

There wasn't any answer, even though I could hear her phone ringing inside the studio. I looked both ways down the hallway and pulled out my digital lockpicking kit, making quick work of the entrypad. When the door opened, I gasped and ran forward.

"Hannah!"

The woman in question was sprawled on the floor, a small pool of blood spreading around her head. I dialed Emergency Services as I checked her pulse. Still alive.

"Emergency. What is your location?"

I rattled off the address, urged them to rush Medical, and turned back to Hannah. She didn't appear to have any other wounds except for the bash on the head, but I wasn't about to move her and make things worse.

Within a minute, there was a brisk knock on the open door, and the Medical team pushed me out of the way. What I wouldn't give to live somewhere with a response time like that.

As I squeezed myself into a corner, I noticed that the closet door stood open, and a long narrow box lay on the floor, empty. I stepped over the bed (sorry, Hannah) and used my stylus to move it just enough to see the label. Sure enough, it was addressed to Thomas. Looking around to see if the note might have fallen out, I found nothing.

The Med staff interrupted my snooping. "You coming with us, or ...?"

I shook my head. "I'll wait here for Security and explain everything."

They didn't wait any longer and took off with Hannah on a backboard. Even if I didn't like her, I still hoped she survived this. Nobody deserved to get caught in the middle of a smash and grab.

As the Med staff disappeared down the hall, Chief turned the corner and scowled when he saw me in the doorway. "I take it I have you to thank for this callout."

"If you mean, did I discover an injured woman and

render aid before she could die, then yes, I'm your girl." I gave him the rundown of everything I knew — which wasn't much, to be honest.

The chief snorted as he surveyed the empty box. "That all you've got? I remember you having more spring in your step back in the day."

"Aww, you just said I was competent." I fluttered my eyelashes at him. He growled.

"Get out of the way of my techs, but don't leave the Station. Think you can follow that order?"

"Yes, sir, happy to be at your disposal, sir!" I made myself scarce before he could think of something more to keep me there.

I started back to my office, mulling over what I knew so far, the likely players, and their motivations. As a thought occurred to me, I changed course and made for the Communications office instead. While everyone could make vidcalls through their tablets, all communication on or off the Station had to be routed through the servers in Communications. And I still had a guy who owed me a favor.

"Bae!" I clasped hands with the guy at the front desk. "It's been too long."

"Yes, yes it has! My sister's doing great now. Thanks again for taking care of that whole ... mess." His smile was easy and warm, a far cry from the emotional wreck of a man who had begged me to get his sister out of an abusive relationship. It was a balm for my fraying nerves.

I leaned on his counter. "I'm so glad. She's a sweet kid. I was wondering, could you check on something for me?"

Bae didn't miss a beat, opening up his search terminal. "Sure thing, what do you need?"

"Yesterday morning around 7 am, a call went out to

Representative Tarmel. Could I get the details of that comm?"

"Just a minute, let me find it … Here it is. I sent it to your tablet." Bae's easy smile turned on me once again. "You free for drinks tonight? It'd be great to catch up."

"Not tonight, I'm afraid. The case I'm in the middle of is a little high-profile." At his crestfallen expression, I hurried to add, "Soon, though. I'll drop you a line when this is done, all right?"

"Great! Just let me know when!"

I thanked him again for the call log and left him grinning foolishly at his computer screen. Bae's interest in me had gone right over my head until now; some detective I was. But he wouldn't make such a bad date. I made a note in my calendar to call him after this weekend, since the case would be over one way or another by then.

I scanned the call log, and what I saw made me pick up my pace — not towards the Ghert residence, but towards Medical. I slowed to a stop in the doorway and panted at the receptionist, "Hannah. Where?"

Wide-eyed, the receptionist shook their head. "I can't tell you that unless you're family."

"She could be in danger! Has she had any visitors?"

"Just the family assistant, Charlotte. She went back a few minutes ago."

I cursed and blew past the reception desk, ignoring the shouts of the receptionist behind me. I scanned the emergency bays, looking for my target, and almost missed her because Charlotte was hunched over Hannah.

"Charlotte!" I called, trying to catch my breath. "Thank god I caught you!"

The woman's back stiffened, and I saw her tuck something into the bedclothes before she turned to me. "Gina, it's kind of you to visit Hannah here, but shouldn't you be out pursuing the culprit? She's not even conscious yet."

"I just needed to ask you another question." I wandered over to the hospital bed, moving to hold Hannah's hand in such a way that forced Charlotte to step back from the bed.

"Of course. I'm at your disposal." She folded her hands in front of herself, but I could see them shaking, just a little.

"Your call yesterday morning with Tarmel. It was live?" I didn't bother to watch for her reaction, I knew what it was going to be.

"Yes, of course."

"That's interesting, because you also know that Friday mornings are when he plays squash. And if you look here …" I pulled up the record of her call on my tablet, "You'll see that it wasn't a live call at all, but a recorded blast sent from your phone. You pre-recorded the call and sent it out before you impaled your employer on a walrus tusk."

"What? No, don't be silly." She shook her head vigorously enough to dislodge a hair pin. "There's no way for you to know that."

"Isn't there? Right here, this little number? It indicates a pre-buffer only used for recording transfers." I carefully set down the tablet and readied myself for whatever Charlotte might do next. Was she the sort of woman to run? Or the sort who would launch herself at me?

Charlotte reached some sort of decision and calmed quickly. Not a good sign. "Why would I want to murder Mrs. Ghert? There's where your theory falls apart."

"Yes, I was confused about that as well. You went so far out of your way to hand me the draft of the will that cut Thomas out and implicated his bride. But then there was the walrus tusk sent to Thomas with a phrase only his grandfather used. I think Hannah here was just collateral damage as the killer was trying to retrieve the tusk from her room. Which they needed because a DNA test will reveal that it came from the same walrus as the one in Mrs. Ghert's chest — am I right?"

I shifted my weight, watching Charlotte gauge her options as I laid out the trail in front of her. "Then there were your very visceral reactions: negative to everything Hannah and a vested interest in everything Thomas, including him trying to sign away his patrilineal inheritance. And now you've come to finish Hannah off because she might be able to identify you as her attacker. My only question is, first or second?"

Charlotte blinked, confused by the sudden turn. "First or second what?"

"Cousins with Thomas, of course."

At that question, Charlotte bolted straight into the waiting arms of Chief, who had snuck into the doorway behind her. He would have been called by a receptionist following protocol after a security breach (i.e. me).

"Chief! Thank god you're here! Gina's gone crazy! She attacked me!" Charlotte collapsed into the chief's arms, but he rolled his eyes and handed her off to one of his security officers to cuff.

"Don't try that with me, girl. I've been standing here long enough to know what's going on." He sighed as he looked me over, hands on his hips. "I suppose *you* are proud of yourself."

I grinned and flipped up the blanket at Hannah's side, exposing a syringe. "I think you'll find that that's a lethal dose of whatever it is. With Charlotte's prints all over it."

He carefully retrieved the needle and placed it in an evidence bag just as Thomas came into the room.

"What is going on here? Hannah needs rest, not ... Charlotte? Why are you in cuffs?"

I gently guided Thomas over to the chair beside his

fiancée. "Good news, bad news, I'm afraid. Bad news is, she killed your mother. Good news, you have a new cousin!"

The look he leveled at me was very clear that he didn't appreciate my dramatic reveal. "Maternal or paternal?" he asked, wry.

"Oh, definitely paternal. When your mother started the paperwork to cut you out of the will — the will that would ensure you received your birthright as a walrus-killing descendent — she tried to stop it, I think out of some confused sense of familial responsibility and love. Or lust? Whatever. When that didn't work, she killed your mother before she could finalize those details. Charlotte even sent you her tusk, hoping you'd think it was a message from your ancestors and take a stand against your mother."

"And Hannah?" He smoothed the covers, his face showing nothing but concern for his love. No accounting for taste.

"Collateral damage, though I'm pretty sure it was a side benefit to Charlotte." I turned back to the woman in cuffs. "You didn't like Hannah much, did you?"

"She was just going to be another damn harpy, like Thomas's mother," Charlotte snapped. "He would be better off without her. We are *Gherts*. And he was willing to just sacrifice his birthright? His legacy? Just to marry this, this —"

The chief gave her a little shake. "That's enough out of you."

I rolled my eyes and turned back to Thomas. "Now, we'll leave you with your fiancée in peace. Call me when she wakes up, okay?" He nodded, but his eyes were fixed on Hannah. Sighing, I followed Chief out of the room, sure I was in for a long lecture and an even longer debrief.

"Are you sure you didn't want to head over to the wedding? They *did* invite you, after all." Bae shifted nervously in his seat while we waited for our drinks.

"Very sure. I may have saved Hannah, but I still don't like her. Besides, being at an ex's wedding is weird." I happily accepted my mojito from the waiter as Bae took his piña colada.

"Only if you haven't talked to them in forever. I've been to two exes' weddings, but that's because we stayed friends afterwards." He took a sip of his fruity drink and hummed his pleasure.

I snorted in amusement. "That is a skill you'll need to teach me."

"Happily. So, if you're avoiding all things wedding today, want to go catch the new movie? I think it's something about mutated land monsters."

Groaning, I added an eye roll for good measure. "Another one? You'd think they'd get tired of the same damn story all the time."

"Do *you*? I mean, not all your cases can be high-profile murders and daring rescues." He seemed genuine in his question, so I quashed the flippant answer I was about to give.

"You know, I used to love boring when I was in Security. Nothing new ever seemed to happen; I could work a case in my sleep. Until something interesting *did* happen, and it ruined my life. You'd think I would stay away from the interesting ones now, but I just can't seem to stop now that I've started."

I smiled a little sadly, thinking of the woman I had been so many years ago. Maybe it was time to let her fade into the past and embrace what was in front of me now. That thought had me draining half my glass in one go.

Changing the subject, I told Bae, "Tell you what: get me drunk, and I'll go watch another kaiju monster movie with you. As long as there aren't any walruses."

He laughed, waiving at the waiter to order another round. "Deal."

Learn more about this author at:
https://rebeccademarest.com/.

# ALL CLEAR

## M.M. DE VOE

THE STINK of the dusty air made Daniel cough: notes of diesel and burnt meat, with a mouthfeel of some ancient, between-the-walls mold that hadn't met fresh air for decades. Above his head, the roughly-hewn edges of a cluster of thick copper pipes caught the setting sun. They dangled freely, as if sheared off by a saw. In the moment they had broken, there had been a loud shriek as if metal was tearing, reminiscent of a movie monster's agonized wail. Thing is, when Daniel replayed the moment, the sound happened before the pipes broke off. Monsters do not exist, but Daniel couldn't quite believe the news report of an earthquake.

One of these pipes suddenly gushed filthy water, adding the stench of sewage to the already malodorous air. Daniel gagged as much from the sight of it as from the smell. The pipe emptied onto the place in his living room where a plate glass window used to separate him from the sky. His high-floor apartment overlooked Houston's flashy EaDo district — named so by marketing firms and not by the locals, where property values had been going steadily up, before plummeting to toxic levels in the last hour. There was nothing Daniel could do to stop the wet mass of solids and pungent liquids from splashing in an arc across the patterned tile floor, splattering his suede Eames sofa, then waterfalling down ten stories to the destroyed street below his shattered apartment.

Just this past Tuesday, a nude streaker had run up and down Fannin during rush hour to protest the immoral shows on Netflix. Daniel's next thought made a similarly stupid and pointless appearance, and it caused him to wonder if the event had snapped his brain. Despite the devastation of his apartment, despite the possible loss of *life* in his building, his neighborhood, and adjacent neighborhoods in a jagged line for who knows how many miles, despite the loved ones who wondered if he was okay, and the ones he needed to check up on — despite all that, he wondered whether he should run down to street level to try to recover the Persian rug that KP had given him as a fourth anniversary gift, just before leaving him for the coder in the next booth. He'd treasured that rug, with its red-for-passion pattern of lotus blossoms. The rug, the baby Steinway that had rested on top of it, and the entire back edge of the room had plummeted out onto the traffic below. Daniel's loft now ended in a concrete cliff ten stories above ground level, the floor broken off, patterned tiles missing like a meth addict's teeth.

Picturing himself searching the ruin of city for the sentimental rug, Daniel started to laugh and could not stop. The wind off the street was hot and carried the stench of METRO buses. His laughter turned to tears at the realization that, of course, the blessed central air would never work again because the ducts that used to carry it were hanging like modern art from his ceiling and out of his walls. This was his reality. The teary laughter overwhelmed him, and he sank to the floor, holding his head in his hands.

*All clear. The emergency is over. All clear. The emergency is over. All clear. The emergency is over ...*

Cole Weingarten stared at Penny's body, splayed out on the driveway. He had thought they'd been untouched by the disaster. Their modest two-bedroom home in Greater Eastwood had not been smashed. Their lawn was unblemished, mowed just this Wednesday. The trees were all intact, including the new pecan and the four rosebushes that the landscaper had added at considerable expense. The roses were budding and would be in full bloom by next week. And there was Penny, lying near their extra carport with her hand reaching out above her head.

She had been killed on contact by the Audi when it had struck her in the owner's panic to evacuate their neighborhood, the city, the state, reality. She looked as if, after she had fallen, she had hoped that Cole would find her, reach down and comfort her. He was a man who prided himself on being her protector — and he had failed her. He had stayed hidden in their panic room until the emergency alert had been recalled by the same triple blast that had sounded the alarm.

He stooped down to brush a long strand of red hair back from his wife's bloody forehead. Telluride or Whistler seemed like such a stupid fight now. Everything seemed stupid.

Mrs. Allen had accounted for all her cats and had stockpiled fresh water for them in a row of jugs, mason jars, juice pitchers, flower vases, pots, and pans. She sat quietly on her sofa, stroking Brave Bill as the others circled around them. Before her power had cut out, the TV announcers had blamed the destruction on an earthquake. It had certainly felt like an earthquake, but when had there ever been a quake in Houston? Tornados, yes, and plenty of hurricanes. But even Bill — who was afraid of nothing — had vanished under furniture when he'd heard the eerie, throaty grumble approaching. Now he was shaking on her lap, and all the petting in the world seemed unable to soothe him.

*All clear. The emergency is over. All clear. The emergency is over. All clear. The emergency is over …*

Over on Louisiana Street, Bob's three sons piled tires back into large pyramids at Bob's Tire Shop. They didn't talk much as they cleaned up. There was no internet and no power, so Frankie couldn't run his playlist. He'd started to whistle at one point, but Jazz had glared at him, and he'd fallen silent.

The three brothers piled the tires in the hot sunlight and fought the biting mosquitoes and irritating flies and tried not to let the smell of hot rubber overwhelm them. Bob sat in the small office staring at his hands. There was his wedding ring, worn for 22 years without a break. There was the scar left by a game of mumbledy-peg when he was a teenager. There were the recent wrinkles, the age spots, the tufts of gray on his Irish knuckles, the ever-looser skin. His father's hands at the end of his wrists.

The phone didn't ring. There would be no customers. The investment he had made in his father's store would never pay off. The highway bridge that the city had just opened was a pile of rubble blocking off his newly paved parking lot from the rest of the world.

He had survived the Harvey flooding with minimal damage, had escaped Florence entirely. Had survived drought. Had survived the construction of that bridge. But this disaster took them all. The ground had shaken in an ominous slow rhythm that could have been drumbeats announcing the arrival of God's Vengeance. Every terrible movie he had ever seen had come rushing back like an accusation. There would never be customers at this location again.

His boys knew better than to bother him. They just stacked tires and picked up debris, in hopes of someday clearing the front lot.

*All clear. The emergency is over. All clear. The emergency is over.*
*All clear. The emergency is over …*

The gas oven still worked, so Stasia Green baked cookies. Her husband's favorite: spice cookies shaped like moons that reminded him of his childhood in Syria. They filled the air with the scent of cardamom. He had spent precious seconds telling her the safest places to hide — informed by memories of wartime attacks in his native land. He and the boys had taken their rifles from the safe and gone to see what could be done to save the convenience store.

Her hallways now ended in empty air; the east end of her home, where all the bedrooms had been, was flattened into a stone pancake. She let the tears roll down her face as she searched for the oven mitt to remove the perfect cookies that no one was alive to eat.

∿

The last of the looters were still scouring the shelves in the dark supermarket. It was almost funny how picky the couple of tattooed musicians were: leaving the blueberry Pop-Tarts upended on the floor, but taking the last two boxes of the strawberry, even though both boxes were damaged.

Roger, the daytime manager of this particular Kroger's, considered shooting the couple, as he had done to so many of the others before. But he overheard them talking in delighted voices about a huge monster and caught sight of the fierce, yellow-eyed bald eagle tattooed on the girl's shoulder, and suddenly he felt a warm compassion for them both. Given the guy's green hair and pierced eyebrows, and the girl's midriff-baring black t-shirt (Roger also admired the string of eighth notes descending the small of her back and vanishing below the black thong and beltline), the couple was probably visiting from Austin, and how were they supposed to survive here as tourists? No one would be getting into or out of this part of town for a long time.

The store had already lost everything, so screw it. This really wasn't his job anymore. He couldn't manage a store that had no electricity, nearly nothing on the shelves, a parking lot full of upturned cars blocking the entrance, and dead bodies in the aisles.

The girl clutched her boyfriend's arm and pointed at Roger. He lowered his gun and shrugged. Let them take what they wanted and go.

∿

Polly and her mother climbed out of the bathtub where they had hidden. It was strange to see the sky from the bathroom — so blue that it looked as if her mother had used it as a reference when she bought the matching towels.

Her mother was still sobbing, curled up over her knees in a yoga position she could never have achieved if not for the sheer panic of the day. Polly put her hand on her mother's shoulder, and felt it redouble its shuddering.

She asked if her mother was okay, but she already knew the answer. Why should she be okay? Brandon was gone, snatched from life like a worm from a hole. Still wriggling.

Polly had watched. She had reached for her little brother's chubby foot but had been left holding only the tiny canvas shoe with its dinosaur pattern. Then she had grabbed her screaming mother and had dragged her to the bathtub to hide.

Why didn't she feel something, after what she had seen? Why was she so calm? She wondered if the math test would still be given tomorrow, whether she should bother to study tonight, whether Mr. Fish had even survived the attack. Would school reopen tomorrow? Would it ever? And when school reopened, would they expect the ninth grade to pick up right where they had left off?

Perhaps she *should* study, just in case. Would people still use math? Maybe for creating new weapons. Maybe to count the dead. Her mother rocked, holding her knees. Above them, the clouds made glorious white shapes against the towel-blue sky.

Erika Shilter walked through the arboretum on the Alice Brown loop, taking dazed notes in her park admin workbook. The black-eyed Susans had survived, but one of the oldest sycamore trees had been uprooted and flung into the pond. She swallowed hard, wondering if it was in any way her fault that Shiro Yokohama, the visiting cellist, had been killed by that falling tree, mid-performance on the Ravine Overlook Deck. She had organized the midday concert, after all.

It had been her fundraiser that had brought the glitterati of Houston together for a Victorian boating picnic. Upended boats bobbed in the murky water along with wrappers from the imported pepper crackers and plastic champagne flutes. She listened for the "jug-o-rum" calls of the bullfrogs, but nature was subdued. Not even the mockingbirds were talking. Sticks cracked underfoot as she walked, but otherwise nature was as quiet as a guilty child. As well it should be. There had been nothing natural about the event.

Erika had given her life to protecting nature. How could it have turned so horribly against her? She looked down at her notes, and finding only incoherent scribbles, sighed, and turned to a fresh page to try again to make sense of all this.

*All clear. The emergency is over. All clear. The emergency is over. All clear. The emergency is over …*

Helen buried her Labrador. She hadn't been able to get Rusty to hide in the closet with her. The foolish dog had given chase instead. Afterward, she had found her faithful companion in Mrs. Bloomhaven's tomato garden: barely strong enough to whimper, an iron I-bar pinning his broken body to the freshly watered loam, his front paws tracing tiny circles in the air, his back paws disastrously still.

She could not imagine where the monster had gotten the

iron bar — had he carried it all the way from downtown? Had it become caught between his toes or in his scales somewhere? Did he even have scales? She had seen only a glimpse of brown, bigger than the First National Bank building. The household rifle she'd used to put Rusty out of his misery would have been of no use against such a monster, but she should have tried. Rusty's courage shamed her.

She laid his twelve-year-old body to rest in a lovely chest that had formerly held photographs for her ancestry work. Her funeral service was long, for she read aloud the entirety of *Dr. Doolittle*, the children's book that had inspired her to get a puppy in the first place. It took an hour to dig a hole in the red clay deep enough to bury the chest.

When it was all over, Helen brushed pine needles from her knees and returned to what was left of her house. Ancient family photographs were scattered all over her living room, blowing in the breeze from the busted wall.

No one in the old photographs was smiling.

Rajesh drank all the whiskey his roommates had locked in the liquor cabinet that now was surrounded by the remaining glass shards of the window all three had fallen through, in their quest to film the creature as it passed by. He no longer wanted to be a surgeon. If he couldn't be a god and bring his people back from the dead, then he would just drink until he forgot their names.

Stephanie pounded on the door again, begging him to come outside with the other residents to help on the streets. He stared into his glass. So many people needed his help. Too many.

A freight train carrying cattle had been thrown half a mile and now lay across Mr. Muller's cotton field. No one seemed to care about the oil spill or the pathetic mewling of the broken cows. No one seemed to care about the train that lay on its side, twisted by the uneven ground. They only cared about the footprints, six feet deep at their shallowest.

Mr. Muller had often complained in Town Hall meetings that erosion was making the topsoil dangerously thin over the hard red clay. No one seemed to care about that now either.

Mr. Muller walked to the county sheriff's office a mile from where his pickup truck had run out of fuel. He had brought his tools. "Take me to wherever I can do some good," he said. The sheriff wasn't in, but the receptionist put Mr. Muller to work, fixing doors that had come off their hinges. She helped him because, of course, the landlines were out. Sometimes they both stopped as if sharing some kind of psychic link and checked their cellphones for messages. Sometimes this ended in laughter, sometimes tears.

Steve Capalowski, who had yearned to be a contractor all his life, took his hard hat off and let it fall from his fingertips as he stared down the endless trench the monster had left — not just through his worksite where the teamsters had been building a new hotel, but through thirty-five miles of city and suburban streets. After causing this devastation, it had unfurled giant leathery wings and taken flight: three steps forward, then upward. Cellphones had recorded the monster vanishing into the clouds.

Social media buzzed with commentary; it was instantly the world's most-watched meme. Trouble was, the power was down in all of Southwest Texas, and how long would it be before all those phones were nothing but doorstops with drained batteries? 48 hours at best? Steve's own phone had died ten minutes ago, in the middle of a call to his mother in Port Arthur. She'd just wanted to hear his voice, she'd said. He had reassured her that he was fine; there would be major construction work forever. He might even get rich.

Steve wished he hadn't given up smoking. He wished he had a cigarette in his hand, to help steady his breathing. He worked his jaw as if chewing gum and punched his crane operator on the shoulder rather harder than necessary.

*All clear. The emergency is over. All clear. The emergency is over. All clear. The emergency is over ...*

Blood pooled in many places on Margarita Hinojosa's wedding dress. The entirety of St. Thomas's Roman Catholic Church had been destroyed, apse to nave, with one flick of the creature's tail. Nothing was left of the crushed wedding party but a mass of gelid skeletons in tuxedos and tea-length chiffon in a shade of eggplant remarkably reminiscent of a bruise.

The photographer had fled without taking a single photograph of the monster, an omission he would regret for decades afterward. The flowers that Maria had painstakingly chosen, fought over, and won were now as irrelevant as the fact that the long line of fancy rental cars outside the front door had been spared. There was no one left to drive them, and no one from Avis, Enterprise, or Alamo would ever come pick them up. Margarita herself lay forever single in Miguel's arms, unmarried yet mingled with him; their two chaste bodies now melded, coalesced into one in a way that no married couple could ever hope to achieve.

Father Anton cowered in what remained of the dark wood confessional booth, screaming and praying, sometimes simultaneously. The altar was strangely intact, its chalice shining gold, linen altar cloth perfectly white, purificator folded tidily and laid to the right of the chalice. However, the enormous crucifix bearing its suffering Jesus had been torn from the reredos behind the altar and lay stabbed into the ground near the wedding carnage like an enormous grave marker. The bloody streaks painted on the agonized face of God's only son looked as fake as ketchup on a fourth-grade stage when compared to the congealing blood on the surprised faces of the actual corpses.

What shoddy work on the part of the creator of this Jesus. What artist had thought that a betrayed man would ever look sad? Betrayal, as was evidenced by the entire wedding party — down to the three flower girls in their frills of white taffeta and the three mothers whose bodies had attempted to protect their little girls and failed — naturally expressed itself as anger.

Dr. Langone argued with Dr. Chen over where they should go for lunch, though they both agreed that they would go nowhere alone. The staff caf had been destroyed by a thrown Jeep (which was still stuck up there), and neither scientist knew whether the nearby Chinese place or Al's Pizza had survived. Without signal or landlines, they couldn't find out.

The restaurants were in opposite directions and Dr. Chen didn't think her Buick held enough gas to visit both. She proposed they skip lunch altogether and just get the hell out of town, but they both knew that their division of NASA would be needed. It was only a matter of time. Never mind that their budgets had been cut deeply enough to render them impotent in the aftermath of an attack that no one in their department had had the budget, resources, or freedom to predict. Their former department head, Dr. Evans, would have been saving everyone's ass right now, but he had been let go a year ago — and last Dr. Langone had heard, the former Navy Seal had eased the pain of his sudden dismissal by chemical means and was now living on the streets like a lot of other affronted veterans.

Dr. Langone wanted to rub that slimeball president's nose in those budget cuts, but instead, he started up the Buick and drove to the Chinese place. When they saw the lights were on, their breath caught in tandem. They sat an extra second in the parked car, in case it was a mirage.

Inside, everything was normal. They placed their usual order of cashew chicken and steam fried rice. Dr. Langone's voice trembled as he added an extra order of fried pork dumplings. For the first time in as long as they had been going there, Dr. Chen asked the lady behind the counter her name and had a brief conversation with her. No one had more information than what the news had related four hours ago. *An emergency. Leave the area. We will inform you when it is safe to return.*

Later, when the scientists were sitting at a cheap table with their heaping Styrofoam plates and plastic cups of water, Dr. Chen gently cleaned her glasses with a napkin that said, inexplicably, "Best Bamboo Location." The gesture made Dr. Langone want her more than ever. Now was *not* the time, he reminded himself, his eyes glued to her careful fingertips. And yet it was also the *only* time. Still, it would be inappropriate.

He satisfied himself with watching her eat with chopsticks while he used a plastic fork, and they talked about their current project just as if everything were normal.

*All clear. The emergency is over. All clear. The emergency is over. All clear. The emergency is over …*

Across the entire city, dozens of people slowly regained consciousness and inched carefully out of precariously dangling automobiles that had been tossed halfway across town.

Those in the areas where signal hadn't gone out were huddled over their phones placing call after call or group texting or posting "I am safe" in response to a Facebook check-in. Some of the drivers sat and clutched their steering wheels, as if they still had any control at all. A few of the cars had exploded — one with the family of five still inside. Some of the luckier passengers had run from their cars when the monster reached the scene and had therefore survived — but now they struggled in vain to find cars that had been thrown in random directions. The missing vehicles could be anywhere: caught in a construction crane, upside-down in a fenced-in schoolyard, sunk to the bottom of a water hazard on a golf course. Insurance would not cover any of this damage. Insurance would not cover any of the damage in the entire city. It was a colossal loss.

*… today, we speak to Mary Hertz, a Johns Hopkins assistant professor in the Krieger School's Department of History of Science*

*and Technology. Hertz specializes in looking at environmental catastrophes through "the Godzilla lens," and we ask her how last week's surprise attack in Houston could affect global response to environ ...*

*... please welcome Jahna Guardward, chair emeritus for SETI Research, who will help us understand whether the astonishing attack on Houston could have originated in outer space ...*

*... we are pleased to bring you live to Ann Arbor, where a helicopter team of LA Firefighters has airdropped twenty senior citizen survivors of Houston's horrific attack ...*

*... speaking to the former preschool teacher who became a hero using first aid and her love of art ...*

*... Next up on* Reality Dysfunction: *three weeks ago, an enormous winged monster attacked Houston. Now, scientists from the Centre for Genomic Regulation face off against researchers from MIT ...*

*... no news on when Houston and its surrounding areas will regain power ...*

Six weeks later, Polly still flinched and hid under her covers whenever she heard a loud bang. She wished her phone worked. Her mother had said she should never expect it — or anything electronic — to work again. There had been a sonic weapon, she reminded Polly in that toneless way that she spoke now. An effective sonic weapon, but the government had pulled funding. The attacks were spreading. It was a conspiracy. The monsters were everywhere now. None of what her mother said was grounded in reality.

They had no way to contact the outside world, no way of knowing what had actually happened, only gossip sourced from the few people who still had working generators. There had been a monster, that much was clear — but maybe only one, and no official story agreed on the why of it all.

Polly's mother repeated herself a lot these days. Too much. She forgot some things and repeated others. She forgot that her baby had been snatched from her arms and eaten whole. She repeated Polly's name a lot. Polly often caught her staring at walls while humming strange tuneless melodies.

Sleep provided a reprieve, but even that was no longer the same. The covers smelled of old pizza. This bed was getting too small for her. The way the dog nosed his way up to her under the covers was both endearing and infuriating. She threw off the quilt, ruffled Solo's head, and called him a good dog. The beagle shook his head in a way that made his ears flap like a propeller, making Polly laugh. Laughing was her favorite thing now. It should always have been, but now she recognized its importance, how similar it was to crying.

No matter how his accountant tried to explain it, Cole Weingarten could not understand how he could be bankrupt. He'd done everything right, had invested in insurance companies, drug companies, things that were unable to fail in times of calamity.

The worst was the insulting letter he'd received from MetLife — though he was a stockholder, the life insurance company wouldn't pay out for Penny. The form letter merely stated that her death wasn't on the job, even though, as a YouTube sensation, she was always on; every moment of her day was for her fans. She had been one of the few to post a good shot of the monster before that car plowed into her, and … and there was no reasonable explanation for his financial situation unless his accountant was ripping him off. To add insult to injury, Cole had been unable to get diesel for his generator this week, so he sat in candlelight, feeling like one of the stupid unprepared.

He poured himself two fingers of bourbon and added another splash for good measure. The monster had stormed through only six weeks ago. Cole's hand shook in bringing the glass to his lips. It wasn't possible for his entire life to change like this in such a short time. He took a slug of the woodsy liquid. Or maybe that was the only way reality ever changed: in an instant. He opened and closed the clamshell of his dead laptop and listened to the sounds of his neighbors singing at a backyard bonfire party.

The homeless man on the corner of Polk and St. Charles settled himself on the red patterned Persian carpet that had fallen from the sky the day the first monster had passed through — it had fallen along with a piano, a shower of glass, and a large portion of an apartment building, none of which, other than the rug, had held any interest for the ex-Navy Seal.

He washed three pills down with a celebratory slug off the Smirnoff someone had tossed into their kitchen garbage half-empty (God bless Houston's alcoholics and their remorse). Just as the former NASA scientist was nodding off into a happy, drug-induced slumber, he felt that deep, double-throated growl shake his sternum again.

His eyes snapped open. His breathing stirred. His heart rate doubled, and he clutched at the filthy edge of the plush carpet. In the distance, he could hear the city beginning to respond with barking dogs, alarms, gunshots, and desperate screams. He roused himself to one elbow and rolled up the carpet. He was ready for the sequel. This time, Dr. Evans had a plan.

Learn more about this author at:
https://mmdevoe.com/.

# INSIDE JOB

## MEL GREBING

EVERY MORNING when Tay wakes up, they make sure it's a complicated process, slowly coming to and reorienting themself in their life — because that's no way to start a story.

Tay runs through the rest of their day as best as they can — because running, too, is no way to start a story. And the last thing Tay wants is to start a story.

Tay never considered what would happen if they broke their ankle. When they do, Tay can't think of a worse thing to happen. Ever since the accident, they are painstakingly careful to be as boring as possible. Not broody, though. Tay doesn't want a pessimistic lit fic claiming their body and steering them into a poetic suicide.

So far, Tay has avoided three supernatural encounters and a sad detective who followed them around for a day, and the number of talking animals they've had to ignore was astounding.

Tay is close to getting away with it, too. They can walk again now; in a few weeks they'll be able to run. And you don't start a story with the protagonist running away, even if they're running away from the story itself.

And then you turn up. You and your constant expectations: *Do something interesting. Have an adventure.*

Thank you, but no. Tea and scones is adventure enough for Tay.

Still, you keep poking your nose where it doesn't belong. Your eager eyes browse over Tay in their living room. They're reading, legs stretched out on the couch. The scar from their operation is a red welt against their white skin. Not the angry red of inflammation, but the soft pink glow of healing.

You lean over Tay's shoulder, peering into the book they are reading. Why do they devour fantasy when they refuse to participate in it? A portal fizzled out in the other corner of the living room only an hour ago. You circle the couch Tay lies on, trying to descry their motivations.

Tay gets up. They favor their left foot while walking. Now and then the right shoots memories of pain up their leg. You follow them into the kitchen, where Tay puts the kettle on.

What goes through their head as they wait for the water to boil? Unlike more amenable protagonists, Tay doesn't talk to themself. They have no pet to share their thoughts with. If they know of your existence, they ignore you.

Instead, Tay peruses their collection of teas. Dark rose petals embedded in black crumbs smelling of citrus. The scent of jasmine wafting up from a light green tea when they open the tin. Their hands wander — a familiar ritual.

Finally, Tay scoops a teaspoon of black tea with highlights of blue cornflower into the tea egg. The kettle chirps and Tay pours the steaming water gently into their cup. While the tea steeps, they busy themselves in the kitchen —

putting away dishes, wiping down counters, sorting through the fridge and writing up the next shopping list.

Finally, they pull the tea egg from their cup and return to the living room. Tay lounges back on the couch, putting down the tea and picking up their book.

Nothing happens.

And yet you linger.

And yet you stay.

Day after day, you return to Tay. And day after day, they ignore you. They ignore you and beckoning adventure in favor of their teas and their books. You see spaceships float past their window, mages who poke their heads through the holes in Tay's reality. Tay avoids all of that carefully.

You follow Tay to physiotherapy and watch them slowly regain full mobility and strength in their foot. *It makes sense they want to heal before going on an adventure*, you reason. When Tay goes on their first short jog, you follow.

It's not easy. You can't remember the last time you ran. You'll sprint to catch a bus now and then, but jogging is not one of your favorite activities. Still, you follow them. Instead of loafers, you arrive at Tay's place wearing sneakers, ready to follow in case they try to run off into adventure without you.

Tay doesn't. They also slow down whenever you lag behind. It's kind of them, in a weird way. An acknowledgment of your existence of sorts. So you do your best to keep up. It's not that bad to be a little in shape. It's something you can get out of this until Tay yields and goes on their grand adventure.

Only they still don't. Once they can run again, it's what they do each day, every day. They allow you to follow, but

Tay is never tempted by the mysterious strangers on the streets or the magical cats and stray Wolpertingers squeezing through their running feet.

"Stop following me!" they order a gentleman in historical garb carrying a briefcase and serious expression. "I am not inheriting anything!"

And then Tay is off again, fleeing the perfect opportunity for a happily-ever-after with a most eligible bachelor. You are disappointed. Tay has a way with words; the banter would have been a joy. You are not sure how appealing Tay might be to a duke or duchess, though. They are exceedingly boring on purpose.

After watching Tay doing nothing but run and read for some time, you turn your attention to their home. Bookshelves line all walls of the living room — shelves upon shelves of fantastic stories: spaceships, dragons, vampires. Your fingers run over the spines, some of them broken by many re-reads. Trinkets collect dust in front of the volumes: colorful, campy memories of past travels.

The only reason the fourth wall isn't bricked up with more books is that it's a window front. A slim glass door leads out to a strip of balcony. Flowerpots are attached to the rail and overflow with herbs, decorated with metal butterflies in bright colors on tall stems. The glass door creaks softly when used, its frame warm from the sun.

Your footfall is soft on the laminate. Tay has placed rugs only where their feet rest often: in front of the couch, under the kitchen table, in front of the bed.

Their kitchen is tiny, and the bright highlights of color can't hide that. A window has been painted around the tea shelf with more love than craft. Summer yellow fabric has been stapled to the wall in imitation of curtains.

You only peek into the bedroom. It feels stalkery, even for you. But there are more bookshelves at the head of the queen-sized bed. The blanket and pillow lie askew on it — no attempt at making the bed was made. Books are stacked on both bedside tables.

A cupboard takes up one wall of the room, facing the foot of the bed. Photographs of blue skies over far-away landscapes decorate the wall opposite the door. An octopus lamp stretches its tentacles across the ceiling and brings warm yellow light into the room. Air fresheners fill it with the smell of wildflowers and breezy days at the coast. You close your eyes and can almost feel the gravel underfoot, crunching cozily as you walk along the shoreline, gulls screaming overhead.

You even peek into the bathroom when you know Tay is safely tucked away in the kitchen, making another cup of tea. The stark white tiles glare under the neon light, and a thin line of charcoal gray runs around the room at head height. It feels exceedingly cramped — and personal, with Tay's soap and shampoo on display, and their toothbrush naked on the small shelf over the basin. You close the door quickly.

The life of Tay doesn't get any more interesting. And still you return, day after day. You jog. You watch: Tay doing laundry. Tay doing the dishes. Tay cooking dinner and eating alone. *Where are their friends?* you wonder. Talking mice steal the leftovers and Tay ignores them.

You pace their small flat. By now, you are as familiar with it as with your own. When you enter, the kitchen and bathroom are to the right, the bedroom to the left, and the living room straight ahead. The latter is the only room with windows. Tay spends most of their time there. They read. Now and then, they watch a show.

Tay likes mac and cheese with a side of gherkins. They like twelve-tone music and the sound of Wikipedia. They never walk when they can run, because you don't start a story with the protagonist running, and Tay doesn't want to get involved.

They allow your presence, though they never acknowledge you openly. They may slow down while running so you can keep up, hold a door longer than they need to so you don't slam into it face first.

Sometimes you consider leaving Tay and their little life behind, finding somebody more amenable to the idea of great adventures or at least petty crime. And then you don't. It is a comfortable routine, following Tay through their days. You even start to like the amount of running it entails.

You return after a shower one day, knowing Tay has done the same. They had enough time to make themself a cup of tea, though their hair still clings damply to their skull.

With the cup in one hand, Tay turns and stares you down as you stand in the door to the living room.

"You're really into domesticity, huh?" Tay says.

It's the first time they acknowledge your existence. For a moment, you hesitate. *Do* you like watching them in their everyday life? Or were you simply hanging around in the hope that something big and terrible would happen to them?

"Maybe." It seems to be the safest reply.

They squeeze past you and return to the couch, where they sit down cross-legged. The cup of tea steams between their hands.

"You've hung around very long for 'Maybe,'" they say. "What are you waiting for?"

You follow into the living room and stand awkwardly at the head of the couch. "I don't know. Anything, really?"

"Good luck then." Tay tilts their head at you before they leave you standing.

You wonder if there is a way to entice Tay to go on an adventure. All those magical books — how can they not be tempted? You choose one for the number of creases on the spine. It has to be a favorite.

It's an okay story. When you finish, Tay watches you from across the room. It's a first. You lower the book slowly, start turning it over in your hands.

"So?" Tay prompts.

For a moment you stare down at the cover. At some point, Tay bound the paperback with adhesive foil so it wouldn't fall apart. "I don't understand," you say.

"The plot?" Tay raises a brow.

You shake your head. "You read this so many times, and yet—" You wave the book around vaguely. "The wizard this morning, the magical sword, the speaking griffons — you ignore them all."

"Yes." Tay nods happily. "Yes, I do."

"Why?"

Tay lowers their own book and frowns. "What do you mean, 'why'?"

"You obviously love adventures." You gesture at the books surrounding you.

"I love *reading* them," Tay corrects.

"Everybody can read them," you reply.

"Exactly." Tay throws their book at you, and you have to drop the one you're holding to catch it. "Glad you tried it."

"I can read books at home." You pick up the fallen novel and put it back on the shelf.

Tay takes a sip of tea before putting down the cup and reaching for the next book on their pile. "Then what are you here for?"

You don't know what to reply to that. This is where stories are born, where protagonists are chosen. And Tay is a novelty. Not many protagonists like them are having

fantastic adventures. You'd hoped for some new excitement, for the familiar with some fresh spice thrown in.

A friend of yours followed his protagonist through
portals into worlds of hive-minds and warships. Another
found a storyteller to tag along with, and she speaks of their
stories with gleaming eyes. You had hoped for that kind of
adventure. Finding Tay, you downgraded your expectations
to a mystery, maybe a thriller — lit fic if you had to.

But Tay resists all of the stories reaching for them.

"I'm not here for your entertainment." They look up
from their reading for a moment. It rings true. You will not
find adventure here.

And yet you linger. And yet you stay.

Quietly, the routines fall into place. You try to break them
up less and less. There isn't much to explore you haven't
seen already. And some things, you cannot bring yourself to
intrude upon.

The lighting adjusts to the needs of the observer; you
can see even in the pitch-black darkness of Tay's bedroom
with not a single ray of light intruding through the blinds
from the outside.

You can easily make out Tay in their bed, fast asleep: a
fuzzy blanket pulled up over their head like a protective
shield against the world, with a weighted blanket on top of
it, pressing the soft microfleece against Tay's skin. They
turn over in their dream and you are an intruder on this
moment, on the only time Tay has to themself.

You wonder if a story can start within a dream. It feels
like a dark betrayal to risk having Tay snatched away like
this. Still, you cannot make yourself return to your own
empty home in the small hours.

If Tay knows about your transgression, they never mention it.

Maybe they are getting as used to you as you are to them. Maybe they are as lonely as you are. How much time do you spend watching Tay? Is there nothing more interesting keeping you in your home?

Tay doesn't appear to be sad or unhappy with their life. But what can you know, when you cannot see into their head? So there is nothing stopping you from asking. "Aren't you lonely?"

"No?" Tay snorts in disbelief.

"But you have no friends, nobody—"

"Oh, don't even go there," they interrupt you. "Of course, I have friends. But if you think I'll drag them into this by contacting them with you around, think again. I love my friends. I'd never do that to them."

You are taken aback. You never thought about it like that and now that you do, you feel a little stupid. It's obvious that Tay isn't interested in going on an adventure. You never considered that their friends mightn't either.

"Oh," is all you manage to reply.

"Oh, indeed." Tay shakes their head and returns their attention back down to their novel. The curve of their neck makes your fingers itch — to run them over the smooth skin there. To be close enough to lean against Tay's shoulder, smell the scent of their hair. Wrap a bold arm around their shoulders.

It hits you like an avalanche that none of the things you desire have anything to do with two bodies writhing against each other in the pursuit of short-lived fulfilment. That only makes it so much worse.

You take an unconscious step towards them and Tay looks up.

"So, are you gonna stay?" Their eyes sear straight into

your soul. "Because it won't be easy and domestic all the time."

You bite your lip. This isn't how it's supposed to go. There is no great adventure, no quest, no plight. The smell of the tea rises to your nose, soft and beguiling. "What if I do?"

"Then we start running." Tay grins, and it lights up the room. They hold out their hand. "We run and live our lives. As best as we can."

"We run," you echo, and your eyes can't rip themselves from Tay's offered hand. You are not that good at running. But when you watch Tay, life looks comfortable. "Why do we run?"

Tay's grin broadens into a smile. "Because you don't start a story with the protagonist running, not even if they are running away from the story itself. We run and stay safe."

Understanding dawns on you. This *is* Tay's story — your story. Or it can be. What is it after all, that you leave behind?

Learn more about this author at:
http://melgrebing.com/.

# ABOUT THE AUTHORS

*You can learn more about the authors in this anthology by connecting with them on social media or on their websites.*

**Melody Alice**: https://www.melodyalicevo.com/author
**Matthew F. Amati**: https://www.mattamati.com/
**Mia Dalia**: https://twitter.com/Dalia_Verse
**M.M. De Voe**: https://mmdevoe.com/
**Rebecca A. Demarest**: https://rebeccademarest.com/
**Laura Engelhardt**: https://lauraengelhardt.com
**S.D. Gibson**: https://stephendgibson.com/
**Mel Grebing**: http://melgrebing.com/
**Bruno Lombardi**: https://www.facebook.com/profile.php?id=100051709043140
**Mike Morgan**: https://perpetualstateofmildpanic.wordpress.com/
**Spencer Nitkey**: https://www.spencernitkey.com
**Marisca Pichette**: https://www.mariscapichette.com
**Jason Sharp**: https://www.amazon.ca/Jason-Sharp/e/B01B8Y669U
**Matias Travieso-Diaz**: https://mtravies.wixsite.com/mysite
**Richard Zwicker**: https://www.amazon.com/author/richardzwicker

# ABOUT THE EDITORS

**Hannah Terao** holds a B.A. in Creative Writing from Hamilton College. In addition to her work with the Wandering Wave Press, she has served as a head editor for Red Weather literary magazine and an archivist for the American Prison Writing Archive. She would like to thank her family and her mentors (especially Ed Gonsalves) for their support of her writing throughout the years.

**Brandy Hussa** holds a B.A. in English Literature and Theater from Hamilton College and a M.A. in Teaching (Elementary Ed.) from Lewis & Clark. She currently works as a freelance writer, editor, and audiobook narrator. When not immersed in text, Brandy hikes the hills of Astoria, Oregon with her husband and son.

The production staff of *Tumbled Tales* all share a common foundational background: Hamilton College. Our bicoastal, multigenerational team includes alumnae who attended Hamilton in the early 1990's and those who have attended in the last five years. The campus and staff have changed drastically in the intervening decades, but the alma mater's motto, "Know Thyself" remains the same. Through the process of creating this anthology, we have connected, shared skill sets, and learned from each other. This is not just a case of alumnae mentoring a younger generation. We have all gained new insights and experience as lifelong learners.

Wandering Wave Press

www.ingramcontent.com/pod-product-compliance
Lightning Source LLC
Chambersburg PA
CBHW031756260626
47154CB00027B/1970